Advance Praise

This powerful first novel tells a riveting and supernatural story of angelic forces pitted against the power of the devil. An intimate account of betrayal and salvation that requires no translation to engage us. Although parts of *Flightless Bird* are raw and excruciating to read, the book in its entirety is marvelously written.

—Anthony Laurino, retired publishing executive at Penguin

If any young writer knows how to channel the traditions of gothic fantasy and horror to spin an elegant tale full of beauty and bad things, it's Bret Bucci. *Flightless Bird* delivers on familiar themes of love, betrayal, revenge and vindication, but through the vision and voice of an author who uses her influences as a mere origin part for something totally new and sweeping and stark. Open it and disappear for a few hours. That's what a good book is all about.

—Kenny Herzog, Pop-Culture Critic

Flightless Bird

Flightless Bird

Bret Bucci

Apprentice House
Loyola University Maryland
Baltimore, Maryland

First Edition

Printed in the United States of America

Paperback ISBN: 978-1-62720-069-1
E-book ISBN: 978-1-62720-070-7

Design by Natalie Bello

Cover: Image of a white feather by Joao Estevao Andrade de Freitas

Section Icons: Image of a black feather by Warren Lynn, licensed under the Creative Commons Attribution-NoDerivs 2.0 Generic

Published by Apprentice House

Apprentice House
Loyola University Maryland
4501 N. Charles Street
Baltimore, MD 21210
410.617.5265 • 410.617.2198 (fax)
www.ApprenticeHouse.com
info@ApprenticeHouse.com

Contents

For my little sister, Bianca.

Preface

Some questions only have one answer. How much would you give up to save the person you love? The answer is everything, and anything less than that can't be called love. I gave up everything once.

When I was eight years old, I made a deal with the Devil; and I mean that literally. I summoned him, I asked for his help, he asked for my soul, and we shook on it. I guess I shouldn't have been surprised when he cheated me, went back on his word. He was the Devil after all, the original fallen angel, the prince of darkness, the king of demons and now my soul belongs to him. I have spent the last ten years desperately, foolishly searching for a way to redeem myself. Death is inevitable, but Hell is a choice. I don't want to burn in never-ending fire and choke on sulfur for all eternity.

I need to find a way back into His good graces, so until I discover a way to save my soul, I will help rid the world over whatever evil I come across. Not people— although I've run into plenty of rotten people— but there are dozens of sinister creatures that poison the night. They haunt your homes, influence your bad deeds and want nothing more than to watch the world burn. I've sent a handful of them back to the underworld, which is another reason I want to avoid going there. I would prefer not to give the monsters of Hell such an easy opportunity for revenge.

I gave up everything to save the person I love, but she died anyway, so now I want it all back.

1

This Will Hurt

He looked like a man, but I knew better. I chased him through the darkest hours of night, in the grittiest city on the east coast. Bridgeview was an eye sore resting along the majestic Hudson River; but for better or worse, it was home.

I caught up with him in the alley that connected Tarquin Boulevard to Mona Drive. I heard his maniacal laughter ring out before the shadows parted and I could see him clearly.

The man's slim shoulders were rounded and his spine was severely curved, similar to the letter C. If he ever stood up straight, he would've been close to seven feet tall. His stick-thin arms hung like dead branches at his sides and his emaciated frame made him appear skeletal underneath the burnt orange glow of the street lamp.

I heard Jack release a threatening growl as we approached the lanky man in pinstriped slacks and a matching waistcoat. I let my hand rest in the patch of white fur between his ears and my canine friend settled down. As we drew near, I watched the slender man's long, scratchy dreadlocks bounce as his shoulders jumped up and down with each breath. Even hunched forward he towered over me. When his laughter subsided, he studied me with vibrant hazel eyes, flooded with specks of green and gold that shone beautifully in contrast to his coffee skin and black hair.

"Bon nuit, cherie. You have exhausted me. May I ask what I did to deserve your attention?" A charming French accent was paired with each word. "I have to say that I am flattered you are so desperate to make my acquaintance. I never dreamed I would be face to face with the legendary Sage Barnaby."

"Legendary?" I scoffed.

"I have heard of you, through friends. I believe you have met Ronove and Abaddon. Oh, and Murmur. Although I am not sorry he is back in the lake of fire. I never much cared for him."

Ronove, Abaddon, Murmur… they were demons, and I had exorcized all of them. When I removed Murmur from the world, he left bucketfuls of blood in his wake.

"Do you have a name, demon?" I asked.

It had been so obvious that body didn't belong to him. This creature wasn't used to commanding such stretched limbs. I noticed it when he ran from me. Every step required too much focus; he was clumsy. He probably hadn't been living inside of that flesh-suit for very long.

"Why would I tell you my name, cherie? That would just make it easier for you to exorcize me, and I have no intentions of ever going back to where I came from."

I flashed a playful smile. "You can't blame a girl for trying."

The man pursed his dark lips and leaned back against the brick wall of the alley. "How many of my kind have you returned to the lake of fire?"

"As of last week, the total comes to thirty-six," I answered smugly. "But that's not why I followed you tonight. I can exorcize you some other time. I'm here to ask for your help."

He cocked his head to the left in a bird-like manner. "You want me to help you?"

I nodded. "I know you've been traveling with the Creole sorcerer for years. I want to meet him."

"Ha!" the demon shouted into the brisk night air. "You must be in a lot of trouble if you need to speak with West Laveau. Let me guess what happened, you sold your soul and now you are having second thoughts."

I was stunned. How could he have known that? I never mentioned it. I must have seemed baffled because the demon felt the need to explain.

"Ah, so it is true? Cherie, do not fret, it is more common than you think."

The gaunt creature circled me in the alleyway. Now that I needed his help he had regained some confidence— realized that he had the upper hand. Jack snarled again. Whenever the demon stepped too close, the dog would bare his teeth, a string of drool trailing from his black lips. I had faced lots of demons without Jack there to protect me, but I always felt better when he was.

"I will require something in return for my help," the demon said.

I felt my stomach turn. I spent most of my free time hunting demons. I had never done a favor for one before, as a matter of principal.

I rolled my eyes. "What do you want?"

"I want to drink some of your blood, just a taste."

"Gross," I shook my head. "I don't think so."

"Then I will not tell you where to find Monsieur Laveau," he shrugged. "Quel dommage, cherie. Have fun spending your afterlife in the lake of fire. Would you say hello to my brothers for me? They have been stuck in the pit for a long while now, and there is not much hope for them venturing to Earth anytime soon."

I watched him distance himself from me, shuffling his feet across the gray pavement. Without the sorcerer, my chance for redemption plummeted greatly. I had spoken to the most respected clergymen of Rome while I studied demonology in Vatican City. I sought advice from the wisest Buddhist monks in Tibet while learning to read dreams. I'd even undergone soul purification in Japan where I trained in defensive martial arts. Unfortunately, the purification only left me with a brutal hangover and ten pounds lighter (I gained the weight back). While I was now adequately prepared to fight evil, I was no closer to reclaiming my soul. This enigmatic so-called sorcerer was my last hope; I had explored every other option.

"Okay," my voice cracked through the darkness, and I instantly heard the demon's lazy steps cease.

"D'accord, very good." He leisurely made his way back to where I stood by the street lamp. "I will arrange a meeting between you and my friend, the sorcerer."

I watched him remove a slip of paper from his waistcoat pocket and toss it casually onto the ground in front of me. I reached down for the business card inscribed with thick black letters.

> West Laveau
> Owner of Marie's N'Orleans Café
> 40 Talbot Place, Bridgeview City

"Come to the address on the card tomorrow at midnight," the skinny demon instructed.

I held it between my fingers and felt a tinge of hope swell up from somewhere deep inside of me. There were plenty of rumors attached to this mystical figure. When I traveled across the country to hunt demons or cleanse haunted houses of troubled spirits, I'd heard Laveau's name often. It seemed that everyone had a different take on him, what he was and what he was capable of. A man in Lawrence, Kansas suggested that West had been roaming the Earth since the dawn of time. There was woman in Buffalo, New York who swore he was a shape shifter; and a couple in Casper, Wyoming who told me that Laveau was no more gifted than your dime a dozen carnival palm reader.

However, there were far more people praising his talents than denying them all together. The thing most often said about him was that he was well connected both upstairs and down below, and that he never favored one side over the other. Creatures from the Devil's Court and the Kingdom of Heaven had equally benefited from their friendship with Laveau.

Another recurring whisper surrounding the Creole sorcerer was the he might be part angel. Almost everywhere I went people told me that his ancestor Marie Laveau of New Orleans, Louisiana had relations with an angel. Supposedly, that love affair resulted in a child of whom West is a descendant. Honestly, I didn't care which story was true. I just knew that if Laveau couldn't find a way to liberate me from my deal with the Devil then no one could.

"Now, I have held up my end of our bargain," he lowered his voice and his French accent sounded like purple velvet. "Cherie, it is time that you did the same."

I swallowed and tried my best not to seem intimidated. He was just going to drink a little of my blood after all. How bad could it be? The creature took an aggressive step toward me and I instinctively stepped back. Jack could sense my panic and placed his massive, white, furry body between the demon and me. The hair along Jack's spine stood on end as the dog persisted to threaten the demon with violent growls.

I watched the dark creature marvel at Jack, as he fearlessly protected me. The rail-thin man tilted his head and narrowed his eyes, examining the dog with the utmost concentration, and then he smiled. It was a broad, toothy smile that stretched from one side of his face to the other. At first his smile appeared inviting, amiable, but slowly I saw it was something quite the opposite. My breath quickened with the terrible realization that each of the demon's ivory colored teeth had been shaved down to fatal points. His entire mouth was lined with tiny, triangle shaped chompers. I knew that they would sink into my flesh with absolutely no effort.

I glanced back up at his face and the demon was no longer focused on the dog. Every bit of his attention had been redirected to me, his next meal. He stared at me with an unnerving, mad-eyed grin that I am not ashamed to admit rattled my bones, and I don't scare easily.

"Don't you think the razor sharp teeth are a little dramatic?" I asked in an attempt to stall for more time and maybe talk myself out of the situation.

"Do you like them? I did it myself. It makes feeding so much simpler."

"Well, I know for a fact that there are no such thing as vampires, so that must make you a bloodlust demon," I deduced. "Since the Devil only created about a thousand of you, I should have your name by the end of the week. I will be exorcizing you in no time. Thanks for the hint," I winked.

"Perhaps." Another demented smile graced his face. "But I will be the envy of every demon in Hell because I will know what Sage Barnaby tastes like."

Jack was still growling, but I silenced him with another reassuring pat on the head. The demon moved across the alleyway so that we were standing no more than a foot apart, reached out his spaghetti arm and wrapped it around me, drawing me nearer.

I unconsciously pulled away again, but his grip was uncompromising. I was so petite compared to him, barely eye-level with his chest. The demon let the back of his hand caress the porcelain skin of my cheek. My face grew hot beneath his touch, embarrassed by the unwanted intimacy. I was very, very rarely this close to another person.

"Cherie…" his voice was soft and trailed off, waiting for me to reply.

I released a long sigh in a vain attempt to calm my nerves. "Yes?"

"I just wanted to tell you," he bent over until I could feel his warm breath tickle the spot where my shoulder becomes my neck. "This will hurt."

He was right. I winced as he drank from me. His pointed teeth dug into the tender flesh of my neck, and I questioned if I would do it all over again. Would I have sold my soul to save my sister's life knowing that ten years later, after countless trials and disappointments and injuries, she'd be dead anyway?

"Merci pour le petit verre, cherie," the demon was breathless. He wiped his lips dry with his forearm. His eyes were glassed over as he staggered away from me in a daze.

"How do I taste?" I asked. I pressed the cuff of my sleeve against the open wound and felt my blood soak into it. The demon's so called "petit verre," meaning "small drink," had left me light headed.

He turned back around with his arms swinging lifelessly at his sides. His face was vague, almost expressionless yet blissful. "Unlike anything I have known in this world."

I crinkled my nose, puzzled by his lackadaisical behavior. "Can you narrow that down?"

"Dark," he purred. "The darkest blood I have ever sampled."

Well, that's not creepy…

Then, rather unexpectedly, a familiar song began to play. It was a terrible upbeat song with a catchy chorus line. The tall man was pulled out of his seemingly drunken state, and I watched him slide his thin fingers into his pocket to retrieve his cell phone.

He placed the device to his ear and the music stopped. "Oui, monsieur?" I recognized the French greeting. "Oui. Je suis avec la fille maintenant."

I suddenly wished I paid more attention in my high school French class. Nope, I learned Latin instead. Latin was a breeze. I was fluent in a dead language. Maybe if I ever met the Pope we could have a nice chat. However, there hadn't been much use for French when it came to hunting demons, until now.

I watched the gangly creature nod and speak into the phone. His voice was so smooth and melodic it sounded like a song to me. He spoke in whispers for a minute before abruptly slamming the small device shut. He looked back over his shoulder and a perverse smile played on his lips.

"Cherie, I have some good news to deliver. Laveau has taken an interest in you, and he wants to help. He has an idea."

I waited for the demon to say more, but he let the silence linger as his dramatic pause took affect. "What are you waiting for? Trust me, you have my attention," I said and tried not to appear too anxious.

"I would hope so. The fate of your soul hangs in the balance," he beamed. "Sage, how would you feel about meeting your guardian angel?"

It was decided. I would go to Laveau's café the following evening and we would summon my guardian angel, but I still had no clue why. Laveau would be shedding light on the answer to that question when I met him. Summoning angels is not a common practice and very few even know how it can be done. Even with all my experience in the supernatural, I had never heard of summoning an angel before. There were no texts on the subject. Whatever happened tomorrow evening would be an entirely novel experience for me.

Apparently a guardian can only be summoned at a specific time every day, the exact time you were born. For me, that was 12:08

a.m. So, if everything went according to plan this time tomorrow, I would be standing beside an actual angel.

I liked the idea of a guardian angel. It was nice to think that someone had been watching over me during the worst moments of my life. On second thought, my guardian hadn't done a very good job, had he? Actually, I think it was safe to say that he hadn't even done a halfway decent job protecting me.

"I think my guardian angel drinks," I told the demon, and he chuckled softly.

While we're on the subject of drinks, this demon had just ingested my blood. I allowed it because he told me he said he would arrange a meeting with Laveau, but... West Laveau just called to say he would take my case, which meant he knew about me before tonight.

I should've realized it sooner, but I was blinded by my desperation. A man as powerful and deeply private as West Laveau wouldn't have let me track him down unless he wanted to be found. Why else would he have set up shop in Bridgeview? Laveau traveled here with the purpose of meeting me. I hadn't trapped the demon in a corner. He wanted to be caught.

"Hey," I called out as the creature started to make his exit. "You all ready knew Laveau wanted to meet me, didn't you?"

"Oh, you are clever, cherie."

"Why did you pretend this was a coincidence? Why did you act like you were doing me a favor?"

"I think that much is obvious now," he sneered, and his pointed teeth were stained red. "You cannot gain someone's favor without first doing them a favor."

"Damn." Sage Barnaby, you idiot. "You needed me to feel like I owed you one."

"It worked beautifully."

I brought my hand to the open wound on my neck. "My

blood," I shuddered. "I don't understand. How come you were so desperate to drink my blood?"

"You do not have to understand; it is done and it cannot be undone."

I took in a sharp, worried breath.

"Rest well, cherie. You have quite a night ahead of you tomorrow."

We ended our meeting there, and I watched him move away from the streetlamp and disappear into the unlit part of the alley. I didn't look away until the dog's tail fell limp and his face regained its docile, big-eyed expression. Jack and I wandered in and out of grainy side streets and through the unforgiving smog that hung in the air, until we made it back to our apartment on Gretchen Road.

I drew the curtains closed as the sun began to rise over Bridgeview City, painting the sky a cardinal red. I went to the bathroom and stared at my reflection in the cracked mirror. It was a sight I had grown very familiar with: a young, dark-haired, brown-eyed woman, pale and covered in blood. A wave of fatigue crashed over me, and I hurried to bandage the small holes in my neck. When I entered the bedroom, I found Jack making a nest for himself. He clawed and rubbed his snow-white face into the extra blankets I had laid out for him at the foot of the bed. I collapsed onto the plum colored sheets, not even bothering to remove my blood stained sweater.

My exhaustion was well worth it, despite being tricked by the demon. I finally had an address to go with the name I'd been hunting. West Laveau wanted to summon my guardian angel. I wasn't sure what that would accomplish or how it would save my soul, but I was grateful for a plan. I just prayed it did not require some kind of sacrifice on my part because I had nothing left to give.

2

Freckles: Part I

I don't know when I fell asleep and I don't remember what I dreamt about, but I woke up with a start. There was an onslaught of relentless knocking at the door. Jack erupted into an orchestration of barks and howls. It was official. I was up.

I groaned into the downy pillow and rolled over onto my back. The deafening ruckus persisted. I came to the conclusion that the only way to silence the insufferable noise was to answer the door and punch the person standing there in the face. I even toyed with the idea of breaking his hand, so he wouldn't be able to knock again.

I sat up and forced myself from the bed. I dragged my feet across the wood floors; they felt like cinder blocks attached to the end of my stumpy legs. Jack followed me to the front door. He continued to yelp as he announced the person's presence on the other side.

I noticed the clock on the microwave read 5:12 PM. Just under seven hours until I would summon my guardian. Honestly, I wouldn't have minded another hour of shuteye, but that wasn't an option anymore. Now that Jack was awake, he would need to go for a walk. Whenever I ignored his whines to be let out, he always lifted a leg against a piece of furniture in the apartment. Once he even defecated in my favorite boots.

I yawned and rubbed my eyes. Maybe this person was a solicitor of some kind, extremely desperate to make a sale. Maybe they'd just been in a car accident and needed to use my phone. All I knew was that there better be a good reason I was being disturbed.

"I'm not interested," I said from inside the apartment.

The knocking stopped instantly. There was a pause, and then a mannish, resolute voice answered, "I am looking for Sage Barnaby."

An uneasy feeling seeped down into my palms and left them with a clammy, tingling sensation. I'd never had a visitor before. Hell, no one other than my godfather and his wife, Ned and Lena McGreevy, knew where I lived. I was estranged from my parents and I had no friends apart from Jack. I never even had mail delivered to this address. It was always sent to the McGreevy's house.

When I took too long to respond, the banging started up again. "Hello?" the voice spoke into the door.

"Go away. I'm not interested," I repeated more aggressively this time.

"Please. I am only asking for one minute."

I leaned in and put my eye up to the peephole. He wasn't unattractive. The tall stranger was around my age with ocean blue eyes and brown hair that stuck up in every direction. His white button up shirt was wrinkled and his blue jeans were ripped. Despite his unkempt appearance, the young man had a kind face. He nose sloped perfectly between his high cheekbones, and there was the slightest cleft in his strong chin. Although I couldn't be sure from this distance, I swore there was a line of faint freckles sketched across the bridge of his nose and beneath his eyes. He looked vaguely familiar, but I wasn't sure why.

I watched as he nervously shifted his weight between his feet and chewed on his lower lip. I still hadn't answered him. When I saw him lift a closed fist with the intention of knocking again, I immediately unlocked the door. As soon as Jack realized that this young man wasn't a threat, he stopped barking.

"What do you want?" I used one hand to prop the door open while the other rested on my hip.

His eyes passed over me with a hint of trepidation in his gaze. I was certain I looked like a train wreck. I was dressed in yesterday's clothes, there was gauze and tape plastered to my neck, and I was caked in blood with bleary-eyes and thick matted hair. "Um, are you Sage?" he asked cautiously.

I didn't speak. If he found me here then it meant he was looking for me. He must have known who I was.

"My name is Shane— Um," he stopped mid sentence and continued examined me with curious eyes. "I think you're bleeding." He pointed to the bandage on my neck.

I stepped back, as if stunned. "You don't miss a thing, Sherlock."

"Are you okay?"

"Peachy."

"Sorry, you just weren't what I was expecting."

"Well, I wasn't expecting you either," I said, irritated by the way he stared at me.

I decided to avoid making eye contact. I noticed a small rectangular black object clutched in his hand. I could make out three of the five letters printed across the front cover.

"Oh, I see. Did word get out that I need to be saved?" I asked, disgusted.

"What?"

"Aren't you here to save my soul? I'm sorry, but you're too late. I gave that thing away years ago."

"What—? No." He shook his head. "I don't know what you're

talking about." He looked around the hallway, as though a camera crew was going to pop out at any moment and fill him in on the joke.

"I can see the Bible in your hand, Shane."

He glanced down at the thick black leather bound book in his hand. His gray-blue eyes widened with understanding.

"I appreciate the gesture," I said. "I know you have good intentions, but I'm not really in the mood to listen to you read scripture. Actually, I would rather be doing anything else."

I turned my back on the door, leaving it open, and retreated into the apartment. There was a direct line of sight from my front door into the bedroom. I could feel Shane's eyes follow me as I moved away from him. I was shocked when I heard him step forward and enter without an invitation. That wasn't very Christian of him.

"I need to talk you. I won't read anything from the Bible. I promise," he shouted from the doorway.

I refused to answer him. I didn't want to encourage him. I had read the Bible more than enough times. I had even read passages written by the disciples that were excluded from the Bible. There was nothing Shane could tell me that I didn't all ready know. I did not need to be enlightened. At the moment there was only one thing I sincerely needed, and it was a big, hot cup of coffee.

I shut the door to my room and stripped off my clothes before pulling on a fresh pair of faded black skinny jeans and a gray sweater. While I was lacing up my boots, Shane started to call my name. "Sage, you might want to come out here."

I pushed open the door, and my eyes were immediately drawn to the massive white marshmallow of a dog standing on three legs. Jack was relieving himself against the television stand in the living room. I walked into the kitchen, grabbed a dishtowel and threw it down over the yellow puddle of liquid on the floor.

I crossed to the front door. "Okay, well I would love for you to stay and chat but—"

"Wait. There's something I want to ask you."

"I told you. I am not interested." I tried to push past Shane, but he held out his arm and blocked my path. "What are you doing? Move."

"Would you just stand still for a minute?"

I made a second attempt to get around him, but again he prevented me from leaving. I tried to force my way through, but he continued to awkwardly obstruct the exit.

"Move!" I shoved him, but Shane kept his feet firmly planted on the floor. He stood there, almost a foot taller than me with an unwavering determination. I could see in his stormy eyes that he wasn't going to move aside unless I made him. I took a step back and sized him up. Then a wonderful, mischievous idea crept into my mind. "Jack," I hardly breathed the dog's name.

I didn't have to say anything else. I knew he would understand my tone of voice. In a flash the dog's demeanor changed, hardened. Jack reacted the same way he had to the demon the night before. His fur raised, his ears fell flat against his head and he bared his teeth. It was a threat, and based on the fearful look splashed across Shane's face, the message had been received.

Shane watched anxiously as the dog crouched, resting his weight on his hind legs, ready to lunge forward and attack if I asked him to.

"Logan Forester," his voice was low, grave and his words were a blow to my chest. Hearing that name knocked the wind out of me. I was breathless, dizzy. I had been up against some of the foulest creatures in existence and never lost my nerve, but one human boy says one name and I feel like I might faint. I was overcome with the desire to run as far away from Shane as possible. I knew he looked familiar, and now I knew why.

3
In 1976

I left Shane standing in front of my apartment with more questions than he arrived with. I wish he hadn't found me, and on that note I wish his brother hadn't found me either. Logan Forester was my one failure. I thought of his sweet face and childish corduroy pants every day. I couldn't help Logan then, and I couldn't bring myself to help his brother now. Shane swore he would find me again, that he wouldn't leave the city until he unraveled the mystery surrounding his brother's death. Of course I could have given him those answers. Shane deserved to know, but I was too chicken to say anything, so I ran away.

I moved through the city, over cracked pavement and breathed in the smell of old pizza and dirty river water. Bridgeview City was nothing special. It rested towards the northern end of Westchester County in New York. The government had abandoned Bridgeview a long time ago, and it had been at the mercy of its residents ever since. The city had become a forgotten place, not far from being considered a ghost town. People wouldn't move in unless it was their absolute last resort; and since it wasn't exactly safe or pretty, Bridgeview only attracted a certain crowd.

The skies were gray most days, and even if the weather forecast suggested they should be blue, nearby factories pumped out a thick fog that infiltrated every street and created a permanent haze. This didn't affect the citizens of Bridgeview. We had somehow evolved passed choking on the pollution that hung in the air. The buildings were crumbling brick by brick; the neighbors were criminals; and if things ever changed, they would only get worse.

I cut through the alley where I had met the demon, walked up two blocks and found myself on the corner of Rice and Louis Street, the location of a city treasure. 1976 was a humble, worn out diner in the center of the city. There were only six parking spaces out front, and the neon sign meant to indicate whether the diner was opened or closed wasn't very reliable. Plus, one of the windows had been boarded over and gone unmended from a break-in eight years earlier.

None of that mattered though, because you could smell the bacon and hash browns from the opposite end of street, which somehow caused you to forget that how ugly the city was for a minute or two. The smell of fresh coffee even managed to dull the sound of constantly screaming police sirens.

The food came second to what I really loved about 1976. The diner's owners, Ned and Lena McGreevy, happened to be the most kind-hearted people I'd ever known. They were two of the very limited number of people I could stand to have a conversation with; and while I rarely showed them signs of affection, I always stopped in to say hello, and eat for free.

The bells hanging over the door chimed as I walked inside and moved through the diner. I felt a rush of judgmental eyes sear into the back of my head. I was used to being on the receiving end of criticizing headshakes from the 1976 patrons. They assumed I was taking advantage of the McGreevy's kindness. I had definitely played into everyone's disapproval over the years. I'd caused a scene or two in the diner, but the McGreevy's always defended my embarrassing behavior and told the customers to mind their own business.

I tried not to pay attention to people's opinions of me though. This was Bridgeview City, after all. No one here was squeaky clean. I took a seat at one of the padded stools in front of the counter. To my right were Mr. Munch, Mr. Finn and Mrs. Cragen, and each of them had piles of dirt swept under the rug.

It was clear that Mr. Munch had a drug habit with his sunken cheeks and missing teeth. Mr. Finn liked to pickpocket the diner's utensils and often walked out before paying his bill. Mrs. Cragen didn't even try to be inconspicuous with her spending after she collected the life insurance money from another husband who mysteriously kicked the bucket. It seemed that apart from Ned and Lena, no one was innocent in Bridgeview.

"There's my boy!" a sweet voice chirped from behind the counter. "Jack, I am going to cook up a greasy plate of bacon for you. How's that sound?"

Lena McGreevy was all ready making her way into the kitchen to fry up a stack of fatty meat for Jack. The pan sizzled as she placed the cold strips of uncooked bacon into it. The dog followed her and began salivating as the bacon cooked just a foot above his head.

A large grisly hand reached across the counter and took hold of my wrist. I looked up to see that it belonged to Ned, who met my gaze with a tired smile. He was a man who believed in hard work. It showed in the lines next to his eyes and in the corners of his mouth, still the years had treated him kindly.

"Barnaby," he nodded.

"Old man."

"Watch it."

He pointed a cautionary finger in my direction. He turned away from me to grab my favorite coffee mug from the shelf above the cash register. It was the bluest blue ever, and it nearly matched the color of Ned's eyes. He poured me a fresh cup and added a heaping spoonful of sugar. He'd been preparing my coffee for years now. He slid the mug across the counter to me.

"How's your day?" he asked and ran a hand through his salt and pepper hair.

"To be perfectly honest, it just started."

"Why doesn't that surprise me?" he glanced down at his wristwatch and grunted. I knew Ned disapproved of my sleeping habits.

Whenever Ned was upset with me, I made a point to quickly change the subject. "Can I ask you something?"

"Shoot."

"Why do you and Lena call this place 1976?"

He didn't answer me right away, but his face changed. In fact, the atmosphere in the diner seemed to change; it became overcast and gloomy. Ned wiped his face with an open palm and shot a quick look over his shoulder towards the kitchen.

"How come you want to know that? You've never asked about it before."

I shrugged. "I guess it just occurred to me how strange it is to name a diner after a year, a very specific year."

I watched his fingers shake as he raised them to his lips and silenced me. "That story would best be told without Lena standing so close by."

I nodded and offered an apologetic smile.

I was taken aback by Ned's secrecy. I had always felt welcome to question every part of his life, from his terrible taste in footwear to his terrible taste in football teams. I hadn't meant to set him on edge. He was unfocused, the color drained from his face, and he cleared his throat one too many times.

"Excuse me." His voice was hoarse. "I have to make a trip to the John."

He hurried to the back end of the diner towards the restrooms. Half a minute later, Lena was placing a steaming hot plate of eggs benedict drowned in creamy yellow hollandaise sauce on the counter. Her cocoa brown skin was glowing, as usual. Her perky attitude and bright smile perfectly complimented the way she sashayed through the dining area, clearing trays and taking orders.

"Sage, could you pass me that bottle of ketchup?"

I handed it to her and she placed it on an empty table.

Lena had grown pleasantly plump over the years without losing any of her youthful beauty. I often imagined her as Mrs. Claus, always ready with a freshly baked tray cookies and a cold glass of milk. There was something undeniably jovial about her, and it was infectious.

"How are you, honey?" she took the open stool beside me.

I lifted a forkful of eggs to my mouth. "Fine."

It was strange that Lena and Ned probably knew more about me, my favorite foods, my insecurities, my temper, etc. than any other person. However, they had no clue that I spent my nights hunting monsters. It never occurred to them that every time I went out of town to visit a friend I was really working a job. I had no friends, after all.

Sometimes I wished I could tell the McGreevy's the truth so that I wouldn't have to suffer all of it alone, but I would never do that to them. Once you realize that the supernatural actually exists, that it's not some bedtime story your parents told you so you'd behave, there is no forgetting it. Suddenly ninety percent of the situations you're in become a matter or life and death. The biggest decision of the day isn't whether you should order a medium or large coffee (because let's be serious, small was never an option.) It is whether or not you should kill a shape-shifting kitsune with a silver blade to the heart or by setting it on fire and reciting an incantation. Trick question, you have to cut off all of its tails; there can be as many as nine. Anyway, I don't think the McGreevy's would welcome that much gore and Latin into their simple lives.

"Sage, when was the last time you went on a date?" Lena asked. "I was just speaking with Raquel Lori, her nephew's in town and—"

"Oh God," I threw back my head dramatically. "Lena, please don't set me up with anyone. I am not interested."

"Do you plan on just going through your whole life alone?"

"I'm not alone. I have Jack."

"Are you referring to the slobbering animal licking grease off a plate on the floor?"

I shrugged.

"Honey, you need to meet some new people, emphasis on the people. I love Jack, but that's a very one sided conversation." Lena always had a maternal way of telling me like it is, never judgmental, but always brutal. "I just want you to be happy."

"I know you do." I stared into my coffee.

"Meet a nice boy, fall in love—"

"Okay, now you're pushing it!" I laughed.

She nudged me and played with a curl of my dark hair. It made me think of an interaction a mother and daughter might share, although I had no memories of something so gentle taking place with my own mother.

I wanted to ask for a hug, but I didn't. I wasn't accustomed to physical contact in a nonviolent manner. Sure, Jack would snuggle against me on the couch while we watched the food network, or lean against my leg while we waited for the light to change before crossing the street, but sometimes I longed for a little human contact.

A second later the moment between Lena and I had passed. She was back in the kitchen reprimanding one of the cooks for dousing the tomato sauce with too much salt. Ned made his way back behind the counter and blew his nose into an old rag. I jumped at the sound, which could have been mistaken for a foghorn.

"You know, kid, if you ever decide to start sleeping through the night and you want a more productive way to spend your days, I would be glad to take you on as a waitress."

"No," I said without missing a beat. "Stop asking."

"Hey, you know what else I was thinking—"

"Ned please, anything but that. I can't remember the last time you had a thought that I agreed with," I warned him.

He pushed forward, undeterred by my disinterest. "I was just thinking that you should move back in with Lena and I."

"I have an apartment."

"Your apartment is a dump."

We had had this conversation before. When Ned took me in, he thought he could fix me; and eventually I would like the color pink and sneak out at night to meet up with boys and cry when I watched romantic comedies. While my godfather had done more for me than any other person alive, his dreams of a little girl who liked the color pink never came true.

Even though I didn't live up to his picture of an ideal child, Ned still wanted me around. Who was I kidding? Ned was the only one who ever wanted me around, and it made me feel loved, in a way my own parents didn't love me.

"I like my apartment," I repeated. "Besides, I see you and Lena almost every day."

"I just feel like you're gunna run away again."

Ned was referring to my year abroad. He thought I went there to find myself, but really I was learning how to be an expert in all things supernatural. Truthfully, it wasn't enough time. I was in no way an expert. There were still a lot of things I didn't know, but I'd managed to avoid being killed so far, and in my line of work that is a huge accomplishment.

"You're just a kid—" he continued.

"Ned, I am eighteen, and legally that makes me an adult."

"Sage, you sleep until four in the afternoon, I've never met any of your friends, and sometimes you leave town for a week or two at a time and I can't get in touch with you. That is not mature, adult behavior. For Christ's sake, you're wearing a sweater in August! That's just dumb."

I rolled my eyes. "I can't believe this."

"I am just saying that it might not be a bad idea for you to move back in with us. We'd love to have you," he tried to sound optimistic, but he knew how I was going to react. "What do you think?"

I looked down at Jack, who had returned from the kitchen and was lying beneath the counter by my feet. "Are you listening to this?" I asked the dog. "Yeah Jack, it does sound familiar. I'm sick of hearing it too."

Ned let out an exasperated sigh. "You cannot be serious. Don't avoid our conversation— don't talk to the damn dog," his cheeks turned red with frustration.

"I am not avoiding the conversation," I shot back at him. "I have it memorized, because we've had it a dozen times!"

"Would you lower your voice please?" he hushed me. "You're making a scene."

"Come on, Ned, you know what it looks like when I make a scene, and this is tame. This doesn't even come close to me making a scene."

He shook his head. "You know what, kid? Just get out of here. Go."

I choked. "What?" I almost spit a mouthful of hot coffee across the counter.

Ned had never asked me to go before. I was completely out of my element, shaken even. I gathered my composure and looked up from the blue mug.

"Go," he said again.

I glanced around the diner, unable to believe that Ned was really telling me to leave. His scowl must have been meant for someone else, right? I brought my eyes back to him, and he was still glaring at me with the same burning contempt.

I hesitated to answer. I wanted him to take it back. I was waiting for him to take it back, but he didn't.

"Go?" I asked naively. "A minute ago you asked me to move back in with you, and now you're asking me to leave?"

"That sounds about right to me, Blondie."

Blondie. I couldn't stand being called that. I hated that nickname. It was a reminder that I was forever the black sheep.

I was a brunette. There was no mistaking me for anything else, but that wasn't normal for the women in my family. For dozens of generations, every female on my mother's side had been blonde, until me. I wasn't adopted and I don't dye my hair. I am the great mystery of my bloodline. Since I was a young girl, my mother, father, grandmother and Ned have been calling me Blondie. It was meant as a joke, but it never made me laugh.

I think my godfather perfectly understood my aversion to being called that name. I think that's the reason he used my nickname now. Ned was angry with me, and he wanted to make sure I knew it.

"Did you hear me, Blondie?" he said the name again and it stung, like a vicious paper cut. "Go."

I stood up and jetted for the exit. I was halfway there when I stopped in my tracks. I just stood there in silent fury. How could he ask me to go? I looked around at the customers smiling over their cheeseburgers and stacks of pancakes while Lena sauntered through the crowded diner. I knew I shouldn't act out, but I was so angry I couldn't help myself. Therefore, in the middle of the diner, I threw a temper tantrum that any three year old would have been proud of.

I turned back towards the counter defiantly. "Ned."

He looked up, surprised to still see me there, and braced himself for my next move. I rushed up to the counter. I heard Jack's nails click across the tile as he trotted after me. In one quick movement, I swiped the blue coffee mug off the counter and threw it against the wall just above Ned's head. Well, that burst of excitement captured everyone's attention. Lena immediately assumed the position of disappointment. She stood behind me with her hands firmly placed on her hips, while everyone else in the diner gasped and joined together in stunned silence.

"What the heck is the matter with you, kid?" Ned asked with a dramatic hand gesture and a bewildered expression.

I did my best to hold his gaze. I could face down unimaginable foul creatures, but my godfather was something else. "Why don't you trust me to take care of myself?"

"Because you can't! Do you remember how I found you in New York City? Do you remember how long it took for you to recover?"

"That was almost two years ago. It was nothing."

I watched as his eyebrows drew together, which made him appear somewhere between puzzled and hurt. "Nothing? Sage, you were…"

Ned stopped. His eyes darted around the room, and mine followed. Everyone was staring at us. Ned was clearly embarrassed about losing his temper in front of customers. The regulars at 1976 knew him as a laid back, easy to smile, average Joe kind of guy. At the moment he was teetering on the verge of madness, hand curled into a fist, white knuckled and making every effort not to raise his voice. Honestly, Ned was one of those people who didn't need to scream to be heard. All he had to do was give me a hard look, and I understood what he was trying to convey.

"You can't fix me, Ned. I know you tried, but you can't. I'm broken."

I remembered when he tracked me down. I was lost in a jungle of skyscrapers and underground bars. I had vanished into a world of white powder and pink pills and brown drinks. He pulled me out. I hadn't touched drugs or alcohol since then; but that didn't mean I was cured, and it didn't mean I was happy.

"That is such bullshit, and you know it," he let the words drag out. "Listen, you're my girl and I love you, but there are some days you make that really difficult. So would you give a break? Let me nag you a little bit. At least pretend to entertain the idea when I ask you to consider moving back in. Just give me a break."

I crossed my arms and fell into that moment of reacting or not reacting. I wanted to hurt him. I wanted Ned to back off, but should I say the terrible thing that came to mind? I knew it would burn, blister and cut through to the core of him. Maybe I should have thought about it for one more second, but instead I said, cool and clear, "I have never been your little girl, Ned. That's just a pathetic dream you're hanging onto. Wake up, would you?"

He let my words sink in, but I knew he'd hide his pain from me, pretend that my contempt had no affect on him.

"No, you're not mine," he agreed, and I could see emotion sweep across his face. "But I am the one who took you in when your parents didn't want you anymore."

"Ned Heathcliff McGreevy!" Lena shrieked, horrified that her husband had lowered himself to my level.

He ignored her protest and carried on seamlessly. "I think I'm starting to understand why they made that choice."

It never crossed my mind that he would retaliate, but I pushed him and he shoved back. Bravo, Ned. I didn't say another word. I retreated. I was in such a hurry that Jack couldn't catch up before I slammed the door shut, leaving him trapped in 1976.

I paced in the front parking lot. It was the only thing stopping me from crawling onto the hood of Ned's gold '69 Cadillac Eldorado and kicking in the windshield. I clawed at the unruly mess of dark curls that flew in front of my face, obscuring my vision. My argument with Ned had stirred a familiar tinge of vulnerability, worthlessness, which I hadn't experienced for nearly two years.

I had been conducting some supernatural business in Massachusetts when things got out of hand. For the first time since I'd started hunting demons I was in over my head. Technically, the exorcism had been a success. The demon was cast out of this world, but so was the innocent soul of a young man. I had promised to keep him safe. I specifically told him that everything would be okay, and I failed. His death was on my hands.

After that, I cowardly hid myself in the darkest, filthiest corners of Manhattan until my godfather found me, brought me home and took care of me. He made damn sure I got better. For weeks he asked what happened that caused me to fall into such a severe depression, but I never told him. It was for his own good. That was when I decided to move out and rent an apartment. Ned was against it, but there wasn't much he could do to stop me.

I finally stopped pacing and was hit with an incredible urge to chain smoke an entire pack of cigarettes, but then I remembered I don't smoke. I was stuck. My pride would never allow me to go back inside and apologize, but I didn't want to lose the McGreevy's because of my short-fused temper. In place of smoking, I chose to walk it off. I barely made it half a block when I heard the heavy thud of Ned's work boots galloping up behind me.

"Hey!" he called out in labored breaths. "Hey, Barnaby! Slow down!"

I slowed my walking to a more leisurely pace, and he caught up with me. We strolled down the street, side by side, towards

Merrick Park. I refused to make eye contact with him because I was certain that once I witnessed their sincere blue I would forgive him completely. I wanted to hold onto this anger; it was easier to be upset than to admit that maybe I was wrong.

"Well, aren't you gunna say something, kid? I mean, I followed you out here."

I turned a cold shoulder and lifted my chin. "I assume you have a good reason for doing that." My voice was flat.

"Lena made me come after you," he whined. "You know she can't stand it when we fight."

"I always liked her more than you," I meant to provoke him, but he didn't bite.

"Lena accepts you for the pain in the ass you are, and I challenge you to be less of a pain in the ass. Sage, we love you, and we take our roles in your life very seriously," he explained with a satirical twinkle in his eyes.

Golden light clung to his hair and drew attention to the lines of silver just starting to show. His strides were wider than mine and I had to hurry alongside him to keep up.

"You asked me why Lena and I named the diner 1976," he said when it was clear that I wasn't going to be the one to break the silence between us. "Do you really want to know?"

"Yes," I answered sheepishly, not wanting to seem too eager. I was afraid he'd change his mind, and I was truly curious to learn why that year was so important to the McGreevy's.

"Okay," his voice was rough.

Ned took a seat on the bench at the end of Rice Street and patted the empty spot next to him. I sat and we stared across the busy road, our eyes danced past whizzing cars until they settled on Merrick Park, a grassy area that sat in the center of the intersection. There was one tree, which had provided Jack and me with cooling shade during the summer as I read out loud to the dog. There was a small flower garden, that had gone untended and become mostly weeds, and one empty duck pond.

I always thought it was strange that the duck pond remained empty. There was even a small sign indicating that the pond was meant to house ducks, but the feathered creatures never occupied the small body of water. For years the pond had remained vacant. Its only dwellers were a handful of coins people had wished on, trash that failed to find a garbage pail, and fallen leaves from the nearby tree. Otherwise the water stayed uninhabited and still.

"Remember when you asked about the tattoo on my shoulder?" Ned asked, his blue eyes cast down, lost in a crack on the sidewalk.

I nodded cautiously, shocked that he would bring that up. I remembered. It was a few weeks after he rescued me from New York City and brought me home. Ned never did tell me what the tattoo meant. I wondered if it was somehow connected to 1976.

He cleared his throat and began to tell his story. "I met Lena on New Year's Eve, 1975. I'm sorry to say I don't remember what she was wearing or the first thing I said to her, but I loved her immediately. Actually, we were at a party your father was throwing. He was dating your mom at the time; you know we went to college together. June made this incredibly pungent eggnog drink, and Walter hung a disco ball from the ceiling. The music was awful and the beer was warm; but it was the best party I had ever been to. We all huddled around the television to watch the ball drop in Times Square at midnight, and that was the first time I kissed Lena, and I have kissed her everyday since.

"Things between Lena and I progressed quickly from there. We were the epitome of young and in love. We were blind. We were fools. We were totally irresponsible. Three months later Lena was knocked up. Normally when something that big and unexpected happens it kills the relationship, but it only made us closer. We saw the pregnancy as a result of our love, and how could that be a bad thing? So I proposed, we dropped out of school and rented an apartment in Bridgeview. The rent was dirt-cheap. Sage, we were so damn happy, you know? It was like the universe had tried to pull one over on us, and we were too in love to notice."

"You never told me any of this before," I said with a touch of surprise.

He gave me a tender look that made my heart sink in my chest.

"There's more," Ned said like he wished it weren't true, like he wanted the story to end there.

"On December 8, 1976 Lena and I became parents. We had a daughter. We named her Kelly." His voice softened when he said the name. "Kelly McGreevy. She had a mess of dark hair and gray eyes. She was the most beautiful thing we'd ever known. She was perfect, so you can imagine our surprise when the doctors said there was a hole in her heart. They tried to do corrective surgery, but it wasn't enough. Kelly was too small, too weak. It didn't matter how much Lena and I loved her. She passed away New Year's Eve, 1976. It was exactly one year from when Lena and I first saw one another.

"Meeting Lena and bringing Kelly into the world are the greatest moments of my life, what I am most proud of. 1976 was the year Lena and I felt most alive. And after Kelly left us, we just stopped. I mean, we couldn't look at each other without seeing our daughter; we had no purpose and no desire to have another child after losing our first.

"Fast forward a couple of years and a few hundred bottles of whiskey later, Lena's parents buy us a hole in the wall on the corner Rice and Louis. They accused us of wasting away and becoming shells of the people we were. We didn't know what it was going to be right away. Lena wanted to open a pet store, but I'm allergic to cats and rabbits. I wanted a bike shop, but she hated that idea. Finally, we agreed on scrambled eggs, pie and French fries. 1976 is a tribute to the good stuff, when Lena and I were the best versions of ourselves."

He exhaled a long, tiresome breath, relieved that he was finished with his tale. I could see it had taken a lot out of him.

I placed a quiet hand on his shoulder. "Thanks, for sharing that with me."

"I wanted you to know. It's a big part of who I am. Sage, I don't want us to have secrets from each another."

I nodded, but I had no intentions of opening up to Ned today. I could feel a burst of sentiment rising in the air, so naturally I tried to avoid it. I tried to think up something trivial to say, but nothing came to mind. I let out a shaky breath and waited impatiently for the moment to pass.

A distant ringing, a familiar shrieking that pulsed and grew louder, found its way to my ears. It was the sound of sirens, and they were approaching us. Ned heard the noise too and craned his neck, waiting for their imminent arrival and wondering what all the fuss was about.

Suddenly, in one thunderous movement, a fleet of police cars, ambulances and fire trucks dashed past us. The sirens were deafening now. We kept our eyes on the safety vehicles as they came to screeching halts at the opposite end of the street. That's when I noticed the smoke. A screen of murky black smog ascended towards the Heavens and shrouded the sun's view of Earth.

I could all ready smell the thickness of it, which filled my lungs and shortened my breath. Ned stood up, hands planted on his hips, as he peered towards the source of chaos. In the midst of the clouded, hectic scene were screams that rose above the smoke. I could scarcely make out the figures being swept up and carried off in police officers' arms or the blurred images of firemen pulling gas masks down over their faces as they raced into the building. There was so much going on in the crazed scene, but it all happened in a few brief moments, well before either of us could put two and two together.

Then we heard the unmistakable sound of a gunshot. The noise hung in the air and resonated around us. Another gunshot sounded. Another rush of screams escaped the building. A fury of hysterical barking erupted and traveled down the street to where I stood. My blood ran cold. A wave of sheer, terrible panic crashed into me. Jack.

"Ned," I could barely say his name. I was paralyzed by my sudden realization.

"No," he answered, his voice quiet and somber. "No."

4

Hours Ago

There was no time for words beyond that. We sprinted frantically down the street towards 1976. My eyes stung from the oncoming storm of smoke. The scene was much worse up close. My senses were overwhelmed. Jack's barking persisted from inside the diner. Ned and I pushed past the frenzied crowd in an attempt to make our way to the front door. Upon reaching the parking lot, a police officer held out his hands to stop us from advancing beyond that point.

"This is my diner!" Ned hollered without being asked. "Where's my wife?"

The officer wouldn't let up. The man kept his arms extended, denying us entrance. "I'm sorry, folks. I can't let you inside. Be assured that we are doing everything in our power to control the situation."

"Where's my wife?" Ned demanded. "Lena! Lena!"

"Sir," the officer cut him short. "We have men inside clearing the diner now. If you would please take a step back and let us do our jobs—"

"Lena!" Ned called over the officer's head. "Get out of my way!"

"Sir. I cannot let you in there. You'll have to move over to the sidewalk—"

I watched my godfather's face turn red. Faster than I could blink, Ned's knuckles cracked against the policeman's cheekbone and knocked him to the ground. Ned proceeded to hop over the man's unconscious body and disappear into the diner.

I followed but quickly lost Ned in the smoke, which had invaded every corner of 1976. I shut my eyes to keep them from burning and listened for the sound of barking. I tracked Jack back to the farthest part of the diner. I blindly felt my way past the counter and into the kitchen, tripping over fallen pans and utensils that were scattered across the floor.

My foot caught on the inside of a pot and I toppled over, face first towards the ground. Thankfully I had the good sense to put my hands out in front of me. My knees smashed down onto the tiled floor and the pain shot through me like a firecracker. I cursed and continued crawling towards Jack's voice. I placed one arm in front of the other and pulled myself forward on my stomach.

"Ned! Lena!" I called out for help.

There was no answer, but someone did come to my rescue. There was a plush body looming over me. I stretched out my hand and took hold of the furry figure. After I managed to stand on my feet, Jack led me through the kitchen's back door.

The smoke still engulfed us, but at least we had made it outside. I opened my eyes with caution and was grateful to see Jack, who was covered in soot and equally pleased to see me. Unfortunately, that was the last pleasant moment of the day. Several feet from where I stood were Ned and Lena. He was kneeled over her shivering body and cradling her in his arms.

She was badly burnt. Lena's eyebrows and eyelashes had seen singed off. The skin on her left hand was melted, her wedding ring welded to the flesh of her finger. It was a painfully graphic image. Part of me wanted to look away, but I couldn't. This was Lena, after all.

Over the years she had become more of a mother to me than my actual mother ever was. She bought me an abundance of under-things and socks because she believed you could never have enough. She turned me on to pistachio ice cream. She introduced me to bands like The Talking Heads and Queen. Maybe Lena hadn't challenged me the way Ned did, but she made sure I had fun.

"Sage," her voice was cracked and dry. "You should know that Jack was quite the hero."

"What happened?" I basically shouted at her in a panic.

"There was a man with a gun. He took the money from the cash register, but he wanted more, and there wasn't any. He got very angry with me…" Lena trailed off.

She was weak. That frightened me.

Ned hadn't even noticed me standing there until Lena spoke. He supported her head with one arm and wrapped the other around my leg. He didn't say a word, only held tightly to both of us. Perhaps he did this in the hope that we wouldn't drift away from him.

"Does it hurt?" I immediately regretted the question.

I looked at her and thought, of course it hurts. The pain radiating through her body must have been so extreme that just taking a breath was pure agony. I could hear the shallow wheezing every time she inhaled.

"No, sweetheart." Lena smiled up at me. "It doesn't hurt."

I knew she was lying. I think she lied more for Ned's comfort than my own, but I loved her for it. Lena had always been selfless, whether it was volunteering at the animal shelter or letting Ned have the last slice of pizza. She lived for other people's happiness and in turn found her own.

Her smile made me confident that she would pull through. We would take her to the hospital where the doctors would put her back together, and then we would take her home. It would be a while before we found a way to laugh about this, but in time, we would forget how afraid we were and how hard we prayed.

Lena winced suddenly; her muscles tensed with a sharp pain. Ned responded immediately. He gave his full attention to his wife, brushing a few rebel strands of black hair from her face. I don't think he knew any other way to comfort her. The sensation struck Lena again and this time she moaned with it. I watched her teeth clench and her hands curl into fists, but the pain carried on without mercy.

"Oh God," I gasped. "Ned, look at your boots."

His boots were resting in a pool of blood, which continued to expand over the pavement. I took a step back as it stretched towards me. I couldn't believe that neither of us had noticed the small hole in Lena's stomach. It seemed so typical that Lena would not mention a gunshot wound for fear of worrying us. I could see that she'd lost a lot of blood, and Ned couldn't disguise the concern on his face. The color in his cheeks faded, leaving him with a ghostly complexion.

Ned shouted for help. I had never heard such guttural sounds come from a man. It was as if he was all ready mourning her. There must have been medics within earshot because seconds later there were two men running towards us with an oxygen tank and a stretcher.

I honestly have no memory of how I got to the hospital that day. I'm sure that Ned went in the ambulance with Lena. I must have told him that I would meet them there. I wasn't even sure where I left Jack, but he wasn't with me when I came to my senses in the St. Anne's Hospital waiting room.

The hospital in Bridgeview City was nothing in comparison to Lazarus Hospital in Tarrytown where my sister, Nola, had been treated. St. Anne's had a competent staff and up to date medical equipment, but its reputation was poor. Most of the patients were recovering addicts or victims of domestic violence. There was severe neglect from the maintenance department. Panels in the ceiling were missing and it appeared as though the corridors had never been introduced to a wet mop.

I wasn't alone. There were plenty of loved ones waiting to receive updates on hospital patients. There was also a news team parked in the waiting area. They were reporting for channel twelve, covering what had just occurred at the diner. At the moment, there was no one to interview. The hospital was busy aiding the people who'd been injured in the fire and during the shooting. It was hard to accept that Lena was among them. It was even harder to accept that all I could do was wait.

I had two cups of coffee in thirty minutes. My anxiety level was through the roof. I found a corner of the room and made it my own. I focused all of my attention on the wall opposite me. I glanced down at my watch. It had been almost two hours since Lena was taken to the hospital, but I hadn't heard anything about her condition, or seen Ned, since I arrived.

"Jerry!" A crazed voice erupted from the other side of the room. "Jerry, get the camera. Hurry up! Honestly Jerry, a trained monkey could do a better job than you."

A woman, who can be most accurately described as a real live Barbie doll, shot up out of her chair and trotted towards the nurses' station. She had spotted a recently admitted patient who was busy filling out paperwork. Following at the Barbie doll's heels was Jerry. Beads of perspiration accumulated on his forehead as he struggled to balance a hefty camera on top of his shoulder.

He had the look of someone who was constantly on the verge of quitting his job or telling off his boss but could never find the courage to do so. Instead he lived in a quiet misery that was obvious to everyone he encountered. Jerry had an air of exhaustion about

him that resulted in tired red eyes, a permanent furrowed brow
and premature wrinkles. Meanwhile his co-worker was made with
almost the same amount of plastic as the doll she clearly idolized.

"Hello, this is Rebecca Brinkley reporting for New Channel 12.
We are at St. Anne's Hospital where the victims of a violent robbery
are being treated. At around six o'clock this evening a masked man
entered 1976, a diner in the heart of Bridgeview City. Here with
me is Mr. Raymond Keylor who was present at the time of the
incident. Mr. Keylor, can you tell us a little about what happened at
1976 earlier today?"

"Well, the robber came in and told the woman behind the
counter to empty the cash register, and she did. Then he told her to
empty the safe, and she said, 'This is a diner, not a bank. There is
no safe,' and then he shot her. I guess he didn't believe her."

Throughout the interview, he never once made eye contact
with Brinkley or the camera. His voice lacked any emotion. Keylor
must've been in shock.

"And how did it feel to have a crazed gunman in you presence?
Did you feel that your life was threatened?" Rebecca asked, blinking
wildly.

When you're in school, your teachers tell you that there are no
stupid questions. While that may be true in school, it is not always
true in life. Leave it to a woman like Rebecca Brinkley to ask a
totally stupid question. Her scratch-the-surface reporting reflected
her fake blonde hair, fake breasts and fake tan seamlessly. Of course
Raymond was going to claim that he was terrified; he had been
standing within a few feet of a madman with a gun.

Keylor scratched at the wound on his arm. It was still bleeding.
"No."

"Did I hear you right, Mr. Keylor? You were not afraid of the
robber even when faced with potential death?"

"No," he repeated calmly. "I mean, the guy even said please."

Wait. Was this man really defending the gunman? It was always the whackos who called Bridgeview home. Even the shallow Rebecca Brinkley seemed taken aback by Keylor's offhanded response.

"I see you were injured during the nightmarish scene," Brinkley continued the interview and gestured to his bloodied bandages.

"Uh, yeah. The doctor said there might be a permanent scar."

"We're sorry to hear that, Mr. Keylor. Thank you for sharing your experience with us." Rebecca flashed a perfect smile into the camera. "There you have it. An attempted robbery gone horribly awry and leaving innocent people wounded in its wake. News Channel Twelve will be bringing you updates as this story progresses. Once again, this is Rebecca Brinkley reporting from St. Anne's Hospital in Bridgeview City."

The moment the camera stopped recording, Rebecca fell back into her normal behavior. Brinkley didn't bother to say goodbye to Raymond Keylor. After the interview ended, he managed to slink away while she was distracted adjusting her bra. She flipped her platinum blonde hair before shrieking at the cameraman.

"How did I look, Jerry? I think the lavender blouse was a good choice for today, don't you? Ugh, let's get out of this place. It smells like old people."

The questions were rhetorical and everything else was unkind. To people like Rebecca Brinkley, the biggest obstacles in life are fighting the urge to order dessert.

I closed my eyes and listened to Brinkley's heels clicking down the hallway as Jerry shuffled after her. Eventually the clicking grew distant and then ceased altogether. The hospital grew still for a few minutes and I used that time to recite silent prayers in my mind.

I knew I wasn't one of His favorites, but I prayed to Him anyway. I asked that He watch over Lena and make her well again. I might not have deserved His attention, but she certainly did. In my opinion, the McGreevy's had filled their quota of tragedies for one lifetime. First they lost their daughter, then they got stuck taking care of me, and now Lena was fighting for her life. They were entitled to a happily ever after.

Every time a doctor paid a visit to the waiting room my stomach flopped. I thought they might be bringing me news about Lena, but the messages were always for someone else. I stayed seated in the corner hugging my knees to my chest. It was awful, waiting. I grew uneasy and prescribed myself another cup of coffee. Ned had yet to emerge from Lena's room.

Another hour passed.

I bought another cup of coffee and a stale muffin. It was blueberry.

I drank the coffee and tossed out the muffin.

Another hour passed.

I counted the squares on the ceiling— two hundred and thirty-four.

I almost dozed off. I drank another cup of coffee.

It was dark out now. Every time I started to go crazy with worry, I reminded myself that no news is good news. I pressed my palm into my chest and felt my heart beat.

"Bum bum. Bum bum. Bum bum. Bum bum…" I gave it a voice.

Just as I felt myself start to relax there was commotion down the hall. The sound was explosive. Someone was trashing one of the hospital rooms. A swarm of doctors and nurses fled towards the excitement. There were half a dozen men forcing Ned into the hallway. The man I always knew as gentle and decent was cursing and kicking like he was rabid. I overheard someone at the nurse's station notify security. Ned was pinned to the wall, but he wouldn't let up. He roared as though he had lost the ability to communicate with words.

"Hey, that's my dad!" I heard myself say before I could form a real thought. It was sort of true; Ned was the closest thing I had to a father.

A young man at the nurse's station addressed me. "I'm sorry, but we're going to need to escort your father from the hospital. You can meet him out front."

"What happened?"

A middle-aged woman in a white coat approached me. "Miss, are you with that man?"

I nodded.

"I apologize about all of this. He didn't want to leave her. We said he could stay a while longer, but rigor mortis has begun to set in and we need to remove the body. You understand."

Time should have stopped but it didn't; time is selfish. The world warped around me, broke up into bits and pieces then came back together in one great, terrible rush. This new world was one without Lena McGreevy.

My mouth was dry. "When did—? You know."

"Hours ago," I heard the sympathy in her voice.

I was breathless. I had been around tons of violence and death before today, but it hurt so much more to lose someone you care for. First Nola when I was eight, then Logan Forester two years ago.

I couldn't believe this was happening. I thought I would have felt it if she died. Ned had been with her body for hours and I hadn't been with him. I didn't want him to suffer through this alone. But I guess that's the only way people can suffer, alone.

I watched several large security guards pull Ned towards the stairwell. The sounds coming from him curled my blood, as he protested and insisted he be left with his wife.

My head raced as the room spun around me. I didn't know which way was up. The woman in the white coat gave me a few seconds to pull myself together before addressing me again.

"I am sorry for your loss, but there is some paperwork that needs to be filled out."

5

Ghost Secrets

A police officer was parked outside of St. Anne's and offered us a lift to the McGreevy's home at the outer limits of Bridgeview. I would pick up Ned's Cadillac from the diner for him in the morning.

Ned was too weak to cry and too disturbed to say a word. On the car ride home, I watched his eyes glaze over as he retreated into a sad trance. The officer helped me carry him into the house and rest him down on the living room sofa. I thanked the man in blue, who in turn tipped his hat and left. Five minutes later, there was scratching at the front door. I answered to find Jack sitting on the porch, patiently waiting to be let in. I had never been happier to see him. There was still gray soot in his white fur, along with splotches of what could have been blood or ketchup around his muzzle. It was hard to tell.

Jack trotted right past me, without so much as a look. What did he think, that the door magically opened for him on its own? He moved into the living room where Ned had been staring at the wall. The dog jumped up onto the couch beside him and laid his body over Ned's lap. The two of them sat there like statues.

I walked past the room periodically and questioned whether or not they were breathing. I stood in the doorway until I saw their chests rise and fall, then I would give them another few minutes of privacy.

I could see that Jack was grieving too. Dogs have a sixth sense and I think he knew that Lena wasn't coming home. He never said it, but I am pretty sure he loved her for more reasons than plates of hot bacon.

I wanted to be useful, maternal even. I would go mad if I just continued to pace around the eerily quiet house while Ned and Jack remained in their catatonic states. I decided to cook whatever I could find. I whipped up scrambled eggs, chicken cutlets, spaghetti, waffles and grilled cheese. I assumed that most of it would get tossed out. With Lena gone, I doubted Ned had much of an appetite; I didn't. Normally Jack would have been salivating profusely if someone in the house were cooking, but he stayed jarringly stoic in Ned's lap. I guess it was for the best. I wouldn't have been surprised if my inexperienced cooking led to food poisoning.

It was starting to get late, and I worried that I would miss my appointment with West Laveau. Still, I didn't want to leave my godfather alone when he was clearly struggling with a mental break down. I went into the living room, convinced that I could pull him out of whatever door he was trapped behind in his mind. I stood in front of him with my arms crossed.

"Ned," I said. "Can you hear me, old man?"

He didn't say anything. He stared absently at the far wall. If he heard me, he gave no indication of it. Other than breathing, there were no signs of life in him. In a couple of hours, Ned had become pale and drained. I really should have allowed him to detach from the world. God knows he put up with me during more than one dramatic meltdown.

"Ned!" I screamed into his face, but there was no reaction.

"Hey, talk to me."

Silence. Now I was scared. I had never witnessed the deterioration of such a strong person before, someone I had always relied on to be stable and present. It wasn't unusual for me to act out when I felt vulnerable; and at that moment, I got the urge to throw something.

I noticed a stack of dark green marble coasters resting on top of the coffee table, between the couch and where I stood. I picked one up and let the heaviness of it weigh down my hand.

"Ned, please. Look at me. Blink. Give me a sign so that I know you're still in there."

He said nothing. He did nothing.

"Fine," I said, still not sure if he could hear me. It was time for drastic measures.

I threw the coaster over Ned's head. It crashed into the wall behind him, knocking a picture frame off the mantelpiece. Shards of glass flew to every corner of the room. Jack was on his feet. He whined, not sure what to make of the disruption. Ned never even flinched.

I hurled the next three coasters while screaming at Ned, demanding that he snap out of it. Once the last coaster hit the ground I could see dust drifting through the air, the wood panels of the walls were splintered, the pictures on the mantel had fallen and one of the windows was cracked, but it had been worth it. Ned moved.

He shifted his weight on the couch; his eyes flickered and bounced around the room, taking in the catastrophic scene.

"What the Hell happened in here?" he grunted. "Barnaby, did you do this?"

I guess he had been hidden some place in his subconscious all that time. He was wide-eyed and innocent while he waited for an explanation. Ned was clearly still in shock from the day's events, but I was thrilled that he was no longer comatose.

"Uh..." I stalled. I took a flannel blanket from the trunk in the corner of the room and wrapped it around his shoulders.

"What the Hell did you do? You broke my fireplace, damnit!" He was perfect at playing the quintessential grumpy man.

"Jack did it." I pointed a finger at the dog.

Ned pushed himself off of the sofa and placed a hand on my shoulder. I couldn't bear to look at him anymore. Where he had been emotionless only moments ago now he was filled with sorrow. I could see it in his wrinkled brow and tensed jaw line. I knew I wouldn't be able to ease his pain. Only time could do that and it would take a lot of time.

"Would you do me a favor, kid? Stay here," Ned said with a frog in his throat. My heart went out to him. "Would you stay here tonight? You can sleep in the guest room."

I nodded.

"Good. I'm gunna go to bed. I'll see you in the a.m."

I watched as he dragged his feet up the stairs and disappeared into the bedroom. I went back to the living room and started to tidy up. I picked up the heavy coasters, placed a few picture frames back on the mantle and tossed out the broken glass. Jesus, I thought. Lena would have a fit when she got home—

I put a hand to my chest and shuddered. What was I thinking?Lena was never coming home. I would never stop seeing the sadness in Ned's eyes. He all ready looked ten years older than he did a few hours before. She would never fuss over Jack or ask me if I met some special ever again. From now on, I'd have to buy my own socks and underwear.

After cleaning up, I sprawled myself out on the couch where Ned had spent the last few hours. It molded perfectly to my body after a trying day. It wasn't long before I had to head over to Marie's N'Orleans Café, but exhaustion had taken its toll on me. I drifted off, against my will, and fell into the world of dreams.

For a minute, I thought I was awake. I sat up and stretched my limbs. Jack was asleep on the armchair. When I looked around the room, I realized it was not how I had left it. There was no broken glass, no broken fireplace or holes in the wood panels. The living room was immaculate. It was exactly as Lena would have kept it.

Suddenly the lights began to flicker. The temperature in the room dropped. I could see my breath when I exhaled. I looked back at the armchair, but Jack was gone. He had evaporated from the room. There wasn't even a patch of white hair blanketing the spot where he'd been curled up. The windows blew open and an arctic blast of wind rushed in. Out of the darkness, a voice found its way to me, and a blurred figure was made clear.

"Hello, dear."

I held my breath. I realized why she had chosen to meet me in a dream. The living can't always sense spirits in the waking world, but in a dream you can't escape them. "Lena," I answered the voice.

She didn't speak right away. She watched me with warm eyes. She was glowing, just as she had in life. Lena McGreevy stepped out of the shadows towards where I sat on the sofa.

"How have you been?" she asked sweetly.

"What do you mean, since you died? I've been better."

"I'm flattered," her closed lips turned up into a demure smile.

"I had no idea you were such a narcissist, Lena."

She laughed, rich and infectious as always. She'd never taken my teasing seriously in life. I guess that hadn't changed. She used to say she admired my dark sense of humor because it proved that I was both insightful and clever.

"I can't believe you let that monster drink your blood, Sage. You should have never agreed to that. There are some lines that are not meant to be crossed."

I was shocked. How could she have known about the demon

in the alleyway? I gave her a puzzled look. My nose wrinkled at its bridge.

"Yes, I know you met with the demon," she explained. "The laws of time have no hold over me anymore. The past, present and future are one in the same. Although, there is still time to change your future, Sage."

"I can't believe you went snooping into my past," I scolded her and grabbed a hand full of my curls. "That is none of your business."

"Maybe not. I guess selling your soul to save your sister is none of my business, and your interest in the demon is none of my business, but what happened between you and my husband…" she narrowed her eyes, their deep brown color matched her cocoa skin. "That might be my business, what do you think?"

I flushed, and my cheeks grow hot with embarrassment. I couldn't find the words to defend myself. I cast my eyes to the floor. It had almost been two years since that pathetic, desperate low point in my life. I felt sick remembering it.

"I forgive you," she said, and I knew it was genuine.

"I never asked for your forgiveness."

"No, you did not, but one may wait a very long time for an apology from Sage Barnaby, and I'm in a bit of a hurry, dear."

"A hurry for what? I thought you were free of time restrictions."

"I am, but right now we're having a conversation inside of your head; and since you're not dead, you are going to wake up sooner or later."

I nodded so that she knew I understood.

"I wish I could have come here with the sole purpose of saying goodbye," she started with a tender smile. "Unfortunately, I have only been allowed this visit because you need to warned. Do not meet with West Laveau. Do not summon the angel."

"I have to. You know I have to."

"Nothing good will come of it. Things will remain as they are meant to be."

"How else will I ever get to see you again, Lena?" I frowned. "It's not like someone is going to hand me a day pass to Heaven."

I knew I should trust Lena. She had passed into the world of spirits and immortality. At this point she was wiser than any living person. Still, I couldn't practice blind faith. I screwed up ten years ago and this was the one chance I had to change my ill-fated future. If I didn't attempt what West Laveau had planned, then I would undoubtedly be doomed to an eternity in fire.

"Lena," I continued. "I did something that is unforgiveable; and even if I could take it back, I wouldn't. Nola deserved to live. I tried to make sure that she did. I crossed a line, but I don't regret it. She was sick and I was her sister. It was an easy decision, an obvious choice—"

"Sage," she shook her head gently. "You were dealt a tough hand, but you play with the cards you were dealt. You don't cheat. You don't make deals with the Devil."

"I'm scared," I confessed. I felt warm tears spring into my eyes. I had never cried in a dream before. "I had good intentions, really I did. I just wanted to help, but I was only eight years old. I was naïve, stupid— and now…" *I am damned.* I wanted to say, but it seemed unnecessary. Lena knew my sins; there was no point saying them out loud. "Could you put in a good word for me? I don't want to go to Hell. Lena, please."

"I have put in a good word, several in fact," Lena's lips pressed into a smile, but her tender expression quickly faded. I don't believe she wanted to give me false hope.

I felt a sudden pull from the room, like the first steep drop of a roller coaster, that moment when your stomach vanishes for a few seconds and then plummets back inside of you. I was waking up.

"Lena!" I shouted into nothingness. The room had blurred

and gone. I was adrift in a hazy darkness. "Help me, please." I was trembling, afraid of losing her a second time, afraid of waking up with more questions than answers.

In a flash, her face was clear again; her eyes were bright and inches from mine. She held my face in her hands, which were soft and surprisingly warm. I had thought they would be cold. I don't know why she felt so warm, maybe it was the dream or maybe it was because Lena was at peace.

"I can't save you from the path you're on. I wish I could," her normally cheery voice dropped into a low whisper. "I loved in life and that feeling has only been amplified in death. Therefore, I will help you in one small way."

"How?"

Lena shrugged casually. "I can give you a name." A teasing smile played on her lips.

My brow furrowed with curiosity. "Whose name?"

Lena's dark eyes twinkled with unfiltered delight. "I think the world could use one less demon in it, don't you? Besides, pinstriped slacks and a matching waistcoat— Can you say out of style? It's tasteless and tacky and I won't have it!" she waved her finger at me. "Sage, if you wake up now you can sneak in a quick exorcism before meeting the Creole Sorcerer, if that's still what you plan to do."

Lena was referring to the demon from the alley, the bloodlust demon. At least one good thing would come from today. "Lena, tell me. What's his name?" I inched nearer to her, tingling with excitement. Discovering a demon's name pre-exorcism was like Christmas in July.

She leaned in, wrapped me in a hug and delicately whispered the creature's name in my ear. I nearly collapsed at the sound of it. I knew exactly who this demon was. He was infamous among demons, revered by his own kind. Even his enemies admired his wicked conviction, his unholy accomplishments. Oh, he was very bad, and I would be the one who cast him back to Hell. Thanks, Lena.

She released me from our embrace. I tried to mask the sadness in my eyes and swallow the cry in my throat. "Goodbye, sweetheart," she whispered before quietly retreating back to where she came from, the light.

Then I woke up.

6

The Devil's Masterpiece

Ned·

Out walking the dog. Jack has an embarrassingly
small bladder. We will be back when he's
good and empty. Don't worry. Sleep well.

-S.B

Bridgeview City was its haunting self on the walk from Ned's
house to the café. My boots scuffed along the sidewalk, as I dragged
my feet around corners and down unlit streets. I couldn't help
feeling hopeful, despite Lena's warning. Tonight I would meet my
guardian angel.

I made a quick stop at my apartment on Gretchen Road.
It never hurt to take a few precautions before dealing with the
supernatural. I strolled past the plum colored walls of my bedroom
and slid open the closet door. Before me was a sea of black clothes.
I shoved the black sweaters, jeans, leggings and t-shirts to one side
of the closet to expose the back walls' wood paneling. I pushed my
weight against two of the wood panels and it triggered a release. I
removed the planks from their place in the closet, revealing a secret

compartment within. This was where I hid my toys, if you can call them that.

I owned an array of knives, from pocket to machete; and while I tried to stay away from using guns, I recently purchased a vintage English pistol and a Colt Python revolver. They were racked one on top of the other and both were fully loaded.

There were also less obvious weapons, which happened to be the more commonly used. These items consisted of bags of unprocessed salt, boxes of school board chalk and gallons of holy water. I always kept a flask of holy water in my pocket whenever I worked a job.

Every weapon had a story to tell; some more than others. Tonight I took the Colt Python with me. Its wood grip perfectly fit the curves of my hand. The smooth, cold black barrel of the gun had never failed whenever I made the choice to aim and fire. I would be lying if I said I didn't love the way the chamber clicked into ready position. It might not have been the prettiest gun, but I trusted it in a tight spot.

I slipped the flask of holy water and a bit of white chalk into my jacket's side pocket, and stuffed the barrel end of the gun down the back of my pants, the wooden handle peeked out over the top of my jeans. I grabbed my apartment keys off the coffee table, locked the door behind me and set out to meet the illustrious West Laveau.

Even though it was August, the night carried a cool breeze with it and I hugged my black pleated military coat tight against my body. A muggy fog had settled in the air and Jack's stark white fur made him look like a ghost lost in the darkness. I wondered if I looked just as inhuman, dressed in black with pale skin, wild dark curls and russet brown eyes.

I turned onto Talbot Street, closing in on my destination. I looked down at the watch on my wrist. It was almost eleven, which meant this would have to be the quickest exorcism in history. After all, I had an angel to summon at 12:08 a.m.

I slid my right hand into my jacket pocket and removed a tiny bit of chalk. It seemed silly that such a small, fragile thing could be ultimate weapon against a powerful demon.

I approached Marie's N'Orleans Café and took note of the "Grand Opening" banner beneath the title sign. The neighboring buildings weren't exactly friendly looking, but that only made the small cafe shine brighter. It was a humble looking place that gave off the appeal of southern hospitality. The exterior was brick, which had been painted white, and the front door was made of glass encased in a black cast iron design.

I walked to the front door and pressed my nose to the glass. The lights were switched off inside, but I could still make out the black white-checkered tiles of the floor and small bistro tables accompanied by two or three matching chairs. It was small, less than half the size of 1976, but it certainly had charm.

I gently tapped on the glass door and waited for a figure to emerge. A tall, lanky shadow appeared and crossed the length of the café towards to front door. I immediately recognized him as the thin demon with terrible posture from the alleyway. He flashed a pointed smile at me before gently pushing the door open and taking a step outside.

I tried to conceal my excitement as butterflies swarmed in my stomach. The demon had no clue that he'd just walked right into a trap.

"Bon nuit, cherie," he pleasantly greeted me. "Oh, and you brought your furry friend." He sounded disappointed upon noticing Jack, who was standing at my side with his tail limp and his ears alert.

"Can I ask you something, demon? Who does that body really belong to?"

"What does it matter?" he scoffed, his French accent pressed onto every word. "I wear it so much better than he ever did."

"Can you even remember his name?"

"The name on the clipboard was Darryl Stephens, but he checked out years before I found him. I could see that there was no soul in this frame. The body was wasting away in a hospital bed. He had been in a coma, cherie. There were machines keeping his body alive, but Mr. Stephens was long gone."

"I don't believe you."

"I am proud of my wrong doings; I would not hide them from you. I needed a physical form and this body was unoccupied. It is much easier than taking one by force. People tend to fight back; and even when I win, they are still there, sitting in the corner of my mind. I endure them as they whine and scream and cry, but I can always hear them. It can be distracting."

"I bet," I agreed nonchalantly.

His amiable expression darkened. The corners of his mouth turned down. "Why did you want to know about this body's original owner?"

I loved this moment, when I was still one step ahead of them, just before the demons realized that this would be their last night on Earth.

"I wanted to know who I would be speaking with once you were gone."

The demon cocked his head to the left, unsure of my meaning.

Being so close to him should have made me nervous, but I had never felt safer in the presence of a demon. I pointed to my feet and watched as his eyes followed the direction of my finger. When he saw what I wanted him to see, a flood of rage pumped through him. A surge of color rose in his mocha skin as he wrenched his hands into fists and cried out in distress.

"Sage Barnaby, you will undo this demon's snare!" He was

beside himself with anger.

I was completely enthralled by his panic. Who needs Netflix when you can exorcize demons?

He was standing in the center of a demon's snare, which I had drawn with the bit of chalk I had tucked in my pocket. I was surprised he hadn't noticed the white powder that caked my fingertips. A demon's snare is comprised of a circle filled with specific pagan symbols and a few forgotten words. When a demon steps inside the circle, it cannot step out. That is, unless the circle is broken.

I didn't have much time to show off my artistic abilities so the trap didn't consist of much detail. The one drawn under my bed was much more impressive. The snare he stood in was simply a circle encompassing the evil eye and several very old words few people would be able to read.

"This is silly, Sage," his voice went up several octaves. "You cannot exorcize me. You do not know my name, and this will not work unless I tell you my name."

I cracked a winning smile. "I might be damned, but I have friends in high places. I know all about you, Alastor."

The demon's eyes widened and quivered in their sockets, as though he'd just suffered a monstrous betrayal. "That is not possible."

Jack sat at my side and we shared a sense of amused satisfaction while the demon paced hopelessly inside the trap. I wanted nothing more than to be the girl who sent the infamous Alastor, whose cruelty is unrivaled, back to Hell.

"Give my love to your scorned brothers," I said complacently.

"No! Cherie, I beg you! Do not send me back. Let me stay. I will do whatever you ask. Do not send me back!"

I began to recite the exorcism ritual I was taught under an experienced priest in Rome. The Latin fell off my tongue without difficulty. I didn't stammer once, which was often the case when I first learned the language. While I spoke, Alastor's body moved in unnatural ways and the sounds that came from him were unnervingly inhuman.

His stretched limbs twisted and contorted into horrifying positions. His arms entwined behind his back in such a way that I was certain they had broken. If there was another person dwelling inside that body, they would need medical attention after I exorcized Alastor.

I wasn't surprised that Alastor was so desperate to stay on Earth. After what he had done, I would be scared to face my brothers too.

"You know who I am, cherie!" he wailed as I continued to speak the Latin verse. "I am the Devil's Masterpiece! I am the most wicked of his children, the most senseless and cold-hearted! You cannot do this to me!"

Alastor didn't need to introduce himself. I knew exactly who he was. Originally the Devil's Masterpiece was made up of six demons, they were brothers—

I should explain that demons were never angels. They did not fall from the Heaven. They were born in the fires of Hell. While humankind and the angels were merely created in His all mighty image, demons were made from the Unholy One. Lucifer carved them from his flesh and brought them to life with his blood. Humans were crafted from the clay of the Earth, and because of that we're weak and easily manipulated, molded. Demons, however, are insufferable and destructive all the way through. They will stop at nothing to inflict pain and conflict into the lives of others and nothing pleases them more.

Alastor was the youngest of six brothers who traveled the circles of Hell and cities of the world together. There was Sarpendon, Neleus, Clymenous, Pylos, Nestor and finally, Alastor. His older brothers were simple-minded demons. They sought to tempt men into betraying their loved ones. They hoped to be the reason an honest man took off his wedding ring when he noticed an attractive woman or when a normally reasonable person used their kid's college savings to keep gambling. Alastor wanted to cause more damage than that. He strove for greater things.

"Cherie!" the demon called to me. His voice strained; his eyes bloodshot. "If you send me back to the underworld, I will placed in the deepest part of Hell, the ninth circle."

"Yes, the place where betrayers are imprisoned. You belong there after what you did to your brothers."

"You know, it is a wonder you are so quick to judge," he continued, falling into a rant. "I was created in the image of evil. I am a demon of bloodshed and bloodlust. It is in my nature, and therefore out of my hands. As for you, you are requesting aid from Monsieur West Laveau. You claim to be a moral upstanding child, but you have done something so terrible that you are desperate for my friend's assistance. You want Laveau to save you from what it is you have brought down on yourself, a mistake you made of your own volition! So do not be so quick to judge me, the demon. I have a better excuse for my bad behavior than you do."

I was speechless and a little embarrassed. I did my best not to show that he'd shaken me. The demon had successfully called me out on my foolishness and defended his cruelty. At least he could blame his wickedness on instinct. I had chosen to go off course and do something I knew was wrong, all on my own.

"I will let you in on a secret," Alastor proceeded. He was stalling. "Demons, like angels, do not want to be restricted to their homes for all time. The idea of remaining in one never changing place is unbearable to supernatural beings. Life on Earth is exactly what we are looking for. We envy what you have here. The way your world is constantly changing and how human emotions come and go so quickly. We are amazed that the sun will fill the sky one day and storm clouds will command it the next."

I had actually thought about that from time to time. I would lie awake at night and imagine how angels and demons view humanity. I came to the conclusion that angels and demons, God and the Devil, must be unendingly fascinated by how we can endure and cause the worst kind of harm, destruction to our world and each other. Still, we are capable of love and forgiveness. Humans are well rounded. We're three-dimensional but any other creature in existence is not. I always felt that we were something to be admired. There is nothing quite like being human and the rest of creation knows it; they envy it. Not every day, but most days, knowing that is enough to get me out of bed before Jack urinates all over the apartment.

"I was the youngest of six brothers and wherever we made our home on Earth chaos followed," the demon explained. "We grew stronger throughout the decades and the centuries. The madness we created was so brutal and heartless that the Devil himself often referred to us as his masterpiece, but it was my desire to be the worst. It was my dream to surprise Lucifer with the depth of my callousness. Does that shock you, cherie? That even demons can dream?I decided to send each of my brothers back to Hell without the prospect of ever returning."

My eyes sparked with intrigue. "A permanent exorcism?"

He lifted his eyebrows. "Precisely."

"How?" I asked.

I didn't even know permanent exorcisms were possible. I could save so many lives with that knowledge. I had never sent demons back into Hell without the fear of them returning. As it stands now, you can send them back but the really clever ones always manage to crawl out again. "Alastor, tell me how."

"No. I cannot," he said. I knew pushing him to speak further on the subject would only ensure his silence. "Moving forward, I started with Nestor who never saw it coming. He was the second youngest of our family. I suppose I thought it would be poetic to work my way up to the eldest. Pylos was next, which I have to admit was the most difficult for me because we were a good team once upon a time; he could always get a laugh out of me."

Alastor paused here and for the briefest moment his smile faded, remembering his lost brother, Pylos. Not a second later, he shook his head and dismissed whatever nostalgia he'd felt.

"Regardless of my near hesitation, I knew that Pylos had to die. It was all part of my master plan. Kill my brothers, an act so heartless even the Devil himself would be surprised; and as a result, I would go down in history as the cruelest demon in all creation. We have little else to aspire towards where I come from.

"After Pylos was gone, Clymenous and Neleus caught on. In vain, they tried to overcome me with force, but they had always been wide, clumsy characters and I was much too quick for them. It took next to no effort to dodge their blows and catch them off guard. It was almost too easy to be rid of those two.

"Finally my eldest brother, Sarpendon made an appearance. He was wonderful, the way his eyes dashed about the room and focused on each of our fallen brothers. It was magical from where I stood. Sarpendon's face twisted in anguish and his hands tightened into shaking fists. It was a delicious sight, and I drank it in, every last drop.

"While demons are not capable of love, my brothers and I did have an understanding. We trusted one another. We relied on one another. We had agreed in the beginning to torment the souls of this world together in the name of our creator, and I had betrayed that promise. My eldest brother was furious with me to say the least.

"I can recall hearing Sarpendon's shoes click across the halls of our home until he found his way into the grand library and his eyes feasted on the gory scene. All of his brothers' bodies were lifeless and broken, save one. I stood before him and was beside myself with excitement. I had nearly achieved my goal. I could barely control my laughter. I had gone mad and I relished in that madness. Sarpendon crossed the room, stepping over the bodies as if they weren't there and approached me.

" 'What have you done, little brother?' he asked.

" 'It seems I have made a mess. I am afraid we may never be able to remove those stains from the carpet.' I couldn't help making light of the situation. Especially when Sarpendon was being so perfectly dreary.

" 'Our brothers…' He looked dejected as his eyes passed over their corpses before resting on the object in my hand. 'They can never return to Earth.'

" 'That's right,' I sighed, bored with the sad expression on his face.

" 'Why?'

"I repeated Sarpendon's question to myself. Why? Why? I had thought it was obvious. I wanted to be great. And when one is not born great or has greatness thrust upon them, he must achieve it. However, achieving greatness means making sacrifices, which is why so few people ever acquire it. I had been looking forward to this moment for a very long time. With the rest of my brothers all ready back in the lake of fire, news of my diabolical plan was surely moving through the circles of Hell. I was almost famous. There was just one more thing to do.

" 'Why?' Sarpendon repeated in a booming voice.

" 'Why not?' I responded coyly.

" 'This is wrong.'

" 'Which is why it feels so right.' I began to circle him like a vulture waiting for its prey to die. 'You have become very sentimental in your old age, Sarpendon. I am amazed that you feel sorrow over the loss of our brothers. I did not expect that from you.'

" 'Not sorrow, brother. I feel regret for the suffering we could have caused this world. The six of us were made for each other and we are strongest when we are together. We are the Devil's Masterpiece.'

" 'Do not worry about the suffering the people of this world will endure, brother. I will take care of that.' I brought my face close to his. I could smell the adrenaline rushing through him. His eyes were solid black and seething. He was ready to fight. He hated me and I found that very stimulating.

" 'You are the final piece of the puzzle, Sarpendon. '

" 'Yes. I figured that out for myself,' he nearly laughed. My eldest brother always had a dark sense of humor. 'I'm stronger than you are, Alastor. You know this.'

" 'Je sais,' I answered in French. 'You are better than me.'

" 'Then how do you intend to kill me?'

" 'I want you dead more than you want to live.'

" 'Well, it seems we're past the point of words. We must now speak through our actions. You first. I insist.'

" 'Always the gentleman, Sarpendon. Goodbye, brother.'

"Sarpendon was right. He was stronger than I was. He had been older than me by a millennium or so and it certainly showed during our final time together. To be honest, there were a couple of moments when I doubted whether or not I would come out on top. But like I said to Sarpendon, I wanted him dead more than he wanted to live. Needless to say, my brother did not retreat into the eternal fire easily.

"I couldn't tell you how long our battle raged. Perhaps we fought for over a century because the state of our home was unrecognizable by the time we were through. The wood was rotting, cobwebs had piled up and my brothers' bodies were severely decomposed. But time isn't so important to immortal creatures.

"I am the last of the Devil's Masterpiece to roam the Earth. My plot to achieve greatness and become a legend among my own kind was a success. I am now the patron demon of familial bloodshed. When a parent harms their child or there is brutality between brothers, you can find me just around the corner with a smile on my face.

"I am the most heartless of Lucifer's children; and because of that, I am one of daddy's favorites, although I have been told he was quite angry with me at first. After all I did betray my own kind, my own blood. Eventually he realized that I was a mad genius and praised me for my actions. My older brothers do not share his appreciation of my wickedness, which is why I am in no hurry to return to the lake of fire. My brothers will want a word with me and I am not ready for that conversation or the violence that will follow."

I stood in front of him, arms crossed, watching the demon recover from his tale. Alastor was hunched over, his hands on his knees and his breaths labored. I had never officially called off the exorcism so he remained in a state of total distress and unfathomable agony.

"That was one Hell of a story," I complimented him.

"But you're still going to send me back."

"It's sort of my thing."

"Then I would like to request that you make it quick," he wheezed. "I feel as though I might turn inside out any second."

I was about to grant his request when a question jumped to the front of my mind.

"Laveau must know you committed a crime against your own kind," I noted. "How can he trust you after what you did?"

"Damned if I know," he spat back at me.

"You're damned either way."

He almost laughed, despite the excruciating pain he was in. Alastor's eyes were rolling back into his head while his neck was twisted at such a sharp angle I worried it might snap. "If you must know, I owe Laveau a favor, several in fact."

I wanted to know more but time continued to press on. "Okay, I have to summon an angel in less than an hour. Goodbye, Alastor."

I started to recite the final section of the exorcism ritual, picking up where I left off. Alastor was fighting it. He didn't want to go, but he couldn't escape my words and my will. The wind blew up around us and the surrounding street lamps flickered on and off. I was nearing the end of my chant. Alastor knew it. There was fear pouring out of his honey colored eyes.

A sudden, unexpected sound made itself known from inside the café, and it rose over the ugly screams coming from Alastor. The noise persisted and I recognized it as clapping. A lone figure emerged from the café and walked out into the faint glow of streetlamps. His skin was as dark as the night. His eyes were darker still. There was no hair on top of his head, which was perfectly round and looked as though it had just been polished.

"That was quite a show, Miss Barnaby." The applause stopped. "However, Alastor still owes me a couple of favors so I would prefer if he wasn't sent back to the furnace just yet."

The man then smeared the chalked circle with his shoe and the demon's snare ceased to possess any power. Now that Alastor was no longer in throbbing pain, he straightened himself out and exhaled a sigh of relief.

Alastor gave me a relaxed salute. "Do not beat yourself up, cherie. It would have been a beautiful exorcism if you had been given the chance to finish."

Jack was on full alert again as Alastor stepped out of the demon's snare. The bald man approached me with one hand extended, the other resting comfortably inside his pantsuit pocket. The gray suit was perfectly tailored, accompanied with a skinny black tie resting over a white button up dress shirt.

When I shook his hand, I saw that he was also adorning skull cuff links. It was a bold look but it suited him.

"You must be Sage Barnaby. I have heard so much about you. You may have guessed that I am West Laveau."

7

The Creole Sorcerer

"Hello," I shook his hand, very business-like.

"I gather you've been trying to meet me for some time." His eyes sparkled despite their ink black color. "It seems we have time for a quick chat before we call on your angel. Alastor, you may leave us. Miss Barnaby, please follow me."

Alastor watched Jack, Laveau and I disappear into the unlit café. Just before we were out of sight, I glanced back over my shoulder and Alastor shot me another nonchalant salute.

We moved towards the back of the café where an enormous grandfather clock rested in the far left corner of the room. It was an antique and it tock-ticked rather than tick-tocked, which drove me a little mad.

West reached out and opened the clock's door where the pendulum swung back and forth. He pushed at the wood panel behind the pendulum and it gave way, revealing a narrow corridor that led to a solitary red door.

"This way," he smiled and savored the surprise in my eyes.

Jack and I stayed close behind as we followed West down the hallway. The red door was unlocked, and West walked in ahead of us. I shut the door behind me; and when I turned to face the room,

I found myself staring into a mirror. I faced my reflection and took in a pair of large brown eyes, a button nose, heart shaped lips, cascading curls and a soft curved body. Yeah, that was definitely me, but the mirror seemed somehow peculiar.

It was certainly an antique, same as the grandfather clock. The mirror's frame was made of cast iron, similar to the front door, and the black metal hugged the glass in place. The design created from the cast iron looked familiar to me. I studied the mirror trying to figure out where I had seen those symbols before, and then it dawned on me. I was staring at the Egyptian symbol for truth, an ostrich feather, which was connected to the goddess of truth, Ma'at.

"Do you like it?" West watched me admire the object.

"Sure, but... there's something off about this mirror. I don't know. It's just a feeling."

West's smile broadened.

In a way, he hadn't stopped smiling since I met him. He had a constant twinkle in his eye, a small spark of electricity pushing through the black abyss. It was as though Laveau had a secret lurking just beneath the surface. His eyes were constantly suggesting that he knew something everyone else didn't. He had the answers while the rest of us where fumbling around aimlessly in the dark.

"You have strong instincts, Miss Barnaby. You're right. That is no ordinary mirror. It is called a tell-all and they are quite rare. I'm a collector of priceless items, you see. My sources have reported that there are only two tell-alls in the world and I own one of them."

"You have sources?" I asked. "I thought you knew everything."

He chuckled. "If only that were true. I know so much because I never stop asking questions, and one question inevitably leads to another."

"What makes this mirror so special?"

"It shows things for what they really are. Let me explain," He was proud of the trinket and crossed over to the object. "When you stand before the mirror, you see your reflection; nothing has changed. That is because you are human and that is what's reflected in the tell-all. If Alastor were to stand in front of the mirror, he would not see the body he's taken over; he would see the creature within. The tell-all would show his true demonic form."

"Have you seen what he really looks like?" I asked, sounding naïve.

"I have. What an incredible sight. It would be hard to describe accurately, but I will say there is something both sick and elegant about his tortured, skeletal and almost metallic appearance."

Laveau walked across the room where he kept a large cupboard. I took a moment to scan my new surroundings. It was a large, open space. There was no clutter. Apart from the cupboard to the right of the mirror, there was a long bar fully stocked with a variety of liquors and a poker table in the center of the room. The florescent lights seemed to cheapen the room, which West had clearly put a good deal of money into.

"How much time do we have left?" he asked. Laveau had taken a dozen white candles from the cupboard and was placing them sporadically around the room before lighting their wicks.

"The time to summon my guardian is 12:08 a.m. We have twenty-one minutes until then."

"Perfect. Enough time for a drink then. Would you like one?"

"No, thank you."

West Laveau slowly made his way to the bar. He seemed perfectly relaxed in his movements. I quickly concluded that this man had not compromised in any part of his life. He was in control of his destiny. He poured liquor from a bottle with a label that had the word Rhum written on it. I could also make out a bit of the fine print that noted the liquor was imported from Haiti.

He took a long, indulgent sip of the beverage before addressing me. "What do you think of my café?"

"It's hard to say. I haven't tried the food."

"All the southern desserts are made from my great, great, great-grandmother's recipes. She lived in New Orleans in 1794. She was born free, you know. Marie's N'Orleans Café is just a small tribute to her."

"A small tribute to one of her many talents," I added. West Laveau must have known his great, great, great, grandmother was famous for more than baking.

"What do you know about Marie Laveau?"

"That she was known as The Voodoo Queen of New Orleans."

He flashed a smile, beaming with pride for his ancestor's reputation. "She was brilliant, you know."

I had heard many rumors involving Marie Laveau's connection to voodoo and supernatural forces. Some of those rumors affected West Laveau. No one knows for sure; but it's whispered that Marie had an affair behind her husband's back. More specifically, a love affair with an angel in the early nineteenth century and the consequences of that affair resulted in a child. The child was called "the hybrid," and if the rumors are true, West may not be entirely human. He may have a touch of divinity in him. It would make sense given his supernatural line of work but like I said, they were only whispers.

Of course I didn't mention this to him. If it were true, then West obviously wanted it kept private. After West finished his drink, he set the glass aside and returned to the cupboard. He proceeded to burn a bit of sage and outlined the pool table with a thick line of red powder, which I knew to be brick dust.

"You're taking a lot of precautions," I said.

"In order to summon your guardian, we will need to open a portal between this world and the world beyond. It won't be a very large opening and I don't suspect anyone will notice; but there is a chance that something other than your angel will find its way through. Sage, the herb not Barnaby, cleanses the room of negative energy and any creature that means us harm won't be able to cross the line of brick dust."

After prepping the room for an angel summoning, West crossed back to the bar and took another sip of rum.

I heard ice cubes clink together as he stirred the glass in his hand. "Miss Barnaby, you've noticed by now that I haven't asked for anything in return for my help."

The thought had crossed my mind. In ordinary life people rarely do something without an incentive, or a reward; in the supernatural world it is unheard of.

"What do you want?" I wasn't sure I had anything to offer him. West Laveau was a collector of priceless objects. What could I offer him that would compare?

"I love a good story," he said.

I pursed my lips, thinking. "I don't know any."

"Then I will settle for yours," he teased, large teeth shining through his smile. "What brought you to me? I have heard stories, but it is so hard to know what's true unless one hears it from the source."

"You want to know about my deal with the Devil."

He leaned forward, and I watched his pupils dilate. "So there was a deal."

I felt my cheeks blush. I hated to admit I had ever done something so terrible, even if it was for a good reason, a noble cause. I took a seat at the bar and wished I could reach out and pour myself a drink, something to take the edge off. I was fully committed to the idea that a shot of rum would make sharing this story a whole lot easier, but I resisted. I made a series of sighs and groans before words started to form. It wasn't poetic, but it was the truth. It was my truth, for better or worse.

8

To the Moon & Back

"Nola was three years younger than me."

I hadn't said her name in years. That was a whole new kind of hurt.

"She had leukemia and time wasn't on her side. I was her big sister. I just couldn't accept that. I can still recall every floor, staircase and elevator of Lazarus Hospital because that is the place where my childhood died. The overpowering smell of cleaning products, the cold stale air and the awful cafeteria food will never leave me.

"Even in a hospital gown, she was the most beautiful little girl— the personification of innocence. My parents tried to hide what was going on from her, but I think Nola knew she was dying. Throughout the duration of her treatments, she never cried or complained even though it was clear she was in pain. Some of her golden hair had fallen out and at times her skin looked frail and gray.

"My mother and father were beside themselves and followed the expected behavior of a grieving parent. Hopeful and strong in front of their child but belligerent and broken behind closed doors. My father drank more and my mother smiled less. I don't blame them for falling apart while Nola was sick, but I can't forgive them for rejecting me after she died.

"My parents, June and Walter, were holiday Catholics. However, when Nola got sick my mother had a renewed sense of faith. She prayed constantly in the hospital's chapel, the church in Tarrytown where I grew up and at Nola's bedside while my sister was asleep. My mother really believed that words would save her little girl.

"Personally, I've always put my faith in actions. Without actions to back up our promises, our words mean nothing. Maybe that's part of the reason I lit a red candle on a night when the moon was full and read from a very old book.

"The truth is that I had close to no idea what I was doing in the hospital basement that night. I actually discovered the book in the Tarrytown library when I wandered away from the childrens' section and found myself upstairs in a room I had never explored before. The windows stretched from the floor to the ceiling, even taller than the bookshelves. I remember the carpet under my feet being an unattractive faded green. The smell in the room overwhelmed me. It was an intoxicating musk that can only come from old books, the smell of magic.

"I breathed in and it was like discovering a new world. My eyes moved over the spines of the books that surrounded me. I raced in and out of the aisles, past millions of pages, thousands of characters and hundreds upon hundreds of stories. I was stopped in my tracks when one book flew off the shelf and landed, with a thud, at my feet. I jumped at the sudden noise in the silent library. I stared down at it, unable to figure out how the book had suddenly come loose from the shelf. It was as if the book wanted my attention. Like it had been reaching out, just waiting for me to come along.

I can't even remember if there was a title inscribed on the cover, but the book was so heavy my eight-year-old hands could barely support it. I brushed away the dust and opened it up to where a marker had been placed, page one hundred and sixteen.

"The first set of words were written in English.

> *Only to be read out loud when your faith in Him*
> *has failed you.*

"The next line was written in Latin.

> *Quando periit fides estis quaesivit, et sub luna*
> *plena, i quaerunt vestry vexillum hac nocte.*

"When faith is lost you are sought, and beneath a full moon, I seek your company this night.

"Following the Latin was a checklist of necessary items and quasi directions. I needed to light a single red candle in an underground location while the moon was full. I was to repeat the Latin phrase three times out loud before blowing out the candle.

"I never checked out the leather bond book from the library. I simply tore that page from it, folded the piece of paper and shoved it into my pocket. When I got home, I hid the page under my mattress. I was sure it would stay safe there. Since Nola had gotten sick, my mother and father rarely cleaned the house, did laundry or made dinner. All of their conversations focused on taking shifts at the hospital or medical bills.

"Most of their responsibilities regarding me had been pushed onto my godfather, Ned McGreevy. He lived about a half-hour north of Tarrytown in Bridgeview City, but he made the drive south every day so that someone would be there to pick me up from school. He made sure I did my homework, we would watch old movies together, and he always gave me an extra scoop of ice cream for dessert. On the weekends he would visit Nola at the hospital and read her favorite stories to her. She loved books by Dr. Seuss."

I stopped for a moment to collect myself. Memories of Ned reading *Horton Hears a Who* had gotten me chocked up.

"Would you like a refreshment, something to ease your nerves?"

Yes, a thousand times yes, I wanted to say. "No, thanks," I answered instead.

"At your leisure, Miss Barnaby," he waited with patience and genuine interest.

I nodded. "One night Ned stayed over the house while my parents stayed in the hospital. He had fallen asleep in my father's armchair; and not wanting to be alone, I curled up on the couch. It must have been close to three in the morning when the phone rang. He was startled out of his sleep and jumped over to the source of the sound. He grabbed the phone's receiver and pressed it to his face. For a couple of seconds Ned appeared groggy, eyelids half closed and his hair flat against one side of his head. His bewildered state didn't last long. In a flash, his full attention was on the voice streaming in through the phone. His expression collapsed.

" 'Okay.' His voice was grainy. It was the only thing he said before he hung up. He rubbed his forehead with the palm of his hand but it didn't produce any calming effects.

"Ned looked up and found me watching him. He kept his eyes locked on mine. I could tell he wanted me to know something, but he couldn't bring himself to say it. I didn't matter. The message was clear to me.

" 'Okay,' I said. 'I'll get my coat.'

"Ned was taken aback, but tried not to show his surprise. He slipped into a pair of loafers and waited for me by the door.

"I wasn't really going upstairs for a coat. That was a diversion. I ran into my bedroom and pushed my hand beneath the mattress until I found the slip of paper I had taken from the mysterious library book. I stuffed it into my coat pocket then pulled open my sock drawer and withdrew a red candle. Before heading back downstairs, I threw open the curtains in front of my window. As if it were meant to be, the moon was full and beaming against the night sky.

"Ned sat in the waiting room while I stood at Nola's bedside with my parents. I could tell my mother had been crying. My father remained quiet in the corner. There were no sobs, cussing or prayers coming from him, but I could see that his hands were shaking.

" 'Sage, why don't you say something to your sister?' my mother suggested.

"You know, I have exorcized demons and run from creatures I don't even know the names of, but walking over to Nola's hospital bed that night was the scariest thing I have ever done.

"I looked down and the first thing I noticed was her petite, milk white hand. I leaned closer and held it. She tightened her tiny fingers around mine with all the strength she could muster, but it wasn't much. I knew what my mother meant when she told me to say something to Nola. She meant that I should say something nice, that I should say goodbye— because it would be the last thing I said to her.

" 'Nola.'

" 'Sage,' she called to me in a soft whisper.

" 'Hi.' I forced a smile. I couldn't bear seeing her in this condition. She was so frail. I was afraid to touch her because she looked as though she would break. 'I miss you at home. I like your braid,' I continued. What was left of her yellow hair was perfectly braided to one side of her head. With gold hair, big brown eyes and a button nose Nola appeared to be a genuine fairytale princess.

" 'Mommy did it for me,' she answered happily.

"That's when I heard a choking sound, a guttural cry escaped from my mother. She smacked a hand over her own mouth and held it there. She turned away from my sister and I, allowing us some privacy.

" 'Mommy did a good job. You look beautiful,' I said.

" 'I'm sleepy.'

" 'I know but try to stay awake a little longer. Please.'

" 'Okay.' She nodded and struggled to keep her eyes open.

"I remember envying her in that moment. Death wasn't frightening for Nola; it was a welcomed nap. My father was in shock, my mother was sick to her stomach and my heart was breaking, but Nola was fine. She was calm and accepting. I knew that I was being selfish for wanting to keep her with me.

"Then something amazing happened. I accepted that I was selfish. I stopped feeling bad about it. I didn't care that Nola was tired or that this was her time. I decided that she needed more. I became obsessed with the idea that she had been cheated and this was not right. I told myself dying at five years old was not going to be my sister's destiny. I wasn't sure what I could accomplish with a candle and piece of paper, but it was the only trick I had up my sleeve.

" 'Nola.' I held back a flood of tears. 'I love you. I love you so much.'

" 'To the moon and back,' she smiled. It was something we had always told one another in my family.

" 'Yes. And much, much more.'

" 'I love you too,' she said.

" 'Nola, do you think you can stay awake for a couple more minutes? Would you do that for me? Don't go to sleep until I come back.'

"She promised she would do her best, and with that, I went racing out of the room and down the corridor towards the stairwell. I sped past Ned in the waiting room. I didn't give him a chance to ask where I was running.

"I tripped over my feet several times while descending to the lowest level of Lazarus Hospital. I managed to catch myself on the rail but I never stopped moving. One foot in front of the other, over and over and over and faster and faster. Eventually the moonlight grew dim and the air around me became cool. I was in the hospital's basement, well underground.

"Maybe if I had taken a moment to think about what I was doing, I wouldn't have gone through with it. Even at eight years old I understood how foolish it seemed, practicing dark magic under the full moon, what a cliché. But I didn't think about it. I ripped off my jacket and emptied the pockets on to the gray concrete floor. I struck a match, lit the red candle and used its light to read from the page I had torn out of the library book.

"The first line had stated that this was only to be executed when my faith in Him had failed. Well, my mother had been praying for months and each plea had gone unanswered. Nola was just a little girl. What could possibly be gained from her death? It was clear that my mother's faith in Him had betrayed her. I was going to do something about it.

"I held the candle up to the paper, casting its light on the Latin words. It took me several attempts to properly annunciate the foreign language.

" 'Quando periit fides estis quaesivit, et sub luna plena i quaerunt vestri vexillum hac nocte.'

"I recited the phrase three times out loud. My voice shook, but I forced the Latin from me; and then in a breath, I blew out the red candle's flame. I was left in the dark. The only sound resonating in my ears were my own shallow breaths. It was freezing in the basement. The cement floor and surrounding walls offered no comfort. I tried to make my way towards the exit and back up the stairs but that proved near impossible without the ability to see where I was going.

"A noise other than my own breathing became present— 'Hello?' I called into the shadows. 'Hello?'

"I couldn't decipher which direction the sound was coming

from. I turned myself in circles until I felt dizzy. When I finally stopped spinning, the basement lights were switched on, blinding me for a moment.

" 'Sage Barnaby.' A tranquil voice made itself known. 'You are unexpected. I never thought I'd hear from you.'

"My eyes eventually focused to the overhead florescent lighting and settled on the person in front of me.

" 'You're a tad young. If I made a deal with someone your age, I would upset a great number of people,' he said. 'All right, I'm intrigued. What do you want from me?'

" 'How do you know my name?'

" 'You summoned me, Sage. Of course I know your name.' "

"The man stepped towards me and I could make out the lines and curves of his face. His eyes were gray, and they were littered with specks of brown and lines of yellow. He was smiling at me; the dimples in the corners of his mouth certainly added a seductive charm to his expression. His teeth were white and mostly straight, which gave him the feel of an average man, but of course that was misleading. He had short, light colored hair that had started to gray and made him look to be in his fifties. However, I knew this man exceeded that age by at least 4 billion years.

"He smoothed out the front of his t-shirt then brought his eyes back to me. I remember thinking that he reminded me of my third grade gym teacher.

"I wasn't sure if there were formalities I should follow. Instead, I did my best to be direct with the man.

" 'My sister is sick and I think she's gunna die,' I began. 'I found those Latin words in a book from the library. I need your help.'

" 'Was it a large brown book, seemingly ordinary?' he asked. I nodded. 'I see. I was beginning to think there weren't any of those left. I call them Ultimum Recursum, or The Last Resort. I made them for the hopeless. They sense only the most distressed souls and make themselves known to those people. I am pleased to know some still exist in the world. I have not been called on through Ultimum Recursum in many hundreds of years.'

"He shifted his weight between his feet. His sneakers were stark white, not a scuff or trail of dirt on them. He studied me, letting his eyes dance across my face and decipher my body language.

" 'I don't give help freely, Sage Barnaby. We will have to make a deal,' he hesitated, about to lose his nerve. 'Oh, but you are so young this hardly seems fair. It's too easy.'

" 'I don't care. I want to make the deal.'

" 'You're not afraid of me, are you?' he looked amazed.

"Even then, at eight years old and standing before the darkest angel to ever fall from Heaven, I almost laughed. 'I'm terrified of you. Of course I am, but I need your help so I can stomach my fear for a little while.'

"The man started to walk in circles around me. I felt like Dorothy, stuck in the tornado that blew her to Oz.

" 'I am impressed and I do not say that lightly,' he inhaled and smoothed out his t-shirt once more. 'Now this deal, what are your conditions?"

"I didn't hesitate. 'Make Nola better.'

" 'What's in it for me?'

" 'Whatever you want.'

" 'Really? Anything?' he looked disappointed. "I'm getting a bit turned off now. You seem rather desperate, Sage, and I should warn you men don't find desperation very attractive. They much prefer a chase.'

"I didn't understand what he meant at the time. I tried to keep my patience while the Devil made light of the situation. 'Of course I'm desperate. I'm asking for a deal with the Devil but that's not what you should be concerned with.' I gathered the courage to meet his eyes.

" 'No?' he took a step forward as if to intimidate me. 'What is it I should be concerned with, darling?'

" 'Your reputation,' I said.

"I wasn't sure if I had convinced him to help me but I certainly had his interest. His eyes burned into mine, but I refused to break away and look somewhere less.

" 'You're right. I am just a little girl,' I started with a clear voice. 'Have you ever made a deal with a little girl? You have quite a reputation to uphold. There isn't much excitement in murders and adulterers anymore.'

" 'Of course there is,' he said quite simply. 'Why do you think soap operas are so popular?'

"I ignored his quip. 'If I were you, I would want to show everyone just how rotten I am. I would be looking for new ways to impress my followers and shock my enemies. The Devil makes a deal with a little girl, that sounds like a good story to me.'

" 'You are very well spoken for a child,' he mused.

" 'I like to read.'

" 'You make a good point. Everyone knows my name, but the angels rarely talk about me anymore; and my own demons and minions aren't nearly as cowardice in my presence as I would like them to be. Sage, you might be just what I need. The little girl who shook hands with the Devil. I like the sound of that.'

"I thought I had him. I thought we were on the same page, but the Prince of Darkness is very clever, and he was chapters ahead of me.

" 'Good.' I nodded. 'You fix Nola and I will lie for you or steal. I'll do worse than that if you ask me to. Whatever you want, I promise.'

" 'Actually I would like to stick to tradition in this matter.'

His dimples winked at me when he smiled. 'I will make your sister better and in return I get your soul. You still get to have whatever life you choose for yourself on Earth but when you die you become my pet in the lake of fire. Is this agreeable?'

" 'Yes.' Adrenaline pumped through me. I wasn't mature enough for such heavy conversations, but at that moment I handled myself with a great deal of understanding.

"The Devil smiled at me again but this time it was the way you smile at someone when you know something they don't. I can see that now but at the time I was blinded by pride. I had saved Nola from the brink of death. My sacrifice would ensure that my sister had a full life to look forward to. Everything else was background noise.

" 'Well seeing as we have come to an agreement, there is only one thing left to do,' he extended a hand towards me, a wicked grin still playing on his lips.

"I took his hand in mine. It was that easy. I don't know what I expected, but it felt just like any other handshake."

Laveau had been still for the duration of my story, and even when I finished he remained stoic. There was no movement in his muscles, no flicker in his eyes, and I don't recall him blinking.

After a minute had passed, he spoke. "What happened next?"

"What do you mean? I told you what happened. I made a deal with the Devil. I lost my soul. I want it back."

"Oh, but there is more to your story. You would not be here if your sister were still alive."

Laveau was right, of course. I often wished the story would end with me shaking the Devil's hand. After that everything would have gone according to plan and Nola would still be with me today; but like I said, the Prince of Darkness is very clever.

"Well, he did what he said he would. Nola got better. Everyone said it was a miracle. It was like she had never been sick. Her pink cheeks and ivory skin returned. She laughed hysterically at the tiniest things. Nothing scared her. Things that I was afraid of Nola was fascinated by— the dark, spiders, the ocean, new foods… Nola had more life in her following her recovery than she ever did before the leukemia. It was amazing. I really believed giving up my soul for Nola's life had been worth it. She was perfect… and two months later she was gone.

"Before I left home, five years after Nola's death, my parents were still arguing over who forgot to lock the front gate. She was only five. I'm not sure why she ran out into the street, but as she did a car turned the corner. The driver didn't see her until it was too late. I'm pretty sure I know who played a part in that gate being unlatched.

"Maybe if I had been older when Nola got sick I would have been more specific about the conditions of the deal I made. You see, he only promised to make her better; he never said anything about keeping her alive. He made the choice to take her from me in the basement of that hospital. He tricked me and I was a perfect idiot. There have been so many what ifs since then. Mostly I wish I hadn't enticed him with my ridiculous speech about reinforcing his reputation by preying on the desperation of one little girl. He certainly went farther with that than I could have ever imagined.

"He took her from me anyway and the crazy part is that I'm still tied to my end of the bargain. My soul still belongs to him when I die because he kept his promise."

West's eyes narrowed on me. "Well, I have to say, I am somewhat beside myself, Miss Barnaby."

He stood up from the bar. Jack, who had been sitting by my feet, kept his attention on Laveau as he strode across the room. A low series of growls vibrated in the dog's chest. Eventually Laveau stopped pacing and turned to face me. His finger scratched his bottom lip as a childish expression filled his face.

"I cannot believe it," he declared. "You are the little girl who shook hands with the Devil? I have heard your story before, but I doubted its validity. Sage Barnaby, what a foolish, proud child."

I was stunned, offended.

"What am I to you? Some kind of twisted fairytale?" I said.

"Oh Miss Barnaby, you are one of my favorite bedtime stories." He was glowing. He drank in my embarrassment, and I knew that I deserved the humiliation. The moment passed and Laveau took another sip of rum. "May I ask how you came across my name?

"Actually, I first heard it through a demon I was exorcizing out of a young boy. He offered it to me as a truce."

"Which demon?" he asked.

"Orias."

"Well, for your sake I hope you showed him mercy," he waited for me to answer.

I shook my head.

"Orias is royalty in the underworld, Miss Barnaby. If you do end up in Hell, he will have a legion of demons waiting at the black gates when you arrive. He will have your head."

"Well, he's going to have to wait a little longer for it."

Laveau grabbed my wrist again and checked the time. "Oh, look at that, we're closing in on 12:08."

He moved to the cupboard for a third time, and when he turned back to face me, there was a long silver blade in his left hand.

"The animal, please." West approached Jack and me.

"What?" I stepped back and rested a hand on Jack. "No."

"Don't be so sentimental. Summoning an angel is nothing short of forcing a miracle. Sacrifices must be made."

My stomach flopped but I kept my composure. "Sacrifices?"

"Yes. Blood must be spilt."

"You can use mine."

West raised a hand to stop me. He looked again at the dog. Jack released a low growl sensing the rising tension in the room.

"I am sorry," he shrugged. "We need the blood of an innocent. We both know that you are not, and I freely admit that neither am I."

"I don't understand why an angel should require any blood in the first place? I thought they were peaceful creatures."

"Some. Yes."

"What does that mean?"

West hurried through an explanation. "I'm sure you are well aware that there are a variety of angels in the great beyond. They serve Him in different ways, based on what they were created for and what abilities He has embedded in them. Humans can change. Angels cannot. You could start taking piano lessons tomorrow or learn how to make sushi. But a cherub could never learn how to wield a sword and an archangel could never be taught to sing.

"All guardians come from within the many ranks of angels. Summoning each one calls for a specific prayer or sacrifice. To summon a cherub, you would need to volunteer a kiss; for a throne, you must recite poetry that reveals the soul; seraphims can only be called through song, and virtues ask that you answer a riddle."

"What kind of angel is my guardian?"

Laveau broke into a rich laugh. "Now I had thought that much would be obvious."

I stared blankly at him.

"An archangel, naturally," he waited for me to catch up. "That is why a sacrifice must be made in blood. Archangels are His warriors. They make up His armies and defend His kingdom. Now, if we were summoning a demon or a dark spirit, your blood would be very acceptable but we are calling forth a creature of light and only pure blood will suffice."

I paused, soaking in this new knowledge. It seemed logical

enough. I had been in plenty of situations and done things that were based on far less logic than this. It was easy to trust West Laveau. Maybe it was because an astounding reputation preceded him. I just kept worrying that if he couldn't help me then who could? This had to work.

"How did you know my guardian was an archangel?" The question popped into my head.

"Since you began ghost hunts and exorcisms, you have never failed to send an ungodly creature back from whence it came, which is quite remarkable because you've been up against some beastly things."

He toyed with the silver blade in his hand. My attention was never far from it.

"You looked into my past?" I raised an inquisitive eyebrow.

He ignored this. We both knew that he researched me before agreeing to meet this evening. "It is uncommon for one so young to have been so successful. You have exorcized every demon you've faced. Alastor would be been back in Hell by now if I had not broken the demon's snare."

"I wouldn't say that all my exorcisms were successful," I confessed.

West's voice softened. "Are you referring to the Forester boy?"

I looked down to the ground. I hated being reminded of the Forester boy, as West referred to him.

"Well, that was unfortunate," he paused respectfully. "Although, you still managed to remove the demon from his body. That creature no longer walks the Earth because of you."

Neither does the boy, I thought to myself.

"We are getting off track. Miss Barnaby, you wanted to know how I could be sure that your guardian was an archangel. Apart from fighting opposite evil, you are also a fire sign, born in early August— Happy belated birthday. You have a protein heavy diet, a short temper, quick reflexes, you take yourself too seriously and your instincts are respectable."

He had done his homework on me. "I hope you're right, West."

"That's why you sought me out," he reminded me. "Now I am afraid we must bring our conversation to a close. We've only a few short minutes until 12:08. Quick, bring the animal."

9

Angel Vomit

West failed to mention that he only needed several drops of Jack's blood. That settled my nerves for the time being. Jack didn't whine as the silver blade cut into his shoulder. He stood still as the blood accumulated in his white coat. In half a minute the fur that covered the dog's shoulder was crimson red. Jack looked up at me with pale eyes, and I praised him with a scratch behind the ears.

West brought the blade over to a candle sitting on top of the poker table in the center of the room. White wax started to drip down the candle's shaft and melt into the green felt of the table's surface. Laveau had the dog's blood fall off the blade and onto the flame. Lena's warning came back to me.

"I forgot to ask you something." I broke Laveau's concentration.

"Ask quickly. We have work to do."

"Once my guardian angel is summoned, how is it going to help me? I mean, my deal with the Devil still stands. It was a mortal sin. That won't change."

"Your guardian will be able speak directly to The Man Upstairs. They can appeal to Him on your behalf, assure Him that you were an innocent child and your intentions were pure. He values His angels' opinions."

I shook my head. "But my intentions weren't pure. I knew what I was doing. I knew that it was wrong."

"Ah yes, but He doesn't know that."

"I thought He knew everything," I crossed my arms.

"He knows a lot, certainly more than anyone else, but even He enjoys some mystery," West paused to make sure I was paying attention. "That is why He defines our character by our actions and not our intentions."

While I spoke West brought the sliver blade, dripping with Jack's blood, to the remaining candles. The room grew increasingly dim as each wick's flame was doused out.

"The angel will know that I wasn't innocent when I shook the Devil's hand. My guardian would have been watching me. They would have heard me accept his offer without hesitation. I practically begged the Devil to make that deal."

"Yes, but there's a loop hole. A guardian angel is assigned to a human with the sole purpose of protecting them, keeping them on a path that will gain them access into Heaven, at all costs."

"Even if it means lying to Him?"

"Precisely," Laveau winked. "Now that you're up to speed and our time has run out, we must begin the summoning ritual."

I looked down at my wristwatch. The minute hand had just moved to eight past twelve. I took a breath. This was a now or never moment.

"Rumpere silentium rerum angelorum quaeritur," West recited the Latin.

In a breath the room went cold. I translated the Latin to: *We seek to break silence in the world of angels.* In another breath, the lights went out and a violent wind rushed through the room. I could hear the glasses behind the bar clang together. Jack barked relentlessly, but I couldn't find him in the dark.

Laveau's voice rang out. "Cruor insons insontis, pario curator."
Blood of the innocent, bring forth the guardian.
The air grew heavy around us.

I stayed quiet, as a deep humming resonated through the space. A foul stench infiltrated the room and choked me. It was the scent of burnt hair and expired milk.I gasped, but no sound came out.

"Abbas, filius quod sanctus phasmatis." The hum had grown into a roar and West hollered above the deafening noise. "Suscipio nostrum nisus. Cruor insons insontis, pario curator!"

I felt the room shake fiercely as the prayers fell from Laveau's lips. The ceiling cracked and crumbled down around us. As pieces of debris slammed onto the ground, I heard a sharp cry escape from Jack.

"Jack." Nothing. "Jack!" Nothing.

"Leave the animal!" West's voice boomed. "Something is wrong, and we cannot leave this unfinished. Take my hand!"

You don't say? I got the sense that something was wrong when the room started falling down around us. I did as Laveau asked and we scrambled towards one another in the dark. I walked into the poker table twice and tripped over bits of the ceiling scattered across the floor. When I managed to get a hold of him, West pulled me close.

"I thought this might be the case, but I hoped that I was wrong. Don't move, Miss Barnaby. This will only sting for a moment."

"What?" I tried to tug my hand away from Laveau, but he refused to loosen his hold on me. I struggled in vain. "Let go of me."

"We must finish the ritual, Miss Barnaby!" His voice lost its silky texture. "The portal is still open. We need to close it. Anything is capable of passing between worlds right now."

"What are you doing? Stop!" I shrieked.

That's when I felt a sharp sensation pass through every nerve in my left arm. I wanted to scream but held my breath instead. I had my share of scars, and blood has never made me queasy but I usually saw it coming. Laveau released me and I collapsed to my knees. My right hand reached up to where he cut me. I felt warm liquid soak into my sleeve. I could smell the salt of my blood as it ran down my arm, covered my palm and trickled onto the floor. As I leaned forward, on my hands and knees, I noticed a pale red light seep out from beneath the poker table in the center of the room.

"What is that?" I asked. Thanks to the new light source I could see his feet planted beside me.

"West," I continued. "Why did you—?"

"I needed more blood—tainted blood—a sinner's blood."

"You said that you needed to blood of an innocent to summon an archangel."

"I know what I said," he snapped.

What could have gone wrong during the summoning ritual? I was worried about Jack. Since the ceiling collapsed, I hadn't heard the patter of his paws, which were always within earshot.

I pushed a handful of unruly curls away from my face. The bottom half of my hair was wet from the blood pouring from my arm. What was the soft crimson light leaking out from beneath the poker table? Where the Hell was my guardian angel?

"Why did you cut me, Laveau?"

"Let me put it this way, your guardian is not exactly what we were expecting. However, you two are very well suited for each other."

"I have no idea what you're talking about!" I shouted. "Have we summoned my guardian angel or not?"

"The simple answer is yes. Yes, we have summoned your guardian, Miss Barnaby, but I'm not sure how helpful he is going to be."

I brought my attention back to the light beneath the table as it expanded over six feet from one end to the other. In one great flash the light vanished, imploded, like a star collapsing in on itself. Before I was plunged into utter darkness, I was able to make out the distinct shape of a male figure where the light had been.

The sound of someone coughing followed and persisted for an uncomfortably long period of time. It was an aching cough. Each painful gasp for air was more agonizing than the last. The sound echoed throughout the room.

West went over to the wall, flicked up the switch and the room flooded with artificial light. My pupils constricted as I adjusted to the brightness. A wave of shock passed through me when my eyes finally settled on the creature in the center of the room.

There was a naked man lying on the ground. He was exquisite, a marble statue carved with Michelangelo's masterful hands. He had soft blonde, almost platinum, waves of hair that fell just over his ears and down onto his forehead. Every muscle tensed as he coughed violently over and over again. His back arched, his arms tightened and his chiseled jaw grew taut. He could hardly manage to take in a breath. Every time he inhaled, it showcased his hard abdomen and perfectly cut pelvic indents. I grew light-headed. It took everything inside of me to stay conscious. The creature surpassed beauty. There was no way he could ever be mistaken for human because he was just so extraordinary to behold. His large hands curled into shaking fists as he tried to gain control of his unsteady breaths.

He lifted his head off the floor and looked straight at me. I was paralyzed. His stare struck me in such a way that I felt completely vulnerable and exposed. There was something unmistakably intimate in the way we looked at one another. His eyes were watering from the hysterical coughing. They were an arctic blue and seemed to be crystallizing as he held my gaze. It was unsettling and magical all at once. I held my breath, unable to look away from him.

When I thought I couldn't bear to hold his gaze a moment longer, that his beauty might actually kill me, my attention was drawn elsewhere. There was weak cry calling out from across the room.

"Jack!"

I rushed over to the source of whimpers. Jack was trapped beneath a block of the concrete that had fallen from the ceiling. I struggled to lift it off of him but was eventually able to move it aside. I wrapped my arms around the white beast but there wasn't reason to panic. The dog quickly regained his strength. Nearly half of his fur was matted with blood from when Laveau had cut into him a minute ago. In fact the dog's appearance suggested that he had been hit by a truck and dragged along the highway, but Jack seemed fine. He proceeded to survey the scene, sniffing each corner of the room and the scattered debris.

I brought my focus back to the newest member of our company. The angel had crawled out from beneath the poker table and pulled himself to his feet. He seemed to have trouble balancing and leaned on the bar's counter for stability. Although his cough persisted, it had subdued greatly from a moment ago.

The angel was still stark naked, with his back turned to me. He had his attention set on Laveau, who was smiling from ear to ear.

West walked up to the creature and pulled him into a firm hug. "Belial."

"Bastard," the angel said, not amused.

"I would say that this is a surprise, but it makes perfect sense," Laveau announced without further explanation.

I tossed my hair over my shoulders and stepped towards the pair of opposites. West Laveau was a stocky man with dark skin, a shaved head, endless black eyes and very well dressed. Belial was completely nude, with eyes the color of ice and a full head of gorgeous blonde hair. If he stood still, I would have sworn he was a statue. It was daunting to be in the same room as these two men. I had little to offer in their company.

"Belial, let me introduce you to Sage Barnaby," West patted my back and pushed me forward.

"You don't have wings," I noted. "What kind of an angel doesn't have wings?"

Another coughing fit took hold of the exotic, wingless thing and grew increasingly hostile. He struggled to breathe. The angel keeled forward, clutched his chest and vomited directly on my boots. The stench was atrocious and I was furious.

"What's wrong with it?" I turned to Laveau. "Is it dying?"

"No, Belial is adapting. The atmosphere on Earth is very different than he's used to. He hasn't been accustomed to fresh air for a long time. He's been breathing in sulfur for many years."

"Sulfur?"

"Yeah," Belial said in a hoarse voice. "S on the periodic table, yellow in color, atomic number 16 and classified as a non-metallic. I guess you never took chemistry."

"I know what it is but you're an angel. There shouldn't be any sulfur where you came from. Sulfur is found in—"

Laveau cut in. "How have you been, Belial? You look well."

The angel scowled. "What year is it?"

"Welcome to the early twenty-first century, my friend."

"Stop calling me Belial. That name makes me sound old."

"But you are old," I said. "I mean you're really, really old."

The angel looked at me like he might lunge forward and tear my throat out with his hands.

"What name would you prefer?" West asked.

"Just Lial."

After that West politely excused himself from the room. He

was going to fetch the angel a pair of pants. After he left, Jack and I watched the angel move over to the tell-all. He stared at himself for a moment and seemed satisfied with what he saw. I looked down at his feet. They were caked in soot and grime. I moved my eyes upwards past his ankles, defined calves, muscular thighs and—

"You're staring." Lial was watching me examine him.

"You're naked," I kept my voice flat and hoped it would mask my complete humiliation.

He looked down at his body and shrugged. He crossed back to the bar and opened the cooler, pulling a bottle of beer from the ice. He opened it with his teeth and took several large, noisy gulps. The brown beer trickled out of the sides of his mouth, moving down his neck and onto his white, hard chest. Lial wiped his mouth with his forearm. He had finished the beer in less than a minute and opened another.

Lial didn't seem to care why he had been summoned. He hadn't asked why we called him to Earth. He'd only thrown up, been discourteous and was now finishing off his second beer. He wasn't the guardian angel I had imagined, but he would have to do. I hoped that his relationship with The Man Upstairs was a good one. I needed his word to go a long way.

I decided to focus my attention on anything other than his naked body, which proved to be difficult. I knelt down beside Jack and gave the dog a once over. His wound had stopped bleeding. I was grateful for that. Jack's always been a real comfort. After the chaotic summoning ritual and Lial's poor attitude, I knew I was in over my head but Jack helped keep me calm. Sometimes knowing you have someone on your side makes all the difference, even if they never say a word.

West returned with a pair of faded black jeans that ended up being a bit too large the angel. They sat too low on his hips, but I was just thankful that he was finally clothed. Now we could get down to business. I had a dozen questions, but before I could begin Lial was halfway out the door.

"This was nice," Lial said, his voice dripping with sarcasm. "But I have to run. Albert owes me money. Is he still in Jersey?"

"You're friend Albert Einstein died about sixty years ago," West said gently.

"Oh, that's right," the angel gave a somber paused. "I forgot you said we were in the early twenty-first century. I guess I have been gone a while."

"I am sorry, Belial."

"Don't be," he shook his head. "People die."

"I know how close you two were. Albert's remembered as a great man if that's any consolation. Everyone knows his name. He was a genius."

"Albert was a lunatic." Lial tried to hide any sentiment in his voice. "When he was a teenager, he had a dream about cows being shocked by an electric fence and somehow woke up with the theory of relativity. That's not genius; it's madness."

I couldn't believe what I was hearing. My guardian had been close friends with Albert Einstein. I immediately wondered which other famous historical figures he might have known. Did Lial ever sit down for tea with Winston Churchill or stand in a sea of people listening to Martin Luther King Jr. speak? Was he at Woodstock? Did he see Rome fall? The possibilities to what Lial might have witnessed were endless and that fascinated me.

"You couldn't have gone anyway. At least not without taking Miss Barnaby with you," West added.

"What are you talking about?" The angel was finally as puzzled as I was.

"We summoned her guardian angel, Belial. You showed up."

"Oh crap," Lial hung his head. "Well that doesn't do anyone much good."

The two men exchanged a look I didn't understand before bursting into an uproar of laughter. Laveau started to cry he was laughing so hard. I grew increasingly impatient as I watched them fall into hysterics. I had no idea what they found so hilarious, and I was in a hurry to have Lial help me save my soul.

I cleared my throat. "Sorry for breaking up the reunion, but would you mind telling me what's so funny?

West became serious, so serious that it frightened me. "My apologies, Miss Barnaby. It hurts me to tell you that we've summoned your guardian in vain."

"No," I blurted out before I could think. Laveau's words crushed me.

"I am afraid so. When we summoned your angel, I had really hoped this wouldn't be the case."

"What's wrong with him?"

"Nothing. Look at me. I'm perfect," Lial announced smugly.

"You noticed it the moment you saw him," West cut in. "You asked where his wings were. You can see that they are not where they should be."

"He is my guardian angel though, isn't he?"

"Yes, but…" he trailed off.

I gathered a fistful of my dark curls in my hand and exhaled. I did not like where this conversation was headed— downhill. I was starting to feel overwhelmed. I was bleeding and covered in angel vomit. There was no way to predict how I might respond to bad news at this point.

Lial finished the sentence. "I'm a fallen angel."

I couldn't speak. The world caved in around me. That one word had ruined everything. *Fallen.* I would never find redemption now. Summoning my guardian angel was supposed to create a link between Him and me, but now we couldn't have been farther apart. That link had been severed millions upon millions of years ago when the archangel Belial had taken sides with the darkest angel of all, Lucifer.

I was damned. It was the only thought I could form. I was damned.

"I did not think this plan through. The fault is mine," West said. "When Lucifer left paradise, he took a third of Heaven's angels with him. Belial was one of them and today his name proves true."

"Ouch," Lial sounded offended.

"Belial means without worth and he certainly is useless, worthless to your cause, Miss Barnaby."

"How could this happen?" I asked.

"Our maker is all-knowing unless he chooses to turn a blind eye. When humans were born into creation, He knew one day that you would walk among them, Miss Barnaby. Your guardian angel has been assigned to you since you were nothing more than stardust. One guardian per human soul. That is how it works. Lial was meant for you; but when he fell from Heaven, he rejected his responsibilities as a guardian, and you have suffered horribly for it."

"I think she gets it," Lial cut in, annoyed. I guess he didn't want to be held accountable. "You have a flare for dramatics, hybrid."

Lial called West a hybrid. Did that mean the rumors were true? Had West's great, great, great grandmother engaged in an affair with angel after all? It would take an angel to recognize if someone else was part angel, right? My head was swimming with questions, but I wouldn't dare ask them, especially after I saw the look on Laveau's face. West spoke to Lial in a fury. His Latin was impeccable.

"Non insultare mihi, delebo eam angelus linguae!"

"Touchy." Lial shrugged off Laveau's threat, but I watched his eyes ice over. He obviously did not like being told what to do but he suppressed the urge to lash out. That was something I could empathize with.

West brought his dark stare back to me. "Do you understand now?"

"Yeah. I have been alone this whole time. You're telling me that he can't help, that I am still alone."

A heaviness sank onto my shoulders and sat there. Before I knew that Lial was a fallen angel, I was hopeful. I believed there was still a chance to work my way back into His good graces. I thought that if I ran fast enough and tried hard enough, I could escape Hell. Lial was the end of the line. He was supposed to be my miracle.

"You're not going to start crying, are you?" Lial asked me. "Nothing is more unattractive to me than tears."

"I'll react to this shitty news however I want. I may have failed but at least I tried. All you know how to do is give up," I said broken-hearted.

I don't know if my response surprised Lial or enraged him. Either way he fell silent, his face still bearing a detached expression. He had no idea how much this summoning had meant to me, or how much I had looked forward to meeting him, and he didn't care to.

A peculiar grumbling came from somewhere in the room. It was so loud the walls seemed to vibrate. I looked down at Jack and realized he was not the source of the noise. I thought the sound might be an after-affect of the summoning ritual. The aggressive growl came again.

West and I looked at each other before bringing our attention to Lial. He was standing on the opposite side of the room, a hand placed on his bare abdomen.

"My stomach hurts," he frowned.

"Ha!" Laveau roared. "You are hungry, my friend. You haven't eaten in over half a century. Let's go upstairs to the café. We will find something to satisfy your empty stomach. You used to have a wicked sweet tooth. What was it you used to say? Pie and pork chops? Chocolate and chicken? I'm can't remember."

"Cake and steak," he answered and then a strange and beautiful thing happened. Lial offered a genuine smile. It was not at someone's expense or the result of a cheap joke. His smile was honest and pure and breathtaking. Watching him smile, with his bright eyes and sweet dimples, made me feel weak.

"Yes!" West exclaimed. "Cake and steak. I am sorry that we do not serve steak here, but I can find you something tasty to eat."

"Why not let him starve?" I suggested.

West stopped in the doorway. "Do you remember a moment ago when I said we summoned Belial in vain? Well, I might have been mistaken. I just had an interesting thought. I admit it's a stretch, but hope is still alive. I will tell you all about it over a plate of beignets."

Upstairs we sat at one of the mosaic bistro tables and were treated to the most incredible assortment of midnight snacks. I fidgeted my leg, impatiently waiting for Laveau to explain his master plan for my salvation. He was distracted by the angel's monstrous appetite. Lial had devoured a serving of bread pudding, pralines, peach cobbler and half of a pecan pie. For such a savage appetite, he still generously shared his meal with Jack, who greedily scarfed down whatever Lial put in front of him.

"If you keep that up, you're going to be sick again," I warned.

"Yeah, but this time it will be worth it."

"Sage, you can't argue with that," West beamed with pride. He loved that his grandmother's recipes were still working their magic. "Eat something, Miss Barnaby."

I had no appetite. I couldn't quite grasp my current situation. I was sitting in a café sharing pastries with a master of dark magic and a fallen angel. Oh, and the dog was relieving himself behind the counter.

"Jack!" I scolded.

"Oh, it's not a problem," West said casually.

"Between the mess in the back room and the dog out here, you have a lot of cleaning up to do," I observed.

"Oh no. I won't touch any of that," West whipped out his cell phone and proceeded to send a text. "Alastor will be more than happy to take care of it."

Lial perked up from his plate of food. He wiped his mouth. I don't think he had taken a breath in the past five minutes.

He looked disgusted. "Is that parasite still walking the Earth?"

"You know what's waiting for him if he ever returns to Hell. I think that he plans to stay here until the sun burns out," Laveau answered.

"Alastor told me about his brothers," I chimed in.

"What did he tell you?" Laveau's voice dropped. I suddenly had his full attention, which struck me as odd.

"Everything— Well, everything apart from one significant detail."

West put down his fork and leaned in towards me, overly interested in what I would say next.

"He wouldn't tell me how he managed to pull off a permanent exorcism. Alastor would murder his own kind— his brothers— but he wouldn't share that information with me. Do you know how to permanently send a demon back to Hell?" I asked.

Laveau ignored my question. I didn't bother to ask a second time. I decided it was probably best to change the subject.

"West, you said there might be another way to save my soul."

"Yes," he said. "There is an object hidden somewhere on Earth that He would love to have back in His possession." West pointed upwards.

Lial tilted back his chair. "You have got to be kidding me."

"I am not, Belial. If you return that book, it might mean salvation for Miss Barnaby and yourself."

"I don't want to be saved," the angel insisted.

"Don't be ridiculous, of course you do— You were the last to fall. Yes, you followed the dark prince, but it took a lot of convincing, and you have never felt good about it."

"Enough!" Lial slammed his fists down on the mosaic tabletop. Blonde locks of hair fell in front of his eyes. "We are not discussing this any further. Liber Alter is a rumor at best and it is barely that."

"I would disagree with you," West argued.

"I am not going on a scavenger hunt when there is no book. It is a myth, not real."

"It just hasn't been uncovered yet."

"That's because it doesn't exist. Am I repeating myself?"

"Then it won't cause you any trouble to go searching for it," West said. "Listen to me, Belial. You are her guardian. Miss Barnaby summoned you and you are bound to her. You have to stay with her and keep her safe, just as you promised eons ago."

"I had no problem breaking that promise," Lial said without missing a beat. I knew it was the truth, but it stung to hear it said out loud.

I spoke up. "You two are doing that thing again."

"What?" Lial huffed.

"When you assume that I know what's going on, but I have no idea— that thing. What is Liber Alter?"

"West, would you please take over this conversation? I think my IQ has dropped just by participating."

"Liber Alter—The Other Book— has been lost for billions of years. It was last seen not long after the Earth was created. Demons say the angels took the book, and the angels swear it went missing at the hands of demons. No one knows for sure." West paused for a breath.

"Why is The Other Book so important?" I asked.

"There are so many theories." He rubbed his head. "It might be a formula to end the world. It might contain the outcome of every future sports event. Some think that its pages hold the meaning of life—"

West could hardly finish his thought before Lial had joined him in a laughing fit. Lial laughed so hard he stopped making any sounds. He just clapped his hands together and looked like an moron. I sat there in quiet frustration, waiting for them to settle down. It took a while. I coughed in an attempt to focus their attention. It had no effect. I looked down at my watch and began to get nervous that Ned would wake up to find Jack and me gone. Even though I left the note telling him not to worry, I knew he would.

"What is so funny?" I screamed.

"The meaning of life," West said catching his breath.

"Stop! Don't make me laugh again!" Lial pleaded. "I still haven't gotten used to breathing. Ouch! I have a cramp!"

"I don't get it," I said.

"There is no meaning to life, Sage," Lial sneered at me. "I thought that was common knowledge."

"Oh come on," I released a breathy laugh. "You're joking."

"No. I'm afraid the joke is on you, human."

West and Lial looked at me with expressions that would suggest they were in the company of someone with multiple heads. The subject was dropped.

"What were we talking about? Right." Lial started. "Even if Liber Alter does exist, and I am not convinced it does, it has been lost since the Earth began. I am not going to waste my time searching for something that can't be found."

"Well, unless Miss Barnaby releases you, you have no choice but to stay at her side. You belong to her for the time being."

Lial's wrinkled brow expressed his disapproval. I can't be sure what was going through his head, but I think it is safe to assume he didn't want to be in the café a moment longer. Lial removed himself from his chair and took several long steps towards the front exit.

West shot out of his seat. "Where are you going? Lial, the girl summoned you here. You cannot leave! You know what will happen if—"

"Watch me," he said and disappeared into the night.

Laveau shook his head. "You should catch up with him, Miss Barnaby, and quickly. Since you summoned Lial, he cannot be more than one hundred yards from you at all times or else there are... consequences," he put a lot of thought into the last word.

"What kind of consequences?"

"You will need a strong stomach," he warned.

I turned for the exit. "I better get going then. Bye, West."

"Miss Barnaby, when you find Liber Alter— if you find it— bring the book here. I can send a message to the angels and they can deliver it to Him."

"I don't even know where to start looking."

"Belial does, whether or not he wants to admit it," his gaze flickered towards the front door. I gave Laveau a parting wave.

"Come on, Jack, he couldn't have gone far."

As I left Marie's N'Orleans Café, I felt invigorated. I really believed that this would end well. Hope is a dangerous weapon in the hands of a desperate person, and it makes them do crazy things. I think West Laveau knew that. I think he counted on it.

10

Freckles: Part II

A couple of minutes after leaving the café, I began to think that Lial had outrun us. Jack wasn't picking up the angel's scent. We weaved in and out of alleyways and down quiet streets, but there was no sign of him.

I passed through the deserted streets. The brick walls of buildings blurred red on either side of me as I walked through the grid-like city. Lial didn't even have a last name, forget about a credit card or social security number I could track down. The angel could vanish with no trouble at all. Just when I thought I would never find him, Jack stopped abruptly a few feet ahead of me. The dog was sniffing a specific spot on the cracked pavement.

When I caught up to the animal, I saw what had attracted his interest. There was a single drop of blood resting on the ground. A foot from the first drop of blood was a second and another and another. The pattern continued as we progressed down the road. We followed the blood trail down two more streets before Jack and I turned off Stan Boulevard. The trail had grown more and more bloody as our search continued. It ended on Claudia Lane. That's where we found Lial, lying in the middle of the street and writhing in a warm pool of his blood. West warned me that upon finding

Lial his condition would be unpleasant, but that hadn't prepared me for what I saw.

The angel was disfigured. His body was twisted in pain and the expression on his face reflected that discomfort. His usually clear eyes were glistened over and staring blankly at the stars above, but I don't think he could see them. I don't think he could grasp anything beyond the burning agony he was in.

Lial was lying on his back, bare-chested with jeans torn at the knees. He must have been crawling on the pavement until the pain immobilized him. I guess he'd been really desperate to escape me, but he wasn't going anywhere now. The most disturbing part of this image were the long cuts that covered every inch of his body. The dark jeans he wore were soaked through with blood. The marks resembled stab wounds, not that there was any skin left to cut into.

It sickened me to look at him. I had witnessed all kinds of gruesome acts but this one was especially heinous. Maybe it was because the angel had been so beautiful the last time I saw him and now he was mutilated beyond imagination.

"How do I look?" Lial asked in a hoarse whisper.

"Are you being funny?"

"I thought so, but you're not laughing."

"Well, you look like shit."

"I know," he choked out. " But I'm beginning to heal now. We're less than a hundred yards from each other. The wounds are closing. Hurts like a bitch though."

"Good," I said. "That's twice you've abandoned me. I think there's a lesson to be learned from this."

"Now you're being funny," he avoided my point. Lial stared at me; his cold eyes were unwavering.

"Is there something you want to say?" I asked.

"There are several things I would like to say, but I would frighten you."

He didn't speak beyond that, but Lial didn't need words to
express the unfiltered hate rising inside of him. It appeared in
the edges of his unblemished face. It seared through his full lips,
impossible cheekbones and thick eyebrows. He wanted me to see
the rage that boiled just below the surface.

"An empty threat from a penguin. I'm shaking," I mocked him.

"What did you call me?"

"You're an angel without wings, a flightless bird, like a penguin.
Penguins are cute; no one's afraid of penguins."

His normally frigid eyes seemed to burn then. If Lial wasn't
in a paralyzing amount of pain, I think he would have struck me.
Luckily he hadn't fully recovered. I watched the muscles in his
jaw clench, but at the moment he was powerless. I thought about
humiliating him further. I could have gone for a long walk and let
Lial hope I didn't separate myself more than one hundred yards
from him, but I still needed his help. I needed our relationship to
be tolerable at the very least.

I stood over him while his body stitched itself back together.
Jack licked the open wounds, and Lial winced but allowed it.
Perhaps he was too weak to push the dog away. When I saw that
most of his cuts had vanished and there were no scars left behind, I
decided to head back to O'Brien Circle.

"Keep up," I called over my shoulder.

Jack immediately began trotting down Claudia Lane at my
side. Lial took a little more time to gather himself. I kept a slow
pace as I made my way back towards the McGreevy's home. I could
hear Lial shuffling behind me. His breaths were shallow and rasping
but he soldiered on, a true archangel.

Back at 181 O'Brien Circle the house sat quiet. Lial had healed
completely by the time we reached the driveway, which was without
the gold Cadillac. I remembered that the car was still parked in the
lot of 1976. I dreaded picking it up in the morning because I'd have

to face the damage done to the diner. I was overcome with misery when I thought about how much Jack, Ned and I had lost that day. I tried to push those thoughts out of my mind for the moment.

For now I walked up the front steps and onto the porch. Lial and Jack stood on either side of me as I turned the brass key and unlocked the door. I could hear Ned snoring upstairs, and I prayed that he was sleeping peacefully. The last thing he needed was to relive what happened at the diner in his dreams. Waking up in the morning was going to be unbearable for my godfather as is; he didn't need to be tortured in his sleep as well. When I pushed the door open, I was caught entirely off guard.

"Sage," a voice called out.

I jumped. My heart pounded against my ribcage. Jack growled at the figure immersed in shadow at the end of the porch. A young man with ruffled brown hair, blue eyes and light freckles stepped forward. I recognized him immediately.

"Shane?" I said, still flustered.

He was still carrying his beat up copy of The Bible.

"Listen, I'm starving," Lial announced. "I'm gunna raid the refrigerator."

"How can you still be hungry?" I asked, truly amazed.

"Just one of my many gifts," he shrugged. "Oh, and I will know if you decide to go for a walk, wonder off… I would appreciate it if you stayed close."

Well, I wouldn't want him bleeding all over the house. I agreed that it would be best to stay on the porch. Jack hesitated but followed Lial inside. I shut the door behind them. I didn't want my voice to travel upstairs and disturb Ned.

I sat down in the rocking chair where Lena spent so many afternoons with the paperback romance novels she treasured. Shane stood in front of me with his back leaning against the rail. He was standing in a flood of moonlight that made his eyes shine.

"I guess you want to talk about Logan."

"Yeah, my little brother— he's dead. I want to know why he wrote down your name in his Bible.

Logan Forester. I didn't want to relive any of this. It was two years ago, but I thought about him every day, as often as I thought about Nola. I had thought Shane's face seemed familiar when I first saw him. It reminded me of Logan. It made sense that they were brothers, but that made it harder for me to look at him now.

"Logan and I were close," Shane said. "He told me everything— Well, I thought he did. He never mentioned you." His knuckles turned white as he clutched the railing.

"I can't help you."

"I don't believe you!" He lost his temper and raised his voice, but quickly regained control. "I deserve to know what happened, Sage. I have to know."

He crouched down in front of me and looked up at me with misty blue eyes that probably made girls melt. All he would have to do is ask and they would follow him anywhere. Shane's freckles were faint; they lined his cheekbones and added a hint of childish mischief to his face. He grabbed the arms of the rocking chair. I sat between them with my hands folded firmly in my lap. My stomach fluttered with nervous energy, but it wasn't being fueled by fear or anger, which was unusual. This was something entirely new. I felt myself welcome the sensation with quiet anticipation.

"Please," he ended our shared silence with a gentle whisper. "Tell me what happened. I was the one who found him. His bones were broken— almost every bone in his body was broken. That was two years ago and no one has been able to figure out how he died. A couple of months back when I was going through his stuff, I found this Bible and your name was the first thing I read from it. Sage, you have to know something. Logan was my whole world. Do you know what that's like? Do you have any brothers or sisters?"

I swore I could hear my heart crack. I couldn't believe I was having this conversation. I wanted to be anywhere else— Back in the hospital waiting for Lena or in a dark basement making a deal with the Devil. I just wanted to get a way from this boy and his sad eyes. He did deserve to know what happened to Logan, but I couldn't find the words to explain any of it.

"I would've done anything to help him," Shane continued. "I thought he knew that, but he never came to me for help. I think Logan reached out to you. Why?"

"I don't know. I'm sorry. I am so sorry." I gave myself away with the second sorry. I couldn't bring myself to look him in the eye. Shane could tell that I was hiding something.

"I knew it," he breathed the words so softly they were barely audible. "Logan did need your help. What did he ask you to do?"

"Stop," I begged. "Just stop this. I can't—"

I stood up, brushing past Shane, and crossed to the front door. I rested my hand on the doorknob. Shane rose to his feet, but he didn't follow me. Actually he was incredibly poised and calm. He went back to leaning against the rail.

"I don't want to see you again," I said.

"Too bad," he answered. "Now that I know you had something to do with Logan's death I won't be able to stop thinking about you, and I definitely won't be able to stay away. Let me ask you something, Sage. If it were your little brother, would you be able to stop before you had answers? Could you turn around and go home without knowing what happened to him? After years of not knowing how or why Logan died, I finally found someone who could tell me the truth—at least some of the truth. I'm not going anywhere. I can be patient. I can wait until you're ready, but we will talk. Get used to seeing this face."

Shane was pleased with himself. I was less amused.

He hopped off the front porch and started walking down the

road. He had been wearing the same white button up shirt and faded jeans from that morning. After taking several long strides away from the house, he turned back around and offered an unexpected smile. He looked so much like his little brother it made my heart sore.

"I'll be back." He did a truly awful Terminator impersonation as he walked out of O'Brien Circle, the moon acting as a spotlight while Shane made his exit.

I pushed open the front door and kicked off my boots in the hallway. A surge of exhaustion weighed on me as I turned the corner and moved into the living room. Lial was there. The angel's bare feet pushed down into the carpet and left footprints as he walked across it.

He studied the pictures on the mantle but gave no indication to what he was thinking as his eyes danced over the photographs. His back turned to me and I noticed two small scars on his shoulder blades. I figured it must've been where his wings once were. I wondered if he missed them, if he missed flying. I thought about how badly it hurt when they were removed. I don't know if Lial saw me staring at him as I kneeled in the doorway, rubbing Jack's stomach, but he moved through the room as if he were alone.

Eventually Lial crossed the couch and started to lower himself onto the worn mustard colored cushions.

"No!" I said in an excited whisper. "Don't sit down. There's still blood on you pants. You can borrow some of Ned's clothes from the hamper."

There was a laundry basket piled with folded clothes at the side of the couch. Lena must not have gotten around to putting them away before going to 1976 that morning. Lial chose a pair of Ned's old college sweatpants from Quinnipiac University and a navy t-shirt.

I turned around to give him some privacy, and stared out into the kitchen, which sat just across from the living room. I heard Lial unzip his jeans and shake them off his legs.

"What? Are you shy all of a sudden, Sage? You couldn't take your eyes off of me at Laveau's place."

"I've had my fill of you for one day."

He must have been comfortable in these new clothes, but they didn't suit him. I thought he looked much more himself in the nude. It didn't help that the sweats were a couple sizes too big for Lial's frame. Ned was a somewhat huskier man although not out of shape.

Lial finally sat down, bouncing himself on the couch cushion. "Who's Ned? This is his house. These are his clothes."

"Ned is my godfather; he's asleep upstairs."

"I hope you don't mind me saying this, but it just came to my attention," Lial leaned forward and he sniffed the space between us. "Sage, you smell like death."

I couldn't decide if I was disgusted or impressed. "You can smell death?"

"Among other things."

I took a deep breath and willed myself to talk about the horror today carried with it. "Ned's wife was murdered today. I'm worried about him."

"Jeez, you humans make such a big deal about death, the same way you dramatize everything in your silly lives. Life is an experience; just one experience of many, many more that He has waiting for you. Death wasn't supposed to be feared, it was supposed to be exciting. Death was meant to be a new experience, another adventure but like so many other things, you humans got it all wrong."

"From a human's perspective death is permanent and unknown. There is no guarantee that we move on after our lives end. Can't you see how that might terrify us?"

Lial burst into laughter. I was afraid he would wake up Ned, but everything stayed quiet upstairs. I stood there, impatiently tapping my foot and eventually my hands found their way to my hips.

"What's so funny?"

Lial settled down, looking up at me from his relaxed position on the couch. His eyes were so striking I nearly lost my balance. Their beautiful shade of unearthly blue made me shudder. "You are. You are funny. Stupid, but funny."

I wrinkled my brow. Lial could see that I didn't follow his train of thought. He rolled his eyes and continued.

"Sage, you're one step ahead of the rest of them. You know that God, the Devil, demons and angels exist. You know that humans have souls that live on after their bodies die and rot and turn to dust, but you still don't have faith."

A smug grin played on his full lips as Lial sprawled his long body across the sofa. He knew he had gotten under my skin.

"What's your point?"

"A sense of faith is necessary. Why else would human life be laid out with so many unanswered questions?"

"Because science isn't advanced enough to answer those questions yet."

He took a moment to consider that. "That might be part of it," he admitted off-handedly. "Listen, there are two kinds of faith, Sage. Faith in humanity can be much more important than your faith in Him."

"I don't need a lecture in faith from a fallen angel. I'm tired."

"Faith is necessary to the human experience," he persisted.

"What are you saying, Lial? Because I struggle with my faith, I am less human?"

"No. No. No. I did not say that." His voice was almost kind. "You said that, but I won't argue with you."

"Over half of the human population struggles with their faith."

"I know and it seems the longer the human race lives, the less faith they have. Faith has weakened from generation to generation."

I didn't want to know if he was right, if I was less than human because I lacked faith in Him and humanity. It had been an excruciating and long day. The sun would be up in a couple of hours and tomorrow would be another excruciating, long day. I would have to deal with Lena's death, Ned's broken heart, my pending fate, a fallen angel and Jack's tiny bladder.

"I am going to stay in the guest room," I told him. "Lial, you can sleep down here on the couch. Jack, go keep Ned company."

The dog hurried out of the room. I heard him climb the stairs and jump onto Ned's bed. Ned didn't stir; he just continued snoring.

I leaned my back against the wall. "Do you know what we're going to do about this mystery book that may or may not exist?"

"Uh, that's where my faith falls short. I have always believed that Liber Alter was a supernatural urban legend, but I know someone who can tell us for sure whether or not we should even bother looking."

I yawned, and turned to head upstairs. "If you get cold, there should be some blankets in the trunk."

"Aren't you going to wish me goodnight?" he called after me. "What? You can't bring yourself to say it, can you? Do you hate me that much?"

Lial was being very bold. "Lial, you would leave me again in a heartbeat if it weren't for the hundred yard rule. Let's just find the book, save my soul and go our separate ways. How does that sound, penguin?"

His smug smile faded. "It can't come soon enough."

It was exactly what I expected him to say and with that remark, I grabbed a fresh t-shirt from the hamper and retreated to the guest room.

I paused in front of Ned's door, which was left open just enough for Jack to slip through. I could see him resting at the foot of the bed; and even though patches of his fur were still stained red, I wanted to nuzzle my face into him. Instead, I just watched Jack curled up on the bed while the sheets covering Ned rose and fell as he slept. For one short minute things almost seemed normal, but then I moved into the guestroom. I hadn't so much as walked past that room in almost two years.

There were unwanted memories waiting for me in there. They were in the floral pattern of the curtains and the archaic, tacky wallpaper I always disliked. The memories thickened towards the center of the room. The bed had been witness to my indiscretions. My sweat and embarrassment and secrets would never leave the white quilt and goose-feathered pillows.

I pulled off my bloody top and replaced it with Ned's t-shirt. I removed my jeans and threw them in the corner before crawling into bed. There were few things in this world more uncomfortable than waking up in denim. I laid on top of the covers and tried to push away the thoughts creeping to the surface of my mind. I hoped I would fall asleep before the memories grew too vivid to ignore. I squeezed my eyes shut, listened to my breathing, made an attempt to meditate but nothing worked. I fell back into my memories. It took no time at all to get lost in the past. I had been through so much since Nola's death, but the despair I knew then was still fresh.

After Nola died, my mother couldn't look at me and my father started spending more and more hours at the office. I never felt so alone. My relationship with June and Walter Barnaby was broken, and neither of them seemed interested in salvaging it. I pretended not to care.

When I was thirteen, I started smoking marijuana in the high school theater with Travis Murcott and Kristen Weisse. They were part of stage crew for all of the school productions. After rehearsals we would sit together on the empty stage and share a joint. At that point I didn't care about the drugs, it was just nice not to be ignored. They always found a way to laugh and sometimes I laughed with them even when I didn't get the joke.

Eventually my mother caught on. She would smell the smoke clinging to my clothes when I got home from school in the afternoon. We fought about my new habit constantly, but she never made a real effort to stop me, never offered to take me to counseling or pick me up after school so that my friends wouldn't influence me. June yelled at me until her eyes glazed over, then she would turn around, walk up the stairs and lock herself in her bedroom. I knew that everyone grieves differently, but I wished she let me grieve with her, instead of leaving me to my own devices. I couldn't blame her though; she was a mother who lost a child, which is one of the worst things in this world.

"Do you ever wish it had been me?" I found the courage to ask her over breakfast. "Do you wish I had gotten sick?"

My mother didn't answer right away. I watched her throw her frazzled golden hair over her slim shoulders. Her green eyes, which had been so bright, were jaded now. She inhaled and stared into her cup of tea. "That is a horrible thing to ask me."

"I know that." I kept my eyes on her. I remember thinking that this was the longest conversation we'd had in weeks. I knew what her answer should have been, but she couldn't bring herself to lie to me. She should have said, "Of course not. I love you, Sage. You're my daughter too."

She just sat there, and after a minute, June managed to shrug her shoulders. It seemed to take all the energy out of her. She rested her elbows on the table.

"Mom?"

"I don't know. I have thought about it. Nola was… and you're—"

"Okay," I said without letting her finish.

I accepted that I would never hear what I wanted to from my mother, but that didn't make it hurt any less. I couldn't talk to my father about anything because at this point he was always buzzed or blacked out or passed out. I was angry with everyone.

I stopped fighting to get out of bed anymore. I didn't want to feel anything. I was done caring, and for a while that worked.

I kept smoking with Travis and Kristen until one day Travis showed up with something stronger than marijuana.

Travis sauntered in through the side door of the theater, which we always kept unlocked. He was sporting the same gray beanie he wore every day. His eyes were bleary and bloodshot. I scooted over so that he could nestle himself between Kristen and I at the edge of the stage.

"What took you so long?" Kristen nudged him.

She had a real alternative look to her, thick eyeliner and a short, pixie hair cut. She was stick thin and I always resented how she could eat fast food tacos, bags of potato chips and boxes of chocolate without putting on any extra weight.

"I picked up something special for us," he said and took out a small plastic bag filled with three white pills inside.

"What is it?" I asked him.

"It will make you believe in magic."

"Oh, I am so in!" Kristen squealed.

That afternoon everything changed. I didn't believe in magic, but I believed in the numbing power of drugs. I could live with myself as long as I was high. My habit grew until I was addicted. I was visibly impaired every hour of the day. I stopped going to school and would get home later and later each night. I was always slouching and stumbling and sleeping. I don't think my parents even noticed. I tested everything I could get my hands on. It was never the fancy stuff, but it always got the job done.

A year later I was fourteen and wondering through the high school parking lot when a '69 gold Cadillac Eldorado pulled up in front of me. The driver slammed the door shut as he got out of the car. He loomed over me and I recognized his warm blue eyes. It was Ned McGreevy, my godfather, to the rescue.

"Barnaby," he greeted me in a gruff voice.

"Old man."

"Get in the car, kid."

"I'm not supposed to accept rides from strangers."

"You know who I am."

"I don't even know who I am right now." I laughed, and pushed past him.

"Hey. Hey, Sage." Ned grabbed my arm. "Stop."

"Back off."

"Sorry, kid. You need help."

"Let go of me!" I screamed.

How dare he? I hadn't seen Ned McGreevy in years and now he shows up and wants to fix me. I wouldn't have it. I was fourteen, immature, erratic and high, which meant there was no way I was going without a fight. I broke free from his grip and started sprinting through the parking lot, but it wasn't five seconds before Ned caught up to me. He wrapped his arms around me and lifted me off the ground. I was hysterical, kicking and scratching him at every opportunity.

He locked me in the back seat. I reached over and grabbed the steering wheel three times before Ned threw the car into park. He pulled me out by my hair and shoved me in the trunk, which was a new low. Every pothole and bump in the road made the ride to Bridgeview City unbearable. About twenty minutes later we pulled into the McGreevy's driveway and I never went back to

Tarrytown again.

I am going to skip the messy details, but Ned and Lena rehabilitated me in their home, in the guest room. The withdrawal symptoms lasted for nearly two weeks, and I still cannot imagine how Hell could be any worse. I threatened to burn the house down.I threatened to kill myself and I called Ned every horrible name that came to mind. Every nerve was on fire, and my body cramped constantly. It was pure agony, but Ned and Lena were at my side for all of it.

Ned force fed me and held my hair back when I got sick. Lena was the one who helped me shower and dress and cleaned the soiled sheets. They were so patient. About three weeks after moving in with the McGreevys, I made my way downstairs and poured a bowl of cereal. Ned and Lena were astonished. They watched me from across the kitchen table. I was dressed in one of Lena's pink silk nightgowns, which was way too long for me. When I finished drinking the leftover milk, I glanced up at them.

"Have June or Walter even asked about me since I was kidnapped?"

Ned and Lena sat in silence. I could tell they were trying to work out how to break the bad news to me. I think they worried that whatever they were keeping from me would send me spiraling out of control again.

"Come on, I promise not to relapse before lunch."

They shared a tender look with each other before speaking up.

"Honey," Lena began the conversation. "Your parents just put a very large sum of money into a personal bank account under your name. As long as you stay clean, you will have access to that money and a home with us."

"As long as you like, Sage," Ned cut in.

"Of course. But your parents—"

"Oh." I breathed and Lena stopped talking. "I can't believe

this."

I knew that I had promised not to relapse before lunch but getting high just became a top priority.

"Barnaby." Ned slid his hand across the table, but I pulled mine into my lap.

"I'm fine. I get it. My parents are paying me off to stay away. They want me out of their lives."

Ned softened his voice. "It's not fair, kid. I'm sorry."

"I think it's for the best, dear," Lena added. "Your mom and dad never recovered after your sister passed away, and they just can't take any more tragedies right now. Sage, you were in a dark place, and your father asked us to step in."

"Walter called you? Could he even speak without slurring his words?"

"That is besides the point."

"Listen kid, you're rich. Sage, you never have to worry about money again. You have a home here with us, and all you have to do is stay sober. That last part is important, you need to stay sober."

I stood up and placed my empty cereal bowl in the sink. "I appreciate what you and Lena are trying to do, but I don't want your generosity. I would rather have a drink. Nola is dead, my parents disowned me— I'm sorry, but I don't have one good reason to stay clean."

I thought it would be best to leave out the part where I sold my soul to the Devil.

"Sage," Ned straightened himself up in his chair. "I know you're hurting, and you're gunna carry some of that pain around with you forever, but not all of it. Just wait and see. With time things won't seem so bad."

Bullshit, I thought.

"Well, now that we're all on the same page," Lena chirped. "Would anyone like a scoop of pistachio ice cream?"

"It's not even nine o'clock, honey," Ned said.

Lena stood and opened the freezer. "There is never a wrong time for ice cream."

I promised to stay clean, and I had a home with the McGreevys. Lena home-schooled me, and it turns out I was pretty smart. Without any distractions or drugs, I graduated high school over the next year, but I had no plans of attending college as a fifteen year old. I decided to take a nice, long vacation overseas instead.

I had been sober for a year and I was rich; now all I needed was a way to save my soul. That was when I decided to expand my horizons. Ned, of course, thought my vacation was a terrible idea, but he had no hold over me. It was my money and my decision. I promised to call him once a day. I sent him postcards, emails and photographs constantly. He never stopped worrying but eventually he stopped asking when I was coming home. A year later I returned to Bridgeview, ready to save the world and redeem my soul.

After several months battling creatures in the night, I started to feel like I had found my purpose. I was sending spirits into the light and casting demons back into the fire. My short temper even made me more suited for the job. Unfortunately it is impossible to work in the world of the supernatural without accumulating a death toll.

One sunny day I received an unexpected visit from a boy with auburn hair and freckles. He seemed too nice to have ever suffered a day in his life. I was celebrating two years of sobriety the day Logan Forester tracked me down.

I was reading in Merrick's Park, just down the road from 1976, when I first saw him. I was sitting by the duck-less duck pond when a shadow fell over me and blocked out the sun. I looked up to find a pair of smiling brown eyes staring down at me.

"Can I help you?" I asked, annoyed. He'd interrupted a good part of the book.

"Is your name Sage Barnaby? I'm sorry to bother you. I know Mrs. Gordy—"

"Eleanor Gordy from Baltimore?"

"She gave me your name and told me you live in Bridgeview City. She said you helped her daughter, Patricia.

"I remember."

Patricia Gordy had been a difficult case. She was possessed by Berith, a demon who influences homicides and blasphemy. Berith broke three of my ribs and bruised the entire left side of my face before I exorcized him from Patricia's body. I couldn't open my left eye for a week afterwards. I told Ned and Lena that I tripped and fell down a flight of stairs. I don't think they believed me.

"I have a similar problem," he said. "Well, I think I do."

"What's your name?"

"Logan," he said with a smile. "Logan Forester. I came here from Boston."

He took a step back and the sun poured onto my face. The light seeped through his auburn hair and for a second it resembled a campfire. Logan reached down his hand and pulled me to my feet, and like everyone else I stood next to, he towered over me. He looked so thin in his old brown t-shirt and faded corduroy pants.

"Let me guess," I said, and flipped the mane of dark hair over my shoulder. "You are missing hours from your life, maybe days that you have no memory of. You can't escape a sour smell that seems to be following you around. You have nightmares even when you're awake. You've become sensitive to sunlight, and lately the smallest annoyances send you over the edge. You don't care about the things you used to anymore. Does any of that sound familiar?"

"It could be mental illness, depression or schizophrenia," he suggested.

"Yeah, it could be. Does your family have a history of mental illness?"

"No." Logan hung his head.

"Possession often gets mistaken for a psychological problem and in a way it is. Medication can sometimes suppress the symptoms of demonic possession but they always break through. You can't keep some monsters caged."

"Can you make it go away?" His voice trembled.

"Yes. I can."

When I look back, I might have been overly confident. A lack of humility can often lead to failure.

Logan and I exchanged information; and whenever he lost time or felt unreasonably angry, he would call me. A couple of weeks after our first meeting in the park Logan phoned to tell me that he had been waking up with unexplainable bruises on his arms. I asked him to set up a video camera and record himself while he slept. The following morning I received a video and a text message that read:

> This is really happening. I'm scared. Please help
> me.
> -Logan

I played the video on my cell phone. The image was Logan's bedroom. He was sleeping. The digital clock on his nightstand read three-twenty in the morning. Everything seemed normal until Logan began stirring beneath the sheets. He was waking up. Logan pushed the blankets off his body and sat up. His hair was unkempt and out of place as he looked around the room. A smile crept onto his lips, but it wasn't the smile I had been so fond in the park. This was malicious and crazed.

Logan scooted to the edge of his bed and reached into the drawer of his desk. He removed a pair of scissors and toyed with them in his hands. His eyes were steady on the sharp blades. He seemed to be falling in love with the tool. He slipped his fingers coyly through the handle then brought the scissors to his mouth. I watched as Logan kissed the blades and for a brief second his eyes flickered towards the camera lens. They weren't the beautiful shade of brown that belonged to Logan. They were black holes, entirely demonic.

What happened next wasn't easy to watch. The demon possessing Logan's body began to mutilate him. He brought the scissors to his skin and pushed down before dragging the blades through his flesh. He did it again and again and again. There were open cuts all over his forearms.

Once he finished, the demon calmly placed the scissors back into the desk drawer. He looked down at his artwork. The sight of Logan's blood thrilled the dark creature. The red liquid raced down his arms. The demon positioned itself back under the covers and blood was smeared across the bed sheets. He chuckled manically before pulling up the comforter and shutting his eyes. Apart from the blood stained sheets, the rest of the night passed peacefully. Logan hardly moved. His breathing was steady. He looked peaceful.

The video cut off before Logan woke up that morning to the bloody scene. I assumed he didn't want me to witness his terrified, possibly manic reaction.

I called him straight away. "Logan."

"Did you watch the video I sent you?" His voice was so low it sounded like he was afraid to talk.

"I am getting on the next train to Boston. Can you pick me up from the station?"

"Yeah."

"Do you live with your parents?"

"Yeah, and my brother."

"Unless you want them around for what we have to do, you need to find a way to get them out of the house," I instructed.

"We have a lake house. My parents go there every weekend so

they won't be home. I can think of something to tell my brother."

"Good," I sighed. "Oh, and think of somewhere we could grab a bite to eat before we head back to your place. It's better to do what we have to do on a full stomach."

I swore that I heard him smiling over the phone. "Thank you, Sage. I will see you in a couple of hours."

Later that day I stepped onto the platform at South Station in Boston. The wind from passing trains gathered my hair and obstructed my vision. When my curls finally settled, I could see Logan standing at the opposite end of the platform. His auburn hair had also been assaulted by the wind but he couldn't have been any cuter. After an awkward wave on both our ends, I made my way over to him.

The walk as I approached Logan seemed to unfold in slow motion. His eyes never left me and a nervous energy spread through my body. I had never experienced this kind of sensation before. It wasn't as dramatic as butterflies or blushing cheeks. I was just happy to see him.

He smiled and kept his eyes on my face. "Hi, Sage. You look nice."

I don't know what he was talking about. I was wearing what I always wore, black clothes and a lot of black mascara.

"Why are you smiling? I came here to perform an exorcism on you."

"Yeah, but that's no reason to spoil dinner."

I brushed off his joke. "Do we have the house to ourselves?"

"Yeah."

"What did you tell your brother?"

Logan's face turned red. "I told him that I have a date."

"If this is a date, it is the strangest one in history," I teased.

"Oh, I don't know," Logan scratched his head, ruffling his auburn hair. "I hear that dinner and an exorcism is the new dinner and a movie."

I couldn't help laughing. His optimism was contagious.

Dinner was great and not just the food. Logan was a gentleman. He held every door, he pulled out my chair and he paid for everything. He took me to this great hole in the wall burger joint. There was dim lighting and good music. The food was messy and delicious. I savored every bite. During our meal, we never even mentioned the reason I came to Boston. We talked about our favorite bands, movies, where we saw ourselves in ten years, what cities we wanted to visit, we told bad jokes and we laughed. We laughed a lot. I hadn't felt that normal since before Nola got sick. It was wonderful. Too bad it was the only dinner we would ever share together.

Eventually the meal ended and the conversation turned from recreational to business. Logan stared at me from across the table. The candlelight played on his face and highlighted his freckles.

"Can you talk me through what's going to happen tonight?"

I paused and tried to think of a way to explain an exorcism ritual without it sounding completely monstrous, but it was impossible. I had to be honest with him. I had to be unemotional and detach myself. I had to ignore the shimmering trepidation in his eyes.

"Logan, this is all going to sound very strange."

I watched him put on a brave face.

I sighed. "We are going to go into your bedroom, and I am going to tie you to the bed. Then I will draw a demon's snare on the ceiling above you. I will call forth the demon and force it to reveal its name. You might still be conscious for this. You might be completely aware of what's happening to you, around you. You are going to hear me speak in Latin, but you will also hear another voice."

"You mean the demon?"

"Yes, but you have to stay level-headed. It feeds on your fear, so you need to trust that you are stronger than the thing inside of you."

He cast his eyes away from mine and whispered. "Do you think I'm stronger than the thing inside of me?"

"Absolutely."

I watched as the light jumped back into his brown eyes.

"What happens after the demon tells you its name?"

"That's the easy part. More Latin. I insert the creature's name into a lost passage from The Bible and it's driven out of you. I will send it back to the place where it was born, Hell."

Logan nodded. I could see him struggle with the horrible reality of this situation. "When this all started, I just thought I'd gone crazy. Now I wish it was that simple. They have pills and therapy to take care of that. Sometimes I pretend this is all part of some epic nightmare I haven't woken up from yet."

I watched Logan finish drinking the water from his glass. His hand was shaking as he placed it back on the table.

"Logan, you are going to be okay. I promise."

"I know," he said with one his perfect smiles. "I trust you."

I got that happy feeling again, and I smiled too. I wanted to keep my promise to Logan Forester, but it ended up a horrible lie.

When we got back to his place, we went straight into his room. I took out some holy water, burned sage, lit candles and then proceeded to draw the demon's snare on the ceiling. He was very still when I tied him to the bedposts. He didn't complain that I had knotted the rope too tight or said that he was having second thoughts.

I took a moment to examine his room before beginning the ritual. I told myself it was work related, but the truth was I wanted to know more about Logan. There were Duplass movie posters on his wall and a really impressive stereo system connected to his laptop. Behind the door was a small basket of children toys. I figured that these were the toys he kept from childhood, his favorites.

I was hit with a startling realization. Logan was just a boy. At fifteen, he was only a year younger than me. There was a whole life waiting for Logan Forester. I would be the reason he got to live it or never got the chance to.

The pressure was unbearable but I didn't express my concern. I buried it deep inside me. I had performed a dozen of exorcisms prior to this one. They'd all been successful. Each possessed individual was freed with minimal injuries. Sure, occasionally there had been bruises, maybe a broken bone or torn muscles but nothing that couldn't be mended. Logan would be fine.

"Sage," he whispered from the bed. "I just— I want to thank you."

I almost laughed at his sincerity. "Don't thank me yet."

"I might not get the chance to later."

I put forth a reassuring smile, but I could see the panic swimming in his eyes. "Are you ready, Logan?"

He nodded. His gentle eyes were locked onto mine. We had no idea just how awful, bloody and crushing the next twelve hours would be. I had no idea what I was up against. It was nearly seven in the morning when I finally got the demon to give me its name. By that time I had been thrown across the room, suffered a concussion, my ears were ringing and I wasn't sure where I was bleeding from, but there was a ton of blood.

Regardless of how I suffered, Logan suffered much worse. He was captive in his own skin. The demon writhed inside of the boy, tearing his limbs from their sockets. The demon felt nothing.Logan, on the other hand, felt everything and he couldn't even scream.

The room had been turned inside out. There was a heaviness that pushed down on my chest and I fought to breathe. I struggled to recite the Latin passages I had memorized but eventually I followed through. The words punched their way out of my mouth.

The demon squealed and twisted in severe discomfort. Logan's eyes changed to the black I had seen in the video. His mouth was gaping and his muscles tightened. As Logan's body lashed about on the bed, I grabbed the bottle of holy water and sprinkled it over him. The sounds that came from the creature were barbaric and crude. I could feel the demon's cries resonating in my bones as the room grew frigid. My teeth chattered, and I wanted it to be over. I wanted Logan to be safe. With every ounce of conviction in me, I commanded the demon to tell me what he was called. I wanted to hear the name that Lucifer had bestowed upon him.

"Loqui nomen tuum. Christo cogit vos!" I hollered over the flying objects and the screeching demon.

"Vocatus sum Murmur," the beast replied against his will.

"Murmur. It has been a pleasure," I said coldly. "Farewell."

"I have hurt the boy too badly. If you send me away, he won't survive his wounds," he warned me. "He won't survive minutes."

"I don't believe you."

I could see that Logan's body had been through a lot. It was clear that he would need a trip to the hospital following this ordeal, but I wasn't convinced that he was dying. Demons are not known for their honesty.

"Lucky for the boy, I am willing to compromise."

"Oh, now you want to negotiate?"

"The boy can have the body Monday through Friday. I want it on weekends," his black eyes glared up at me.

"I don't think so."

"Fine, every other weekend," he was grinning like a comic book villain.

This diabolical creature would get no sympathy from me, but I think Murmur knew that. He knew he wasn't going to spend another day on Earth. But the way Murmur saw it, if he wasn't allowed to stay then neither was his host.

I couldn't have known that the demon was being truthful when he told me that Logan wouldn't survive the exorcism. Even if I had believed Murmur, I still couldn't have allowed Logan and the demon share a human form. The idea was unethical, and forbidden by the priests in Rome who taught me how to execute exorcisms.

After my deal with the Devil fell through, I promised to get rid of whatever evil I came across. I swore to stop the creatures of darkness from destroying this world. Murmur had to be sent back to Hell, even if it meant that the world would lose Logan Forester. I just couldn't let Logan live if it meant Murmur survived.

I hated making that choice. I hated that he found me in Merrick's park by the duck-less duck pond. I hated that he looked so beautiful when I stepped off the train. I hated the way his freckles glowed in candlelight.

"What do you think?" the demon hissed.

"Logan. Can you hear me, Logan? I am sorry. I am so, so sorry."

"Wait a minute!" Murmur roared. "I have more to say. I am a prince of Hell, and you will listen to me!"

I closed my eyes. I listened to my breathing and waited for the room to fall silent. "Dei creatura per terram ambulare. Murmur, natus ex carne et mundo proditorem ignis. Reverti illic nunc. Ubi reditum umbris solis odio flagitiorum quae plus ignis ardebit. In nomine Patris et Filii et Spiritus Sancti."

When I opened my eyes again, Murmur was gone. The bedroom was in disarray. Logan's broken body lay motionless on the bed. My heart sank from my chest into my stomach. I rushed to Logan's side and untied him. It must have hurt, but Logan reached out to hold my hand. His eyes were barely open as we spoke.

"Sage…" he said my name and I nearly fell in love.

"Oh, thank goodness, you're alive."

"I don't think I have much time left to be honest."

"Sure you do. You have all the time in the world."

"I am glad I have the time to thank you again," he squeezed my hand.

"Don't. It wasn't supposed to happen like this. I promised you would be okay."

"Hey, I'm great." He managed to smile. I was astounded that after what just happened he could still find a reason to smile. "That was by far the best date I have ever been on," he joked. "Not a dull moment."

I was horrified.

Logan smiled again, but it took more effort this time. I brought my face closer to his and started to cry.

"Can you forgive me?" I asked.

"No," he answered. "Because you have nothing to be sorry for. You were amazing." I let my free hand stroke his auburn hair. He didn't seem to mind. "You know, there is a reason people keep to tradition. Next time, how about dinner and a movie?"

I was sobbing and laughing all at once. I wiped away hot tears as they streamed down my face. "I can't wait."

I pictured us sitting in the theater. I imagined Logan reaching over the armrest to hold my hand in the dark.

"Promise me that you will leave my body here. I don't want my family to think I ran away or went missing. I want them to have some kind of closure. I need them to know that I'm not coming back."

I nodded.

"I'm so glad we met."

"Logan, don't go. Stay. Please. Stay."

He squeezed my hand one last time and I watched his eyes shut. I could feel the life drain from his body and leave the room. I

was alone. The only company I had was the sharp pain in my chest.
I was pretty sure that this was what it felt like to be heartbroken.
I had only known Logan for a couple of weeks. I don't know if I
would call it love, but it was definitely the closest I had ever been.

11

The Goldfinch

Returning to New York from Boston was soul crushing. I wept the entire train ride back to Penn Station. I was supposed to be saving human lives, not ending them. When I arrived in New York, I couldn't bring myself to walk to Grand Central and board the next train to Bridgeview.

I checked into a five star hotel, stared at myself in the bathroom mirror, hated what I saw and relapsed. I stayed in the city for two weeks. I drank a minimum of three rum and cokes every morning for breakfast. Then spent the rest of the day hunting down every drug I could find. I stopped calling the McGreevys to check in. I knew Ned and Lena wouldn't call the police. They must have assumed I was using again and they were too kind-hearted to have me sent to juvie.

Each night I partied with strangers in grungy back alley bars. I even called my old high school friends, Travis and Kristen, to join me. They had dropped out of school and were working in off-off-off-Broadway theaters as lighting designers and sound technicians. They performed all of their professional responsibilities high. I actually enjoyed their company. I was happy to be around people who would enable my habit. Ned would have forced me to live in a cold, tedious reality. I preferred my cocoon of sleepless nights, booze and drugs.

Travis, Kristen and I were always the last to leave whichever bar we inhabited. Afterwards we would trudge up to the hotel's roof and watch the sunrise. The sky would change from black to gray to navy blue, then lavender and the lavender faded to pink and then bled into a red before it turned orange and finally yellow. We took this time to come down off our high. It was the few minutes of each day when we found a sense of peace, no matter how small or how brief.

Exactly two weeks after my horrible ordeal with Logan in Boston, Ned found me drunk in a biker bar in New York City's meat packing district. It was an incredible place, covered in filth, swarming with unruly men, warm beer and hundreds of ladies' undergarments hanging from the ceiling. I don't know how he found me, but I didn't want to leave.

I vaguely remember that some of the regulars tried to defend me, insisting Ned leave me alone. He refused to go without me and became a victim of a bar fight. I watched him take on four grown men with bad attitudes and plenty of experiences in brawls. The odds were definitely against my godfather but he managed to overcome them. For the next week he had a black eye and bruises. I think someone broke his wrist. Ned would tell you it was worth it, but I'm not sure that's true.

I never said goodbye to Kristen and Travis, but I don't think they cared. They never came looking for me. I spent another long withdrawal period in the McGreevy's guestroom, and it was much worse than the first time because now I had Logan's death eating away at me. I begged Ned and Lena to contact some of my old dealers. I asked for cigarettes and bargained for painkillers, but they were merciless. Every time I mentioned drugs or alcohol, they immediately left the room and locked me inside.

Both of my guardians fell back into their prior care giving roles. Ned force-fed me and Lena washed me. For three days I was convinced they were conspiring against me. I cursed them, and accused them for trying to poison me. I called them terrible names. Once Ned almost hit me but Lena stopped him. I saw the shame in his face afterwards. He was embarrassed that I'd almost gotten the best of him.

My stomach and muscles cramped for days, I threw up every meal, shivered constantly and suffered severe migraines. If death had come for me, I would have welcomed him gladly even if it meant going to Hell. Unfortunately, I was still very much alive, and the withdrawals raged on.

Even on my better days I still experienced flu-like symptoms. Every other hour I was either throwing the sheets off me or asking for more blankets. Ned and Lena always obliged me. They even switched between the air conditioning and the heat to make me more comfortable. I don't know how they did it. I think Lena began spending more time at the diner to avoid not only the house's change in temperature but also my violent mood swings.

One late afternoon Lena was managing 1976 while Ned babysat me. I had been confined to the guest room for six days at that point. I had become victim to an unbearable chill that seemed to steal beneath the covers and crawl under my skin. It was like all of my internal organs were freezing as I lay in bed shivering uncontrollably. I was sweating; my skin was sticky and balmy, which betrayed how cold I felt. Regardless, I was beside myself with the unrelenting torment that is withdrawal.

"Ned!" I called his name from beneath the covers. "Ned! NED!"

He never showed up.

"Ned! Ned, I need you! Come here! Ned! I'M FREEZING! Ned!"

Nothing. I took a deep breath and shouted with everything in me. "OLD MAN!"

That did it. My lungs were sore, but I immediately heard a pair of feet rushing down the hallway towards the guest room.

"Sage, are you okay? What is it?" he huffed.

The door slammed open and I peeked out from under the covers to find Ned, breathless and wearing nothing but a pair of boxer shorts. I tried not to stare at his small tuff of chest hair or the trail of hair beneath his belly button. I brought my gaze to his face. The hair on his head was soaked and matted to his forehead. A puddle of water collected at his feet.

"You're wet," I said.

"No shit. I was taking a shower. Something you should seriously consider."

"Sorry I interrupted you."

"Well, I heard psychotic screaming. I thought I should look into it."

He watched me with immaculate blue eyes, baffled by the young woman I had become. A part of me felt bad. I wanted to be the sweet girl he dreamed of, but I didn't have it in me. I would always be this broken, feral thing.

Ned stood patiently in the doorway. "What seems to be problem?"

"I'm cold."

"Well, I don't know what to tell you, kid. You have every blanket in the house, including the ones that are supposed to be on my bed. Not to mention that it's seventy-something degrees outside."

I shivered all over. "I'm cold. Please."

I was very much like a child then. Ned couldn't help but be sympathetic. I needed him because of my poor choices, my mistakes, but in a weird way I had finally become the little girl he always wanted.

"Turn over, would you?" he said.

I lay curled up on my side as Ned sat at the edge of the bed and rubbed my back over the blankets. While it didn't necessarily warm me up, it was a comfort. Then I heard the most heartfelt, wonderful song that has ever been sung.

> *The way you wear your hat;*
> *The way you sip your tea;*
> *The memory of all that.*
> *No, no, they can't take that away from me.*
>
> *The way your smile just beams;*
> *The way you sing off key;*
> *The way you haunt my dreams.*
> *No, no, they can't take that away from me.*
>
> *We may never, never meet again*
> *On the bumpy road to love.*
> *Still I'll always, always keep the memory of*
>
> *The way you hold your knife;*
> *The way we danced 'til three;*
> *The way you've changed my life.*
> *No, no, they can't take that away from me.*

I felt even colder than before. I couldn't push away thoughts Logan Forester, the boy with the perfect smile. The boy I had killed. A wave of self-hatred crashed over me and I heard myself choking for breath. I sobbed into the pillow while a steaming pile of guilt drove me mad. I knew that I could never share it with anyone. I would have to bear it through tears and silent prayers.

"Hey kid, are you all right?" he whispered in a soothing voice.

"We all make fools of ourselves. That's part of life— a big part of life."

"Is it always this hard?"

He sighed. "Yeah. I'm afraid so."

"So why does anyone bother?"

"Oh, come on. You've read enough books and seen enough movies to know the answer to that."

Ned was such a sap. "I don't believe in love, old man."

"Of course you do. You love me. You love Lena. You love pistachio ice cream."

I sniffled. "And I love coffee."

"See?" he chuckled.

I listened to him, but it had grown too cold for me to respond. I felt my body temperature drop, and the freezing cold burned me.

Ned rested the back of his hand on my forehead. "Jesus, you weren't kidding. Sage, you're frozen."

"I can't feel my fingers," I whispered through chattering teeth. "Or my toes."

"Scoot over, kid."

I couldn't move though. I was too cold. Ned had to push me over a foot before crawling under the blankets beside me. Once he'd gotten himself situated in the bed, Ned wrapped his arms around me and held me close. I was facing away from him and could feel his breath tickle the back of my neck. After a minute my teeth stopped chattering. Another minute passed and I started to get the feeling back in my toes.

"Two years. You were sober for two years. Why? Why did you start using again? What could have gone so wrong that you—?" he sighed and held me tighter. "Don't worry. I don't actually expect an answer. You keep your secrets and I'll keep worrying about you. That's our routine," his embrace tightened once more. "God, I wish you would trust me enough to tell me what's troubling you."

I stopped shaking and my breathing eased as I drifted off to sleep. While my body slept in Ned's arms, my thoughts strayed to Logan. Even in dreams I felt nauseous. His face, his brown eyes and freckles were never out of sight. I dreamed of his broken bones and his dying smile. My heart broke when he left this world and continued to shatter in my dreams of him.

When I woke up, it took me some time to realize where I was. Lazy sunlight poured in through the windows and warmed the bed sheets. I stretched and discovered that my limbs were sore from earlier. I must have been tensing my muscles in an attempt to keep warm. I rolled over and found myself staring at a man's back. That was when I remembered that Ned was lying in bed with me. He must have fallen asleep after I did. I shouldn't have been surprised. Ned often indulged in afternoon naps.

His back was strong and defined with a couple of complimenting beauty marks. On the right side of his back was a tattoo of a small bird with a bright yellow body, and accented black feathers on its tail, the wings' tips and at the crown of its head. The bird had beady ink black eyes and a pale orange beak. I couldn't believe I'd never seen it before. I let my hand move across the piece of art on Ned's bare shoulder blade. I outlined the tattoo with my pointer finger and accidentally woke up Ned.

He turned over to face me and was immediately surprised by who he saw in bed with him. Ned probably expected to see his wife, but instead he got a sweaty, stinking teenager. I watched him play off his confusion.

"Hey, kid. How are you feeling?"

I only smiled. He smiled back. I was feeling much better. My body temperature had normalized and my migraine was gone. My skin was still incredibly sensitive and I was a little dizzy, but that was better than I had felt in days. Ned closed his eyes again.

He wasn't asleep, just resting. I guess he wasn't quite ready to rejoin the waking world. I don't think I had ever been this close to him before. (I had never been big on hugs.) I could make out every piece of facial hair and each eyelash that lined his closed lids. His lips were slightly chapped and his nose was a little crooked, but altogether it was a nice face.

"Ned."

"Hm?" He kept his eyes shut as we spoke.

I whispered because it seemed appropriate given the lack of space between us. "Why did you get the tattoo on your back?"

"You saw that?" he hesitated to answer.

"What kind of a bird is it?"

"A goldfinch. It's a symbol for resurrection or overcoming death, the importance of change. For example, moving from life into death, or moving on when someone you love has died."

Ned spoke with a monotone voice and his eyes stayed closed. Their unending blue was hidden from me.

"Did someone you love die?"

"Yup."

"When?" I asked.

"That's not a conversation for today. Sorry, kid."

He reached up to pat my cheek, but since his eyes were shut one of his lumbering fingers caught me in the eye.

I winced. "Ouch! Jerk."

"Oh, come on. That couldn't have hurt worse than the withdrawals."

"That is not funny! Too soon, Ned."

"If you can't find a way to laugh, you are going to spend all your time crying," he teased.

I decided to test out his theory and slapped him playfully across the face.

"Hey! Ow!"

"You were right. That was hilarious."

"Ha. Ha," he replied sarcastically, pinching my side.

And so a brutal and merciless kicking, pinching, slapping match commenced. It was all in good fun, of course. I don't believe either of us intended to hurt the other, but we both voiced our discomfort before the next retaliation. Our roughhousing ended as quickly as it had started, but it had taken a lot out of us.

"All right! You win. You win, kid! Stop!" Ned smiled and held both of my hands in his, concluding the altercation.

We lay in the bed facing one another with foolish grins on our faces. We were like children. Our breathing was heavy as we settled down from the pathetic brawl and kept our eyes steady on each other, questioning if the match was really over. I worried he would attack again the second I let my guard down. The blood had rushed into Ned's face, and he blushed as his chest fell with each heavy exhale.

My gaze settled on his face again. I studied the laugh lines beside each eye and at the corners of his mouth. His lips were parted. The brilliant smile we had just shared suddenly turned into a somber frown that only a mouth like Ned's could showcase.

I lifted my eyes to meet his, and they held my stare effortlessly. I was happy to be lost in their blue. I realized that we were sharing a near perfect moment together, so naturally I felt the need to ruin it.

I am not sure if I was still recovering from my recent dream of Logan Forester or if I wasn't thinking straight because of the withdrawals, but my mind and body betrayed me. As I stared at Ned another cold front threatened to take hold of me. I couldn't shake it. I wanted to know someone in a way I had never known anyone. I was sixteen years old and I had never kissed someone. Between my depression, addictions, travels abroad and exorcisms, it had never happened. But while bathing in that perfect moment I wanted it to.

I leaned in, ever so slightly, and waited. Ned didn't pull away.

Why would he? He had no clue what my intentions were. I brought my face closer. I could make out a look of alarm in his eyes, an electric mixture of fear and anticipation. I felt it too. My stomach became light and airy, transforming into a dry sponge. The small gap between us was quickly closing.

"Um, Sage," Ned said in a coarse breath. He probably meant to say something that would stop me from advancing, but all he could manage was my name.

I brought my mouth down on his and pressed against him. His lips parted for mine and we kissed, breathing each other in. The nerves lacing my body tingled fervently. The kiss we shared was intimate and chilling and wrong. I like to think that if Ned hadn't pulled away when he did, I would have.

Ned and I were together in that sense for four and a half seconds. We've never talked about what happened that day. It was a great, big mistake neither of us would ever conceive making again.

Ned stared at me with panicked eyes and did the last thing I expected. He pulled me into a firm, unyielding hug.

"Forgive me," he was practically crying. "Forgive me."

I leaned into him. It had never occurred to me that Ned would see himself as the aggressor and me as the victim. Still, he must have felt a sense of responsibility. He had always been the adult, never failing to drag me out of the darkness I threw myself into. Ned always did the right thing as he saw it and rarely lost his cool or sense of honor. It seemed that our four and a half seconds together was unchartered territory for him.

I had plummeted to a new low, which wouldn't have bothered me so much if I hadn't brought Ned down with me. We never told Lena. It was an unspoken agreement between us, which is why I was so unsettled when Lena's spirit approached me and claimed to know what happened between her husband and me. *I forgive you,* she said.

It's amazing how things just happen. How wars just happen. How shopping sprees just happen. How kissing someone just happens... but there is always a moment just before it happens when you can change the course of things. I rarely took advantage of those fleeting moments. I avoided that moment entirely during my time in the guest room with Ned.

It had been nearly two years since then and I hadn't stepped foot inside there all that time. The night that Lena died I slept on top of the covers, not wanting to be further reminded of the time I laid beneath them. The guest room would never be a place of fond memories. I would always cringe knowing that it still existed in the McGreevy's home at 181 O'Brien Circle.

12

Personal Business

"Whoa!" The exclamation woke me. The shouting was followed by the aggressive sound of rattled furniture and books being knocked off shelves. The chaos was accompanied by an uproar of incessant barks.

"What are you trying to do, kill me?"

"Oh, now that you mention it, yes!" My godfather's voice boomed from downstairs. "Would you stay still and make it easy for me? I'm an old man."

There was another loud crash, the sound of glass shattering. Damn. I never told Ned I was having company over. He must have been pretty upset to come downstairs and find a stranger sprawled across the living room sofa. I raced downstairs while simultaneously pulling my jeans over my legs. I wasn't coordinated in the mornings, especially before I had had a cup of coffee. I clumsily made my way into the living room.

The two men were standing across from one another, wide eyed and alert. Jack stood in the corner of the room. The fur along his spine was raised, but he kept his distance from the crazed humans. Ned had a baseball bat raised over his head, and Lial had his hands in the air. The room was in shambles with broken glass scattered across the floor and holes punched into the walls. Between this event and yesterday's coaster throwing incident, the living room had become prey to some violent scenarios.

"Hey, for an old man you've got a pretty good grip on that thing," Lial noted.

"Two and a half years of college baseball. I'm a surgeon with this bat," Ned announced before a puzzled expression came over his face. "Hey, are you wearing my clothes? Are those my favorite Quinnipiac sweatpants?"

The altercation continued, but Lial didn't seem to be very intimidated by Ned's threats. Ned took another swing and slammed the baseball bat into a window, destroying it. The sunlight that had been shining through reflected off the bits of glass scattered across the floor and created a mosaic of rainbow colors, which beamed across the walls and ceiling. While I found the quasi fight entertaining, I thought I should break it up. There was no chance either of them would stand down.

"Ned. Stop," I kept my voice calm.

Ned swung the bat recklessly. The angel managed to avoid getting struck by the weapon. "I want you to get out of here, kid. I can handle this."

"Ned," I tried to focus his attention away from the strange, tall man wearing his favorite sweatpants. Just as my godfather was rearing back take another swing at Lial's head, I screamed. "I invited him! I asked him to come."

"What?" Ned froze with the baseball bat still raised in the air, his robe hung open with his superhero boxers exposed. There were tiny droplets of moisture forming around his forehead, and his blue eyes were shining. I watched as he slowly regained his breath and lowered the bat to his side.

"You know this person?" Ned asked.

"His name is Lial. Lial, this is Ned McGreevy."

"Next time let me know about house guests before they arrive. I could have really hurt this young man."

"You've always wanted to meet my friends," I joked.

Ned sized up Lial, who was standing beside me in the doorway, and a grave look of disapproval washed over my godfather's face. I could see that he was uncomfortable having a stranger in his home, and reasonably so, with yesterday's tragedy was still fresh in his mind. Instead of voicing his discomfort, Ned awkwardly changed the subject.

"Who wants breakfast?" he asked as he moved past us into the kitchen. Jack followed at his heels.

Lial and I stood next to each other in the doorway and stared at the opposite wall, avoiding eye contact. I had been in the presence of dozens of demons but angels were something new. I still couldn't believe that West and I managed to summon my guardian, even it turned out to be somewhat of a disappointment.

"I could have taken him," Lial announced.

"Ned wouldn't have made it easy for you."

"Well it wouldn't have been difficult; he's human," Lial said the word, human, like it was poison in his mouth.

"I think you underestimate us."

"No, Sage. I understand you. I have been watching humans since the first of your kind. As a whole your species is predictable and selfish. Either you focus all of your energy on the past, which only depresses you, or you constantly worry about the future. Either way, humans are always distracted from the present moment. You miss out on so much and you never even realize how ignorant— no— how monstrously stupid you all are. I'm embarrassed for you, really," his eyes darkened. "Free will was wasted on humankind."

"I don't think He would have made that mistake. I think He has more faith in humanity than most of us do in Him," I argued, thinking back on our argument from the night before.

I could feel his ice blue eyes watching me. After a moment I turned my face to meet his stare; it startled me. I don't know why Lial had to say something unpleasant at every opportunity. It's not as though his point of view on God and humanity were a mystery to me. Lial was a fallen angel; he turned his back on his maker. Furthermore, he was a failed guardian because he turned his back on me. His actions spoke volumes. I guess he just liked the sound of his own voice.

"Do you want to know a secret, Sage?" Lial started up again. "Would you like to know why humans were given free will? He was bored. Your kind was meant to be the entertainment. How humans have destroyed this planet and one another was never of consequence to Him. He doesn't care. If He did, He would have put a stop to it by now. Humanity is trashy television. Life on Earth is the ultimate reality series and it used to be much funnier, but lately it's just sad. Not even worth watching."

Lial finished his unflattering theory and a wicked smile graced his angelic face. It took over the fullness of his lips. I turned away and stormed across the hall.

The kitchen had a much cozier atmosphere than the rest of the house. There were quaint wooden cupboards, the wall tiles were adorned with pink roses and the windows faced east, which allowed pale morning light to fill the room.

Ned was whipping up an admirable stack of pancakes and a fresh pot of coffee was brewing. The aroma of coffee always brightened my spirits. I sat down at the table and helped myself. Lial and Ned joined me while Jack ate from a dish of pancakes and dog biscuits on the floor. Ned and Lena had always kept a stash of treats in the cabinet for whenever Jack visited.

Over breakfast Lial and I listened to Ned's plans for Lena's burial. He didn't want any kind of service done, not a wake or memorial. He said he couldn't stand the idea of listening to people say they were sorry for his loss. Men like Ned always appeared unbreakable to the outside world. Only the women in their lives got to see them vulnerable. For Ned, that woman had always been Lena. I believed that when she was buried Ned's heart would go in the ground with her.

"We are going to bury her Thursday morning at dawn in Bridgeview cemetery. We bought a plot several years back. I never thought we would use it so soon," Ned said.

I just listened to him talk. There were no words capable of comforting someone who just lost his best friend.

Then, without warning, Lial stood up from the table. "Sage, we should really get going. Now."

Ned's face dropped. "Where are you going?"

"No. I think we can wait until Thursday."

"No, we can't," Lial pushed.

Lial could wait, but he wanted to get as far away from me as fast as possible. That meant we had to find The Other Book and return it to Him. It was Sunday and the burial was Thursday; we had four days to change my fate. I didn't know how to explain this to Ned, and no matter how I tried to shape the words they would sound selfish. However, the silver tongued angel managed to find the words for me.

"Mr. McGreevy, I was sorry to hear about your wife's death. I am here for a similar reason. You see, my sister is sick and the doctors say it's serious. She met Sage in Rome a few years ago, and they became friends. I thought Sage might want to visit her, just in case she doesn't pull through."

He was brilliant; every word seemed to come from truth, just like an angel. However, every word was a lie, which I suppose is just like a fallen angel. Regardless, it was a better excuse than I could have come up with. I watched Ned sitting across the table, his mind churning.

"I am sorry to hear that. What's your sister's name?"

Lial wrinkled his nose. "Uh…"

"Kelly," I blurted out.

I immediately felt like the worst person on the planet. I could tell from Ned's doe-eyed expression that he would let me leave, and I was disgusted with myself. How could I use his daughter's name as a means to persuade him? I tried to ignore the guilt, but it stuck to me and cloaked me in shame. I was experiencing an entirely new kind of self-hatred. Ned trusted me when he told me about Kelly and I used that information against him.

"Ned, I don't want to leave you alone." I continued.

"I have plenty to keep me busy. I need to assess the damage that was done to 1976. I want to get the diner back on its feet as soon as possible. Just make sure you're in the cemetery with me Thursday morning. Okay?" He paused. His eyes fixed on me. "Don't worry about me, Sage. Go see your friend."

I marveled at how composed he was. "Come on, Jack," I said. "Let's go back to the apartment and pack your squeaky beaver and pig ears."

"No." Lial almost shouted. "The dog is not coming with us."

"Yes, he is." I barked back.

"Sage, if we're taking Mr. McGreevy's car, I don't want the dog having an accident in the back seat, not to mention he sheds."

Lial was playing a game. He acted concerned about Ned's car because he didn't want Jack to come on our road trip. Furthermore, I never mentioned borrowing the Cadillac. Lial just killed two birds with one stone.

"Did you tell him I would let you take the car?" Ned stood up from his seat. He looked as though someone had just slapped him across the face.

"I'm sorry, sir. I thought you knew," Lial pretended to be

shocked. "Sage said you wouldn't mind."

"I never said that—!"

"Jesus, Blondie, were you going to take Sweetie without asking me?" Ned tried to stay composed, but his nostrils flared.

"Ned, I would never—"

"Listen, if you want to take the car for a few days that's fine, but bring her back in one piece. Do you hear me?"

I was stunned by his offer. It must have showed on my face. Ned's gold '69 Cadillac Eldorado was the only thing he loved more than the women in his life. I had never seen him so openly affectionate with something. He would say hello to the car every morning and wish it pleasant dreams each night. Sometimes I asked Ned if they would like to be left alone, but he never saw the humor in that.

"Thank you, Mr. McGreevy," Lial was all ready making his way out the front door.

"Hold up. Can I have a word with you?"

"Sure," Lial said with caution.

"Sage," Ned grabbed my attention. "Wait here."

I wanted to protest but something about his tone made me stay put. Ned and Lial moved into the hallway. Even though they spoke in whispers, I could still hear their conversation.

"I need you to take care of her," my godfather started in a hushed voice. "Sage doesn't handle trauma well. She gets into a mood and that mood gets her in trouble."

"What kind of trouble, sir?"

"Sage has a problem with substance abuse. I hate to even mention it because it's her personal business, but that girl is my personal business; and I need to know you're gunna look after her. Do I have your word?"

Lial didn't answer for a long time and then very softly he agreed, "Mr. McGreevy, you have my word."

"Good boy," I heard Ned slap Lial's back.

As the two men made their way back to the kitchen, I quickly retreated further into the room and took a seat at the table. When Lial walked in he looked miserable. It was clear that he did not want to be held accountable for me.

"Sage, I wouldn't mind if Jack stayed with me while you're away," Ned said. "Actually, I would prefer it."

"Okay," I growled. I couldn't refuse Ned, but Jack and I had been inseparable from the day I got him. It would be hard to leave without him, but I tried to appear indifferent. "See you later, Jack."

The dog looked at me with pale eyes. His pink tongue hung out the side of his mouth while he panted. I rested a hand on his head and scratched behind his ears.

"I promise to take good care of him."

"Make sure you take him for a lot of walks or else he is going to make a mess in here. Jack has no sense of decency."

Ned laughed, then moved in and kissed me on the cheek, something he almost never did. I ran my hand through Jack's white fur one more time. Lial shook Ned's hand before following me out the door.

We stopped at my apartment so that I could pack a bag. I made Lial wait in the hallway. Afterwards we made our way over to 1976, where Ned had left his car the previous day.

We found the two door hard top sitting in the front lot of the diner, but my attention was not focused on the glittering Eldorado. 1976 had suffered terribly. The neon sign that sat front and center on the roof had been melted down and the sides of the building were burnt black. Altogether, the diner looked more like a lump of coal than a restaurant. At least restoring the place would give Ned something to do.

"Lial, this is Sweetie. Sweetie, meet Lial," I introduced the Cadillac to the angel.

"I'm driving," he said.

Before sliding into the driver's seat, Lial looked at me over the top of the Cadillac. "Ned called you Blondie. Why'd he do that? It doesn't even make any sense."

"Blondie is a nickname," I let out a heavy sigh. "Every female on my mother's side of the family has always been blonde, but for whatever reason I have dark hair."

"Are you cursed or adopted or something?" he sneered.

"I think it's just science. I didn't get the blonde gene," I heard myself become defensive. I remembered how I used beg my mother not to call me that name. "Anyway, my family has been calling me Blondie since I was a girl because it's ironic or funny or whatever."

"Well, which is it— ironic or funny or whatever?"

I thought about that for a moment. Whenever my mom referred to me as Blondie, it was only meant as a dig, a reminder that I was different and somehow not good enough. "Honestly, I always thought it was kind of mean."

"I think it suits you," he shrugged.

"How?"

Lial stared at the Cadillac's shimmering hood while he thought. I could see its gold paint reflected in the blue of his eyes. "I guess you're not what you seem."

He lowered himself into the driver's seat and slammed the door shut. I sat next him on the passenger's side, stewing over the last thing he said to me. I am not what I seem. What did that mean? Maybe Lial meant that I wasn't as bad as I seem, or more likely he meant that I was much, much worse than I seem.

Sweetie's engine purred as we headed south. I didn't know where Lial was taking us, but he said it was important. I had no choice but to trust that he would help me find Liber Alter.

The windows were down. Lial's blonde waves of hair and my dark curls flew wildly as the air rushed in. He drove well above the speed limit, but I didn't ask him to slow down. I always loved the feel of wind racing through my hair. I imagined this was what flying must be like.

13

Cake & Steak

Three hours later we were still in the car. Lial made a poor attempt to sing along with some indie rock song on the radio. Laveau was right. I guess you can't teach an archangel to sing, but you couldn't stop one from trying.

His unruly hair bounced as he nodded his head to the music. He tapped the car wheel off beat to the song and screamed the lyrics out the open window. I laughed. Lial might have had the heart of a rock star, but he had the voice of a strangled cat.

"I don't hear you singing any better," he defended himself.

"That's because I don't sing."

"Don't you know this song?"

"Everyone knows this song."

"Go ahead, sing."

"No," I said.

"Come on!"

"No."

"Sage. Sing, damnit!"

I shook my head defiantly.

Lial raised his eyebrows, giving me a smug look, then focused on the road.

"Are we almost— wherever you're taking us?" I asked.

"Yeah, we're close."

A couple of minutes later, Lial moved the gold Cadillac into the left lane, and we veered off the highway. The sign above the exit ramp read: Baltimore.

The last time I was in this area I helped Mrs. Gordy exorcize the demon Berith from her daughter.

"Baltimore?"

"Do you remember when I told you we were going someplace important?" Lial chewed on his lower lip. "Well that's true, but it might be more important to me than to our overall mission."

I felt my temper burn, ready to boil and then possibly explode.

Lial let his eyes settle on me and I glared at him. I was so angry that I forgot how to speak.Did we really just drive four hours for nothing? I shouldn't have been surprised. Lial hadn't wanted to help me from the beginning.

It wasn't long before he switched on the Eldorado's blinker and we turned into a wide-open parking lot. There were a handful of crappy cars scattered throughout the lot, mostly pick-up trucks. Sweetie stood out among the neglected vehicles. After pulling into an empty spot, Lial and I crawled out of the car.

I groaned immediately. "Oh, you cannot be serious."

"Ha! Look at that— it's still here!" he was giddy.

"You mean there was a chance we drove all this way for nothing?" my voice bubbled on the edge of fury.

"This bar has been here for generations. It will grow on you. I swear."

At first glance I was not impressed. On second glance I was even less impressed. I sincerely doubted that this out-house would grow on me. It was nothing more than a wooden shack. There weren't any windows, the roof looked like it would cave in any moment and the wood beams that made up the exterior walls were rotting away. If it weren't for the parking lot filled with cars, I would have never guessed that people were brave enough to step inside, which made me question the type of crowd we would find here.

Lial pushed through the swinging doors, the kind you find in a western film. There was a long counter with stools that took up the left side of the bar and everything else was open space. The place smelled like a barn. I can only describe it as somewhere between dust and urine. There were no paintings on the walls or televisions above the bar. It wasn't a place where people came to enjoy footballs game. This bar was strictly for drinking, and I imagined occasionally for fighting as well. It was fully stocked, not only with beer and liquor, but with grizzly drunken fools.

There was one such character standing behind the counter and pouring drinks. Lial took a seat and I sat beside him. We were surrounded by dozens of people dressed in mismatched, tattered clothing. I welcomed the minimal lighting because every stranger in this dump had a disagreeable face. Everyone laughed too loudly and their eyes were dead. I moved my stool closer to Lial in an attempt to avoid the slobbering man to my right.

"What is this place called?"

"I can't remember," he said.

The squatty, overweight bartender made his way to us, wearing a white-collared shirt with yellow stains and suspenders. His greasy hair was slicked to one side and his black beard was patched with gray spots. When he spoke to us, I noticed that his teeth were the same color as the stains on his shirt.

"You folks aren't from around here," he sounded like he was trying to swallow a pint of gravel. "Welcome to One Way Ticket. What can I get you?"

"I will have a beer and a shot of whiskey," Lial said. "What do you want, Sage?"

I looked at Lial as though he were deranged.

"What do you want? You look like a vodka and soda girl."

"I prefer rum and coke, actually," I corrected.

Lial turned to the bartender. "You heard her."

"Stop," I protested. "I don't want anything."

The bartender looked back and forth between us obviously confused. Maybe no one had ever refused a drink at One Way Ticket before. Lial shrugged and the bartender turned away to prepare his drinks.

I shouted above the music. "You know I can't drink."

Lial rolled his eyes and looked out at the crowd.

"Ned told you about me, he said to keep an eye on me— you promised to make sure I stay out of trouble."

"Relax, Blondie. It was a test and you passed."

I let my rust brown eyes sear into him. "Lial, you have no right to test me— you don't know me, and if I hadn't summoned you yesterday—"

"I knew you wouldn't drink it. Okay?"

"That makes one of us," I said. "And don't call me, Blondie."

The chubby bartender came back with the whiskey and beer. He told the man to start a tab. Lial took his shot of whiskey like it was water.

"Did we really drive all this way so that you could have a drink?"

"Don't be ridiculous. Hey, bartender!" he called.

The man shuffled back towards us. "What do you need?"

"Cake and Steak. Make sure the meat is very, very rare."

"Cake and Steak. Comin' right up, pal."

"Hey, get the girl a shirley temple, would you? She looks lonely."

Lial was smiling like an idiot. He observed the people slither through the bar as he tried to keep rhythm with the music. We ended up watching some drunks play a game of darts in the back.

I was beside myself. I could not believe that we drove three and a half hours for alcohol, cake and steak. We were supposed to be searching for the key to my salvation. Were we any closer to finding it? I fidgeted my leg anxiously. I think Lial sensed my frustration. He looked down at me from his great height and nudged my arm with the bottle of beer in his hand.

"You can have a bite of my cake and steak, if you want."

"No, thank you," I sounded discouraged.

"I needed this," he began. "I needed to speed down the highway in that beautiful gold '69 Cadillac Eldorado. I really needed cake and steak. I was in Hell, remember? Not figurative Hell, actual Hell. One Way Ticket is a small taste of freedom," he lazily sipped his beer.

After finishing Lial called for another shot of whiskey and beer. The bartender came back with that and more. He set a shirley temple with maraschino cherries in front of me and a massive plate before Lial. Resting on it was one enormous slice of yellow cake with pink frosting and one gigantic very, very rare cut of beef. The scent of blood and sugar was intoxicating. Lial was immediately overcome with ecstasy. I have never seen someone that happy before or since.

"You have got to try this!" he stuffed a forkful cake and steak into his mouth in one colossal bite.

I shook my head.

"Come on, it's cake and steak!" He tired to offer me his fork, but I turned away. "Blondie, you're missing out. I've been around a long time, and very few things beat cake and steak."

The stammering drunk to my right cut into our conversation. "Blondie?" I didn't answer, but the drunk persisted. "Blondie," he said again.

I could feel Lial watching me, waiting to see if I would respond to the moron gunning for my attention.

"Hey!" the stranger took hold of my arm.

From the corner of my eye I saw Lial flinch when the man grabbed me. I heard him set his fork down on the glass plate. I turned towards the drunk, who stared at me with bloodshot eyes. I was revolted by his dry, raw skin and overgrown fingernails. He was balding, but obviously in denial about it because he'd given himself an atrocious comb over.

The drunk spoke to me with wheezing breaths. "Blondie? Hey, is that supposed to be your name?"

"Kind of," my voice sounded tired. I was not in the mood to explain the nickname to a man who was barely coherent.

"That name doesn't make any sense," he slurred.

"I try not to think about it."

He chuckled a little too near my face. "Blondie. Ha! What a dumb name. Were your parents blind? You're not even blonde. You're a walking contradiction."

"What's your name?" I asked.

"Uh, Henry," he said and nearly fell off the stool. "My mother was fond of British royalty. She named me after King Henry the eighth. He had six wives, you know."

"Divorced, beheaded, died, divorced, beheaded, survived," Lial recited the fates of King Henry's wives under his breath.

"Funny," I smiled.

Both the angel and Henry leaned in, wondering what I would say next. An uneasy look took over Henry's face.

"What is so damn funny?" the drunk hollered; his breath was foul.

"We have something in common, Henry. I'm called Blondie, but I'm a brunette. And you're named after royalty, but you are the furthest thing from royalty I've ever come across. I bet that my dog, who uses my shoes as his personal toilet, has a better bloodline than you do."

"What are you trying to say?" Henry asked with a stupid look plastered on his face.

"I could word it another way. You. Are. A. Slobbering. Drunk."

I knew that people hated to be called out for what they really were. Lial didn't want to be called a penguin, Laveau didn't like being called a hybrid and Henry didn't want to be called a drunk, even though everyone knew it was the truth.

"What did you say to me, girlie?"

"I think she made herself clear," Lial answered for me. I guess he was as bored with Henry's conversation as I was.

"I'd like to hear her say it one more time, if you don't mind."

"Well, I do mind because you're interrupting my cake and steak. The girl said what she thought of you; now you can either accept that and shut up or we can settle this some other way."

I furrowed my brow. "Lial, what are you doing?"

"Defending you."

"Yeah, but you're gunna get us in a fight," I warned. "I am assuming Henry is a regular here, so if you start something the others are going to join in. Lial, we would be outnumbered."

His mouth curled into a delicious smile, mischief bright in his eyes. "You know, cake and steak isn't the only reason I like this bar. One Way Ticket is the best place for a good old fashioned brawl on the east coast."

"You talk about this place like we're in Disney World."

"For an archangel, it is."

Henry grabbed my arm again, and his hand was rough. "Hey, Blondie! Hey, I am talkin' to you!" he yelled.

I ignored the old drunk. Lial ordered a couple more shots of whiskey, and the chubby bartender obliged him. I enjoyed my pink fizzy beverage until Henry shook my arm so hard he caused the soda to spill out of the glass and down my shirt.

"I am talkin' to you, girlie!"

Henry had gone far enough with his small annoyances, so in one rapid motion I brought a clenched fist across his blotched red face. Henry flew off of his stool and belly flopped onto the floor. I heard him yelp as he hit the ground. When he turned himself over he was bewildered and disoriented.

"All right, girlie. We can communicate your way."

Henry struggled to crawl to his feet. From various corners of the bar, eight men came forward to support the royal drunk. They were each as ugly and ragged as Henry. As they advanced towards me, I suddenly felt I was in over my head.

Upon seeing his drinking buddies lined up on either side of him, Henry got his confidence back. "You know, Blondie, I didn't take you for someone who likes to dance."

"You can only dance if you can stay on your feet," Lial cut in. He took one last bite of his cake and steak and wiped his mouth. He stepped down from his stool. I did the same and braced myself for the inevitable.

While Lial was perfectly at home in the dive bar, he looked incredibly out of place. Lial's skin was so white and unblemished that I was constantly questioning if he was made of flesh or stone. His eyes were piercing and sharp, not bloodshot or yellow like the men we stood up against. He stood apart from the crowd the same way Sweetie stood apart from the rusted trucks in the parking lot.

"Sage, I had no idea you could throw a punch," Lial said.

"I can do a lot more than that, but right now I wish I packed my revolver."

"I don't care for guns; they take away all the fun," he grinned. There was a spark of crazy in his otherworldly eyes.

Lial walked over to Henry and hit him just as I had a minute earlier, only harder. Henry was knocked out in a second and hit the floor with a resonating thud. Six of the eight men rushed in towards my guardian. He avoided their closed fists effortlessly. He was much quicker than the brawny, sluggish drunks he was up against. Lial slipped between them and attacked from behind. If the hooligans managed to get back up after he had knocked them down, he simply hit them again.

I was only taking on two drunkards, but I seemed to be having a harder time than Lial was with six men. I managed to put my basic knowledge of Kung Fu to good use, blocking each of their blows with defensive moves.

The closer the two ruffians got, the more I could smell their stink and see their eyes were glazed and unfocused. Unfortunately, their sight wasn't blurred enough to misdirect their swinging fists. I got caught in the jaw and fell back, slamming my back into the bar counter. It knocked the wind out of me and I crumpled onto the filthy ground. I felt my diaphragm spasm and the air got trapped inside of me. I brought my hand up to my face, which would be black and blue come morning.

I still hadn't caught my breath when the larger of the two men approached me. The man reared his fist back, ready to bruise the other side of my face, but before he could brown glass shattered over his skull and the man staggered. I watched him gradually lose his balance and fall face first into the dirt floor.I climbed to my feet just in time for the last drunk standing to take one final swing at me. I dodged the blow, jumped up on the bar and kicked him square in the face. He hit the floor the same way his friends had. Hard.

I stood breathless, mad with adrenaline. I was sweating through my black clothes and my hair was more wild than usual. I looked over at Lial, who stood with a broken beer bottle in hand. He was glowing, strong and full of life. It must have been the fighting; he was designed for battle.

"You okay, Blondie?"

"Great," I ignored the pain in my face. I could all ready feel it swelling.

"I liked what you did at the end there, when you jumped up and kicked that last guy in the face."

"You weren't too bad yourself, for a penguin."

The entire bar must have been staring at us, but I can't remember. I just remember Lial's eyes. They were a blue I hadn't seen before, less cold than their usual shade.

"I need another whiskey," he said and opened himself up to the many faces littering the bar. "Drinks are on me!" he hollered.

The entire bar was in an uproar. He was their hero, offering free booze to every wretched soul in the joint. The only problem was that Lial didn't have any money, which meant his generosity was going on my tab. We stayed at One Way Ticket for over ten hours and by the end of the night, Lial and Henry even became friends, acting as teammates in a game of darts.

When we left, Lial decided it was too late and that he was too drunk to drive back to New York. Yes, angels can get drunk; it just takes a truckload of alcohol. I offered to drive, but he insisted that being inside a moving car would make him sick, and he didn't want to soil Sweetie. Instead, we walked across the street to a cheap motel and paid for one night's stay in room number four.

The wallpaper in the motel upset me even more than the wallpaper in the McGreevy's guest room. There was a lamp on the bedside table and some pathetic excuses for artwork hung on the walls. The television remote was nowhere to be found and there was a mysterious stain on one of the bathroom hand towels.

I brought my overnight bag in from the car, and after a quick shower I changed into an oversized t-shirt and pajama shorts. I sat on the bed while Lial leaned against the wall.

"I know this road trip sort of took us off track," Lial said. "I want to thank you for not giving me a harder time than you did."

I nodded.

"You take the bed. I can sleep in the chair," he continued.

I looked down at the bed sheets and noted all the extra space my body wouldn't be able to fill. A great sadness got caught in my throat and I choked on it. I few distressed sounds escaped me.

"Sage?" he approached the foot of the motel bed cautiously.

I covered my mouth with my hands. I thought that if I tried to speak I would end up blubbering in front of him.

"Um, I'm not sure what I should do here," he admitted, almost embarrassed. "Come on. What's the matter?" he pushed, with a touch of concern.

I was too proud to admit my weakness to the archangel. Besides, he wouldn't understand. Lial's world didn't exist beneath the surface.

"I know it's gunna sound stupid once I say it out loud."

"Probably," he agreed in a matter of fact tone.

I almost smiled at his brutal honesty.

"I miss Jack. I have never been away from him this long, and this bed is too big for one person," I started. "I know this is the kind of thing you would find hysterical, but if you laugh I swear I will kill you."

"Look at me, Sage," his voice was somehow rough and tender. "I'm not laughing."

I wiped my tears, and was grateful for the fallen angel's unexpected kindness.

"May I make a suggestion? I could keep you company while you sleep. I could lie next to you. Just shut your eyes and pretend I'm the dog. I won't say a word."

I gave him a curious look. "Lial, that might be the strangest thing I've ever heard."

"I know that, but you look very sad."

Lial switched off the lamp on the bedside table and we lay on our backs beside one another. I closed my eyes and listened to him breathing next to me. After some time, the sound of each inhale and exhale settled me.

The palm of my hands moved across the bed sheets' scratchy material. I revisited the past days' events. The angel's terrible voice as he sang along to the car radio, the plate of cake and steak that made him act like a child, the shirley temple I enjoyed too briefly and the look on Henry's face when I hit him. I wouldn't admit it to Lial, but I might have had a better time than he did.

"Are you asleep?"

He groaned, and I knew he was still awake.

"Can I ask you a question?"

"You just did. Goodnight," he rolled over.

"You told Ned that you had a sister. You said that she and I became friends in Rome. How did you know about Rome?"

"What are you talking about?" his voice was groggy.

"When you fell from Heaven you ignored your responsibilities as my guardian angel, so you couldn't have known that I made a deal with the Devil or that my sister died or that I went to Rome. How did you know? Unless you were checking in on me from time to time."

Lial released a loud sigh. "There was a picture of you standing in front of the coliseum at Ned's house, on the mantelpiece. That's how I knew you were in Rome, from the picture. I never checked in on you, Sage. Not once. Don't flatter yourself."

I rolled away from him and drew the covers up around me. We didn't speak after that.

As the sun rose there was still a riot of noise streaming out of One Way Ticket from across the street. The endless shouting and bad music came together like a degenerate lullaby and helped me to sleep.

14

More Blood

The next day Lial and I drove across the New York state line headed north. The Eldorado moved smoothly over the highway. I kept my attention on the white dashes that divided the car lanes. The short lines whizzed past me. I moved my eyes to the trees lining the road, but they became one massive blurred green vision. The Eldorado's gold hood glistened as it raced beneath the sun, which was sitting high in the cloudless sky.

Lial sat in the driver's seat and hummed along to an old song playing on the radio. His hair was a fury of blonde waves, which grew more and more disheveled as the wind blasted in through the windows.

Sadly, his compassionate moment in the motel room was a thing of the past. I had to fight him to wake up, get in the car and pull over for a much-needed cup of coffee. Some time into our drive I noticed something puzzling. Lial had ditched Ned's t-shirt and sweatpants and was now dressed in torn jeans, distressed work boots, a faded gray t-shirt and a well-worn olive green leather jacket. I have to admit, it looked good on him.

"Lial, where did you get those clothes?"

"Would you stop shouting at me?" he whined. "I stole them

from Henry after he passed out at the bar last night. Something told me he wouldn't miss them."

I wasn't shouting but Lial seemed to be suffering from a headache. I'm not sure if angels can get hungover, but I stopped counting the number of whiskey shots Lial ordered after a dozen. His usually white, shining skin exhibited a greenish hue, there was a ring of sweat around the neckline of his t-shirt, and his hair was greasy.

Lial's constant humming, which was more out of tune than his vocals, started to make me itch. I didn't necessarily want to have a conversation, but it would be less painful than enduring to his musical handicap. I made a poor attempt to tame my dark, spiraling curls and repositioned myself in the passenger seat.

"Do you have a plan to find The Other Book?"

Lial flashed a menacing smile. "Yeah, I have a plan, but you won't like it."

"Why doesn't that surprise me?"

"We need to summon two more fallen angels."

"What?" I almost jumped out of my seat. "No. Forget it. No!"

There'd been nothing but trouble since I summoned Lial. One narcissistic, vulgar, wingless creature was enough. I couldn't begin to fathom the idea of inviting two more fallen angels into the world.

"We need to know more about The Other Book," he explained, ignoring the disgusted look on my face. "We need to know if it exists and whether or not He wrote it. We need to know what it does— why it matters. I don't want to waste my time searching for a way to save your soul when it might be hopeless cause."

"You think it's a hopeless cause?"

"It doesn't matter what I think," he answered coldly. "The sooner we figure out what The Other Book does and where to find it, the sooner we can go our separate ways. That was our agreement, right?"

I nodded sheepishly and took a breath. I suddenly wanted to jump out of the Eldorado. Instead I stared out the window. The wind cooled me as it rushed past my face and danced through my long curls.

"Okay. I will entertain this incredibly bad idea. How does summoning two more fallen angels help us find the book?"

"Every angel has a purpose," Lial started. "Even within of our choirs or what you might call our sects. How can I explain this? You know about Michael. Michael is an archangel, but he is also the angel most skilled with a sword; in fact he is unbeatable with a sword. I'm an archangel too, but swordplay wasn't my specialty. Don't get me wrong. I can handle a blade, but I am a master in hand-to-hand combat, plus I make an outrageous grilled cheese sandwich. Zephon is a cherub, which means he is a guardian of paradise and sees everything He has made as a child would, with wonder and innocence, but there's more to him than that. Zephon is also the only angel who has been able to track down Lucifer time and time again since his fall."

"I think I understand. Every angel has a specific gift beyond the general skills of their choir. Just like people. Some of us are better at math, others excel in competitive sports—"

"No, Sage. You cannot compare angels to humans," he huffed, frustrated with me. "Moving on, I have friends in low places, a sister and brother—twins, but they don't belong to the same choir. Procel is an archangel, but she is also the only angel who knows the truth about hidden or secret things. Vassago is a— huh? I think he's a seraphim. I don't remember. Anyway, Procel will tell us what The Other Book does— whether or not it even exists— and Vassago can tell us where to find it."

Lial moved into the right lane and took the next exit, leading us back to Bridgeview.

"Okay, so we are going to summon Procel and Vassago."

Lial kept his gaze on the road in front of him. "What do you think?"

"What do I think of what?" I wasn't thinking. I'd been distracted by his beauty. I had just noticed that his eyes mirrored the sky's extraordinary blue.

"What do you think of the plan, Sage?"

I shrugged. "I wish we didn't have to open more portals between worlds, but if this is what it takes to save my soul then I'm in."

"Good, because this is all I could come up with."

I was struck with a truly horrible thought just then. I shiver sped down my spine. "Wait. Did you say that Procel was an archangel? We have to summon an archangel?"

Lial nodded warily.

"If Procel is an archangel and we have to summon her that means—"

"More blood." He finished my thought.

"We need a blood sacrifice." I buried my face in my hands and groaned.

"Only this time you know that the angel being summoned is a fallen angel, so we can't use innocent blood."

"Then we can use mine. My blood was able to summon you, so it should be just as effective when we summon Procel."

The angel inhaled sharply and shook his head. "I'm afraid that's not gunna work this time, Sage. You only needed to spill a small amount of blood in order for me to cross into the physical world because you and I are connected to one another. I am your guardian, regardless of whether or not I fulfilled that purpose. I was supposed to be with you since birth so a couple drops of your blood was all we needed to find each other. It was— well, it was easy."

Lial stopped there. Perhaps he questioned the tenderness in his voice or the shame reflected in his eyes. A few seconds past and he pushed forward.

"Procel has no attachment to you. You're not bonded to one another or associated with each other in any meaningful way. You have no reason to cross paths in all of time and space."

"Until now."

"Yes, but this was never supposed to be a part of your life. Humans aren't supposed to make deals with the Devil, and if I had been around this might have never— never mind…" he cleared his throat, his jaw taunt. "This is not how the human experience was meant to be carried out."

I didn't argue with him. I knew he was right.

"We are going to need more blood, a lot more blood," he said the words carefully, hoping I would grasp his meaning.

I did understand and a profound heaviness overcame me. "Someone needs to die. Lial, you're saying we need to kill someone."

"Someone human," he clarified.

A troubled silence fell between us.

Demons were rotten through and through. They belonged in Hell with their own kind, breeding evil amongst themselves. Humans were different because they're capable of both good and bad. They always have a choice, a chance to do the right thing, because they can change.

Taking a human life was completely against my moral code. Regardless of whether or not I felt someone deserved to die. I would never make that choice. I could barely accept the idea of killing in self-defense.

Lial glanced over at me with the corners of his mouth turned down. "Selling your soul was a dark act; retrieving it is going to require several more."

I hit a brick wall in my mission for redemption. I couldn't find out more about The Other Book without summoning Procel, and I couldn't summon Procel without taking a human life.

We were back in Bridgeview City and cruising down Gretchen Road, which was home to my apartment building and the seedy characters that dwelled there. When I unlocked the door to my apartment, Lial walked in without being invited. I immediately felt uneasy because this had always been a private place for me. Ned and Lena hadn't even visited since they helped me move in.

The walls changed from room to room; there was hunter green paint used in the kitchenette, rich navy blue in the living room and a shade of purple called evening woodland in my bedroom. Dark curtains were draped in front of all the windows.

Lial collapsed onto the couch. The angel slouched and rested a long leg on the coffee table in front of him. He tossed the decorative pillows Lena had bought across the room and pulled the remote control out from between the cushions. I watched him click on the television and began flicking through the channels.

I decided to change my clothes and retreated into the bedroom. I pulled one of the countless black shirts I owned over my head and lifted my hair from beneath its collar. I was checking myself in the mirror when I heard a familiar voice come from the living room. I hurried down the narrow hall and plopped down next to Lial on the couch.

"I know her," I said. "Rebecca Brinkley. She was reporting from the hospital when I was waiting for Lena. She covered the robbery at 1976."

I took the remote out of Lial's hand and turned up the television's volume. Rebecca Brinkley had outdone herself in a hot pink skirt and matching blazer. Her hair was bigger and blonder than ever, and her saucer eyes blinked relentlessly.

"Two days ago a co-owner of 1976 was shot and killed after the diner was held up by a man who has yet to be identified.

Lena McGreevy was waiting tables when the masked man walked into the establishment, threatened her at gunpoint and set fire to the building. After being shot Mrs. McGreevy was brought to St. Anne's Hospital in Bridgeview City. Lena McGreevy's death has been a great loss to both her family and the community. The Bridgeview City police department continues to search for her murderer. I will be bringing you more news as the story progresses. This is Rebecca Brinkley, reporting for News Channel Twelve."

I turned off the television and threw the controller aside.

"I was watching that!" Lial threw up his hands in protest.

A brilliant and cruel thought took hold of me. The gears in my mind turned until I came to a heartless decision. "We need to find Raymond Keylor," I concluded.

"Raymond who?"

"Raymond Keylor. He was the witness Brinkley interviewed at the hospital. I think he was more involved with what happened at 1976 than he let on."

"You think that Keylor murdered Lena?" Lial chewed his bottom lip.

"Jack—" I started.

"You think that the dog murdered Lena?" he shouted, confused.

"No!" I corrected him. "When I found Jack after the robbery he had blood all over him. I just assumed the blood was Lena's. I never considered that Jack might have attacked the person who hurt her. Keylor's arm was torn to shreds when I saw him in the hospital. How else could he have gotten that kind of injury? I think that Jack took a bite out of him."

"That's a nice theory, but where's your evidence? We can't go after this man unless we're pretty sure he's guilty."

"Wait, you just need to be pretty sure that Keylor is the bad guy before we kill him? I would have thought you'd want to be certain about something like that."

Lial almost laughed. "Look at me, Sage. I'm a fallen angel. Even if I hurt an innocent person, there are no consequences for me. My existence is as bad as it's going to get. I was banished from paradise, thrown into the pit and now I'm stuck with you. Certainty is overrated. I am perfectly okay with pretty sure."

I closed my eyes and tried to put my mind elsewhere. The idea of summoning one of Lial's delinquent friends through an act of murder only days after Lena had been killed was near impossible to stomach. However, my conscience was settled when I realized I would be sacrificing Lena's murderer to further my cause. It would be an eye for an eye, a life for a life. That was justice, right? The truth is I wasn't sure. I wasn't even pretty sure.

"Now we just need to figure out how we're going to find Keylor."

"I guess there's one more book we need to get our hands on," Lial said.

"Oh, come on. I'm already worried about finding one mystery book. I really don't want to add another to the pile," I complained.

"Well this new book is nowhere near as rare as Liber Alter. In fact, it's painfully common. But I trust that such an ordinary book can help us track down this Raymond Keylor."

"Please, enlighten me," I answered dryly.

"I think you'll know it when you see it," Lial said smugly.

He rose from the couch and rummaged through my apartment in a fury. He searched through the cabinets and drawers, flung the small wooden doors open and slammed them shut again.

"Can I help you find something?" I offered.

"You must have that book in here somewhere," he mumbled, his icy eyes dashed over the apartment.

"What book? There's a bible on top of the nightstand in my bedroom, young adult romance novels on the shelf in the living room next to some required reading from middle school and old newspapers in the bathroom. That's just about all of the reading material you're going to find here. Oh, and there might be a box of stale crackers in the kitchen. You can read the nutrition label if you want to, but I don't know how that will help us find Raymond Keylor."

"Ah! I knew you had it hidden somewhere!" he flashed broad smile.

Lial reached into the back corner of the cupboard beneath the kitchen sink, and removed a substantial book with white and yellow pages.

"The phone book!" he beamed with pride.

I crossed my arms. "I hope Keylor is listed."

"I hope he used his real name when that reporter interviewed him."

That hadn't occurred to me. What if the man I suspected murdered Lena used a fake name? A feeling of dread swept through me. For all I knew Keylor could have fled the state by now. We might never find him, and if that was the case, who else could Lial and I sacrifice to summon Procel?

Lial flipped through the white pages until he had reached the letter K. He flipped through several more pages, reading names aloud. "Morgan Kelly, Bridie Kennedy, Brian Kinney— Oops. I went too far," he thumbed back a page. "Sage, you are pretty sure it was this Keylor person who hurt Lena, right?"

"Yes."

"I am asking because if we find his name in this book, are you going to be ready for what comes next? Ending a human life is nothing like exorcizing a demon, even if the human has demonstrated certain demonic qualities. I'm telling you this because you have to summon Procel. Only a human can summon an angel. I can't sacrifice Keylor for you. You need to be the one who drains him. The blood of a sinner for the company of a fallen angel. That's the deal. It's not negotiable."

I retreated to my former reservations. I always told myself I would never take a human life, but this was an exception, right? I had to stay focused on the big picture. My immortal soul was at risk. Besides, I was pretty sure Keylor had murdered Lena.

She was the closest thing I had to a mother and the love of Ned's life. My godfather would never stop missing her. He would never be able to push away the gray clouds that her death had brought on.

Sometimes bad things happen and there is no one to blame. But when there is someone at fault, why shouldn't they be punished?

"Don't worry about me. Help me find him and I can take of the rest."

"Sage, do you know what you're saying? You are actually considering—"

"No. No, I'm not considering anything. When we find Keylor, I am going to make him pay for what he did to Lena, an eye for an eye."

Lial smiled but he wasn't happy. I think he pitied me. "Yeah. Well, an eye for an eye leaves the whole world blind. An old friend told me that. I disagreed at the time. I wish I had listened."

"Don't lecture me, Lial. You're not that kind of angel."

He kept his gaze steady on me for a moment, and his eyes were a frosty, arctic blue. He turned his attention back to the phone book. "Here. Raymond Keylor. Can you believe that? The son of a bitch used his real name. 14 Magnus Drive."

"Lial" my chest tightened. "He lives right around the corner."

15

Penny Loafers & Stars

Lial and I waited until dark to make our move. It had taken us under a minute to drive the gold Cadillac to Magnus Drive. It was nearing two in the morning when we made our way onto the stoop of Keylor's dilapidated home, the last house on the left.

I hoped Keylor would be asleep but every light in the house was switched on. There would definitely be more of a struggle than I wanted, but Lial was an archangel. I didn't foresee a fight against Keylor being much of a problem, especially since Jack had ruined the use of his arm.

The exterior of his home looked more run down than the current victimized state of 1976. Several of the windows were boarded up, most of the paint had been chipped away and the steps leading to the front door were partially caved in.

"Should we knock?" Lial whispered.

"I thought we agreed to sneak in and take him by surprise."

"Well, he would never expect us to knock."

I shook my head, but Lial wasn't deterred. He jumped up and down in place to pump himself up before we invaded Keylor's home. I thought he was being ridiculous but I realized that apart from the One Way Ticket brawl, this was the most action Lial had seen in decades; and as an archangel, he must've been aching for more.

"Okay. Ready?" he winked.

Before I could stop him, Lial made a fist and knocked at the decomposing wood of the front door. Much to our surprise the door yielded and cracked open. In this neighborhood only a deranged and potentially psychotic person would leave his door unlocked. I immediately tried to recall whether or not I had locked my apartment. I honestly couldn't remember.

"Humans first," the angel gestured to the open door.

I stepped into the house and was immediately unhinged. It was like stumbling into one of Alfred Hitchcock's nightmares. Everything looked normal and decent at first. But the longer I explored the interior, the more unbalanced I felt. I could see into the living area and dining room from where I stood in the doorway. Both rooms were perfectly furnished and tidy but somehow unlived in. I kept imagining myself inside a child's dollhouse, and it disturbed me.

Keylor had arranged the space disproportionally. The dining room table was massive, but the chairs were too low to the ground and the chandelier was too close to the ceiling. There was a large gap between the china cabinet and the cupboard. I didn't have to be an interior designer to notice something was off. The living room suffered from similar symptoms. Not to mention the artwork on the walls was hung in a disorderly fashion. They were spaced out unevenly and held no relation to one another. My eyes moved over framed landscapes, a caricature, and several portraits. In my opinion he had gone through all this trouble in an attempt to make himself appear normal. But once inside for more than a minute, he wouldn't have been able to fool anyone.

Lial tapped me on the shoulder and I flinched. He brought a finger to his mouth and gestured for silence before he pointed to the ceiling and nodded towards the staircase. There was the sound of creaky footsteps coming from somewhere upstairs.

We crept to the second floor of the house. Lial led the way and I timidly held onto the sleeve of his leather jacket as we climbed the stairs. Keylor's house shook me to the core. I believed that if I let go of Lial I would get lost in that horrible place forever.

Upstairs, the footsteps were drowned out by the sound of classical music, streaming out from the room at the opposite end of the hallway. The door was open less than an inch, allowing a small sliver of light to seep through. Lial turned to me and his eyes were completely dilated. He was full of adrenaline while I was full of nerves. We advanced towards the room. When we reached our destination, a terrible silence fell upon us. The music had stopped.

Lial's eyes met mine in the dark. Had Keylor heard us making our way towards him? Lial must have seen that I was worried and he rested a heavy hand on my shoulder to calm me. I felt a warm, thrilling sensation zip through my body, and leave me covered in goose bumps.

The only sounds in the house were the soft breaths that escaped Lial and me. In that quiet moment it dawned on me that neither of us had thought about what we would do once inside the house. The goal was to kidnap Keylor and take him to a somewhere we could summon Procel, but we hadn't actually discussed how we were going to accomplish that. Since Lial and I had absolutely no idea what we were doing, we'd have to improvise. We exchanged one more glance. I could see by the crazed look in his eyes that it was show time.

Lial kicked in the door with so much force I thought it would break off the hinges. We burst into the room only to find it empty. There was a record player in the corner spinning a disk, but there was no music. I took a couple of steps further into the room. It was a small, bare space and Keylor was nowhere to be seen.

"Did he leave through one of the windows?"

"No. The windows are locked from the inside," Lial checked. "Besides, that would be a long fall for a mortal man. I don't think Keylor would risk it."

Lial turned back around and shrugged in defeat. There was no way out of the room apart from the door we came in through and the windows. Unless Keylor had the power to evaporate, I was stumped as to how we could have missed him.

The record player's needle scratched along the surface of the disc and filled the room with an unpleasant static sound not unlike white noise. I stood in front of the open doorway. Lial paced through the room, tapping his knuckles against the wall and sniffing the air.

"What are you doing?" I asked.

"I'm searching for a hallow spot. There might be a hidden room behind one of the walls."

"What are you smelling for? Death? You smelt it on me after I summoned you, the day Lena died."

"No. I am trying to catch a whiff of fear."

I raised my dark eyebrows. "Now I know how Alice felt when she fell down the rabbit hole. You get curiouser and curiouser by the minute."

"I can smell fear and death," he explained. "In most cases they go hand in hand but they each have a specific scent. Fear reminds me of urine, sweat, hot metal and the salt water. Death... I would compare death to the smell you find inside a black hole."

I stepped forward excitedly. Lial had been inside of a black hole in deep space. I couldn't begin to guess what other mind-blowing experiences he must've had in his lifetime. It was no wonder he thought so little of humanity. Life on Earth must fall short in comparison to everything else out there.

Lial's eyes flickered over the room again, looking for potential clues. "I can tell that this house has known a great deal of fear and death. Oh, and you still stink, Sage."

Lena had only died two days ago. I guess the smell of death can linger.

"There is something wrong with this place, Lial. I don't like it here." I had a stabbing gut reaction to the house, which told me to run and I wanted to. I always trusted my instincts, and that trust had saved my life on more than one occasion.

Lial studied my face. I wondered if he could smell the fear rising inside of me now. Even in the poorly lit room his skin was white as rain. I got lost in the striking details of his face, the angles of his jaw and the perfect curve of his ears, but when my eyes rested on his mouth something seemed amiss. His full lips weren't pursed or sporting a playful smile. Instead they were parted, almost frowning. I brought my attention back to his eyes and was struck by what I saw.

It happened before I had time to form a proper thought, but when I stared into his eyes I couldn't find the clear blue I had enjoyed only seconds earlier. They were turbulent and growing darker every moment. I could see my own plain face reflected in them. I could make out my dark eyes and blustery curls amid the specks of gray and blue.

And I saw another figure looming in Lial's eyes. It was a latent shadow, standing over my shoulder.

Lial blinked and reached for me. "SAGE!"

It was too late. Someone had taken a hold of me. I knew it could only be Raymond Keylor. I struggled but my kidnapper's arms were all ready wrapped around my waist and pulling me out of the room.

"Lial!" I screamed his name, sheer panic in my voice.

Just before Keylor slammed the door shut, I could see the angel lunging forward with outstretched arms, but he wasn't quick enough. Keylor locked the door with Lial still inside. I heard him scream my name from behind the door that held him captive, and shout depraved threats to Keylor.

"I swear to Christ if you hurt her I will tear every limb from your body— I will burn you— Sage! Sage!— Keylor I am going to peel the flesh from your wasted human form and feed it to the hounds of Hell! Don't you touch her! Don't— Sage! Blondie!"

Lial's demented cries grew faint as the villain proceeded to drag me down the hallway towards the stairs. I kicked and clawed at him in an ungodly fury but Keylor was strong, even with one bad arm. My skull felt like it was on fire as he pulled my hair and forced me down the stairs. I tried to defend myself. I made several attempts to reverse the position of power between us but he anticipated every move.

"Get off of me! Get off! Stop—!"

My voice was shrill, but it didn't seem to matter how much I screamed or begged. Raymond Keylor remained perfectly calm. He was confident that I wouldn't be able to escape his grip and that Lial would have trouble finding his way out of the upstairs room. We stopped at a door just beneath the staircase. Keylor turned the knob and pushed it open.

"I am NOT going down there! NO!" I don't think I had ever been more scared.

"You came over uninvited. I assume that you want to have a play-date."

Keylor spoke without inflections. His voice was soft and awkward, paired with a perverse and unnatural face. Suddenly the unsettling feeling I got from this house made perfect sense. The bad artwork and disproportionate furniture reflected the twisted soul responsible for them.

Keylor took a fistful of my hair in his thin hand and tugged me towards the stairway that led to the basement. I had no intention of going without a fight. I was hunched forward at the mercy of Keylor. I could see his penny loafers and velour pants, but nothing from the waist up, which is when I realized that he had left one sensitive area exposed.

With all the strength I could gather I kneed Keylor in the groin. He immediately fell forward and moaned in agonizing pain. I pulled away from him, but he still clutched onto my hair. I felt the sharp sting as I tore myself from his grip. I lost a handful of curls in the process but that wasn't an immediate concern. I sped past the maniac towards the front door; hope was on the rise. Unfortunately, that is usually the exact moment when reality catches up with you.

I was running as fast I could, but Keylor had long legs and a longer reach. He grabbed my shoulder with one hand and held back of my head with the other. I felt myself being forced forward at a dangerously accelerated rate. I saw the wall coming towards me. I felt the dizzying pain when Keylor slammed my face against it. I saw stars and a hot, tingling sensation overwhelmed my forehead. My vision blurred and a loud ringing drowned out the noise around me. I knew I was bleeding, and as I lost consciousness, I prayed that I would wake up.

16

You're Late

I don't know how much time past, but when I came to, I immediately regretted my prayer. Keylor's basement was more than just a storage space for forgotten junk, old tools and broken pieces of furniture. This is where he kept his toys, and I am not referring to pogo sticks and jump ropes. Keylor's toy collection was a smidge more cryptic than that.

When I regained consciousness, I could feel dried blood stuck on the side of my face and matted in my hair. My eyes were heavy. It took a minute for my vision to focus, but I could hear an array of eerie sounds in the mean time. The most prominent was the sound of metal clanging against metal.

My head was throbbing and the sound of metal grinding and banging only made it worse. The first thing I saw were my hands and legs tied to the chair I was in. I struggled against the knotted rope but it wouldn't loosen. The awkward sensation of pins and needles overwhelmed my feet. The rope was tied so tight around my ankles that my toes had fallen asleep.

"Oh, good. You woke up," a queer voice greeted me. "I thought maybe I hit your head too hard against the wall. I couldn't stop the bleeding for a while. If you had died, it would have been a real shame. You would have missed all the fun. I must say this is a nice surprise. I never get volunteers."

I picked up my head and stared at the man I had been hunting, the man who captured me instead. Raymond Keylor was just as I had remembered him from St. Anne's Hospital. He was a thin man, just over six feet tall with bulging brown eyes and a receding hairline. His lower jaw jutted out, making him even more unattractive. When I looked at him now, I could see that he was clearly an unstable man. I wondered how I missed it back in the waiting room. Maybe I was too distraught over Lena's condition to notice, but it didn't matter now. I finally saw him for what he was, evil.

Keylor strolled over to a tray in the corner of the room. He glanced back at me before showing off a skin-crawling grin and breaking into a cackle that I feared would never end.

"Do you have a preference, little one? Since you volunteered, I am giving you the opportunity to choose your poison."

"I appreciate that, but believe it or not I'm fairly new to this kind of torture. Could you make a suggestion?

"I would be happy to," he answered with the utmost sincerity. "I have pliers to extract your fingernails, a taser, a barbed-wire whip— Oh, I have a branding iron. I could burn my initials into your skin."

"Well, that is tempting, but what else have you got?"

"Oh, I like you. Let me see… I could blind you with mace. I could pull out your teeth. I haven't done that in a while. Oh! I have a butcher's knife. That's an oldie but a goodie. I think it's still sharp."

I paused, weighing my options. I tried to come up with a way to keep the conversation going. I hoped Lial would find me before the torture began.

"Which device are you leaning towards, little one?"

"I don't know. There are so many to choose from."

"If you don't choose, I will be forced to choose for you," he said in a placid voice. "I would like to show the barbed-wire whip some action—"

"Mace," I said.

"Boring. I thought you were better than that, little one. Ugh, I am growing impatient. When I torture someone, I like to see their blood outside their body. The gash in your head was exciting for a while, but it's all ready started to heal. I demand more blood, and you are going to give it to me."

I nodded, and held my breath. "Pick up the butcher's knife."

"I knew you were special," his shit brown eyes gleamed. "This is going to be quite an event, me cutting you open," he grabbed the butcher's knife from the metal tray.

I took a deep breath, knowing how much this would hurt. I squeezed my hands into fists and braced myself. Keylor was going to play with me. I could tell from the psychotic look in his eyes that he intended to savor every moment. He would keep me alive as long as possible, and I would suffer the entire time.

"Should I just get on with it or are you up for a bit of foreplay?" he asked.

"We barely know one another. Take your time."

"Lovely."

The longer I stayed alive, the more time I had to figure a way out of this mess. Should I ask more questions? Should I provoke him? Should I scream for Lial and hope that he could hear me? To my surprise an unexpected thought popped into my head, and I couldn't stop myself from laughing.

"Would you let me in on the joke, little one? I hate not being included."

"Sure, Raymond. I was just thinking that people are unpredictable. This is going to sound strange, but in my free time

I exorcize demons— and not just demons. I send all kinds of creatures that go bump in the night back to wherever they came from. I know to expect the worst because monsters are only capable of the worst, but humans… are capable of so much more. We can do fantastic things, brilliant things that make the world better or we can do terrible, dark things that create a kind of Hell on Earth."

"I am listening," he said.

"Don't you think it's amazing that we get to choose where we stand in all of this— that we have a choice at all? Maybe the demons and ghosts are just animals following their instincts, and humans are the real monsters."

"I don't know that we have a choice," he mused. "For example, you might enjoy going to the movies or bird watching. Those things make some people happy. More often than not it's our hobbies that get us through life; most people hate their jobs.

"Anyway, I was not built to like seventies films or snow owls. I don't know why— most likely mommy issues but I love hurting people. I want to be the reason they bleed and scream and cry. I want to hear them beg. That makes me happy. I want to see the hope die in their eyes when they know, without a doubt, what they didn't know waking up that morning."

I could feel tears swelling in my eyes. My nerves were getting the best of me. I tried to hide it. "What's that, Raymond?" I swallowed hard.

"That today would be their last," he was completely energized. "I bet you didn't know that when you got up this morning, little one, that today is your last."

"I'm still not convinced," I collected myself. If this was the end, Keylor was not going to see me cry. I couldn't keep my lips from quivering, but I forced myself to smile.

"Let me see if I can convince you."

He slinked towards me and stood over me with the knife in

his right hand. I wouldn't look at his face, but I was sure a perverse smile was on his lips. I closed my eyes and waited for the first burning impression of the knife to hit me. It did and it hurt worse than I imagined. But I refused to scream. I wouldn't give Keylor that pleasure, because knew it was what he wanted. I was sure he would keep me alive until I screamed. Another flash of pain seared into me and I could feel a hot rush of blood drizzle down my arm. I winced but stayed quiet.

"Can I ask you a question, little one?" he sliced me once more. I inhaled sharply. The pain was becoming unbearable. "Why did you break into my home? What did you hope to achieve?"

"I was going to kill you," I admitted. "Well, kidnap you, then kill you."

"Really? How the tables have turned," he cut me again. A loud gasp escaped me. I felt lightheaded. Keylor was invigorated. "I'm flattered, but why kill me?"

"Your arm," I struggled to form sentences. "My dog did that to you at the diner. I noticed it in the hospital when that reporter lady interviewed you. The woman you shot—"

"The woman behind the counter?"

"Her name was Lena McGreevy; she was important to me."

"Oh, I see. Well if I hadn't all ready killed that woman I would have to thank her. After all she is the reason you're here and I am thoroughly enjoying your company."

That's when he stabbed me in the shoulder. The blade pierced into me without yielding. The pain was excruciating. It seemed to blaze through every inch of me. I managed to choke back my scream, but it wasn't without great difficulty. Keylor removed the blade and wiped it clean with his fingers.

"Don't worry. I was careful not to sever an artery. We have miles and miles to cover before I grow tired of you." He looked me over, watching the blood pour from my wounds. His brown eyes widened with unabashed delight. "I have decided to let you in on a secret. Would you like to hear it?"

"Please," my voice cracked.

"Thank you for indulging me. What if I told you that I only held up the diner so I had an excuse to shoot someone in public, with lots of witnesses?"

"Wh— What?"

"I wanted an audience. I wanted to shoot that woman, and see the fear on the customers' faces. I wanted to see the fear that I put into them. I was playing God, you see? I have never felt more powerful. Of course taking what was in the register would have been a bonus but your dog muddled my plans when he attacked me. I had to make a quick exit."

"I would like to apologize on behalf of Jack, the dog. He's a real pain in the ass."

"Are you teasing me, little one?"

"I wouldn't dream of it," I shook my head fervently. "Especially when your knife is still wet with my blood."

Raymond Keylor looked at the knife he wielded and then retreated to the back corner of the room. I could hear him fussing over his tray of toys as he replaced the knife with another torture device. I shuddered, anxious to know which he had chosen.

My clothes were soaked through with sweat and blood. My hair was drenched and heavy on my head. I was starting to doubt if Lial would ever find me in the basement of this peculiar house. I grew more and more certain that if I got the chance to take Keylor's life, I wouldn't hesitate.

The basement smelt like rust and salt. The scent swept over me with a breeze that appeared to manifest from nowhere. I dreaded the sound of Keylor's loafers sweeping back across the concrete floor towards me. His slow and lumbering steps sent a chill through me. I braced myself for the next rush of pain, which came directly.

He had chosen a whip and brought the thick leather thongs down onto my shoulders and neck. I winced and held my breath, swallowing a scream. I was only grateful that there was no barbed wire involved. He brought the whip down again and again, each time with more force. With every stroke of the leather thongs, the skin beneath my shirt burned with unforgiving throbs of pain. My eyes swelled with water, I tightened my muscles until they shook and I stopped thinking about anything other than the physical anguish I was in. I knew the stabbing and the whipping were just the beginning. Tears found their way to my cheeks now. A waft of iron and salt overtook me with another mysterious breeze. Again, the whip attacked me.

"You're very quiet, little one."

"I'm not sure I know what to say," I answered in a hoarse voice.

He turned from me. His thin figure wandered back to the tray and returned. His energy was renewed and childish excitement sprung to his ominous eyes. "You don't have to say anything. I would actually prefer it if you forgot words altogether, and instead graced me with more organic, guttural sounds. I find they can be as descriptive as words, and in my humble opinion, more stimulating."

"What've you brought for me this time?" I asked with trepidation. Keylor was concealing something behind his back.

"A personal favorite," he said and revealed the instrument.

Keylor was holding nothing more than an old rag, a cloth towel. I couldn't understand how he meant to use the seemingly harmless item against me. When I think back on that moment of confusion, I am grateful. Had I known what was coming I might have given Keylor the scream he was waiting for.

Keylor approached me in a slow manner, brought his face eye level to mine and tickled my nose with the dirty cloth. He wiped away the tears from beneath my eyes. I tried to turn away, but he grabbed my face in his hand, forcing me to give him my full attention. He stared into my eyes and his mouth transformed into a cruel snarl. Keylor pushed my face to the side and breathed in my ear; his pointed nose pressing into my cheek.

"I can feel you shaking. I can smell the blood pouring out of you. You smell delicious. I fear I have become obsessed with you, little one." I felt his tongue slide up the side of my face, licking the blood from it. I cringed. "I knew you would taste good."

I squirmed and choked back the impulse of vomit.

"Now let's clean you off," he said.

Keylor backed away and stood upright again. He grabbed two buckets from a nearby shelf and removed himself from the room, wandering to an unseen area of the basement. The sound of running water came to me and lasted about half a minute before ceasing. Keylor returned with the heavy buckets in hand. I wouldn't have thought he was capable of such heavy lifting, but then I remembered how effortlessly he forced me into this damp basement. I couldn't help but feel ashamed that I was unable to defend myself against such a paper-thin man. After all, I had taken on several riled up drunks the night before and come out of that fight victorious. Of course the angel had been at my side then. I wished he were here to rescue me again.

Keylor returned and tossed a dirty rag over my head. It covered my face completely. I felt his hand firmly grip my hair and pull on it, which forced my face to lift upwards. That's when a flood of water poured down on me. I lost my breath. Even if I had wanted to scream, I wouldn't have been able to. He was drowning me, and all I could do was sit there, fighting the rope that kept me in place and gasping for a breath that would never come. More water fell down onto the rag, soaking through to my face and suffocating me further.

I could hear Keylor's fervent laugh ring out above me. "Most people would have passed out by now. I don't know if I am impressed or annoyed that you remain conscious, little one."

I was doused with another bucket of water. I expected to hear another bout of laughter escape Keylor while I struggled to breathe. However, I was thrown off by the sound of a struggle, which ensued around me. I heard obvious banging and thumping that suggested a fight was underway, but I wasn't too concerned about the brawl. My energy was focused on the need to inhale and exhale. I shook my head vigorously from side to side trying to shake the wet cloth free from my face, but it stuck to me mercilessly. I could feel myself fading. It had been too long since my last breath, and my body started to betray me. The more I struggled, the more I came to realize it was useless.

Just as the darkness was about to envelope me, I calmed myself. I didn't want my last waking moments to be spent in hysterics and fear. I wanted to be brave. I tried to be. The murderous rag over my face absorbed the tears falling from my eyes. I waited for the abyss to take me, and then started to wonder if I was dead all ready. I couldn't breathe, and I could no longer hear any sounds of a struggle. I wasn't sure I could even feel the old cloth covering my face anymore. Yes, this was death.

"Sage! Hey! Wake up!" I felt someone slap me hard across the face. I stirred awake. "You're not dead yet."

I opened my eyes and the even the faint basement lights were too bright after my time beneath the cloth. When I opened my mouth I inhaled so deeply I almost choked to death anyway. After a brief coughing fit, I regained the involuntary ability breathe regularly. I could still feel tears running down my face, but I was alive.

In the far left corner of the room Keylor's body was crumpled on the floor. One of his loafers was missing from his foot. There were purple bruises around his eyes and jaw. I saw the red blood that coated the bottom half of his face, as it gushed from his broken nose. There was no doubt the pervert would be in a world of pain upon waking.

I was ecstatic to see a mess of wavy blonde hair just an inch from my face. I could feel the sleeves of a leather jacket brush against my exposed skin as I was untied and pulled to my feet. It was difficult to stand, but a steady hand held me upright.

"Lial," I whispered his name like a prayer.

"I thought you were gone," he breathed his relief into my tangled curls and lingered there.

I should have thanked him, but it didn't occur to me at the time. "You're late. What took you so long?"

"I'm sorry," he offered in a rough voice and held me tighter. The stale leather smell of his jacket was a comfort.

We locked Raymond Keylor in the trunk of the Eldorado and drove the car back to my apartment. Lial insisted that Keylor would be unconscious for some time so we left him under Sweetie's supervision while tending to my wounds upstairs.

"You lost a lot of blood," the angel announced while he stitched up the stab would in my shoulder with some floss and a sewing needle. We sat at the foot of my bed, on top of the gray comforter, and I played victim to his nurse.

"What happened after he locked you in that room?"

"Well it took me a while to break down the door. That wood was dense; five inches thick. I thought about jumping out the window, but it was a long drop and I am in mortal form. It embarrasses me to admit this, but I sustain injuries as easily as you do; however, it takes me almost no time to recover from them.

"Anyway, I broke free, ran into the hallway and waited. I waited to hear you scream. I waited to pick up the smell of fear leading to some other part of the house but nothing came. Finally, I waited for spontaneous stab wounds to cut into me. I thought he had taken you more than a hundred yards from where I stood, but nothing happened. That's when I knew you were still in the house. I wish I found you sooner, Sage. This cut on your shoulder is going to leave a scar," Lial nodded to the wound he had just closed.

"We have Keylor now. He even confessed to murdering Lena so we don't have to be pretty sure, we can be certain. He deserves to die," I said. But I was still not convinced I had the right to make that decision.

"Now we just need an undisturbed place for the summoning ritual."

Even though Lial and I had succeeded in our mission to capture Keylor, there was no sense of victory in the room. The war was far from won and my next task, spilling a sinner's blood, had yet to be accomplished.

I felt as though my face was still cloaked with that wet rag and I couldn't breathe. I got up from the bed, dripping blood across the floor and pulled back the curtains from the window. Sunlight flooded into the room. It was dawn. I unlatched the windowpanes and pushed them open. Morning air flew in and renewed my spirit. I took a breath.

I watched birds sitting on telephone wires, and early risers walking on the street below. This is the way people woke up most mornings. I knew that this was normal, sunlight and morning birds, but it all seemed foreign to me. I turned back to Lial who sat at the foot of my bed, bathed in light. It suited him. His blonde hair was golden and his eyes were their usual surreal blue. They watched me from across the room while I lingered in front of the open window. My mind raced with insuppressible doubts and insecurities. Lial could sense my inhibitions; he could smell the fear swelling inside me.

"What's on your mind?" he asked me in a quiet voice.

"I almost died, Lial."

"I wouldn't let you."

I noticed a change in him. Lial was still course and unrefined, but maybe kind too. "I forgot to thank you," I said.

He broke eye contact and changed the subject. "Are you worried about what you have to do tomorrow?"

"I don't know what you mean," I lied.

"I would be worried if you weren't freaking out about summoning Procel, knowing what it requires of you."

"Raymond Keylor murdered Lena, tortured me, and he would do it again. I am not having second thoughts about tomorrow. Keylor is an evil man and he is going to die and I am going to—"

I stopped there. I couldn't finish the sentence. I guess I had a hard time admitting that I was going to kill a man to save my soul. It made me feel like a hypocrite, even though there was no other way to redeem myself. Spill a sinner's blood, summon a fallen angel to tell me more about Liber Alter, summon another fallen angel to tell me where to find it and return the book to its author. I figured once I took care of Keylor, the rest would be easy.

I moved back over to the bed and crawled beneath the gray comforter. I brought my legs up to my chest. Lial watched me from where he sat, and it made me anxious.

"I am not having second thoughts," I shut my eyes.

"Who are you trying to convince?"

I sighed into the pillow.

Lial flopped onto his back and lay beside me. There was more than a foot between us and I was under the comforter, but I still felt the heat from Lial's body drift over to me.

I imagined him as I saw him moments earlier, basking in the morning light with his white skin aglow and radiating the sun's warmth. He hadn't even squinted against the incoming sunshine. Lial might have fallen, but he still looked most at home in the light. With or without wings, there was no mistaking this exquisite creature for anything other than an angel.

"Don't commit to the idea of taking this man's life unless you're sure you can go through with it," he warned in a low voice. "Otherwise you will have wasted my time."

"Don't talk to me about commitment. You're supposed to be my guardian angel. Where were you when I needed you?"

He kept quiet, hearing the heat rise in my voice.

"Of course I am going to go through with this," I continued. "The alternative is an eternity in Hell."

"Yeah, but Hell isn't so bad once you've been there a millennium or so."

"Lial, I can barely manage life on Earth and I've only been here for eighteen years. I imagine that Hell is going to be a little worse than what I am dealing with now, and forever is a very long time."

"You're right, Sage." He nudged me. "Hell is only a little worse than life on Earth."

He was mocking me. I wanted to smack the sarcasm out of him. How could he make fun of the situation I was in? Actually, when I thought about it, I wasn't surprised. I think it was in Lial's nature to be impossible.

"I know a place we can take Keylor for the summoning ritual," I said. "I am going to get a couple hours of sleep, have a large coffee and then we can call on your friends. You and I are one step closer to being rid of each other."

"Can't come soon enough," he added. "I would've hated being your guardian, Blondie. I've only been with you for two days and I'm exhausted."

"We've been over this. As soon as I can manage things on my own, I promise to release you. Okay, penguin?"

The room fell silent for a while. Lial kicked off his boots and I jumped at the sound they made when they hit the floor. The open window let in a cheerful breeze that warmed me as it swept over bed where Lial and I rested. He tossed about restlessly as he struggled to find a comfortable position.

When I thought Lial had fallen asleep, his voice found me again. He spoke so low the words were almost inaudible, but I heard them and the melancholy they carried.

"I wouldn't have been any good," he whispered. I listened to the angel's confession, not sure what he meant. "You were better off without me as your guardian. I wouldn't have been any good. I would have failed you sooner or later."

I didn't respond straight away. I wanted to be sure Lial had finished his thought.

"Well, you haven't yet," I whispered back.

A playful tug on my curls was his reply.

17

Coincidence

My short nap turned into eight hours. I woke up just before three in the afternoon. I showered, indulged in a cup of coffee and packed supplies for the ritual. Lial and I checked to make sure Keylor was still breathing before we buckled our seat belts and took off in Sweetie. About twenty minutes after we left Bridgeview City, we were in the one place I never thought I would revisit.

"Turn left," I said from the passenger seat.

"You still haven't told me where we're going."

I couldn't believe where we were headed myself.

Tarrytown was quaint, charming and the polar opposite of the Bridgeview. Where Tarrytown had antique stores and homemade ice cream shops, Bridgeview City had seedy bars, unsanitary tattoo parlors and a crime rate double anywhere else in New York State.

I had lived at 179 Union Avenue, towards the dead end. I remember the Japanese Maple Tree in our front yard and the strange pink-ish color of our house. Our front porch was white and we had a brick walkway. My life in Tarrytown was ordinary, and until Nola got sick it was boring. I missed that, ordinary and boring.

Thankfully I knew a way to our destination without passing

by my parents' house. On the north end of Tarrytown was the old high school I once attended, which now lay vacant. It had been reconstructed and moved to a new location on the southwest side of town, closer to the river. Since then, no one had made a decision regarding what to do with the previous school building. It just sat on the hill with empty classrooms, unused sports fields and one unoccupied theater.

I instructed Lial to pull Sweetie up to the theater's side entrance and park. Keylor was awake again. I could hear him shuffling inside the locked trunk. Lial opened the hood and before Keylor could scream two syllables, the angel punched him in the face, rendering him unconscious. I helped Lial carry Keylor by his arms and legs into the abandoned theater. Once inside we tied the murderer to a steel chair, center stage.

I took a moment to remember all of the lazy afternoons I spent in the company of Kristen, Travis and recreational drugs. I thought about all the alternative rock music we listened to and the endless bags of Doritos and Funions we consumed.

There were approximately two hundred empty seats in the theater. The curtains were thick red velvet and stretched from the ceiling to the stage floor. The entire place smelled of dust and velvet. There were incredible acoustics. When the doors were closed, no one outside would be able to hear anything coming from within. If Keylor woke up and started to scream, no one would hear him.

As I closed the side entrance to the theater, I heard a clap of thunder overhead. The sky was overcast and growing darker every second. The sunlight and morning birds Lial and I enjoyed at dawn were nowhere to be found. The summer breeze became an angry blast of wind. A storm was rising and pushed towards us. I welcomed it. Murder and black magic somehow made more sense under a dark sky.

Lial carried the small duffle bag I packed into the theater and emptied it onto the stage. A dozen white candles tumbled out, a piece of chalk, a bottle of holy water, several articles of clothing, a bag of salt and one silver blade.

"Do you want to get started?" Lial asked as he positioned the last candle. "I don't see any point in dragging this out."

"Okay. Light the candles."

"Did you pack a lighter?" he searched through the contents of the duffle bag.

My stomach dropped. I forgot to bring a lighter. Lial saw the embarrassment plastered on my face.

"Don't worry about it," he reached into his pocket. "I have matches."

"Why do you have matches?"

"I like to have a cigarette from time to time. I stole them off that drunk in Baltimore, Henry."

I crossed my arms. "Angels don't smoke."

"Fallen," Lial said and pointed to himself.

He lit the twelve white candles, and after the last one sparked to life, Lial picked up the silver knife and extended it towards me. "Call on Procel first."

I took hold of the blade's handle and turned away from Lial, giving my attention to the unconscious body of Raymond Keylor. I was glad he wouldn't be awake for this.

I knew what I had to do. And if someone had to die, at least I was certain the world would be a better place without Keylor. Still, I couldn't find the strength to lift the blade from my side. I stood motionless in front of my intended victim.

"I wish I could do this for you," Lial said and it sounded like an apology.

"Yeah, me too. Why can't you, again?"

His eyes softened on me. "Only a human can summon an

angel. Since Procel is an archangel, she requires blood; and since she is fallen, it needs to be the blood of someone who has committed sins, the worse the better. Sage, you know this. Do you want me to keep going?"

I nodded even though I understood completely. I knew the rules, but I wasn't ready to bring the blade across Keylor's throat. Lial recognized that I was apprehensive and permitted me another minute.

"You need to bleed Keylor dry because Procel is not your guardian, and a few drops of your blood will not suffice. There is no reason for her to be available to you. Procel requires a greater sacrifice for her services," Lial explained to me for the second time.

"Okay," I heard enough.

"Don't put this off any longer. It won't make it easier."

He was right. I guess he would know. As an archangel Lial had fought and killed before. I wondered if it ever got easier for him, or if his stomach still turned when he thought back on all the violence he was responsible for.

I looked at the man's face in front of me. He had floppy brown hair, a pointed nose and thin lips. I could see the crow's feet in the corners of his eyes. His face was badly bruised from last night's fight with Lial. Keylor was no longer clean-shaven; an invasive five o'clock shadow was becoming visible. I could make out the raised veins in his neck, hands and forearms. I imagined the beating heart in his chest pumping blood through them. I knew that very soon his heart would be still, because of me.

I raised my arm and brought the silver blade to the skin of Keylor's throat. He breathed normally without any knowledge of the imminent danger he faced. Regardless of how hard I tried to keep my hand from shaking, my nerves prevailed.

Raymond Keylor was human. He wasn't a good person, but he was human and who was I to judge him? Did I really think I could justify taking his life? He wasn't even a human possessed by a demon or haunted by spirits and pushed to madness. He was just a troubled man who had made too many wrong choices. He had a sick mind, but was that grounds for me to slide the knife in my hand across his bare throat? I couldn't commit a mortal sin because it might benefit me. I couldn't kill a man for selfish reasons, no matter what he had done. I made up my mind.

I exhaled slowly and glanced back at Lial. After a few seconds I watched his pursed lips relax and return to their regular pout. His almost platinum hair fell in front of his face and swayed as he shook his head back and forth in disappointment.

"Sage—" his voice was deep.

"I can't do it." I dropped the knife where I stood. "Lial, it just doesn't feel right."

"Of course it doesn't feel right!" His temper shot through the roof. "It's not supposed to feel right. It's murder!"

"Raymond Keylor is human, which means he can change. I can't take that opportunity away from him. He can still be forgiven. Lial, I don't think you understand how precious a second chance is to us humans."

Lial watched me with furious, burning eyes. I thought I would incinerate and turn to ash before him. "I think you're right, Sage. I don't understand second chances because I was never given one. I made a choice a long time ago and I am stuck with the consequences forever. The word forgiveness has no meaning for me. A fallen angel does not get a second chance. So excuse me if I fail to sympathize with murderous men like Keylor and selfish little girls like you."

"I resent that," I said.

"I don't care!"

My breath got caught in my throat. I furrowed my brow, baffled. I ran a frustrated hand through my hair. I wasn't sure where to go from there.

"Whatever," I stated. "I can't kill him."

"You summoned me. I am stuck with you. I told you exactly what would be required of you if we wanted to find Liber Alter, and you agreed. Sage, you told me this wouldn't be a problem." He took a breath and collected himself. "You know what? Never mind. Let that murderous bastard walk away with his life. But now that you've made up your mind, you can release me from being your guardian."

I averted my eyes and focused on my feet.

"No. No…" he growled. "You cannot do this to me—"

"There has to be another way to save my soul! There has to be some way out of my deal with the Devil. I still need your help. I can't let you leave now."

"You just proved my point, selfish."

"I am not selfish! I am desperate!" I cried.

Lial and I were distracted from our quarrel when a loud gasp captured our attention. Keylor woke up and lifted his head, which must have felt heavy from being knocked around so much. It wasn't long before his protruding brown eyes settled on us. We waited for him to scream for help, but he seemed unnaturally calm. Keylor just watched us with wide, inquisitive eyes and a gaping mouth.

"Oh, pardon me," he spoke in a gentle manner. "Did I interrupt something?"

Lial carried on as if Keylor hadn't spoken a word. He grabbed me roughly by the arm and dragged me into the wings, just off stage. We stood between two black curtains with their folds enveloping us. I do not know why Lial wanted this to be a private conversation, but he felt the need to whisper. There were mere inches between us, and I could feel his scentless breath tickle my face. I took a step away from the angel, but when I moved back he stepped forward.

"Listen to me, you will spill that man's blood or you will let me go," he practically begged.

"I'm sorry," I said, unable to look him in the eye. "I can't."

"You cannot be incapable of both. So which is it? Killing him or releasing me?" He searched my brown eyes for an answer, but I never offered one. "Christ, you really are just a selfish brat, you know that?"

"Stop calling me that!"

Lial breathed in through his nose and kept his eyes steady on mine. "When you were eight years old you wanted to save your sister so you shook the Devil's hand, and she lived. Now you want your soul too? You made a deal, Sage. You don't get your sister and your soul," he explained. "That is not how it works."

"Nola died! I was cheated!"

"No!" he grabbed my arms. "You weren't cheated. Nola survived her leukemia and lived two more months before the car accident. You gave her those extra days. You gave her time she was never supposed to have."

"It wasn't enough." I fell into his leather jacket and breathed in the musk that clung to it. I hid my tears there.

Lial hugged me and let a hand become tangled in my untamed mane of curls. I melted into him. My sobbing was interrupted by the loud and sudden sound of a heavy door being slammed shut. The floorboards vibrated beneath me. Lial and I rushed back towards center stage. There was only an empty chair, some cut rope and the knife I dropped at Keylor's feet. Lial hurried over to the side door and pulled it open.

"He's making a run for it! He's halfway across the parking lot!" Lial called to me over the thunder and rain. The wind raced passed him as he stood in the doorway with his hair flying away from his face. "Should we go after him?" he asked.

"I might not want to kill him, but he is a murderer. We could turn him in to the police, or you know, hit him a few more times."

Lial nodded and stepped into the thunderstorm to chase Keylor. At that exact moment, a clash of lightening forked its way to Earth. For a split second I was drowned in a blinding white light. When it ended, I found Lial standing in the rain. I ran over to his side. My shirt was sopping wet and clung to my skin while my hair was being thrashed about by the wind. Lial spoke to me, but it was difficult to hear anything above the storm.

"What?" I shouted.

Lial stretched his arm and pointed to a far away spot in the school parking lot.

About fifty yards from where we stood Raymond Keylor's body was sprawled out on the pavement.

I strained to see past the pouring rain. "Um, is he—?"

"That is one Hell of a coincidence," the angel was breathless with disbelief. "I can't believe it. Sage, you couldn't kill him and he died anyway."

The chance of being struck by lightening was one in a million, which meant that either Keylor was the victim of a natural disaster or an act of God.

Lial squeezed my shoulders enthusiastically. "Well, you should have no trouble spilling his blood now."

18
Close Your Eyes

Lial walked into the pounding rain and carried Keylor's limp body inside the dark theater. All of the candles had gone out, and soft gray smoke rose from their dead wicks.

I drew a demon's snare center stage with a piece of chalk. I remembered what Laveau said about summoning angels. The act would cause a rift between worlds and anything could crawl through. If it were a demon, it wouldn't get very far.

While I finished drawing the demon's snare, Lial relit the candles before once again handing me the silver blade. This time I had no cause for hesitation. It was still awkward, cutting into a man's flesh, but at least I hadn't killed him.

"You have to put out the candles with Keylor's blood; it has to fall from the blade," Lial instructed, but I remembered. It had only been several nights since I summoned him.

The theater dimmed as each candle was doused with the sinner's blood. When the last flame was extinguished, the atmosphere became static and buzzed. It was obvious that there was a dark kind of magic brewing.

"Rumpere silentium rerum angelorum quaeritur," I spoke to the air.

I remembered Laveau saying the same words when he summoned Lial. I hoped they would bear a similar effect.

I felt an intense vibration overpower the room. It was the same uneasy feeling I experienced when summoning Lial. Even the stench was identical. The ungodly odor that could best be compared to burnt hair and expired milk, but that hardly did it justice. I screamed the second half of the ritual over the strident humming, which was made louder through the theatre's acoustics.

"Suscipio nostrum nisus. Sanguine peccatoris, producat cecidit angelus!"

I asked that a sinner's blood bring forth the fallen angel.

"You have to call her by name!" Lial yelled to me from across the stage.

"Ego postulo vestri vexillum… Procel."

The moment her name left my mouth the entire foundation of the high school shook. I was certain the ground beneath would cave in and swallow the theater, but instead a cloud of yellow dust formed and hovered over Keylor's body. The thick smell of sulfur burned my nose and eyes. When the cloud of sulfur evaporated, in its place stood a naked woman. She cleared her throat and adjusted to her new environment, the same way Lial had.

She was stunning. Procel had deep olive skin paired with emerald eyes. Her body was slim and toned, yet curved in all the appropriate places, making her the quintessential image of femininity. I was surprised by the tattoo that stretched across her upper left thigh. It was one word written in a very ancient language called Echonian, better known as the language of angels. No human had the ability to master the spoken word of Echonian, but I had studied the written language in Rome. The tattoo simply stated her name.

Procel stepped over Keylor's body and sauntered towards Lial; her hips swaying seductively. Her arrival on Earth had been much more graceful than my guardian's. She seemed at ease in the physical world.

Apart from being naked with black, syrupy tar smeared on her bare feet, she could have passed for a mortal. Procel didn't appear as surreal as Lial did. It was impossible not to notice his clear eyes or perfectly symmetrical face. Procel's beauty wasn't as ridiculous as my guardian's.

"Belial, it has been some time since we last crossed paths."

"You know that time holds no relevance for our kind," he said with a smirk. "Always a pleasure to see you, Procel."

The formality in Lial's voice startled me. I couldn't decide if their relationship was pleasant or hostile. If the angels weren't on good terms, then Procel would be useless to us. I watched their dubious interaction with caution and hoped we hadn't summoned Procel in vain.

"That's quite a mark you're branded with," Lial gestured to her tattoo.

Procel followed his gaze, and discovered the mark for herself. "I was wondering where that would turn up. Where is yours hidden?"

"The bottom of my left foot."

I stepped forward. "Lial, you have one too?"

Procel answered for him. "Every fallen angel walking the Earth has their name branded somewhere on the left side of their body. Always written in Echonian, which is a divine language. Humans are too underdeveloped and flawed to understand it, forget about speaking it."

The dark hair, green-eyed beauty insulted my species with such an enchanting voice that I almost didn't mind. I knew humankind was flawed but who was Procel to hold that against us? She was a fallen angel, after all. I sold my soul to the Devil but she followed him out of Heaven.

Lial moved towards her. "You know how I feel about

humans, Procel."

"Yes, I do. Should I quote you? They are lazy, primitive, self-obsessed creatures and a great waste of His talents."

"I know what I said," he shot me tender look. "This one is different."

My jaw unhinged. Was that a compliment? I tried to hold his stare, but he wouldn't let his eyes settle on me. I think Lial was embarrassed for defending a human to an angel, and friend.

"Oh Belial, you know that humans are all the same. This one is no different than any one that's come before her, or will come after she is gone," she flashed her harsh gaze in my direction. "No doubt this girl summoned me here for some selfish purpose. Tell me human, what is it you need from me?"

I was tired of her cold stare and nasty remarks. I walked over to where the duffle bag had been tossed aside earlier. I picked up several pieces of clothing and presented them to the nude creature.

"Get dressed and we can talk about why I summoned you," I said.

First she put on the old t-shirt advertising my favorite band, The Airborne Toxic Event. Then she pulled a pair of black leggings over her slender legs. Her feet were still bare, but at least the intimate parts of her were covered. I could tell from the look on her face that this outfit did not amuse Procel but that wasn't my primary concern.

"Okay," she huffed. "What do you want?"

"I am looking for a way out of my deal with the Devil—"

"Have you tried praying?" she offered coyly. Both angels laughed.

I hated being mocked but I managed to push my ego aside and ignore the comment. "I need to find Liber Alter. It's the best chance I have to—"

Lial stopped me there. "If it even exists—We thought you

would be able to clear that much up for us. Both you and your brother are the keepers of secret things. If you can tell us whether or not the book is real and why it's so important, then Sage will summon your twin and he can tell us where to find it."

Procel's emerald eyes expanded with revelation. For the first time since she appeared, Procel lost her poised composure and appeared utterly dumbfounded. She spoke very slowly. Her voice was low and expressed complete severity. "You are going to summon Vassago?"

"Yes," Lial said in an equally quiet voice.

Procel looked to me and waited for further confirmation.

"Promise me," she demanded. "Swear that if I help you, you will summon Vassago and allow us to leave here together, free to walk the Earth. I won't say another word unless you swear it."

"I swear," I answered sincerely.

"Then I will tell you anything you want to know."

After instructing Lial and Procel to take a seat, I excused myself from the stage. There was something I deemed necessary before taking our conversation any further. It took me a while to find what I was searching for. The theater hadn't been used in years and it appeared as though backstage had become a storage area for old desks, gym equipment, and music stands. Everything was caked in dust and I couldn't keep from sneezing repeatedly.

Finally I spotted it. The forgotten piano had been backstage since my freshman year. It must have been a long time since anyone played the instrument, which was certainly out of tune by now. I always remembered the piano being covered by a moth bitten quilt and the very same quilt was still resting there. I had found another purpose for it.

I pulled the cloth off the piano and a cloud of dust flew into the air. I immediately regretted the decision as another sneezing fit overcame me. I wiped my nose on my sleeve before walking back on stage. I shook out the blanket and let it fall over Raymond Keylor's body. I couldn't stand to look at his bruised, burnt, drained, lifeless form any longer. It didn't seem right to carry on with business when there was a dead man in the room but I had no other choice. At the very least, I hoped the blanket would soften the inelegance of the situation.

"Human sentiment," Procel was puzzled, disgusted even.

Lial shook his head, expressing similar confusion.

I seated myself at the edge of the stage, looking down at the angels who sat in the cushioned seats of the audience.

"Procel, what can you tell me about The Other Book?"

"Why don't we start with what you know?"

"Is it worth looking for?" Lial interjected. He sat with his legs set wide apart, slouching in the red chair. "Does it even exist? I want to know if it is a physical object that we can get our hands on. Well?"

Procel smiled and her brilliant green eyes shone brighter. "Yes."

What a powerful word, yes. Yes, made a dream become a reality and a wish granted. Summoning Procel was already worth the trouble.

"Yes?" he repeated, astounded. "That's a good start."

"We've heard different rumors about the book," I added. "I was hoping you could sort out which are true?"

"What have you heard?" Procel crossed her legs and folded her hands in her lap. The t-shirt and leggings were completely unbecoming on her. In my opinion, Procel would have felt much more herself in Channel, Prada and Oscar de la Renta. She had an air of high society in her stiff shoulders and long neck.

"We were told that Liber Alter might reveal the meaning of life."

I regretted suggesting the idea immediately. It provoked the same reaction that both Lial and Laveau experienced a few days earlier. The angels shared a peculiar glance before bursting into an unprecedented fit of laughter. They grabbed at their sides, which were cramping from unexpected muscle spasms while they struggled to breathe. The theatre's acoustics amplified carried their laughter to every corner of the building. It took a minute, but eventually the angels' hysterics subsided and our conversation proceeded.

"I nearly died laughing," Procel wiped away a tear from the corner of her eye and her smile faded as she fell back into our dialogue. "Please, tell me what other ridiculous tall tales you have heard."

"That it might reveal a formula to end life on Earth. Maybe the book holds the key to expanding the universe or creating a new one. It could reveal our past lives or show us how we're going to die. I don't know, Procel. This is why I summoned you."

"I only wanted to see how far your imagination stretched," she waved her hand as if to dismiss me. "You bored me."

"I'm not here to entertain you. Procel, if you won't help me then I am not going to summon your brother." I tossed back my hair, still drenched from the rain, and suppressed the overwhelming urge to punch her in her beautiful face.

Procel's demeanor changed; she was suddenly much more amicable. She spoke slowly and over annunciated her words. She probably assumed I wouldn't be able to keep up otherwise.

"The book was actually safe in His kingdom until The Great War. That's when it fell to Earth and has been lost ever since. There is some debate as to whether or not the book was misplaced or taken. Either way no one has been able to locate it. That's because He installed a default setting, in a manner of speaking. Should the book be lost from Heaven then it can only be recovered under very specific conditions."

"A ritual," Lial noted.

Procel nodded. "Now you want to know what is hidden beneath the book's cover. Liber Alter offers one truth to whomever reads from it, and that truth can be different for everyone. The message is always something that the reader wasn't aware of beforehand and that they would never know otherwise."

"It sounds similar to a tell-all," I made the comparison and could see Procel's green eyes flicker towards me. I had impressed her. "They both reveal the truth no matter how simple or unattractive or unwanted the truth might be."

"That's right," she admitted reluctantly.

Lial stood up from his seat. I could hear water pounding on the theater's roof. The rain beat down with so much force it sounded like a shower of bullets. Lial turned towards Procel.

"I still don't see how returning The Other Book into His hands would be enough to inspire Him to forgive Sage."

"I agree," she mused. "I don't know that He will forgive her, but I believe she has a fair chance. Liber Alter is a deeply coveted object because of its potential. Imagine if God could share the book with his angels, like you and me. Belial, we would have known that we were making a terrible mistake leaving His service to follow Lucifer. We never would have fallen."

"Let's examine it from the opposite end of the spectrum," my guardian said with a coarse voice. "Sage could open the book and learn that it wasn't the Devil who took her sister. She might read that He stole Nola a second time because He had decided it was the girl's time to die, not Lucifer."

Procel stood up and approached my guardian. "I am not arguing the possibility of that, Belial. I am just explaining that Liber Alter does not lie and when people know the truth, they make big decisions based on that information. The truth can change everything. One small revelation and people turn their lives inside out; their worlds upside down."

"Would you read from The Other Book, Procel— If you had the chance to?"

''I don't think I would. I'd be afraid to learn the truth about myself and not be able to live with it. I would rather be ignorant."

"Would you read from it, Lial?" I opened the question to him.

"No," he answered in a somber tone after a moment of contemplation. "We should be stuck with the choices we make. The Other Book offers people an undeserved second chance. I think everyone should have to learn the hard way, from their mistakes."

Lial finished, but I could see that his mind was still churning. He focused his attention on me. I found myself counting the gray freckles that littered his irises before he finally blinked and turned away.

"I would read from The Other Book," I said.

"Shut up, Blondie," he snapped.

Procel set our conversation back on track. "Putting aside our personal opinions, the book is a sacred object and He would be very glad to have it back in His possession. I am sure of that. Can I ask who suggested that you bargain Liber Alter for your soul, human?"

"West Laveau."

Procel's dark cheeks flashed red. "The hybrid!"

Her shrieking nearly ruptured my eardrum. Lial instinctively shot up and moved closer to me. It wouldn't have shocked me if he believed Procel was on the verge of tearing my head from my body.

That was the second time I heard Laveau referred to as the hybrid. I took it as confirmation that the rumors I had heard about his great, great, great-grandmother were true. She must have conceived a child with an angel and West Laveau was the distant product of that union. He was more than human after all. It explained his connection to the spiritual world and the friendships he kept with angels and demons alike.

"Excuse me," Procel calmed herself, smoothing down her jet-black hair with the palm of her hand. "The hybrid and I are not on good terms and the mention of his name took me by surprise, which is not something I am accustomed to. As a keeper of secrets, I usually know what everyone else only suspects. I don't have much experience being caught off guard."

"I understand," I said, attempting to relate to her. "I'm always surprised when my dog uses the apartment as his personal toilet bowl. I should be used to it by now; it happens all the time."

I think she was stunned by my simple-minded comment. Procel turned away from me and gave her attention my guardian.

"Belial, I would like to suggest something that would benefit you, my brother and me. Are you interested?"

Lial crossed his arms and let Procel speak her mind.

"After the human summons Vassago, we should dispose of her, track down Liber Alter and use it to change which side we serve."

"What?" I almost shouted, horrified by her suggestion. "Procel, I am standing right next to you. I can hear you."

"You are irrelevant."

"I summoned you, Procel. You wouldn't be here if it weren't for me."

"Then you are irrelevant and stupid," she corrected. "We really should put the poor thing out of its misery, Belial."

"I won't summon your brother if you plan to kill me afterwards." I stood up, blood rushing to my face.

"Then I will kill you anyway," she said in a nonchalant manner. "Belial is bound to you because you summoned him as your guardian. I am not your guardian and therefore you have no hold over me. In order for Belial to be free of you burdening him, one of two things must happen. Either you release him from being your guardian, or you die and he is automatically released as a result."

Procel climbed up the stairs onto the stage. Her bare feet made no noise and she crossed over the floorboards towards me. She reminded me of a jungle cat, composed and focused, ready to attack at a moment's notice. I hate to admit it, but Procel intimidated me. She set me on edge with her disarming smile and emerald stare. I wouldn't allow myself to take my eyes off her. She might take it as an opportunity to lunge forward and go in for the kill.

Lial was quiet while his fallen comrade casually discussed murdering me. His fist was resting under his chin and his eyes were cast down. As Procel closed in on me, he finally spoke up.

"You and Vassago want to change sides?" he asked.

"Of course we do. So do you, Belial. When we followed Lucifer through the Earth's core and down further and further into deeper and darker places, we knew we made the wrong choice."

"You want to bargain The Other Book for our return to Heaven. You mean to give it back and hope we're pardoned of our crimes against Him."

"Yes. Exactly."

"It won't be enough. Procel, we betrayed Him."

"We have the same chance for His forgiveness as the girl has. In fact, we have more of a chance. He loved us first. We are superior creatures."

I was completely bemused and hurt that Lial could even consider what Procel had suggested. "Don't do this. Please."

I wished there was more I could've said to convince him that joining forces with Procel was bad idea. But why would he want to help me? I summoned him and forced him into acting as my guide. Maybe Lial realized that getting rid of me was easier than putting up with me.

Lial's eyes iced over and there was no emotion in his angelic face. I had no clue what he was thinking. He shifted his gaze from me to Procel and cracked a smile. A stab of doubt pierced through me. A nervous sensation coursed through my body. Again I wondered why Lial would help me when he could help himself.

"I knew it," she beamed. "I knew you wouldn't waste this opportunity on a human, not when we might have found a way home."

"You still need your brother to tell you where the book is hidden," I argued. "And you need a human to summon him. I won't do it."

Procel took an aggressive step forward. "You will summon my brother into the physical world or I will personally tear apart the people you love. You are going to die regardless because I find you intolerable but at least you can spare them."

"You don't know anything about me. You don't know who I care about."

"Belial does. I'm sure he knows where to find them too," she inched closer and I retreated backwards.

I exchanged a look with both fallen angels. I could hear my heart pound against my ribcage. I knew Lial could smell the fear pouring out of me. I stood my ground and waited for the fight of my life to begin. I was certain that I would lose. It would be a triumph if I survived a minute.

"I don't stand a chance against two archangels."

"You don't stand a chance against one," Procel corrected.

I took a deep breath and readied myself.

Just then Lial let out a deafening laugh. He slapped his hands together, unable to control himself. The sound echoed and resonated throughout the empty theater. Procel joined in and chuckled along with him.

"Hold on," Lial stopped his nonsense. "Procel, why are you laughing? I'm not sure we find the same thing amusing."

"I don't know what you mean. Belial, your human just challenged us to a fight, in a battle to the death. Everything about that is funny."

"Well of course I can see the humor in that," Lial stated. "But you and I are not on the same page. Procel, you have been a great help. You have put to rest the rumors surrounding Liber Alter and now we know the book's true purpose. More importantly, we know it exists. Sage will summon your brother, but after he tells us where to find the book, our relationship with you is over. You and Vassago will leave us to our business, and you will not interfere."

"You can't be serious," her black eyebrows drew together. "Don't you want you to be allowed back into Heaven? Belial, I know that you have regretted your choice to leave more than any of the fallen angels."

Procel waited for him to say something, but Lial remained silent. He didn't respond, but he also did not deny that what she said was true.

"Get rid of the girl and use the situation to your advantage. Who knows the next time we will be on Earth together? I haven't been here in over two thousand years. Now that I have a chance to change my fate, you and your human are not going to get in the way. I say that regretfully, but I mean it."

"But that is exactly where we are, Procel, in your way," Lial said calmly.

Procel shifted her weight and stared him down with enraged green eyes. "Then we have a problem."

Tensions rose between the angels and it felt like another bolt of lightening would manifest at any moment. Lial had put my salvation over his own, and over his friends'. He was acting as my guardian angel. A warm flush of emotion passed through me.

"Sage," Lial said my name in his usual rough voice. "Get out of here. Procel and I need to be left alone."

I made a swift exit stage right and hid myself in the wings. I saw Lial make his way to the middle of the stage where Procel stood. His steps were wide and heavy. The female angel remained patient while he advanced towards her.

"I don't want to fight you, Belial."

"You threatened Sage. You threatened me. If we summon your brother now, I can't trust that you won't come after us. I'm sorry, Procel but—"

"I know. I know," she sighed. "You can't let me live," she said without a hint of fear in her voice. "Belial, are you sure you can't find some way to trust me?"

He shook his head, tussling his soft platinum hair. "What would keep you from trying to steal the book for yourself?"

She mulled over his question for a moment and then answered with one cold word. "Nothing."

There was no reason for the angels to speak beyond that. They were on different sides and Lial had chosen mine. He looked over his shoulder to find me staring back at him from the wings. His brow was wrinkled and I could see that his eyes were worrisome. He tried to hide his concern with a quick wink, but I saw through him.

The angel that walked away from this fight would have to take the other's life. I hadn't been able to murder Raymond Keylor and he was a stranger to me. Lial and Procel were friends.

"On second thought," Lial said. "Could I have a private word with the girl? I won't be long."

"If you must," Procel scoffed. "You know, I don't recall you being this sentimental," she called after him.

"What are you doing?" I asked when he found me draped in the black velvet curtains.

He brought his face close to mine. His large white hands found their way to my waist and gripped my shirt. The worry in his face was still present. His voice was strained in a low whisper.

"Close your eyes."

"What? Why—"

"Close your eyes, Sage. Procel is famously competitive. I don't know—"

"No. What are you saying? Lial, you are the second most feared archangel in Heaven and Hell."

"I am out of practice," he admitted. "Going against a drunk is one thing; archangels are something else."

My mind reeled. It never occurred to me that Lial could lose a fight. Had he met me in the wings to say goodbye? The thought of it made me sick. I looked down at my feet. A gentle hand lifted my chin and I found a pair of unnatural blue eyes staring into mine.

"Sage, I don't know what the outcome is going to be but either way I want to spare you witnessing this. Angels do not die easily."

"You are not going to die."

"If I do, it won't be on purpose," he joked. "Close your eyes, and when the noise stops, open them. If I have lost, promise me that you will run."

I took one last look into his icy blue eyes, speckled with beautiful bits of gray, and then closed mine. I heard him sigh, relieved that I had yielded to his request. Lial removed his hands from my waist but I could still feel him in front of me. Normally this would have made me uncomfortable, but at that moment I was just glad to know he was still with me.

Just then a peculiar thought occurred to me and I released a small laugh.

"What?" he asked.

"Nothing— Really."

"I am about to engage in a battle to the death and you are laughing in my face. I would like to know what's so funny."

I kept my eyes shut. I would not have been brave enough to say what I was thinking if faced with his unparalleled beauty.

"You are, Lial," I said as sweetly as I could manage. "In the last minute you have been worried, cautious and sentimental. Your humanity is showing."

"Oh shut up, Blondie."

Lial's long fingers combed through my curls and I felt my cheeks blush. Then he left me, alone and in the dark. I wanted to open my eyes but I respected his final wish. I kept them shut tight like he asked, while the sounds of a world collapsing engulfed me.

There were terrible screams and many of them belonged to Lial. The sound of wood breaking and stone cracking filled the theater. It was an orchestra of amplified chaos and echoing disaster. I thought that the roof would cave in any second. The uncertainty this blindness had brought on was maddening.

I jumped at a curious, horrifying sound coming from the stage, like crushed ice being poured into a plastic cup or crackers being stepped on. I wish the explanation was as simple as that, but it was the sound of bones breaking, snapping. I squeezed my eyes shut tighter as Lial roared in immeasurable agony. Procel's maniacal laugh followed. There was another throttle of violent energy that shook the ground beneath my feet and threw me off balance. I slammed into the floorboards and crawled to my hands and knees. With my eyes still closed, I reached out until I felt the velvet curtain at my fingertips. I grabbed at it and pulled myself to my feet.

In a silent flash I was struck with a paralyzing surge of fear. It had grown quiet. In fact there was only one thing I could hear, a faint tapping. I couldn't figure out what caused the sound so I made the bold decision to open my eyes. I expected to be terrified by what I saw, and I was.

The finale was underway. Just left of center stage Lial straddled Procel, who was defenseless against him. His hands, which had been gentle with me only minutes before, were encircling her throat and applying pressure. I watched Procel's face change from a bright red to a deep purple. No sounds escaping from her gaping mouth. Her eyes were wide as they tried to resist the darkness overtaking them. The tapping I heard came from her open palm slapping the wood panels of the stage.

Procel was dying. She was suffocating and my heart broke for her. I had almost known a similar death in Raymond Keylor's basement. I understood the pain and helplessness she was experiencing. Death is rarely graceful.

It was not what I feared most, but it was worse than I could have ever imagined. Lial had won, although the expression on his face would've made you believe otherwise. Part of him seemed vicious and animalistic. I could see the veins in his forehead, neck and arms as he pressed his weight down on Procel. His mouth turned down in a sour frown. Still, there was a part of Lial that seemed sympathetic towards his victim; after all he knew where he was sending her back to. Procel had once been Lial's friend and now he was the reason she was leaving this world. I could see that it bereaved him.

Eventually Procel stopped struggling and accepted that she had lost. She placed her hand against the side of Lial's face and stroked his cheek affectionately. He bowed his head. If the fight had gone differently, he would have been the one lying on the ground, dying. Procel's gesture of "no hard feelings" burdened Lial with a guilt that was difficult to bear. It might have been easier for him if she never stopped fighting. He would be inconsolable after this.

The light left her green eyes and her body went limp. My stomach turned as her hand fell from the side of Lial's face and hit the floor. I wouldn't say I enjoyed Procel's company, but I never wished her dead. If she hadn't threatened to steal Liber Alter she would have been free to walk the Earth with her brother. I suppose humans aren't the only selfish beings in creation. Everyone wants something.

Lial crawled off her lifeless body and climbed to his feet. He might have won the fight but Procel had done her share of damage.

His hair was sticky with blood. His shoulder was dislocated and he was limping.

"Are you okay, Lial?"

He saw the concern in my face. He turned away from me and slammed his shoulder into the cement wall, howling in pain as he did. His shoulder popped back into its socket.

"I'm great," he groaned. "We have to hide her body. Vassago will never help us if he learns I murdered his twin."

"You just sent Procel back to Hell. Won't she tell Vassago what happened? He is going to know that you killed her."

"There are a lot of channels to pass through upon entering Hell. If we work quickly, we can summon Vassago before Procel has a chance to find him and tell him what happened."

"You said you weren't sure which order of angels Vassago belongs to. How are we going to summon him?" I could hear myself growing louder. "We forgot to ask Procel which choir he belongs to before things got out of hand."

"That was unavoidable. She gave me no alternative," he explained. "Don't come undone. We just have to play the guessing game until we get it right. We can narrow down our options based on the process of elimination. I know that Vassago is not an archangel or a cherub."

"What about a dominion or a power?" I inquired.

"No and definitely not. The powers keep entirely to themselves and are only ever available to Him. I've never even seen a power. None of them fell from Heaven during the rise against our Maker."

"What does that leave?" I hurried him.

"The principalities, but that wouldn't make sense. They are deep thinkers, incredibly formal and soft spoken creatures," he said. "Which leaves us with the virtues and the seraphims."

I exhaled the breath I was holding. "Okay. I am going to relight the candles and you can walk me through the summoning rituals for both orders of angel. I hope we have everything we need with us. Which do you want to start with?"

"The seraphim. They are far easier to summon."

After I finished with the candles, I helped Lial move Procel and Keylor's bodies backstage where we hid them among the forgotten instruments and set pieces. We kept the piano cover laid out to cover the bloodstains Keylor left behind, most of which had soaked into the floorboards.

The theater once again held an dreary silence. Since Lial and I had invited ourselves in, dark magic had been conjured and people had died. Now, with some of the dust settled, it was like nothing had happened at all.

"Tell me what to do," I said.

"You aren't going to like it."

"I wasn't expecting to."

Lial's smile was exuberant, and unlike any other I had seen. The last time I'd see him that happy was when he ate cake and steak. "Well, you have to sing."

19
Songs & Riddles

"What? No! No. No. No. No."

"You have to sing. That is how you summon a seraphim."

"No," My blood ran cold.

"When I told you that you would need to kill a man to summon Procel, you didn't put up this much of a fight. Now I am asking you to sing a song and you refuse."

He made a good point but the idea of singing in front of another person made me feel physically ill. Contemplating murder had been easier.

"What song should I sing?" I asked. "A church hymn?"

"No. It has to be a song that holds weight for you. It has to be personal. It has to be a song that touched your soul at some point. You should still be able to feel it there now."

I started to pace back and forth across the stage. "I don't know—"

"Sage, if Vassago is a seraphim and you don't sing, we can't summon him and you will never know where to find The Other Book. Is that what you want? Is that why you summoned me? Is that why you lied to Ned? Is that why two people are dead? So many sacrifices have been made. We're almost there. Now sing a damn song."

I looked down at my boots. The shoelaces were coming undone. I tried to clear my mind and think of some cheerful moments in my life. I searched for a song that would connect me with any one of them. It was difficult to remember happier days. It had been so long since I had one. I went blank trying to recall which songs Lena would play at the diner and the ones I sang in the shower. I couldn't remember what song was playing at the restaurant where Logan and I had dinner the night I spent in Boston.

Just when I thought I exhausted all my options, a steady, whimsical sort of song crept to the front of my mind. I took several deep breaths and turned away from Lial, knowing that I would blush if I looked at him. I revisited the Latin words I had used to summon Procel earlier.

"Rumpere silentium rerum angelorum quaeritur," I said the phrase slowly, to put off what came next.

"Sing," Lial said forcefully.

I inhaled and did what was required of me. I heard my voice, which was almost inaudible at first, rising with the hot air of my breath. The song was being pushed outward, reaching to the very last row of the theater. I wanted to stop but I knew that would mean starting over again, and I absolutely did not want that. I let the words fall from my lips, sending them to linger in the air around me. I could still feel them after they had gone.

> *The way you wear your hat;*
> *The way you sip your tea;*
> *The memory of all that.*
> *No, no, they can't take that away from me.*
>
> *The way your smile just beams;*

The way you sing off key;
The way you haunt my dreams.
No, no, they can't take that away from me.

We may never, never meet again
On the bumpy road to love.
Still I'll always, always keep the memory of

The way you hold your knife;
The way we danced 'til three;
The way you've changed my life.
No, no, they can't take that away from me.

When I started to sing the words out loud, I only heard Ned's voice whispering them to me one late afternoon while I shivered in bed. I could see the tattoo of a goldfinch on his right shoulder. I could feel him rub my back. It was as though Ned and I were in the guest room again, sharing a nap.

But then the lyrics took on a new meaning, something much more rough and tender, just like *him*. I was singing about his smile and the way he sang off key. How he'd changed my life... Lial. Lial. Lial.

Oh, no. Stop it, Sage Barnaby. Stop. I came to my senses.

When the song ended, I waited for the stage floor to shake beneath my feet. I waited for an eruption of light and a naked man to appear before me, but nothing happened. There was no magic present in the room, apart from the riot of butterflies that swarmed in my stomach when I glanced over at Lial.

He was watching me with curious eyes. His soft smile was not an insult or mockery; it was admiration. Suddenly, his grin widened, and his admiration was replaced with a touch of mischief.

Lial burst into applause. His outrageous cheering embarrassed me, and my cheeks grew hot from the unwanted attention. I wanted to look away but his stare captivated me. I assumed that his next move would be to make fun of me. I said something in an attempt to distract him.

"What now? Lial, the song didn't work."

"Sage," he moved towards me with the most serious look I'd ever seen painted on his immaculate face. "Sage, you have a beautiful voice."

I ignored his compliment. "Should we try the summoning ritual for a virtue? Tell me what to do. What is it? You're looking at me funny," I said.

"You're not going to like it," Lial warned. "I just remembered something."

I waited for an explanation, but he hesitated. I watched as he scratched his head and a childish grin played on his face.

"Lial, what is it?"

"You really aren't going to like it."

"I haven't liked much of what's happened in the past few days. Just tell me what you remembered."

"It's about Vassago," he started.

I blinked, dumbfounded, and my hands started to sweat. I suddenly knew exactly what his devilish smile and hesitation were for. "Vassago is a virtue, not a seraphim," I announced.

Lial nodded, containing his laughter. I hoped he would choke on it.

"You did not just remember that—You knew the whole time! You wanted to hear me sing. You tricked me!"

"I meant what I said. You have a beautiful voice," he was perfectly complacent while he defended himself. "You can hit me if it will make you feel better."

I was tempted. "Would it even hurt you?"

"I can pretend it does," he cracked another arrogant smile.

I let my clenched fist smash into his jaw and, as promised, he put on a show. Lial wailed in fake pain and stumbled backwards. His hand covered the point of impact while he complained about the soreness and total discomfort I had caused him. He was a terrible actor, but I appreciated the gesture.

"I do feel better," I said. "Now tell me how to summon a virtue and it better not involve more singing or blood."

"No, but we need to make a fire."

I found a metal trash bin, next to where we had hidden the bodies. I dragged it on stage and Lial proceeded to fill the garbage can with wood set pieces from past musicals and drama productions. I took the brief interval of peace as an opportunity to clear up a few things I was unsure about.

"Lial, I want to ask you something."

He looked at me with suspicion.

"I didn't know that angels could die. I knew you could bleed, but I didn't think you could die."I must have sounded ridiculous, but I ignored that. Logic didn't always play a part in supernatural matters.

"That's not a question," he noted. "No one really dies, Sage. Not angels and not humans or dogs or birds or fish or trees. Yes, we all have to leave our physical life behind us, but death doesn't mean what you think it does. Death is not permanent. It is a transition. The physical world that you and I are living in is not the reality. It's the dream. When we wake up from that dream, it's called death."

"It still scares me," I confessed.

"It scares me too."

I was amazed. The idea of an angel being afraid to die never occurred to me. "How? Why? You know what's going to happen. You've seen it."

"The more time we spend in the dream, the more we forget what's waiting for us when we wake up on the other side," he explained. "I've all ready started to forget what it's like where I come from and it's only been a few days. Imagine how little you can be certain of after a lifetime."

"I guess even angels have to rely on faith from time to time."

"Maybe we're not so different."

"Lial, if this is a dream then why does it matter? Why should we care about who lies or who gets hurt or who gets sick or who doesn't try their best?"

"Of course it matters," he sounded annoyed. "Life is a dream but why should that make it less meaningful? Some people live more in their dreams than they do in the waking world. Some people feel more and do more and are more while dreaming. Of course it matters, Sage."

"I don't understand."

"No. I don't think you can right now, but you will," he said. "We should get back to work."

Lial removed the matches from his jacket pocket and set fire to the materials in the metal bin.

"Now what?"

"More Latin," he cleared his throat. "Rumpere silentium rerum angelorum quaeritur. Vis ei mittas, nescio. Tecum munera probe respondeant. Vassago, quasi in ignem."

Lial was asking Vassago to send us a question. If we provided the correct answer then we would be rewarded with the angel's presence. After Lial spoke, the fire began to hiss and roar. It spit orange and red light into the air before suddenly bursting into a mammoth black cloud of smoke. I cowered at the explosion and waited for the air to clear. The smoke faded and a thin sheet of soot covered the stage floor. When I looked up, I saw the riddle Lial requested hanging in mid-air. The words were written in fire and burning bright before us.

If I appear too often, I no longer exist. Who am I?

Lial nudged me. "What do you think?"

"How should I know?" I kept my eyes on the question.

"You better hurry. We need to summon Vassago before Procel finds him."

"You keep reminding me."

I repeated the riddle silently to myself. Time was ticking, but my mind wasn't any closer to a decent answer. I was sure it was obvious. It seemed riddles were always obvious once you'd solved them. I decided to walk around the theater and hoped that inspiration would strike.

Lial sat on the stage and stared up at the words scribbled in flames. He mouthed the question to himself. He seemed just as baffled as I was. Twelve simple words had made idiots of us.

I stood by the stage door. I propped it open and watched the rain pour from the sky. Claps of thunder still rolled in and lightening flashed from several miles overhead. As I stared out into the empty parking lot, I could still see Raymond Keylor running across the pavement. A strange thought occurred to me. If Keylor hadn't run away, he would still be alive. I certainly wouldn't have been able to take his life.

It was incredible that the lightening bolt arrived on the Earth's surface at the exact moment Keylor was escaping. That unpredictable act had given me access to a sinner's blood without having to murder someone to acquire it. Furthermore, the madman who killed Lena was dead. It had worked out so well, like it was meant to be. Lial had said it was just—

I caught my breath. I solved the riddle. I was so ecstatic that I could barely form a sentence as I hurried back to the stage. I raced towards Lial, unable to stop myself, and tripped. I tumbled onto the floorboards beside him. I tried to settle down, drew in a slow breath and exhaled one word.

"Coincidence."

He raised a questioning eyebrow. "What?"

"The answer to the riddle," I said in a rush. "If I appear too often, I no longer exist. Who am I? Coincidence. If random luck or ironic circumstances happen over and over, you have to assume they might not be random at all. If coincidences occur too often, then it can't be coincidence; it has to be something else."

Lial looked at the words in fire and then back to me. He narrowed his arctic stare while contemplating my theory. After several seconds passed I watched the corners of his mouth lift. He smacked my forehead with an open palm.

"Good," he laughed. "Now say the word again, but in Latin this time."

"Coincidentia."

The riddle began to crackle and spark above us. Then, without warning the words erupted in a spectacular explosion. The blast threw Lial and I back several feet and we rolled off the stage. Our landings were ungraceful to say the least. I fell directly on top of him, our faces were no more than half an inch apart.

He looked up at me. His bitter stare seemed warmer than usual. The weight of my body pressed into him. I could feel each breath he took. I felt his heart beat against his chest and I knew he could feel mine. As the seconds passed, neither of us moved; we only took in one another through the black smoke that was settling around us. I had never noticed the precise shade of his blonde hair until then. The yellow was so faint that it wasn't yellow at all. It was just light.

I wish I knew what the angel saw when he looked at me. Was I as beautiful and rare in his eyes as he was in mine? I don't think that would've been possible.

A chill crept up my spine, and a wonderful numbing sensation followed. Lial's hand had found its way under my shirt and rested on the small of my back. I don't know how to explain the angel's touch, but it reminded me that I was alive, like fire and ice had come together and completely overwhelmed my nervous system.

"Are you okay, Sage?"

I nodded.

His jaw tightened. "You're bleeding."

Lial brought his free hand to my face and wiped away some blood from the corner of my mouth. His thumb moved across my lower lip. The numbing sensation was now pulsing through me. It spread to my fingers and toes. It was hot on my lips.

"Was that supposed to happen?" I said in an attempt to distract myself from Lial's hands. "The explosion— was that a part of the summoning ritual?"

"Let's check," he shrugged. "Hello? Vassago? Are you there?"

We immediately heard footsteps patter across the stage. I crawled off of Lial. Vassago appeared at the edge of the stage and looked down into the orchestra pit. His hair was darker than Procel's and his eyes were even darker still. He possessed the same rich olive skin as his sister, and he was the epitome of tall, dark and handsome. His name was written in the Echonian alphabet across his left collarbone.

"Belial? I did not expect you to be behind this," his voice was delicate. "Um, you wouldn't happen to have a pair of shorts or a towel, would you? I'm a bit underdressed at the moment."

The t-shirt and sweatpants I brought for Vassago were much too small. They hugged his body tightly. I could make out the curve of his ribs and the muscles in his calves. He didn't seem to mind that I had dressed him in ill-suited clothing. I think he was just excited to be back on the surface.

The angels embraced as old friends and shared a quiet laugh. They were pleased to be in one another's company. Lial introduced us but we were interrupted when Vassago heard the sound of rain falling against the theater's roof. He raced to the door and flung it open, stepping out into the storm. He threw back his head and allowed his clothes to soak through to his skin. He was smiling with an open mouth, catching the water as it fell from a gray sky. His dark eyes were wide with wonder and through the rain I heard him laughing. In that moment Vassago experienced bliss.

"I have been taken from the fire and given to the rain. I feel like a newborn. I am so happy I could cry! I think I am."

Vassago was smiling from ear to ear. He must have been miserable wherever we stole him from. He walked in from the storm and shook his head. Water splashed onto my face. I wiped it away with the sleeve of my shirt. The fallen angel paced the length of the theater while Lial and I stood off to the side and watched him adjust to living.

"I have missed walking," Vassago almost sang the words.

"You've been given good legs for it," Lial said. "You're taller than I am now."

"Ha! Look at that. I am taller than you," Vassago was delighted. "Now I know this visit is not entirely for pleasure. You must be the young lady who brought me here and I assume you have a reason for that. Seeing that you are already in the company of another fallen angel, my interest is raised further. Tell me how I can assist you in return for this gorgeous pair of legs?"

I had expected him to be cold and scheming like his twin, but Vassago was quickly proving to be the kinder of the two. Although, there was no denying that both siblings were equal in beauty. I started to wonder if there were any mediocre looking angels.

"I did summon you with a specific reason in mind," I confirmed.

"Don't be shy. Tell me what I can do for you so that I can leave this rotting theater and start living again. I want to go back out into the rain. I want to run through it!"

Vassago was beside himself with joy. He was experiencing the world again for the first time. It wasn't tarnished or disappointing, not yet. For now everything was astonishing, shiny and new.

"You are the angel who can discover lost and hidden things. You can tell us where to find The Other Book."

"Liber Alter, you mean?" he laughed. "That book is nothing more than an ancient rumor. It is smoke and mirrors, scattered whispers throughout history that lead to no end."

"We know it's real," Lial interjected. "You can't lie to us, Vassago."

The fallen angel was upset with Lial's tone. He yielded and brought his ebony eyes back to me. "My apologies. Yes, I know where you can find the book."

"Where?" I asked impatiently.

He narrowed his stare and spoke with smiling eyes. "Resting on a bed of satin and beneath green sheets, in the company of many, makes for the best sleep. Never to be awakened by the morning sun or a lover's kiss. Your face has been washed, the prayers have been said, climb the stairs and off to bed."

"What? Vassago, just tell us where the book is," Lial's voice boomed.

"I have."

My guardian stepped forward. "We summoned you by answering a riddle so that we would be given a simple, absolute answer to our question. We don't want more riddles. Tell us where the book is hidden, Vassago or I will send you back to the lake of fire!"

"I am sorry, Belial, but I cannot answer you directly."

Lial leapt onto the stage and grabbed the front of Vassago's t-shirt. "Well, you should be able to do better than useless rhymes."

I understood how frustrated Lial felt. So much had happened

since I dragged him to Earth. It was only natural that he wanted to avoid more obstacles, especially when we were so close to getting our hands on The Other Book.

Vassago shook his head apologetically. "If I could say more, I would. You have brought me back to life. I am happy to help you, but information does not come without a cost. The answer is obvious once it's realized. Resting on a bed of satin and beneath green sheets—"

"I heard you the first time!"

I could see the blood rising in Lial's cheeks. No one likes to be contradicted or talked down to but Lial despised it more than most. I watched him try to control his temper. He shoved his hands into his jean pockets, glanced over at me with perplexed eyes and shrugged, defeated.

"I'm not good with words, Sage. I'm good in a bar fight or in a war, but not with words."

"We figured out the last riddle. We can figure out this one," I assured him.

"You start thinking. I am going to stand over here and do something else."

Lial wasn't even making an effort to help solve the riddle. I turned around to have a quiet moment with my thoughts. I repeated the descriptive pieces of the riddle silently to myself. Satin, green sheets, in the company of many, face washed and prayers said. Who sleeps in the company of many? My mind began to wander. I knew that pride of lions sleep together or a herd of walruses, gorillas, wolves, a hive of bees, ladybugs, a colony of vampire bats... I turned back to Lial and Vassago. My brown eyes wide with realization.

"I know that look," Lial said excitedly.

"Vampires."

"Vampires?" he paused in confusion. "The answer is vampires?"

"No. The answer is not vampires," Vassago stated.

I positioned myself between the two angels and explained. "Where do vampires sleep?"

"Where the sun can't get to them." Lial sounded unsure.

"Yes, but more specifically they sleep inside coffins and underground. Vassago started the riddle with a bed of satin and beneath green sheets. Coffins are often lined with satin and the green sheets must be the grass growing over the burial site. He mentioned sleeping in the company of many. I think he is talking about a cemetery, a final resting place for the dead. Am I right, Vassago? Is The Other Book hidden in a cemetery?"

Vassago nodded. "Well done."

"Which cemetery?" Lial asked.

"You are one more riddle away from knowing."

"Another one?" Lial's voice tightened with aggression. "Fine, but when Sage guesses the correct answer, I am going to punch you in the face."

Vassago lowered his stare. "I really wish you wouldn't do that, Belial."

"Too bad. I don't like these words games but you insist on them. Therefore, I insist on some violence to even the playing field."

Vassago shot me a curious look. "Is he always like this?"

"Only when he feels inferior."

"Watch it, Blondie," my guardian warned but I couldn't take him seriously. He focused on Vassago again. "Recite your silly riddle."

"Very well, one last puzzle," the angel shifted his weight between feet." Predicted one thousand years beforehand and for one thousand years to come. One of eight standing in the dark, opposite the sun. When such a creature flies over a place of eternal sleep, you must find one man who has rested over a hundred years, but will never rest in peace. Uproot him from the Earth, tell the man why you are there, reveal one secret truth, open the box and handle with care."

"Sage, figure it out so I can hit him," Lial ran a hand through his soft waves of hair.

"It seems obvious," I started. "It has to be something we're able to predict, that is part of a series of eight and can fly."

Lial's pale eyes flickered towards me. "The moon."

"Yeah, a full moon. We can find The Other Book in a cemetery on a night when the moon is full. Then we have to find the grave of a man who has been dead over a hundred years but will never rest in peace. It has to be someone who committed a mortal sin and never asked for forgiveness."

Lial nodded in agreement. "When is the next full moon?"

"That's where the two of you are in luck," Vassago said, happy to deliver the good news. "There is going to be a full moon tomorrow night."

One more day and night of this ridiculous scavenger hunt and my soul might belong to me again. Since tomorrow was Wednesday, this could all be over before I had to be back in Bridgeview for Lena's burial on Thursday morning.

My thoughts were interrupted when Lial walked up to Vassago and slammed a closed fist across his face. Vassago collapsed to the floor immediately. My guardian let out a crazed laugh.

"Lial!" I scolded him.

"He did warn me," Vassago said in a groggy voice.

Lial extended a hand to the fallen angel and pulled him back to his feet. He patted Vassago affectionately on the back.

"Okay," Vassago clapped his hands together. "Now that I have done my part, you can stop hiding her from me."

Lial and I exchanged an apprehensive look.

"Who do you think we're hiding from you?" he asked.

Vassago showed off a broad smile. "Procel, of course, my dear sister."

"Vassago, she's not here—"

"I know that you summoned her. You called on me because you wanted to know where Liber Alter is hidden. You could not have been certain the book existed unless she told you first. I assume that you also asked her its purpose. Not to mention there is a pool of blood beneath that cloth center stage. You sacrificed someone to bring her here. I do not require blood."

"Vassago, your sister—" Lial started but Vassago spoke over him.

"Did she put you up to this? That wouldn't surprise me, and it wouldn't surprise me if you went along with it, Belial. You two were always a poisonous combination. I mean that as a compliment," he beamed. "So where is she? Procel!"

Vassago took off running, in and out of the aisles and peeking down into the pit of the orchestra. He even climbed the ladder up to the catwalk, which hung above the stage. I felt like there was a snake writhing in my stomach. I wanted to suggest to Lial that we should leave before Vassago discovered her body. Then I saw the look on my guardian's face and I couldn't bring myself to say anything.

Lial was wracked with guilt. I saw it taking hold of the lines in his face; an angel's face that usually resembled white marble was now tragically human. He was experiencing regret, remorse. I knew those emotions well, but to see a divine creature succumb to them was hard to watch.

Vassago disappeared into the stage wings and Lial bit his bottom lip. His eyes filled with a quiet panic. I couldn't comfort him, and he couldn't undo the suffering Vassago was only a few steps away from experiencing. All we could do was wait for the inevitable, and it came.

A horrible scream echoed through the theater and hung in the air. The keening continued, the sounds of mourning rose and fell like waves crashing onto the shore and being pulled back to sea. It was unbearable to listen to. Eventually Vassago emerged from the wings, his arms open, dragging his feet, snot and tears streaming down his beautiful face.

"Belial!" he roared and staggered towards us. "How could you—?"

"Vassago, I am sorry. Procel said she would murder Sage and use The Other Book as leverage for your pardons back into Heaven. I couldn't let her—"

"Why would you oppose her? That is what we have always wanted."

"I told you. She was going to kill Sage—"

"Belial, you have committed a crime against your own kind! Now I want nothing more than the human's death as revenge for your betrayal."

"Vassago, you know that I would end you before you could take three steps towards her. I am an archangel and you are a virtue. It would not be a fair fight," Lial's voice became dangerously low.

"Then I will wait and I will come back to avenge Procel when you least expect it. When you are your most vulnerable, I will come for the girl and there will be nothing you can do to save her," he cried.

"Vassago, do not threaten—"

"When you sent my sister back into the fires of Hell, you fixed that poor human's fate in stone. You have denied me the pleasure of walking the Earth at Procel's side. I can never forgive you for that. You have chosen that pathetic example of creation over your brothers and sisters! What the human has coming to her is your fault, Belial."

"I will not let you hurt her." Lial's eyes iced over.

"You won't be able to stop me," he announced and briskly exited through the side door.

My first impression of Vassago had been that he was a light-hearted, simple-minded creature. However, in those few minutes, he proved to be even more frightening than his sister. He looked back at me one last time. I saw nothing in his ebony eyes. There was no mercy or hesitation. There was no light. He was going to come back for me one day, maybe soon, and I hoped I would be able to defend myself. When that day came, Lial might not be acting as my guardian anymore. As soon as we returned The Other Book to its proper place, I had promised to release him. I meant to keep that promise. I would face Vassago's wrath on my own.

"Lial, are you sure we should let him get away?" I asked.

"I can let him go or I have to kill him," he hung his head. "I can't take another friend's life today. I don't have it in me. As much as I love a good fight, I can't do it again. Please don't ask me to."

Lial's pale eyes found mine. He looked down at me with parted lips. The sadness I saw in my guardian spilled over and filled me. Today had not been easy, and neither of us knew if it had been worth it. We would find out tomorrow, grave robbing under a full moon.

Lial and I stood beside one another and watched Vassago disappear into the mist. The falling rain would hide his tears as he continued to mourn the loss of his twin. I did feel bad for the fallen angel even though he had sworn to kill me. I knew what it was to live without the company of your sister, when she had barely gotten the chance to live at all. I knew how awful that could be, to live when she was gone.

20
Whiskey vs. Shirley

Lial and I spent the rest of Tuesday burying Keylor and Procel's bodies beneath the bleachers of the old football field. When I say that we buried the bodies, I mean that Lial dug the graves and pushed in the dirt while I supervised. I stood shivering beneath the metal bleachers in my rain-soaked clothes and drenched hair. The task ended up taking much longer than expected. Since it had been raining, the water soaked through the grass and into the dirt. Mud was almost impossible to dig through.

Afterwards we drove Sweetie to a local motel in Tarrytown. It was much nicer than our room in Baltimore. The curtains were red and the carpet was blue. The bedpost and other furniture pieces were a dark brown wood, maybe mahogany. I took a warm shower and changed in the bathroom, leaving my wet clothes to drip dry over the bathroom's tiled floor. Lial did the same.

We ordered in. Lial insisted on cake and steak, so we called up a diner from down the road and had food delivered. I asked for eggs benedict and one very large coffee. It had been about ten hours since my last cup; I was having caffeine withdrawals. The food wasn't as good as what the McGreevys served at 1976, but it was edible and we were hungry.

After we ate, I tucked myself beneath the covers. Lial was already snoring gently beside me. He hadn't bothered to crawl under the sheets. His day had been a challenge physically, but the angel was more than overrun emotionally. It didn't surprise me that Lial found sleep so quickly.

A few minutes passed before I tip-toed out of bed. A rush of spontaneous, child-like curiosity had come over me and I surrendered to it. Lial's left foot was hanging off the side of the bed. I crouched down and saw his name in the Echonian alphabet. It was printed onto the sole of his foot, just like he'd said. The black ink curved and stretched in thick lines. It was not as obvious as the names branded on Procel's and Vassago's bodies. I wondered if Lial was glad his dark mark was placed in an inconspicuous location. Since it was indisputable proof that he was a fallen angel, cast out of His kingdom forever. This mark branded him as the bad guy.

I must have been leaning too closely to Lial's foot and tickled his bare skin with my breath. Lial kicked out his leg, nearly making contact with my nose. I quickly scurried away and shoved myself back underneath the covers. I shut my eyes and was waiting to drift off when I felt a playful tug on my curls.

The next morning I woke up feeling weighed down. I rolled over to discover that Lial had draped his arm around me while we were sleeping. The nearness of him startled me, but not because it was unwanted. I felt a sense of harmony in his arms unlike anything I had known before, but it was a fantasy I had to let go of. I mean we weren't even the same species. Besides, there was no chance Lial felt anything remotely similar to the lightening storm of butterflies I experienced when I looked at him. Can angels even engage in romantic relationships? I was doubtful.

I crawled out from under his arm and raced to the bathroom. I realized that I hadn't seen Lial excuse himself to use the toilet once. Maybe angels don't have to. While I relieved myself, the doorknob turned, and Lial entered the small motel restroom. I was mortified. I could feel the color drain from my face and my bodily functions stopped abruptly. His presence during that private moment gave me instantaneous performance anxiety.

"Get out! I'm going to the bathroom!" I attempted to cover my delicate parts.

"Oh, come on. This is so human of you, Sage," he mused.

"I am human!"

"And I am your guardian angel. Nothing about you can ever be too personal. In a strange way, we're an extension of one another."

I don't know why, but I lashed out. I was probably just humiliated that Lial had caught me in such an exposed position. There's something about watching another person go to the bathroom that was beyond intimate, and that intimacy, that unfamiliar level of comfort, terrified me.

"That's not true, Lial. We've only spent a couple of days together. If I hadn't summoned you, you would have never known I existed. You never wanted to be my guardian. We're just a step above strangers. Now, I need to pee. Get out."

He appeared stunned, even hurt by my statement. He cleared his throat. "Oh yeah? Well, since you summoned me, how many times have I saved your life, stranger?"

He left the room and slammed the door shut behind him, giving me the privacy I asked for. I felt terrible. Lial had saved me more than once, first from the drunks in Baltimore and then from Keylor and Procel. He even defended me from Vassago's rage, not to mention that we were going to spend the night in a cemetery. There was no telling what sort of danger we might run into then.

Lial was not the cuddliest of creatures, but he had done his part this whole time. He kept me safe and was leading me closer and closer to my potential redemption. I couldn't believe that I said something so careless and cruel to him.

I came out of the bathroom dressed in black skinny jeans, combat boots and an old faded black t-shirt with holes in it. I had no intention of trying to tame the wild mane of curls around my face. Lial was wearing the same jeans and olive green leather jacket from the day before but he'd borrowed one of my oversized t-shirts. The more Lial wore that jacket, the more it seemed to become a part of him. His light hair was tussled and fell down on his forehead. When his eyes found mine, they turned a frosty shade of blue. He was upset with me. I could see it in the tightness of his jaw and his pursed lips. I wanted to take back what I said.

"Lial—"

"I'm hungry," he cut me off. I could hear the heat in his voice. I decided it was probably a good idea to let him cool off before I tired to apologize.

We drove Sweetie down the road to the diner we'd ordered food from the night before. The restaurant was quiet. There were only two other couples eating. We sat across from one another in a booth by the window. I wasn't very hungry, but I drank two cups of coffee and stole a piece of Lial's toast. He scowled at me when I did that. Only after he'd eaten his meal did Lial break the silence between us.

"What now?" he finished his orange juice and slammed down the glass. "Which cemetery are we going to? Whose grave should we vandalize?"

"I all ready figured that out," I boasted and placed my mug on the table.

He stared at me from across the booth with contempt. "What are you waiting for? I'm not going to congratulate you. If you hadn't summoned me, I would have never known you existed, right? What do I care? Get on with it, Blondie."

My stomach turned at the way he said my nickname, with such disdain. It sounded just like the way my mother used to say it.

"You know what, you don't even have to tell me," he continued. "I can follow you around until we find the book and then you can release me. That's all I really want. This whole thing has been more trouble than it's worth."

I smiled, in spite of his grouchiness. "I went online and traced back Raymond Keylor's bloodline. I figured that kind of demented evil couldn't be random. Something that consuming in a person must be genetic, passed down from generation to generation. Sometimes a person's sickness is just a matter of bad blood. I figured there had to be a distant relative of Keylor's just as twisted as he was."

I let my eyes rest on Lial's face a moment but he wouldn't look at me. He'd become a stoic, living statue again. I continued to explain while he stared out the window.

"Malcolm Webster Ford," I announced. "He was an athlete and disinherited by his family because he refused to stop competing and get a real job. Later in life he worked as a journalist and attempted to launch his own publications but failed every time. Malcolm asked his brother, Paul, for financial help but his brother denied him. On May 8, 1902 Malcolm went to Paul's home and shot him dead, then turned the gun on himself and took his own life."

Lial turned his gaze from the street scene to me. "What'd you say his name was? Malcolm something-something?"

"Webster Ford."

"How is he related to Keylor?"

"Ford is his great-great-great something— who cares? I found someone we can dig up and guess where he's buried?"

Lial raised his thick blonde eyebrows and waited for an answer.

"Sleepy Hollow Cemetery, which is just one town over from here."

"Well, that is convenient," he finally started to show genuine interest. "Sage, you said he died in 1902. That was over one hundred years ago. If Ford killed his brother and then himself, he committed two mortal sins."

"There's no way he's resting in peace," I agreed.

"Once the moon is out, we can go to the cemetery, find his grave and dig up the poor bastard."

Even though we had slept through half of the day, there was still plenty of time left before the full moon rose. It took us five minutes to drive from Tarrytown into Sleepy Hollow. We arrived with hours to spare and nothing to do. I suggested going to the cemetery and finding Ford's grave. That way we would know where to look once it got dark. Lial wasn't interested.

I think he had grown tired of me. He was sick of following me around and saving me when I got in trouble. I could tell by the way he looked at me, or more accurately, the way he refused to look at me. We needed some time apart otherwise we might kill each other before sunset. The problem was that if we separated too much, Lial would break out in open wounds and bleed all over himself.

Instead we walked in silence next to one another, wandering through the village of Sleepy Hollow. It was a quiet Wednesday afternoon and most people were still trapped behind their desks at work. There wasn't any traffic or much movement in general as we strayed up and down the streets. There were a couple of teenagers having a conversation on the sidewalk, enjoying summer break. But in my opinion, it was too humid to be outside. I would have been much more comfortable in an air-conditioned room. I could feel the sweat on the back of my neck, hot from being cloaked by my thick head of hair. It dawned on me that wearing all black was not the smartest choice on a clear summer day.

Lial and I were in front of the post office on Beekman Avenue when I noticed a bar directly across the street. The bar's name was printed in white letters across a green awning. I was struck with the urge to walk inside, take a seat and order a drink or two. I knew

I shouldn't. I knew that if I swallowed a drop of alcohol, it would mean that I had relapsed, but it was suddenly all I could think about.

It would also be nice to be around someone who could bring themselves to have a conversation with me. Since the bathroom incident, Lial had spent the day acting as though he didn't know me. A couple of days ago, I couldn't have cared less what he thought about me. Now he was shunning me and it was driving me mad. I stretched my gaze further along the street. Several doors down I noticed a hole in the wall convenience store and it gave me an idea.

"Hey, Lial."

He didn't answer. In fact, he started to walk faster.

"I know you're sick of me, okay? I have asked a lot of you in the last few days. Tracking down The Other Book has been a nightmare, and I think we need a break. I bet having a smoke would make you feel better. Do you see the bodega over there?" I handed him some cash. "Why don't you buy a pack of cigarettes and chain smoke them while I hang out in this bar and have a shirley temple?" I lied. "How does that sound?"

I saw his eyes light up with excitement and then narrow with suspicion. "Really?"

"Yeah, we won't be more than one hundred yards from each other, and I think we deserve to have some fun."

"If a shirley temple is your idea of fun, I'm worried about you. But there's no way I'm passing up a smoke."

We crossed over to the south side of the Beekman Avenue and I pulled open the door to the bar. "I'll wait for you here," I said.

"Whatever, Blondie."

He didn't bother to say goodbye before he walked off, moving towards the bodega on the street's corner.

I walked inside to find the modest looking bar practically

empty. I could hear the rumble of an air conditioner that pushed out a cool, merciful breeze.

I imagined that this bar was the kind of place adorned by the regulars who frequented it. On the left was a dining area, about ten tables with chairs, and to the right there was a bar that stretched from the front wall to the far back. A brass pole that ran horizontal over thick, dark wood panels separated them. There was only one other customer seated at the counter. The section for dining was vacant.

The man at the end of the bar was in his late fifties and surrounded by half a dozen beer bottles with red labels. He was wearing a worn letterman jacket and faded blue jeans with tan work boots. He smiled lazily at me as I walked in. By the time I sat at one of the bar stools, the man had started to doze off.

I took a seat to the left of the beer taps, towards the back wall of the bar. The bartender waited for me to get settled before walking over. He was in his early forties, with silver hair and eyes that were almost the same warm blue as Ned's. He wore a button down shirt with jeans and old sneakers. His gentle face and easy smile made me trust him immediately.

"Hello," he approached me. "We don't get a lot of new faces here, especially on a Wednesday afternoon."

I pushed the curls away from my face. "Hi."

"Is it safe to assume you're not from around here?"

"Yeah."

"So what can I get you?"

It was a simple question but I took my time answering. Did I really want to do this? Was I feeling that low? Would I regret it? Did I even care? After all the blood and death I had been around, I just wanted to forget.

"Do you need a minute to think it over?" the bartender asked, bringing me out of my thoughts. "I can bring you a menu."

"No. I'm going to have a glass of red wine—"

"You got it." He started to walk off.

"I wasn't done."

"Oh, sorry about that," he turned back around.

"The red wine, a rum and coke, a beer and one shot of whiskey."

"Are you meeting a group of friends here or something?"

"No."

"What is it then?" he asked. "Can't decide what you're in the mood for so you order one of everything?"

"I'm thirsty."

"I don't know anyone that thirsty," he teased. The bartender smiled at his own joke and stepped away from the counter.

After two years without drugs or alcohol, I thought this would be a more difficult decision, but it was easy. In that moment, nothing seemed more important than the wine or the rum or the beer or the whiskey. There was nothing in my world apart from the bartender serving me a drink and the warm feeling that flooded through me when it slid down my throat. I wondered which beverage I would taste first.

My conscience took hold of me then. Would I actually be able to take a sip once the bartender set a drink down in front of me? It was almost the moment of truth. He returned with my order and placed the drinks in a line, from the tallest glass down to the smallest. I let my eyes pass from one drink to the next and I could already taste them. Their sweet pungent smell made my mouth water.

"I thought you said you were thirsty."

I glared up at the bartender, irritated by his comment. He seemed to understand my stare perfectly.

I finally made a poor attempt to engage in conversation, taking the focus away from me. I sighed. I never cared for small talk and I could tell that the bartender excelled in it. "Um, it's been hot out."

People were always talking about the weather, right? That was normal, wasn't it?

"Yeah. Well, it is summer," he laughed.

Right, I thought. Duh. Summer. Hot. I felt stupid.

"What's your name?" he asked.

"Sage."

"Nice to meet you, Sage. Can I ask why that other guy called you Blondie?"

"Oh, that's just a dumb nickname."

"Huh." He watched at me with unsure eyes. "I just thought it was strange, because you're not—"

"I know," I said before he could finish. "I know."

The bartender did something unexpected then, and it caught me off guard. He reached across the counter and took one curl of my dark hair in his fingers. He trifled with it for a moment then casually walked away to serve the regular at the other end of the bar another red labeled beer.

It was an intimate gesture, something that should not have been shared with an unfamiliar person. That being said, nothing about his touch seemed unfamiliar. Maybe it was because he had kind eyes like Ned or maybe there was something more to the immediate informality between us. But it made me feel vulnerable and unsure. I brought my attention back to the temptations within arm's reach. The inexplicable contact with the bartender made me want to consume all four drinks even more.

He crossed back over to me. "Which is it going to be?"

"The beer— No. The whiskey. I don't know yet."

"Let me guess, you're having a bad day."

"I could handle one bad day but… I'm just tired of being scared all the time. Does that make sense?"

The bartender shook his head, disappointed. "Listen, at your age everyday should be Saturday. You are too young to look so sad."

"You think I look sad?"

His easy smile faded for a moment. "Sage, maybe you're not as thirsty as you thought you were," he offered in a gentle voice.

I gave him another hard stare; my brown eyes burned into him. Once again the silver-haired man changed the subject.

"So where are you from?"

"Bridgeview City," I said.

"Oh, yeah? I go there from time to time. In fact, there is a great little diner on the corner of Rice and Louis. It's called 1976. Do you know it?"

I was ecstatic and devastated all at once. Hearing someone mention 1976 made me choke up. I tried to bury all thoughts of Lena and Ned. I wasn't crazy about the idea of crying in front of a perfect stranger.

"Yeah. I know it," I answered casually.

"There's a couple that owns that diner. The Mc— somethings. I can't remember their name but the Mrs.… She burnt my bacon to perfection. I like my bacon burnt. Yeah, that's a great place. Is it still there? I haven't been to Bridgeview City in a while."

I could hardly believe I was having this conversation. "It's undergoing some renovations, but yes, 1976 is still there. The owners are Ned and Lena McGreevy."

"McGreevy!" he slammed the counter with an open palm. "That's their name! I hope you let me know when it's up and running again."

"Sure," I said reluctantly.

The bartender's compliments of 1976 were a heart-warming surprise. I welcomed his compassion. I could suddenly think of nothing apart from the diner, Ned and Lena. For the moment my desire to drink evaporated thanks to the kindness of this man.

The best part was that the bartender didn't know how much

good he had done. I wanted to say something, but I could tell that my words would be wasted on him. A man like that never does nice things to receive praise or be appreciated. He does them because it feels right, nothing more and nothing less. This man was one of those rare individuals.

My newfound restraint didn't last very long. Half a minute later, another wave of sorrow overwhelmed me. 1976 would never be the same. Most of it had been burnt to ash. Lena would never fry another plate of bacon for the bartender or Jack or anyone else. Ned would be changed forever. I thought things couldn't get any worse after Nola died, but since then my life had been nothing but one long struggle.

The Other Book might not even be accepted as redemption for my mortal sin. I had no guarantee of that. I deserved Hell. I made a selfish choice and brought this fate on myself. So what was one more drink or another sixty years of drinking?

"Sage," the bartender said my name in a hushed, polite voice.

I heard him take a deep breath. "I don't know what you're going through, but you are not going to feel any better once you finish that drink, or the others. I think you all ready know that."

"I don't want to feel better. I don't want to feel anything."

I watched the corners of his mouth turn down and it dawned on me how attractive this man was. He had such an inviting smile, but he was irresistible when he frowned. I could see that the bartender was genuinely troubled on my behalf. "I'm sorry, Sage. I am, but I have to cut you off."

I lifted my chin and let my brown eyes settle on his face. He stared back, preparing himself for how I would respond. He probably expected me to cry or scream or throw a glass at his head.

"Thank you," I said.

"Don't mention it."

I watched him shrug his shoulders like it was nothing at all—

like he hadn't just saved me from the only thing worse than demons or monsters or Hell. He saved me from myself.

"I'll pay for the drinks you poured, but could you take them away?"

"Your drinks are on the house," he cleared the glasses from the counter. "Can I get you anything else?"

"Yeah, a shirley temple, please."

"Coming right up."

I spent the next half hour splitting my attention between a sweet pink soda and the bartender's cheerful conversation. My visit to the bar had become a very successful break from the scavenger hunt. I left there feeling refreshed and what I think might have been happy. It was hard to say because it had been a while since I'd experienced happiness.

I did harbor some guilt over feeling that way. I'd caused so many people so much pain, from my parents to Ned to Logan and Lial. It didn't seem fair that I should be happy, even for a moment. Still, I held on to the light feeling rather than repressing it. I knew better than most that life was tragic and unfair and really, really hard but that afternoon, between maraschino cherries and small talk, it wasn't so bad.

I left a ridiculously large tip on the counter and threw the bartender one last look over my shoulder. He waved and gave me the same infectious smile he'd greeted me with. It felt like the most natural thing in the world to smile back.

21
Tibet

That night Lial parked Sweetie across the street from the cemetery. He grabbed a shovel from the trunk before we crossed the road and walked through an opening in the stonewall that surrounded the Old Dutch Church. It was well past visiting hours and we were trespassing on this historic piece of New York. The smell of rain was still fresh from yesterday's storm.

We moved through the Old Dutch Church Cemetery and passed into the Sleepy Hollow Cemetery, which had been started by Washington Irving and named after the fictional town in perhaps his most famous haunted tale. The graveyard was the resting place for a handful of popular historical figures, including Andrew Carnegie, John Archbold and William Rockefeller.

There were walking paths that rolled up and down the graveyard between stretches of grass. We moved past worn statues of angels, mausoleums, vine-covered vaults built into hillsides, towering markers, hundreds of names and even some blank headstones. Their colors ranged from bronze, white, green with age or one of a dozen different shades of gray. The sky was clear of clouds and thousands of stars joined the full moon. I heard the rustle of leaves rise and fall with each warm gust of wind.

Lial walked several yards ahead of me. My short stature was no match for his long legs and wide strides. "Do you know where this Ford person is buried or are we wandering around aimlessly in the dark?" he asked.

"Um…"

"Sage, am I even headed in the right direction?"

"Have we been walking north?"

"No." He stopped in his tracks. A grim look took over his angelic face. "We've been going east."

"Then we need to change direction." I turned away from him as quickly as possible. I was afraid to see the disappointment on Lial's face once he realized I was directionally impaired.

"You know, this wouldn't have been a problem if we came here and found Ford's grave during the day like I suggested. Then we would know where we were going," I called back to him, refusing to take all the blame. "Sleepy Hollow Cemetery is ten acres. We could be here all night."

"We know Ford's grave is in section 65," he said. "That's what the website said."

"Yeah, which is on a hill somewhere close to the Bronze Lady statue, and the Rockefeller's mausoleum."

"Okay, so we have to find higher ground."

We quickened our pace as we moved toward the northern central area of the cemetery. The night seemed to grow thicker as we carried our feet along the paved path. Lial claimed he had no problem seeing in the dark but he pulled a small flashlight from his pocket and handed it to me, since my human eyes were "inferior," as he put it. We followed the road as it began to incline. The stars overhead seemed to draw nearer to us. I was panting when we reached the top of a hill but grateful to discover that we'd stumbled upon William Rockefeller's giant resting place.

I took a minute to study the religious symbolism etched into the graves surrounding us and bask in the stillness that a night among the dead provided. I set my attention a few yards ahead of where I stood and a small gasp escaped me when my eyes settled on the larger than life image of a seated woman.

I pointed in her direction. "That's the Bronze Lady, which means that Ford has to be somewhere nearby."

"Wait. Did you say that's supposed to be a lady?" Lial asked as he squinted against the night. "Whoa! Check out her hands. They're huge!"

He walked ahead, to get a better look at the unusual statue.

I wasn't concerned with her hands. I was solely focused on locating Malcolm Webster Ford. I pushed forward on the path. I moved past a tall gray column and a lesser mausoleum with a crescent moon inscribed over the entrance, which stood beside an enormous, somewhat misplaced boulder. Gradually, I felt my breaths grow shallow and then my vision blurred. There was an emergent pressure pressing down on me and soon every step became an incredible challenge. In a few short moments I collapsed onto the damp grass in front of the gigantic boulder.

"Sage, you have to take a look at her hands," Lial shouted back at me without realizing I'd fallen. "They are massive! Are you sure this is supposed to be a lady?"

"Lial," I wheezed and reached out for him. "Something's wrong."

In a flash Lial abandoned the Bronze Lady and rushed to my side. "What is it? Sage, tell me what happened!" he threw down the shovel he'd been carrying and shook me.

"I don't know," I pushed the words out of me. "It hurts. I can't breath."

He looked around frantically for the source of my problem. I could only lock my eyes onto his and silently beg that he save my life one more time. Lial stared back, but I soon realized that he wasn't looking at me. He was glancing over my left shoulder. I had no idea what had captured my guardian's attention.

"Sage," he said my name in a panicked whisper. "Did you bring any salt with you?"

"In my pocket—" but I couldn't say another word. I felt my throat being constricted. I forced myself to remain still while Lial fished through each of my pockets.

"Stay with me— stay awake," he demanded and shoved his hand into my jean pocket where I kept a small plastic bag filled with salt.

Lial untied the plastic and flung its contents directly into my face. I shut my eyes and winced as the soft pellets made contact with my skin. However, the moment the salt flew from Lial's hand, I found myself able to breath again. I took in a mouthful of air, coughing violently as oxygen rushed into my starved lungs.

When I opened my eyes, I could see that Lial's attention was still focused somewhere behind me. I looked over my shoulder and stifled a scream. There was a deranged, almost sad looking man standing over me. He appeared to be around forty, and the skin on his face resembled leather. He stared down at me with hateful eyes, which were dull and sunken in. It was clear that this man wanted to hurt me. Then, very unexpectedly, the brooding figure spoke.

"The first time the gun went off it was an accident. The second time, I meant it," his voice shook. I had never seen a ghost cry before, but this one did.

I suddenly realized who was speaking to me. It was Malcolm Webster Ford, the ghost of the man whose grave we were searching for. I felt compelled to speak to the tragic creature, probably because he appeared so shattered. (However, I should forewarn that speaking to ghosts is a big no-no. It only empowers them, and just like Ford, most ghosts are not friendly.)

"Are you talking about what happened between you and your

brother? Are you talking about Paul?" I asked.

"Don't say his name!" Ford roared at me, losing every hint of sadness and replacing it with an immeasurable surge of anger.

"You said that the first shot was an accident." The figurative light bulb clicked on over my head. "You never meant to shoot Paul, did you?"

The ghost's image was pulsing with rage. "Don't ever say his name!"

The man lunged towards me. I covered my face in a vain attempt to defend myself. Thankfully, Lial doused the ghost with another blast of salt. This time the image of the man froze, flickered erratically and disappeared altogether. He left nothing in his wake.

Lial grabbed my hand and helped me to my feet. The crippling, breathlessness was gone, but I was still shaken from the encounter with Ford's ghost. Thankfully, the salt had served its purpose. The malevolent spirit had left us and was unlikely to return. I suddenly realized that Lial was still holding my hand. I pulled away from him and played with my hair.

"Are you okay?"

"Never better."

He responded with a modest nod. "That was your friend, Malcolm Webster Ford. He just tried to strangle you to death."

I was disturbed by his nonchalant attitude towards my most recent near death experience. Lial stood in front of me with a broad grin plastered on his astonishing face. "Yeah. But I don't think that's something to smile about."

"There's a reason he attacked you, Sage. Look at where we're standing."

I cast my eyes down and immediately understood Lial's out of place smile. On the large, misshapen boulder were four letters, engraved on an upward slant. F-O-R-D. I circled the rock, and found a number of small rectangular plaques named for the Ford

family members buried in that spot. On the far left was Malcolm
Webster Ford's copper plague, which was a weathered sea green
color now. It was dated 1862-1902.

"We found him," I announced. "A man who has rested over a
hundred years but will never rest in peace."

"I think something is down there that Ford doesn't want you to
get your hands on."

I stared down at the Earth a few feet below me. The cold grass
felt spongy beneath my boots. "We should start digging," I said.

It was a tough dig. The ground refused to cooperate. It took
us almost three hours before we struck the top of Malcolm's coffin,
not to mention a handful of his relatives. I dropped my shovel and
knelt down to get a closer look. His coffin was a common looking
and cheap, made of wood.

I gripped the edges of the coffin's lid and tried to pry it open
but nothing happened. I tried again to no avail. I heard Lial snicker
over my shoulder. I turned and glared up at him.

"Move over. You're only human."

"What does that mean?" I huffed.

"You have trouble opening pickle jars. Let me take care of
this," he laughed.

I moved back and gave the angel some space. He reached
down and pulled at the coffin's lid until his knuckles turned white.
He tried again but it remained stuck. Then Lial lifted his leg and
crashed the heel of his boot down onto the wood. The coffin's lid
didn't even crack. It appeared to be indestructible.

He gave up. "We must have forgotten something. What else
did Vassago say about the grave? What comes next?"

I had memorized the riddle when Vassago recited it. "He said
to uproot a man from the Earth, tell him why you are there, reveal
one secret truth, open the box and handle with care. That was it."

"Then start talking, Sage. Go on, tell Ford why we dug up his grave."

I brought my eyes to the wooden box in the ground. "Okay," I said feeling awkward. "Hi, Malcolm. We met a couple of hours ago. You tried to strangle me. Um, you've been stuck in purgatory for over a hundred years. I bet that can be frustrating. I understand why you—"

"What the Hell are you doing?" Lial interrupted.

"Having a conversation. You told me to talk to him."

"He's dead, Sage. You're conversation is going to be a little one sided, don't you think? Just tell him why we're here so we can get on with it."

"Give me a minute!"

"We have to be back at Ned's before sunrise, remember?"

I faced Malcolm's coffin and took a breath. I collected my thoughts. "I'm sorry about bringing along the fallen angel. Listen Malcolm, we're here because I made a deal with the Devil. I sold my soul and I want it back. I would be fine with spending my afterlife in Hell if he'd kept his end of the bargain, but he cheated me. I just thought you should know that. I was told that I could find The Other Book inside your coffin tonight. I want to trade it for my soul. I am asking you to let me in. Please."

"That part is over," Lial stated. "Now tell him a secret."

"I don't want to," my voice dropped into a shy whisper.

"That's not a choice you get to make. Come on, do you always have to argue with me? Just tell the dead guy a secret."

"Fine, but after I share my secret, I don't want to talk about it. I don't want your thoughts or opinions or bad jokes," I instructed.

"Okay."

I braced myself. I hated to even think what I was about to say out loud.

"I was fourteen. It was the night after Ned told me that my parents wanted me out of their lives. I downplayed how hurt I was.

I tried to act like I cared more about the money my parents were giving me than the fact that I'd been disowned.

"That night I snuck out of their house and took a bus to Tarrytown. I walked from the bus stop to the house on Union Avenue where I grew up. It was a pink house. My mother called the color sand. I think she was embarrassed that it was actually very pink.

"I planned to storm up the front steps and knock on the door. When they answered, I would cause a scene, wake the neighbors, refuse their money and curse them for pushing me off on someone else. They were my parents. They should have wanted to keep me close. It should have been their instinct.

"I was about to step over the curb and onto the front yard when I saw a light on in the dining room window. I could see my mom and dad inside, and they were laughing. I hadn't seen them smile, yet alone laugh, in such a long time. Since Nola died they'd been inconsolable, completely gutted, and now they were laughing, without me.

"At first all I could think was how dare they— I was their daughter too. They couldn't stand to lose Nola, but they wanted nothing to do with me. I hated them for it. I did more to save her than they would ever know. I was just as heartbroken when we lost her. I guess they would rather be childless than have me as a daughter.

"I kept staring through the window, watching them laugh. I watched my father reach across the table and hold my mother's hand. They looked happy, and I realized I could never do anything to hurt them. Not when I had seen firsthand how much they had suffered. I could hate them from afar, but I wouldn't ruin this moment for them.

"I walked back down Union Avenue towards the bus stop knowing that I might never see my mother and father again. That was okay. They had each other and I had the McGreevys. I went back to Bridgeview and haven't been to Tarrytown since, until yesterday.

"How was that Malcolm?" I asked like I was expecting an answer. "Will you keep my secret? Well, of course you will, you're dead. What do you think? Can I look inside your coffin now?"

I grabbed the edges of the lid and pulled, but it still wouldn't budge. I tried to push the lid off but still nothing happened. What more did this ghost want from me? My patience had given out.

"I did everything I was supposed to, now open up!" I kicked the wooden box with the toe of my boot. "I don't know what else to do. Was my secret not good enough for you, Malcolm? I gave you something no else knew! It was personal, embarrassing— Open up!"

"Sage, calm down—" Lial stepped forward, sounding concerned.

"No!" I yelled, and became more out of control, kicking the coffin repeatedly. "This has to work, Lial! The Other Book is in that coffin right now. I know it! We are so close. It can't end here, in this stinking grave! This has to work! Open! Open Sesame! Abracadabra!"

"Sage, you're being ridiculous. Stop."

I ignored him and kept screaming like a mad-woman at the coffin's closed lid. "Veni, vidi, vici! Carpe diem! Et tu, Brute?"

Lial stepped forward and rolled his pale eyes. "Now you're just shouting random Latin phrases! Get a hold of yourself!"

I couldn't. I'd come apart at the seams. The angel pulled me into his arms. I struggled to free myself, but he was too strong. I was forced to settle down. His open palm rubbed up and down my back, and he whispered into my dark curls.

"Sage, you are not the only one looking for this book. I'm here too. The coffin won't open unless I confess something as well," he released me.

"Oh," I blushed, flustered. "Why didn't you say that before?"

Lial stood over Ford's coffin. He scowled at it, resenting the idea that it would not open unless he shared something he would rather not. I thought he was a little hypocritical in that sense. Lial expected me to sing, to tell my secrets, to pee in front of him, basically be totally out of my comfort zone, but he wanted to remain distant and mysterious. Well, not this time. I waited for him to speak, curious to learn what an angel's dark secret might be.

"Tibet," he sighed.

I waited for more but he said nothing, just the one word. Tibet.

"What?" my forehead wrinkled. "Tibet? Is that your secret?"

"Yes," he answered somberly. "The Potala Palace, home to the Dali Llama."

"I know what it is. I was there a couple of years ago."

"Sage—" Lial paused, and gathered the courage to continue. "The picture in Ned's house, the picture of you he keeps on the mantelpiece, you weren't standing in front of the coliseum in Rome," he explained. "You were standing in front of the Potala Palace... in Tibet."

My mind reeled as I frantically tried to piece together the puzzle scattered before me. I lost my ability to speak. Lial was right. That picture had been taken in Tibet, and not Rome. I couldn't believe what he was admitting to.

"The night we stayed in Baltimore, you asked how I knew about your trip to Rome," he proceeded. "You accused me of keeping an eye on you. That it would explain how I knew you had been to Italy. I said I saw the picture of you in front of the coliseum. I told you I never checked in on you. I lied. I'm sorry."

"You knew I had been to Rome without ever seeing a picture of me there."

He gave me a diffident nod.

"You were keeping an eye on me," I said and my heart skipped a beat.

Lial was confessing to being my guardian angel. I could have sworn I felt the world shifting beneath my feet.

Lial quietly composed his thoughts. "The little girl who shook hands with the Devil. It's a popular story where I come from. Some time after word about your deal spread through the circles of Hell, a demon learned the girl's name. It was yours. Sage Barnaby. The moment I heard that name I knew you were the human who was supposed to be in my care. I was meant to be your guardian. I could feel you. It was like you were a part of me. You always had been. I can't explain it beyond that.

"I started to ask myself if you would've made that deal had I been around. I wondered if the Devil would have cheated you if I were acting as your guardian. The truth is I started to feel guilty about abandoning you, so I asked my friends in low places for a favor whenever they ventured to Earth. I asked them to see where you were and what you were doing. I wanted to know as much as I could about you.

"It wasn't long before demons would fall through the channels of Hell, and you were the one who sent them back. You became infamous among the damned. They called you Belial's girl. When someone said that, it always made me feel worthless. I was proud of you, but I couldn't take any credit for the way you turned out."

"Proud?"

"Yeah," he said as if there were no other answer. "Sage, you've give everything you have. I mean you struggle, but you never give up. You demonstrate that hope is more powerful than fear. You're the reason He loves humans more than the angels."

Lial's secret was almost too much to bear. I went into a quiet shock. My mind, my heart— it was all fireworks. I was beside myself. I fought back a smile, wanting to remain humble in the glow of his compliments.

Lial knelt beside Ford's coffin and slid off the lid in one fluid motion. Our secrets had been accepted as payment for entry into his resting place.

I spent the past ten years of my life waiting for an opportunity such as this. I was within an arm's reach of a second chance. I could live and die without being afraid of what came afterwards.

Inside the coffin was Malcolm's skeleton. It was discolored and brittle. I moved my eyes downward from the skull to the shoulders and ribs and finally his hands. The gray bones of Malcolm's hands clutched the small sacred object. We had found Liber Alter. It was a pocket-sized book that could easily be lost or overlooked. It had a bright red leather cover and in delicate gold lettering were the words *Tractandum Cum Cura*, which translated to "Handle With Care."

It was just as Vassago said, open the box and handle with care.

I took the book from the dead man's hands and stared down at the cover. I let my fingers trace along the book's edges and toyed with the idea of opening it. I wondered what truth it would reveal to me. I wondered whether or not that truth would split open my world. My curiosity was burning. I brought my fingertips beneath the book's cover and lifted it less than a centimeter.

"No!" Lial threw his hand down. "Don't do that."

"Why not?" I asked. "Procel said the book would show whoever read from it something they didn't know, something that could change everything."

"Exactly. Sage, you wanted to find the book so that you could return it; and if you return it, there's a good chance your soul will belong to you again. Who cares what the book would show you? We are here for your soul and your soul alone."

He was right. Lial and I had been through so much in the search for my redemption. I needed to keep things in perspective.

My soul was more important than any secret truth I might uncover. My curiosity would have to remain unsatisfied.

"Okay. We should go." I shoved The Other Book into my jean pocket.

"Where are we going?"

"Laveau said he would help us send the book back. We need to head over to Bridgeview, to the café."

Lial was about to climb out of the grave when he stopped and looked at me. I watched as his eyes pierce through the darkness, while mine became a part of it.

"Congratulations," he said.

"We'll be done with each other soon." I ruined the moment, because otherwise I would have melted under his stare. "After tonight, I should be able to release you from your responsibilities as my guardian."

"Right." He answered coolly. "Good."

Lial pulled himself out of Ford's grave and then reached down to give me a lift. It took no effort on his part, and while I'm not a particularly large person, I am also not a size two, four or six for that matter.

Lial and I started to make our way back down the path. Several minutes had past when I could make out the walkway that would lead us out of Sleepy Hollow Cemetery. As I glanced over to tell Lial I noticed his face change. I watched as a bolt of panic jumped into his normally confident eyes. He frowned and stopped in his tracks. Something had set Lial on edge. He reached out and grabbed my arm, forcing me to stop at his side.

"I need you to stay behind me, and when I tell you to run, run," his voice was very low, less than a whisper.

"Okay."

I could tell by the tension his voice that this was not a good time to question him. I looked ahead and suddenly realized why

Lial was acting so strangely. There were three shadowy figures advancing in our direction. Two of the men were a few inches shorter than Lial, but nevertheless threatening. The third man had about three or four inches on my guardian. Even with Lial standing beside me, I couldn't help feeling intimidated by these ominous strangers.

"Do you recognize these men?" he asked.

"No."

The three figures drew nearer and were no longer cloaked in the darkness of night. I could make out the details of each face. They had dark skin and dark eyes. I could see their muscles outlined beneath their clothing. I stayed close to Lial, my hand gripped the back of his jacket. The men gradually slowed to a stop about ten yards from us.

The tallest spoke first. "We have come to take something from you, and you will not keep it from us," he demanded.

"What do you call yourselves?" my guardian shouted.

"These are my brothers Hypnos and Thanatos. I am Nyx," he bowed his head.

"You are not human," Lial announced, much to my surprise.

"We are mostly human, unfortunately, but not entirely," Nyx broke into a wide smile. "However, I believe you would find a fight against my brothers and I to end rather quickly, angel."

"I'm afraid you're right," Lial said. "If you had more brothers, this would almost be a fair fight. As it stands now, I would win in no time."

Nyx laughed pompously. "We might have the chance to test your theory tonight. That being said, for all parties involved, it would be better if you simply handed Liber Alter over to us."

The brother, who Nyx had referred to as Hypnos, stepped forward. He was thinner than the other two and possessed a crafty, serpent-like resemblance. "This encounter can only end one way, ours. Do as my brother has told you. Give us the book."

"We don't have the book," I said. "We spent most of the night looking, but it never turned up."

"You must be Sage Barnaby, or should we call you the little girl who shook hands with the Devil?" Nyx replied with a touch of delight.

"I wish we had found it, believe me. I was counting on The Other Book to save my soul, but we don't have it."

"You are lying to us. My brothers and I have been trailing you and the angel for days. We know all of the filthy deeds you've committed. We know how many coffees you've had, and where you buried the bodies. We know that you have the book. I advise you to give it to us, so that we are not made to take it from you. Like my brother Hypnos said, this only ends our way."

"Who sent you here?" Lial asked.

"I have had enough conversation," the third brother, Thanatos, called out in a disgruntled voice. "We are wasting time and I am bored."

I found Thanatos to be the most frightening of the brothers, who'd been completely silent until that moment.

He was the stockiest of the trio. His hands hung heavy at his sides. If he were to make a fist, I was fairly confident that Thanatos could punch through concrete.

"You heard my brother," Nyx said. "Last chance before this situation becomes especially unpleasant for you."

Nyx, Hypnos and Thanatos started to march slowly and inevitably towards us. I wondered how confident Lial actually was about his odds in a fight against them. After all, Nyx said they weren't entirely human, whatever that meant. Lial placed a firm hand on my shoulder.

"Do you remember what I said to you?" His grip tightened.

"But I could help you fight."

"No. I told you that when I say run, you run."

"You know what will happen if I run too far—"

"Don't start worrying about me now. You have done such a beautiful job of not caring up until this point," he mocked me; a smile teased at the corner of his mouth. "When I say run—"

I shook my head furiously. "Lial—"

"I will catch up with you." His speckled blue eyes held my stare.

I looked back to the brothers who would be upon us in another ten seconds. I let out a long sigh and could feel the adrenaline bubbling inside me. It coursed through my veins and pulsed through my limbs. Normally in a fight or flight situation, I would never pass up the opportunity to fight, but Lial had made his wishes clear. I stared at the men moving towards us and realized that I would have to run more quickly than ever before. They were nearly a foot taller than me, with much longer legs than my own. If I didn't get a decent head start, it wouldn't be much of a chase.

I was suddenly overcome with a crippling dose of fear and guilt. I was afraid of not being with Lial. I felt safe with him. I knew that if I ran, he would be at the mercy of Nyx, Hypnos and Thanatos. Plus, he would break out in more and more spontaneous open wounds the farther I separated myself from him.

"Run," he told me in a calm voice but I couldn't move. "Run!"

"I can't. I'm sorry. I can't."

"You are impossible, Sage!" He gave me a hard shove and I stumbled back. "I am trying to look out for you, but you are making it very difficult! You had one job to do. When I said run, you were supposed to take off! I could not have given you an easier instruction to follow, just one word, run. I should have known you wouldn't listen. Do you have to make saving your life such a chore? I mean, come on! Sage, you are the most—"

"Watch out!" I shouted, as Thanatos was about to bring a

closed fist across the back of Lial's head.

Lial avoided the blow and managed to make contact with his attacker first. Thanatos fell back and was momentarily stalled but nowhere near being defeated. Hypnos was the next brother to start swinging at Lial while Thanatos climbed to his feet. Nyx didn't seem too concerned with the angel. In fact, he didn't seem to notice the fighting at all. The tallest brother appeared to be much more interested in me. I took several steps back as he closed in.

"I'm going to start running now!" I called to Lial.

"Run? Are you sure? That's a great idea. I wish I thought of it," he blocked another attack from Thanatos. "Oh, wait. I did!" he growled before Hypnos landed a fierce kick into Lial's ribcage. I saw the angel fly backwards and crash into a tombstone, which in turn cracked down the center. I waited an extra second, just to be sure that Lial found his feet again, then I ran.

As soon as I dashed away, I heard Nyx hurry after me. The heavy sound of his feet slamming into the Earth was daunting, and I pushed harder and harder to keep ahead of him. I could feel the small book in my pocket, pressed against my thigh, the seemingly everyday object that had brought chaos into the quaint old cemetery.

I hurdled over tombstones, weaved in and out of graves, up one hill and down another. Suddenly the sound of running water came to me, and I remembered a small brook near the cemetery's south entrance. I was nearly clear of the graveyard. There would be a gas station just across the road. If could make it there, Nyx would be forced to stop pursuing me. He wouldn't cause a scene in front of civilians, not without being seen anyway. It was the best chance I had to escape him.

Nyx's voice boomed from a few feet behind me. "A wolf chasing after a rabbit. Why do you bother running?"

The same reason that rabbit runs, I thought. I'm scared for my life.

I sprinted across the bridge that fell over the cemetery's brook and raced towards the dim light coming from the main road. The gas station wasn't far from here. I just had to keep running. I was amazed that my legs hadn't failed me yet. They were short, stumpy, unimpressive limbs but they moved quickly when I needed them to.

I had been moving as fast as I could since I left Lial alone with Hypnos and Thanatos. I wondered how far I was from the angel now. I hated that he was in danger because of me. The thought of him lying on the wet grass, cut up and bleeding was enough to make me wish I had never summoned him in the first place. Sure I had gotten him of out of Hell, but at what cost?

Because of me, he had kidnapped a man, murdered his friend, and betrayed his own kind. The worst part is that he never volunteered for this guardian business. I forced Lial into this, and then I left him alone with two ruthless psychopaths. The three brothers did not seem like the merciful type.

The streetlight blazed in front of me. But Nyx was close behind. He was so close that I could hear him breathing. I had to move my stunted legs twice as fast to stay ahead of him. The south gates of Sleepy Hollow Cemetery were unlocked and I raced through them. I'd made it to the main road when my legs finally started to grow heavy. Thankfully, the gas station was only several yards ahead of me.

As I rushed into the road, a black van pulled up and screeched to a halt, blocking my passage. I almost slammed my body into the vehicle but managed to stop short and prevent it. The side door slid open and revealed the massive frame of Thanatos. I immediately turned to run in the opposite direction, but Nyx had caught up with me. Before I could scream, he clapped a large hand over my mouth and shoved me towards the van. I was hysterical as Thanatos and Nyx lifted me into the back and slammed the door shut, trapping me inside.

The car took off and carried us farther and farther from Lial and the cemetery. Hypnos was driving while the other two brothers kept their black eyes and callous faces fixed on me.

"He said to leave the girl out of this. He is not going to be happy with us," Hypnos noted from the front seat. "We should have taken the book and left her in the cemetery."

"He said to leave the girl out of this if possible, but turns out it wasn't. He also said that we are not permitted to harm her, not one scratch," Nyx added. "If we tried to take the book from her, she would have fought us. This way, the book is safe with the girl, and the girl is safe with us."

It was quiet in the van for a minute or two before I made an attempt to reveal the three brothers for what they really were. "Deus!" I blurted out the Latin word.

Nyx and Thanatos glanced over at me like I was crazy. Hypnos gave me the same bizarre look through the rear view mirror.

"What did you say?" Hypnos spoke up from the driver's seat.

"Deus," I repeated, less sure of myself.

In a thunderous uproar, the inside of the van was overcome with the brothers' laughter. Hypnos was laughing so hard he started to cry. His blurred vision nearly caused him to run us off the highway and into the guardrail.

"Deus? Do you think we're demons?" Nyx asked rhetorically. "What were you expecting? Did you think our heads would spin and our eyes would turn black? Did you think we would tremble at the mention of His name?"

Another riot of laughter fell upon the brothers. They writhed and rocked in silence apart from occasional wheezing breaths.

"We are not demons," Nyx corrected when he regained his ability to speak.

"It was an educated guess," I defended myself. "I mean, if you're not entirely human, what else was I supposed to think?"

"It doesn't surprise me that you cannot see us for what we are. There are not many like my brothers and me in the world."

Hypnos picked up his brother's train of thought. "Your friend, the angel, could not even see us for what we were initially."

"He saw us for what we are once the fighting began," Thanatos added.

"What did you do to him?" I asked.

"Not much. Just when the fight started to get interesting, he collapsed and began bleeding. It was like someone had taken a knife and made a thousand tally marks across his skin. We left him in the cemetery to get the van and cut you off."

"Your timing was immaculate, brothers," Nyx complimented.

We'd been traveling for about twenty minutes when Hypnos switched the gear into park. Nyx slid open the door and hopped out of the van first. Just as I was about to make a run for it, Thanatos's massive hand came down on my shoulder and applied enough pressure to keep me in place. When the three brothers ushered me out of the van I instantly knew where we were.

I was standing at 40 Talbot Place in Bridgeview City. I remembered the white brick walls and the intricate cast iron design covering the glass on the front door. It was the small N'Orleans style café named for Marie Laveau. The brothers who kidnapped me were the henchmen of the very same man who sent me on this impossible mission to recover Liber Alter.

22
Five Words

Thanatos guided me to the back corner of the café, through the grandfather clock, down the narrow hallway, through the red door and into Laveau's secret poker room. When I walked in, I saw my own human reflection in the tell-all, just as I expected. I saw brown eyes, brown curls, curves and fair skin. I noticed that my face was still bruised from the brawl at One Way Ticket. I was annoyed that I'd entered the room first because I didn't get a chance to see the brothers' reflections. I wondered if the parts of them that weren't human would be displayed in the mirror.

The brothers forced me to sit on a barstool. When I looked across the room, I expected to see Laveau waiting for me in a well-tailored suit, but instead there was a lanky man in a pinstriped waistcoat. The demon Alastor stood opposite the bar with his hands palm to palm, as if in prayer. I knew it had only been days since I had seen him, but it felt like years. Alastor's hazel eyes stood out against his coffee skin as he stared at me. His dread locks fell over his shoulders and a welcoming smile swept across his lips.

"Cherie," he extended his arms. "Ah, it is so wonderful to see you again."

Nyx stood behind the bar while Hypnos and Thanatos seated

themselves at the stools on either side of me.

"Alastor. You did this? Laveau should have let me send you back to Hell when I had the chance," I sneered.

He laughed at me, which only made me more enraged. I gripped the sides of the barstool to keep myself from lashing out against the demon. I knew I wouldn't get very far with the three stooges babysitting me.

"Cherie, would you be kind enough to let me take a look at the precious object you are hiding in your pocket?"

I looked down and saw the small book perfectly outlined in the black denim. "You know I won't."

I wanted to sound intimidating, but it was useless. I didn't threaten Alastor. I knew what would come next. He would take The Other Book from me. There was nothing I could do to stop that from happening, but I didn't have to make it easy for him.

"Then I must take it from you," Alastor said. "Nyx, Hypnos, Thanatos would you mind keeping the girl still a moment?"

"With pleasure," Hypnos hissed. His stringy voice made my skin crawl.

That was my cue. I made an attempt to bolt from the room, but just as I predicted, the second I left the stool six rough hands were all over me. The brothers' hold on me kept me planted where I stood. I struggled ferociously against their grip but it was pointless. I was stuck.

Alastor sauntered towards me from across the room. He flaunted a narcissistic grin and his hazel eyes danced over me. The demon slid his slender fingers into my front jean pocket and wrapped them around the book's leather cover. Before removing the object, Alastor leaned in and whispered in my ear.

"Too bad, cherie." The demon's French accent had a degrading edge to it. "You wasted a great deal of time," he elaborated. "You worked so hard, you tried, and you suffered, and still you failed."

I cast my stare down to the floor, defeated. Alastor was toying with me, berating me for his own sick pleasure. This was somehow worse than being tied to a chair in Keylor's basement. After ten years, dozens of exorcisms, solving supernatural cases, summoning angels, staying sober (mostly), and recovering a sacred book only rumored to exist— I failed.

"You were the little girl who shook hands with the Devil, and now you are the girl who almost— the girl who did not," he spoke slowly, wanting his words to sink in and poison me. "Quel dommage."

"I think that could've gone without saying, Alastor."

"No, you see I had to say it out loud, because that is what makes it cruel."

He was proud of his malice, which didn't surprise me. Alastor had a gift for it. He murdered all five of his brothers, after all. His sole reason being to further his acts of wickedness, not only against the human world but against his own kind as well. He succeeded in that endeavor.

The demon took the red book from my pocket and held it up against the light, reading the gold inscription. "It is such a small thing," he noted. "I wonder what the fuss is all about."

Just as he was about to pull back the book's cover, I shouted. "Wait!" I'm not sure why I did that. I suppose I felt the demon deserved to know what he was asking for.

"What is it, cherie?"

"Alastor, if you open that book, it is going to show you something about yourself that you don't know. It might change you."

"The truth does not frighten me. Words are not magic. They are not a cure. They are empty and easy to come by," he explained as though I were a naïve child.

"Yeah, I know. People abuse words all the time. They say I love

you or I'm sorry when they don't mean it, but The Other Book
is not a book of men. It is sacred. What you read won't be fiction
scribbled down by human hands. It will be the truth— His truth.
Be careful," I cautioned.

"You did say that none of us should read from it—" Thanatos
added.

Alastor smiled at Thanatos, but it was demeaning. To Alastor,
the three brothers were nothing more than moronic henchman, all
muscle and no brain. I'm not sure if the book called to the demon,
asked to be opened, or if Alastor was too curious to pass up such a
rare opportunity. I watched as he pulled back the red leather cover.
His light eyes dashed from left to right across the page. It took
Alastor no time at all to finish reading the book's message.

"What did the book show you?" Nyx asked.

Alastor looked up at the three men and then brought his eyes
to me. His face was twisted in quiet terror, the color drained from
him. His eyes were brimming with tears. Alastor's hands went limp
and the book slipped out of his grip, landing on the floor in front
of his large feet.

"I cannot believe it," Alastor's voice cracked. "It is the truth.
The message is genuine, cherie."

Alastor began to pace and flail his arms. The three brothers
slowly loosened their grip on me as we watched the frantic demon,
not sure what to expect.

"Every word was the truth! I am changed— You were right,
cherie! I am new." Alastor was in tears. He was laughing and crying
simultaneously. He'd become short of breath, lost in the excitement
on his revelation, but managed to repeat Liber Alter's message.
"Even though you were born of darkness, you are not condemned
to remain there. When you are ready to change, I will carry you
into the light, bathe you in my love and show you how."

The atmosphere in the poker room altered. Alastor's voice

hung in the air and pulsed around us like a lingering miracle. All of the demon's previous cynicism and arrogance was gone. He was altogether a different being. Alastor was giddy and hysterical, very much like a child.

"I am not beyond saving!" he shouted to the ceiling. "I am ready. I am ready! I want to change. I want to see all the good that you see. Do you hear me! I am ready to be saved! I know now that I am good enough," he beamed. "I never thought that I was good enough."

In the midst of Alastor's dramatics, I crouched down and retrieved The Other Book. Nyx, Hypnos and Thanatos all stood back and stared at the demon in amazement. He proceeded to cry his praises into the air with closed eyes and open arms. I knelt on the floor and scooped the red book into my hands.

"Tractandum Cum Cura," I mouthed the cover's inscription.

Then I did the one thing I knew I shouldn't. I opened the book. I pulled back the cover and was surprised to find another gold inscription written inside.

Periculosum est Veritas. For the truth is a dangerous thing.

I hesitated. Should I turn the page? Could I handle the truth or would I fall victim to an emotional and spiritual meltdown like Alastor? Pride, experience and reason told me to shut the book and slip it into my pocket, but there was one more element whispering to me. My heart had the softest voice, but spoke with the most conviction and I listened.

I flipped to the center page, and an elegant script materialized on the blank sheet of paper before me. I passed my eyes over the message that appeared. The book revealed five ordinary words. Five words that changed everything.

I don't think I would call it a miracle. I did not fall apart or feel like a new person, but the ground shifted, and I knew I would stray from the path I was on. I was happy to walk away and start off in a new direction. I shut the book and climbed back to my feet.

"Nyx, Hypnos, Thanatos you must read from Liber Alter," the demon instructed. "You must."

The three men took a step back from the found-again demon. "Alastor, you are not yourself. There is something wrong with you," Nyx's voice tightened.

"No, No. I have never felt so alive! I thought I could never be more than what I was made for. I thought I would never evolve beyond chaos and depravity, but I have a choice. I can be more than a monster. I can be better. Is that not wonderful? Cherie—" he looked at me with bright, animated eyes. "I am sorry that I had a hand in this plot against you."

"What? I thought all of this was your idea. You were the ring leader," I said.

"He used your good nature against you. He wanted Liber Alter, and you were so desperate to get your soul back he knew that he could use you. Cherie, West Laveau is not on your side."

"No— After everything I've been through the past couple of days— After everything I put Lial through—! West lied to me."

Alastor wept uncontrollably. "I am so sorry! The guilt is going to kill me, but how magnificent it is to be burdened with guilt!"

I fought back my own tears. I had been nothing more than a pawn in a game of chess. I was expendable. "Getting my soul back was never an option, was it?" I asked. "It was just the motivation I needed to find The Other Book and bring it to Laveau."

"I am sad to say that is true," Alastor grabbed my hand. "Come now, we must go before Laveau finds us here. He will take the book from you, and afterwards he will take your life. You are no good to him any longer. We have to leave, cherie."

"You're not going anywhere, demon," Thanatos stepped forward and blocked the red door. "You shouldn't have read from the book. You have made an unwise choice. You and the girl will stay here until Laveau arrives. He will decide what is to become of you."

"I have a feeling it is not going to end well for either of you," Hypnos added with a hard chuckle, and his brothers followed suit.

Alastor and I stared at them, and fear rose inside us as they inched closer. The brothers continued to laugh while the demon and I stood trapped between them. Their chuckles and snickers mocked us relentlessly. Alastor squeezed my hand as I watched him desperately search for an exit.

"Cherie."

"Alastor," I answered.

"Is this what it feels like to be human?" he asked. "I feel weak. I feel regret. I feel sad. I have never known these things before now, but I have seen them time and time again in your kind," he said. "But there is more. While I am sad, scared even, I am still not without hope. Does that sound familiar?"

"Yes, hope is very human," I confirmed.

He nodded pensively.

I looked up at the demon's face, which no longer appeared sinister or malicious. His eyes had been growing more vibrant and tender with each passing moment. His fears were humbling. He was undoubtedly better than his former self. I'm not sure how long Alastor and I shared that look, but I remember exactly when it ended.

I must have heard an extra pair of footsteps in the room, or the unmistakable swoosh of a dense object cutting through the air. I must have noticed West Laveau advancing towards Alastor from behind him. I must have seen the flaming sword in his grip, but what I remember most vividly was the look on Alastor's face when the sword thrust into him and pierced through his chest.

The demon's eyes immediately glazed over and his face twisted in horror. I think he went into shock before he could experience any real pain. Laveau removed the sword from his body and Alastor's legs gave way beneath him. He collapsed onto me and his head fell down onto my shoulder. I wrapped my arms around him and struggled to support his large frame.

I have to admit that my heart went out to the creature. He had been given a second chance, but not the time to make good of it. Even though Alastor had committed millenniums of unforgivable acts, in a peculiar way, he never knew better. He had been carved from the Devil, born into fire and despair. Until Alastor read from The Other Book, he had no idea that he was capable of anything other than brutality.

"Cherie," he said in a rasping breath.

"Alastor, I am so sorry—"

"No. I am happier than I ever thought possible. I truly am. Cherie, I want you to know something."

I knew Alastor only had seconds left. I was surprised he lasted this long. "What?"

"I will meet you at the black gates when your time comes. I will do everything in my power to keep you safe. The others will not touch you without answering to me," he took in a final, staggering breath. "You will have one friend in the lake of fire."

23

Beetlejuice

After that Alastor exhaled and his body went limp, becoming dead weight in my arms. He was gone. I tried to be gentle with him as I laid his body on the cold floor, but I must have looked ungraceful. I took a step away from the body and brought my attention to the man who put it there. West Laveau stood tall with the flaming sword still in hand. He looked down at me with unwavering jet black eyes.

"You wanted to know how a permanent exorcism is done, Miss Barnaby. It's quite simple once you get your hands on a flaming sword. It's not as rare as the tell-all but still exceptionally uncommon," he waited for me to respond, but I had nothing to say. "I really did mean to keep you out of this, but don't worry, your involvement doesn't spoil my plans. Give me the book, Miss Barnaby."

I did. There was nothing else I could do. If I refused, Laveau would've had the brothers remove The Other Book from me anyway.

"It has been a pleasure working with you, Miss Barnaby." He grinned at the sacred book resting in his hand.

"You tricked me."

"Yes. I tricked you, not unlike the Devil did ten years ago." A vicious smile flashed across his face. "Which would not surprise you if you knew who I really was. Are you curious? Have I peaked your interest?"

I acted indifferent, but of course I wanted to know. Laveau betrayed me. I needed to know who or what he was so that I could find out how to kill him.

"First allow me to introduce the young men who brought you here," he gestured to the three brothers. "Nyx, Hypnos and Thanatos share my blood and my ideals. I am very fond of them. They are my great, great grandsons, and they have proved their excellence once again tonight."

I wrinkled my nose, baffled by what he was suggesting. As far as I could tell, the four men in the room were around the same age; there was no way Laveau could be two generations older than the brothers. West must have noticed the puzzled expression on my face because he felt the need to explain.

"Do you think what I have said is not possible, Miss Barnaby?"

"It's only possible if you're not—"

"Human," he raised a smug eyebrow.

Thanatos began to gurgle small breaths before pouring into a bellowing laugh. Hypnos and Nyx joined in, but their laughter died when Laveau shot them a look— the kind of look a parent gives a child who is acting out in public. The brothers instantly fell back into a respectful silence.

"So the rumors are true, you are a hybrid. Your great, great, great grandmother had an affair with an angel, and you four carry some of that divine blood."

"Well, I was stretching the truth when I said Marie Laveau was my great, great, great grandmother," he waved away the previous statement. "Marie was, in fact, my mother, which means that I am half angel."

"You're half human too," I corrected.

"I try to ignore that half."

My eyes widened with a sudden realization. "West, you're really old."

He released a sharp laugh. "Yes, I suppose I am. I was born West Jacques Santiago Laveau on May 12, 1819. Angels do not have last names, so I took my mother's. I am one hundred and ninety-six years old."

"Why do you look so young?" I asked.

"I have discovered that angel blood slows the aging process," he explained. "I have not changed physically since my thirty-ninth birthday."

"Who's your father?"

My hands had started to tremble, so I shoved them in my jean pockets. I knew that with each passing second, the chances of me leaving the room alive were diminishing.

"You will have the pleasure of meeting him soon enough; and when he arrives, I suggest you show him the utmost respect," he warned.

"Is he a fallen angel?"

"I thought that much was obvious. Why? Did you mistake me for one of the good guys?" he asked sarcastically. "Oh that's right, you did. You trusted me when I offered to help you. Miss Barnaby, you should know better. Nothing in this world is free," he laughed again. His great, great grandsons accompanied him with their own heckles and jeers.

West Laveau moved to the back corner of the poker room and knocked on the wall three times, which made a hollow sound. The wall slid open and revealed another secret room. That must've been where he entered from before stabbing Alastor. The space was filled with antique objects, and since Laveau was a collector, I was certain each item was priceless. On the wall hung a second flaming sword. Laveau placed the one in his hand next to the other. The two weapons rested side by side, both ablaze with blue flames. He exited the secret room and the wall closed behind him, perfectly concealing the doorway.

"Alastor borrowed a flaming sword from me once," West mused. "That's why he owes me so many favors. He used it to murder his brothers and ensure that they would never return to Earth. The flaming swords were given to seven of the archangels, to protect and defend His kingdom. They were all lost after The Great War but I have recovered two of them. The other five are still missing. I would assume they're somewhere on this planet."

I persisted with questions. It seemed to be keeping me alive. "West, you're the son of a fallen angel and your grandsons are a part of that bloodline. Do you have the same black marks as the other fallen angels? Are your names written on your bodies in Echonian?"

"No, my dear, we are not marked as they are. When fallen angels come to Earth, their names are branded on them as a reminder of where they came from and serve as a warning to others. My grandsons and I have never been to Hell; we were born on Earth and we have spent our lives here."

I was running short on conversation topics. I could see that Laveau's interest in me was wearing thin. "You said I would get to meet your father. Where is he? Do you have to summon him?"

"No, Miss Barnaby, my father comes and goes as he pleases."

"I could call him for you. Beetlejuice, Beetlejuice..." I teased.

"I don't think I have ever been called that name before," an amused voice manifested in the room, somewhere behind me.

Laveau's eyes widened with panic at the sight of our visitor. "You have to excuse the girl's poor manners. She does not seem to understand her place."

"On the contrary, West. I am impressed with the girl and have been for many, many years."

The man's voice sounded vaguely familiar, but I couldn't remember where I'd heard it before. I realized the easiest way to solve that small mystery was to turn around.

I did, and I nearly fell over when I saw the person in front of me. He had silver hair and laugh lines at the corners of his warm blue eyes. I was staring at the gentle face of the bartender I met in Sleepy Hollow earlier that afternoon. He was even wearing the same button down shirt and jeans.

"The little girl who shook my hand," he smiled. "You are not such a little girl anymore."

I was struck motionless. A flood of memories enveloped me. In my mind, I was back in the basement of Lazarus Hospital, burning a candle and reading strange words from an old book. I could still see the cheap florescent lights. I remembered how level-headed and single-minded I was, so sure that I was doing the right thing. West Laveau's father wasn't any fallen angel. He was the fallen angel. I was meeting the Devil for a second time and it terrified me.

"You've grown into a beautiful young woman, Sage. I know I'm late in saying this, but my deepest condolences regarding your dear sister. It must have been devastating for you, after you gave all you could to save her—"

"You took her from me."

"I can't take all the credit," he confessed in a soft voice. "I only moved Mr. Crimmin's car keys from their normal place on the kitchen counter to his inside coat pocket. That way he would have to speed to make it to work on time. Oh, and I unlatched the gate in your front yard, but your sister ran into the street on her own."

"Why would she do that?" I practically yelled.

"Okay, you caught me! I had a hand in that as well," he added, and I became more enraged. I felt my eyes water with pure unfiltered hatred. "She was chasing a butterfly. Well, she was chasing me disguised as a butterfly— a very lovely butterfly I might add. I used all of Nola's favorite colors for the wings. Children are so easily led into temptation," he said, completely void of guilt.

I curled my hands into fists, but they remained at my sides. I was smart enough to know that I could never win a fight against the Devil. I turned the conversation away from my sister. "What did you do with the bartender? Did you hurt him?"

"No, not at all, he's just fine. I only copied his physical appearance."

"You could choose any face to hide behind. Why would you want to show up looking like that?"

His blue eyes twinkled with cruelty. "You liked him, Sage."

"I thought he was nice," I said.

"Yes, he was, and I wanted to ruin him for you. I wanted to ruin your memory of him. After tonight if you ever think about him, you will also think of me. I have tainted his face in your mind for the forever." The Devil beamed with pride. "That is bona fide cruelty, to destroy someone's memory. I am the absolute worst, aren't I?"

Laveau and his grandsons held their tongues upon the Devil's entrance, and until that point they stood as a silent audience to our back and forth. Now Laveau stepped forward with The Other Book in his hand, which he tossed carelessly to his father. Without even glancing at the red leather cover, the Devil placed it in his pocket.

"Do you want to know why I had West send you to track down Liber Alter? I need this book so that I can keep it away from my followers. I need to keep it secret from the other fallen angels and demons and lost souls plaguing the underworld— not to mention the countless sinners here on Earth. I can't have what happened to Alastor happen to anyone else."

I shook my head. "Alastor is no good to you anymore, not even in Hell. He knows the truth, and it is so pure that fire cannot destroy it. Alastor is not going to forget what he read in The Other

Book. It changed him. Why not let the demon go?"

"Because he is mine!" the Devil roared.

The lights flickered and the air turned cold. I could see that the bartender's face was red with anger, but it was the Devil's words screaming at me. I instinctively stepped back. Even West averted his gaze. "I created him! I carved him out of my flesh! The demon is my masterpiece! If I cannot have Alastor, neither can He!"

The Devil took several deep breaths and then regained his casual, mild façade. He smiled and the bartender's eyes were friendly again. It was as though the monstrous outburst never occurred.

I found myself staring down at Alastor's lifeless body. His long limbs were limp at his sides. His eyes were open and his thick dreadlocks sprawled around his face. The hole in his chest was still gaping and oozing a mess of dark blood. I remembered the demon's final words, his promise to me. He said that I would have one friend in the lake of fire. Now, standing in front of the Devil, I was starting to appreciate that promise much more.

I was about to speak out again on Alastor's behalf, but before I could an eruption of blinding white light filled the room. Following the unexpected blast of wind and a high-pitched shriek that cut through the air. I couldn't determine the source of the sound before it faded into white noise and all of my senses betrayed me. There was nothing but the unbearable light, and for a short time I thought that I had died. When the light faded I glanced down and saw that my boots were still standing on the floor of Laveau's poker room.

West moved to the opposite side of the room and stood by his father while the three brothers cowered against the wall. The Devil's smile stretched wide across his face. I followed his gaze and found a fair skinned, strawberry blonde haired woman. A thin, ivory cloth was draped over her petite frame and her hair fell in soft waves down her back, past her waistline. She was not wearing makeup or shoes or undergarments. The woman's skin seemed to radiate and her pale yellow eyes were fixed on the Devil.

"How long has it been?" he asked in a pleasant voice.

"Since The Great War," she stated plainly.

"Boys," the Devil commanded his descants' attention. "It would seem we have a proper angel in our midst. Would you kindly remove the demon's former shell from the room? She may be an archangel, and therefore not put off by a little bloodshed, but I worry that this vulgar scene is beneath her."

The three brothers said nothing but did as they were told. They lifted Alastor's body and exited through the red door, before disappearing down the hallway. I couldn't say where or how they disposed of the body.

"I may be able to tolerate the sight of blood, Lucifer, but it does offend me. I only fight when I must defend His kingdom. I do not seek bloodshed, and it is always regrettable."

"You have always been so sensitive, Gabriel," the Devil whined. "That is why you were never any fun."

Gabriel. His messenger. The angel, Gabriel. I was stunned. Of all the angels in Heaven, I was standing beside one of the more recognized names. A small burst of excited energy rushed through me and I released a long breath to steady my alarmed nerves.

"I am too sensitive and you are too weak, Lucifer. I suppose we are all imperfect, humans and angels alike. Each of us plays victim to our inadequacies, deficiencies and limitations. But I am not ashamed of mine."

"Weak?" he scoffed.

"Yes. Shall I repeat myself? Weak. You are weak, Lucifer." Her words were about as subtle as an avalanche.

Every time Gabriel called the Devil weak, it appeared to sting him. The world feared the Devil, but not Gabriel, and he did not like that one bit. Since the Devil knew he would never gain the respect of angels, he wished for them to fear him instead.

Gabriel continued, "Faith can only be achieved by the most fervent and passionate beings. You fall short. You were once so much more than what you have become. It hurts me to see you like this."

"It is His fault that I am this way. It is His doing. You know why I left, Gabriel. You know what He and I discussed. He is punishing me for disagreeing with Him. He tossed me aside for expressing free will, and then he bestowed that very gift onto humankind. His precious, useless humans were worthy of free will but I was not."

"This is not the time to relive history that cannot be undone, Lucifer."

The Devil frowned and narrowed his stare with disgust. "I know, but you were not granted free will either. Gabriel, you're here because you are following His orders. You could have been in the middle of a great book or watching the last fifteen minutes of a movie, but He wouldn't have cared.He would have made you stop everything to run an errand on his behalf—"

"No more, Lucifer!" Gabriel warned with fire in her voice. "I will not hear you speak of Him. You don't answer to Him any longer. You do as you please. I chose to stay. I am happy with my choice. Are you?"

The Devil fell silent and the bartender's eyes grew tired. I could see all the negativity of the world brewing inside them. I watched a storm of hate, failed dreams, neglect, war, murder, silent family dinners, wasted time and broken hearts pulse inside those blue eyes.

West and I had remained silent, unsure how to respond to the argument of two infamous angels. It was not a situation we were accustomed to. I suddenly felt very young. Laveau was one hundred and ninety-six; the Devil and Gabriel were probably as old as the universe; so approximately fourteen billion give or take, and I was eighteen. My experiences seemed trivial compared to what they'd been through.

"Why have you come here, Gabriel? You caught me at a bad time. I was kind of in the middle of something."

Gabriel didn't speak. She merely switched her attention from the Devil over to me. Her faint yellow eyes rested on my face, but her stare wasn't invasive or judgmental. It was merely observant. The Devil watched her with great interest and eventually seemed to realize something that had gone over my head. He rushed over to the bar and pushed a dozen bottles onto the floor. The glass shattered and flew across the room, littering the ground at our feet. Laveau and I jumped at the sudden explosion, but Gabriel was unaffected by his violent outburst.

"No! No! No!" the Devil shouted as if he were a toddler having a temper tantrum. "He cannot have her! She belongs to me now. I won. I won her soul. Sage Rose Barnaby is mine and He cannot have her. You tell Him that!"

I decided it was time to interrupt them. "Could someone tell me what's going on?"

"Don't bother," the Devil answered. "You and I shook hands. No one has the power to call off our deal, not Gabriel and not Him."

"Are you going to try and stop us, Lucifer? You may have named yourself the Devil, but you are no archangel," Gabriel cautioned him. "Sage, your good intentions have not been overlooked. You have sometimes made poor choices, but you have never stopped trying to redeem yourself, seek forgiveness. While our actions define us, our hearts are still considered."

"What—? Wait—" I stammered. "Am I getting my soul back?"

She answered with a solemn nod. "Hold onto it this time."

"This is not fair!" the Devil cried.

I almost smiled but something stopped me. This had been exactly what I wanted. This was what I searched and worked and prayed for since Nola passed away. I sighed, thrilled to have the confirmation that happy endings exist. I looked at Gabriel; her face was glowing. I am sure that as His messenger she has not always been sent to deliver good news, so she must enjoy the occasions when she can.

I felt a breeze waft into the room from behind me, which meant that someone must have opened the red door. I would have turned to look but I was in shock. I didn't know how to address the situation from here. I was at a loss for the appropriate words, or any words for that matter. All I could think about was the secret truth The Other Book had revealed to me. The five words repeated themselves mercilessly in my mind.

"Blondie," a deep voice called to me.

I was starting to like that name, but only when he said it.

I spun around to find Lial leaning against the doorway and saturated with blood. At this point in our relationship, the blood didn't surprise me. His hair fell down onto his forehead. A crooked smile played on his lips as we stared at each other. My heart throbbed when I saw him. I don't think I realized how worried I was about him until he was standing just a few feet away.

Now that I knew Lial was safe, my emotions overwhelmed me. I understood how much worse things could have gone for him. I wanted to run into his arms and feel their strength press me against his body. I wanted to hear his heart beat when I buried my face into his chest. I wanted to feel the cool leather of his jacket against my cheek and breathe in the faded scent of cigarette smoke and sweat on his clothes, but all of that would have to wait.

"Lial," was all I could manage.

I should have thanked him right then and there. I should have told him I was grateful he'd checked in on me over the years, even if he couldn't be there. I was touched that he blamed himself for my mistakes. I really appreciated that he had saved my life more than once over the past couple of days. He'd stayed with me and protected me when it might have been easier to let me die and walk away. He kept his word. It was almost time for me to keep mine. Very soon I would release him from being my guardian. I wondered if he was going to miss me half as much as I would miss him.

"You're bleeding," I said.

Lial glanced down at his clothes, which were covered in red stains. "Oh, that's not my blood. Well, most of it is. After you left me in the cemetery, those wounds appeared all over my body. There was a ton of blood, but now that we're together again, it stopped."

"Then whose blood are you covered in?"

"I'll give you three guesses," he winked.

West immediately ran forward and interrupted our reunion. "No— my grandsons—they should have been back by now! What have you done, Belial?"

My guardian grinned complacently. "I think Nyx is on my jacket, Hypnos stained my jeans and Thanatos might be soaked into my hair a bit."

"You better have left them alive!" Laveau hollered fearfully.

"I owe you nothing, hybrid. You betrayed my trust. If you hurry, you might be able to save them, but I doubt it."

Laveau shot a worried look towards his father, who was still disguised as the gentle-faced bartender. The Devil nodded, giving his son permission to attend to the three brothers.

Laveau sprinted from the room. He was so unlike the man I had met several days earlier, that version of him been intimidating and purposeful. Now he was just a scared boy looking to his father and waiting to be told what comes next. Suddenly the flashy suits were too mature for Laveau. His collection of rare items was nothing more than expensive toys. He didn't want them because they were precious or important. He wanted those things so that no one else could have them. It was so obvious now. When I met West Laveau, he put on one Hell of a show but that was in the past. The tables had finally turned in my favor.

Gabriel was going to return my soul to me, which would have never happened if I hadn't fallen for Laveau's ruse. Regardless, I met his challenge. I found Liber Alter and now that I had read from it, I wondered if the book had gotten lost on purpose. The inside inscription said it best, for the truth is a dangerous thing.

"Belial," she greeted him sweetly.

"Hello, Gabriel. Thanks for bringing Sage the good news."

"Sage is not the only one I have a message for," she announced in a mild voice. "He sent me with good news for you too."

"You can tell Him that I'm not interested," Lial replied without missing a beat. "I never asked for His forgiveness."

"That is only because you don't think you deserve to be forgiven, but don't you wish for it anyway? Don't you still pray for absolution in secret? I know you regret the choice you made. If you could do it again, you would not follow Lucifer out of His kingdom."

"You don't know that."

"Everyone knows that," she insisted. "We saw your hesitation, Belial. We know how empty you've been since you left us. Some of the angels have been checking in on you, the same way you have been keeping an eye on Sage over the years. We haven't forgotten you."

"The angels have been checking in on me? Don't make me laugh. Which angels?"

Gabriel lowered her eyes, and stared down at the checkered floor. "In truth it has just been one angel. He's been keeping track of you since you fell. He's often said that he wished he offered to leave with you. Then you could not have doubted his love. He blames himself for your departure. He believes the last conversation you shared is the reason you ran away, and he has cursed our maker many times for letting you go. Belial, you must still think of him. If there is no one else you care to remember from your time with the angels, surely you still think of—"

"Enough!" Lial threw his hands into the air. "I don't want to hear his name—"

"Michael misses you," Gabriel rushed the words. "You were brothers. Nothing you say could convince me that you don't care about him."

I stepped forward. "Lial and Michael, the archangel?Are you really talking about my guardian and the angel who threw Lucifer out of Heaven?"

"Not my finest moment," the Devil grumbled and adjusted the collar of his shirt.

"Certainly your most memorable," Lial noted.

"I don't know about that, Belial," the Devil answered. "I am very proud of World War II. That was a shining moment! One of the more iniquitous influences I've had on humankind."

The two fallen angels exchanged a vile stare. Gabriel moved between them. "Come back with me. You can continue to be Sage's guardian, if you like, and reconnect with Michael and the others. Belial, you can have your wings back."

Lial appeared to be at a loss for words. I knew that he wanted to go home just as much as I had wanted my soul back. I couldn't figure out why he suddenly seemed so unsure. Instead of responding, he changed the subject.

"Gabriel, with all due respect, we are here because of Sage. We should be celebrating the return of her soul. Don't lessen that triumph by wasting your time on me."

I stepped forward. "Lial, are you turning down her offer?"

"Tonight is not about me," he tucked a stray curl behind my

ear. "Sage, you set out to reclaim your soul and you have."

"Gabriel offered me my soul. I never accepted it."

Lial frowned and searched my face for an explanation. Gabriel met my statement with a look of astonishment. Meanwhile, the Devil stood off to the side with a perverse light burning in his eyes.

"What?" he grabbed my shoulders with his large white hands, and leaned in so that we were standing eye to eye. "What do you mean? Sage, you have your soul back, take it and run!"

"Promise me that you are going to take your place with the angels. You should be with Gabriel and Michael."

"Oh, is that what this is about? I don't want you to worry about me—"

"Promise," I said.

"I should not be a factor in your decision."

"I won't accept my soul until you swear—"

"Fine! Yes. Okay? I promise." He kept his eyes locked on mine. "I promise. I will be one of the good guys. Is that what you want to hear? Now take back your damn soul."

"Okay." I felt the hint of a smile creep onto my lips.

Lial believed he'd gotten through to me. He thought we had both received our happy ending. He had no idea that the five words I read in The Other Book ensured there was only one way I could ever be happy. I pulled away from my guardian.

I let my eyes move to Gabriel, whose strawberry blonde hair swayed gracefully against her back as she approached me.

"Sage, the sensation you are about to experience will be unusual," she explained in a placid voice.

Gabriel closed her soft yellow eyes and the room grew still. A peculiar feeling flowed through me. I had suddenly become aware of every cell, atom and molecule throughout my entire body. It felt like there were goose bumps on the inside parts of me. I could actually feel the blood pumping through each artery and every vein.

I heard the echo of my heartbeat in my throat and knees.

Then very abruptly, every hair follicle, organ and bacteria inside me was set ablaze. The heat raced through my body. It was like someone lined my insides with gasoline and set a match to it. It was overwhelming, energizing, and a little uncomfortable. But it was confirmation that I was alive. I knew the burning sensation was my soul finding its way back home inside of me; mine once again.

"Gabriel, thank you for returning my soul to me."

She bowed her head humbly.

"May I ask you something?" It was something I had wanted to ask her since she arrived, but I worried it might be too personal.

"Of course, as long as you're not going to ask me the meaning of life."

The universal joke never seemed to fail. Lial, Gabriel and the Devil all shared a hearty laugh and I almost forgot they weren't friends.

I spoke over their hilarity. "I wanted to ask why you don't have wings."

"I do so have wings," she stated defensively.

"Where are they?"

Lial took over the conversation. "Our wings are only visible to other angels. A person with a set of wings would attract a lot of attention from humans. There would be too many questions, dissections, paparazzi…"

"It's a shame you can't see them," the Devil informed me. "They are exquisite. I always thought so, stark white with bright yellow-golden flight feathers. It's a pity your human eyes are blind to such beauty."

"Cut it out, Lucifer. I'm not flattered by your shallow compliments," Gabriel said.

"Exquisite," he repeated in a charming voice.

Did Gabriel blush?

The Devil retreated to a corner of the room to sulk on his own for a while. I tossed my mane of dark curls over my shoulder and followed him.

The evening had not gone as he'd planned. He knew that Laveau would take Liber Alter from me, but he thought that my soul would still belong to him and that Lial would return to Hell once our adventure was finished. Instead Alastor found his conscience, my soul was mine and Lial had been invited back into His kingdom. The Devil had lost, again. He was good at losing.

Almost a full minute passed since I walked over to him but he pretended not to notice me standing there. I patiently waited for his attention.

"Can I help you?" he asked in a somber voice.

"I think you're the only one who can help me."

I heard Lial step forward. I could feel him standing behind me with a cross look on his face. He anticipated what I would say next.

"You don't need my help, Sage. You got everything you wanted."

"You and I both know there's only one thing I ever really wanted."

"Is that right? What's going on inside that pretty little head of yours?" He was intrigued. The sadness in bartender's blue eyes began to fade.

"I want to make another deal," I said.

I had never been so sure of anything.

24

No Cancer, No Car Accidents

The Devil put one hand over his heart and used the other to lean against the wall and keep from falling over. In no time at all he was smiling again.

Lial grabbed my arm and pulled away from him. He was furious. "Sage, what are you thinking? You can't—!"

"You can't mean it," the Devil said in a quiet voice. He looked at me with suspicion, unable to believe his good luck.

"I mean it more today than I did when I was eight, and you remember how determined I was then."

"What are you asking for exactly? You know what dear, never mind. You can have whatever you like. You can have it all—! The little girl who sold her soul twice. You are a wonder," he mused. "Tell me, what can I do for you?"

"I would love to hear this," Lial growled. He crossed the length of the room and planted himself on one of the barstools.

"Nola deserves a full life."

"You haven't had your soul back for five minutes and you're all ready throwing it away," Lial argued.

Gabriel cut in. "Sage, are you sure you want to do this? You have been given a second chance. You won't get another. Your sister had a life, as brief as it was. She is in a better place. You must believe that."

"If that's true, why are the angels jealous of humankind?" I asked.

Gabriel shot Lial a disapproving look. Perhaps that was meant to be a secret amongst the angels.

"Eternity is a gift and a curse," she said. "Even for an angel in His kingdom, the endlessness can be maddening, but it could be worse. Imagine spending all that time elsewhere. Imagine forever in Hell. Where you spend eternity is your choice. I won't beg you, but I would strongly advise against making another deal with Lucifer."

"You might not want to beg her, Gabriel, but I have no problem lowering myself to that level," Lial moved to my side. "Do not do this! Do. Not. Do. This. I can't help you once you shake his hand. I spent the last ten years hating myself because I couldn't help you. Please, Sage. Don't make me go through that again. How can you trust that Lucifer won't go back on his deal? He cheated you once before."

"I read from The Other Book," I confessed.

Lial's eyes grew stormy and he staggered backwards. He was shocked. "You shouldn't have done that— Why did you do that? You're so stupid! Is that what brought on this change of heart?"

"I never had a change of heart. I always wanted Nola to live. I just thought I ran out of ways to make that happen."

"What did the book tell you?"

"Five words," my voice was shaking. "You can still save her."

He hung his head and grabbed the back of his neck.

"You can still save her," I repeated. "The Other Book meant Nola."

His ice blue stare burned into me before he turned away. I watched him run an aggravated hand through his platinum hair. "Just because you can do something does not mean that you should. I know that you believe it's the right thing to do, but people have done very stupid things because they thought it was right. Look back on the history of the human race. You are notorious for it."

"I'm sorry I let you down, Lial."

"You must be completely bonkers if you think you've let me down." He was somewhere between puzzled and hurt, and it destroyed me to see him that way. "Sage, you are— you are impossible and brave and decent and you have a great voice, you know that? When you order a shirley temple, you eat the cherries first. You drink too much coffee. You can hold your own in a fight. You don't think you're good enough— not for me, not for the dog or that man who puts up with you. You think you deserve Hell. You're wrong. Your sister died because it was her time to die. Your parents couldn't look at you because they were sad. None of it was your fault. Listen to me, you are a good person. You're guarded, but it's only because you care too much… and you're beautiful…. and you are killing me, Sage Barnaby. Don't do this—"

His breath was labored and his eyebrows drew together. I could see him searching for the words that would make me reconsider my pending deal.

"Please," he said. "I am begging you not to do this. I don't think you understand—"

"Just leave me alone, Lial."

He looked at me as though I'd slapped him across the face. "No. I am not going to leave you alone. You asked me to be here. You summoned me to Earth and forced me into a wild goose chase. I saved your life, Sage. I'm your guardian. I am going to save you again and again because that's my job— my purpose—"

"I don't want you to save me!"

I appreciated what Lial was trying to do, but Nola was my only priority. She always had been. There was nothing he could say to change that.

"I won't let you shake his hand. What do you think of that? I will keep you two apart, whatever it takes. I will drag you out of here by your hair."

"Lial, you've done more than enough, and you kept your word," I told him. "It's time I did the same." I let my brown eyes rest on his extraordinary face. I knew what I had to do, but I hesitated. I was granting Lial the freedom to leave but I didn't want him to go. "Nunc absolvo vos, mea sine fuga avis. "

I release you, my flightless bird.

I could feel my heart grow sore as I spoke the Latin. I watched Lial exhale the breath he'd been holding. I saw the light in his eyes dim. He took a step away from me and raised his hands in surrender. "Okay, Blondie. If this is really what you want— Okay."

"Lial, you know why I'm doing this. Nola—"

"Nola! Nola. Nola. Nola. What about the rest of us? What about Ned and Lena and Jack... and me? You don't care what we think. What's the matter? You don't love us enough. Is Nola the only one worthy of Sage Barnaby's love and devotion? Your sister would not want you to sacrifice your soul for her life. I guarantee that."

I didn't know what to say.

He looked at the red door. It had been left open when Laveau ran out of the room. "You know what, I have no idea what I'm still doing here. You released me. I am free to leave, which is all I've wanted since you summoned me. I did my part and now we get to go our separate ways. That was our deal, right?"

It was tough, but I managed to suppress all signs of emotion from my face. I spoke to him like I was indifferent, like my heart wasn't shattering inside me. "Yeah, that's what we said."

"I have been looking forward to this for days, walking away from you."

There was a static, uncomfortable silence that enveloped us. I remembered how thrilled I was when Lial walked through the door. All I wanted to do was run into his arms and stay there. Now I feared I would never get the chance to.

"I guess that's all there is to say." He gave me a somber look. "Well, this has been— oh, never mind."

Lial turned and began his slow exit towards the red door. Maybe he was moving at such a glacier pace because he was waiting for me to change my mind, or maybe I had worn the angel down so much during our time together that he just couldn't move any faster.

"Lial," I said.

He stopped in his tracks. I don't know why I called after him. I think I only meant to keep him with me a little longer.

"What do you want from me now?" he finally asked.

"You have a terrible singing voice, you know that? Um, you love cake and steak. You think that leather jacket makes you look cool. You're right. You think you're worthless. You think you deserve Hell. You're wrong. You are stubborn, and impulsive, but you're loyal and kind too. I wouldn't want any other angel as my guardian. I feel safe with you, Lial. I don't want you to go."

Lial kept his broad back to me. "Are you still going to make another deal with him?" he asked and turned his face towards the Devil.

"I'm sorry that you don't agree with what I'm doing for Nola—"

"You're damn right I don't agree," he said and stormed out.

And just like that Lial was gone. He never even said goodbye. I stood there, probably looking stunned and foolish. He had abandoned me, again.

"Sage," Gabriel's voice delicately grabbed my attention. "I am not judging you because that is not my area, but are you certain you want to do this all over again? Because if you are sure, then I have no more reason to be here."

"I appreciate you delivering the good news to me, Gabriel. Please tell Him that I said thank you, but what I do with my soul from here is my business."

"I do not envy the free will of humankind," her voice sounded like silk. "What a dreadful burden."

Gabriel fixed her gaze on the Devil. "Lucifer, you may keep Liber Alter. It is a gift from Him. He wants you to have it. If humans read from the book, faith would not be virtue because it would no longer be necessary. People would be certain of Heaven and Hell; and if that were the case, we could not distinguish if their actions were done out of love or fear. That is why He got rid of the book in the first place. It was never stolen. Lucifer, hide the book so well that it becomes lost even to you. This once, you and Him want the same thing."

She glanced back at me and seemed to smile with just her eyes. I saw no judgment in their pale yellow color. I watched as she closed them and lifted her head upwards. Her lips moved in a silent prayer. Then in the same fashion she arrived, she was left us. A brilliant flash of white light, a numbing of the senses and the magic trick was complete.

There was no trace of the angel who dressed in a delicate white cloth and spoke in a hushed voice. Lial, however, left quite an impression on the secret room beneath Laveau's café. There were bloody footprints littered across the floor and his scent clung to the air around me. I couldn't believe that our time together had come to its end, especially since we'd parted on such bad terms.

I suddenly couldn't remember what it was like before the angel had come into my world. And even though I knew from the beginning that we were either too similar or too different to ever have a peaceful relationship, it still hurt that he'd made the definite choice not to be with me.

"Sage, shall we discuss the conditions of our deal?" The Devil pulled me away from my thoughts of Lial. "I should warn you, there won't be much room for negotiation."

I nodded. "I want you to bring Nola back and I want her to have a full life."

"Would you like her to have a happily ever after too?"

"I don't care what kind of life she has, as long as it's hers. I don't want you to interfere. I just need you to make sure that she gets the chance to live. I want her to experience what it is to be human. I know that means she is going to struggle and be afraid, and die but she will also laugh and love."

"You think that some jokes and hand holding are worth a life filled with conflict, unjustified cruelty and death?" he asked.

I didn't answer him. He couldn't understand something so incredibly human. How an experience could be bitter and sweet. How people can be beautiful and terrible. How life can be scary and exciting all at once. I have come to learn that the Devil is the farthest thing from human there is. If there were hope for him, he would never seek it.

I stepped towards the blue-eyed wolf in sheep's clothing. "You will not cheat me this time. Nola will have children and grand children if that's where her life takes her. All of that is up to Nola, but I want her to have plenty of time to figure it out."

"Can I ask what makes her so special? If she weren't your sister, would you still care this much? Perhaps I shouldn't be questioning you; I could use the business, but I don't understand why you're giving up everything for her a second time."

"Nola was kind and it wasn't just because she was a child. It wasn't her innocence that made her generous and sympathetic. She was different, better than most people."

I stopped there and observed the monster before me. I assumed that my sweet words would bore him, but he was completely engaged.

"When Nola was five years old, our next door neighbor's husband died. A couple of days later, Nola and I got off the school bus and saw our neighbor, Mrs. Brothers, crying on her front porch. Seeing the old woman look so sad frightened me. I wanted to run inside and pretend I hadn't seen it, but Nola walked right over to her, climbed on her lap and sat there for a while. When Nola came back, I asked her what happened. She said, 'Nothing. I just helped her cry.'

"I was afraid and my sister was compassionate. I don't know if that makes Nola special, but it proves that she has a good heart and the courage to share it with others. Nola will make the world a better place, and I have a hard time just living in it."

The Devil kept his piercing eyes on me. His stare was unnerving, but I forced myself not to fidget in front of him. I just needed him to shake my hand. I wish dreams came true by wishing on stars, but the truth is you have to sacrifice so much to get within arm's reach of a dream. I think that most people end up crazy before their dreams come true. I almost had.

"Okay," he agreed. "I will give Nola Barnaby a life, a full human life, and you will come stay with me in Hell."

I was struck with a spasm of panic. I felt my mouth get dry and my hands swell with anxiety. I would be damned again. I would spend eternity in the circles of Hell. There was no way out this time. My fate was no longer contingent. It was definite.

"There is one more thing, Sage."

"What?"

"Since you are not in a position to argue or bargain, I am not going to help you unless you come with me now. You do not get to have a full life."

"Now?" I asked with a lump in my throat.

"Yes. Shake my hand and follow me into the underworld. Only then will I give your sister what I have promised."

"If anything happens to her that shortens her time on Earth, the deal is off. I walk out of Hell with my soul. I want her to have a long, healthy life."

"Fine," he extended his hand, but I wasn't ready to accept it. "No cancer, no car accidents, etcetera."

"Give me ten years," I pushed my luck. I wanted to be brave, but the thought of diving into Hell at that moment petrified me. I needed more time.

"Absolutely not," he laughed.

"Five," I pleaded. He shook his head. "One! One more year on Earth. Please. What is one year compared to the eternity I am going to spend with you?"

"No."

"Why not? You won!" I screamed. "I belong to you. Once I shake your hand, it's done and there is nothing I can do to call off our deal. I don't see why you need me to come with you right this minute."

The Devil's smile was ruthless and antagonistic. "Because I said so."

I exhaled, defeated and trembling. I was past trying to conceal that I was becoming more and more distressed as our conversation progressed.

I was struck with an image of Ned, alone on a hillside, saying a final farewell to his wife. I couldn't let my godfather face Lena's casket without me. I promised I would be there to bury the woman we loved so much. I couldn't break that promise to him. Ned would be waiting for me at dawn. If I didn't show up, he'd never forgive me.

"One day," my voice cracked.

"No."

"I am begging you. I can't offer you anything. I don't know what else to say— I don't have anymore to give. You have my soul. I just need one more day. It's nothing— it's just time."

The Devil gave me a knowing look, which lit up the bartender's face. "Don't try to fool me. Time is everything to humans. In many ways, it's all you have."

I leaned forward. I cupped my face into my hands and sobbed. I was beyond pride. I had lost all sense of self worth. Rock bottom had come and gone. I was at the Devil's mercy now.

"Please!"

He only laughed at me.

I rubbed my eyes, which were red and puffy. I opened them slowly and gave the Devil a hard stare. "Then we don't have a deal."

"Then Nola is lost to you, and she is lost to this world. Your sister will never have the full human experience, all its suffering and glory."

I shrugged, which only riled his temper.

"She will never live! Which is something you deem so important that you've already sold your soul for it once before."

"But if I lose Nola, you lose me. I get to keep my soul, and I swear I will never call on you again. I want one more day, otherwise there is no deal and you walk away empty handed. What do you say?"

He gave me a curious sideways glance and narrowed his eyes. "Sage, you're beginning to know me better than I would like."

I almost smiled. "I have convinced you to make a deal with me once before, remember?"

"Yes, but back then I was able to cheat you. You've taken all of the fun out of our deal this time around."

I waited in angst as he stroked his chin and mulled over my proposal.

He drew in a long breath and reluctantly answered. "Done.

Congratulations, you can have one more day on Earth."

I would have happily taken one hour at that point. "Okay."

"At sunset you will walk into Hell, and when the black gates close behind you, they will stay closed. You will be my most prized possession." There was a wicked spark in his blue eyes.

I nodded to show that I understood.

"This is your last chance. Your soul is still yours." He leaned in and chuckled softly to himself. "I can't believe I am saying this. Sage, it appears I have a weakness for you. I took advantage of you once before when you were a child. I suppose I feel it is unfair to win your soul twice, and in the same way."

"We both know that's a lie. You love to win and you've never cared about playing fair."

"Ah, you're right. I do love to win. I love winning more than hypocrites and misogynists, but now I am getting off topic. My dear girl, are you sure you know what you're doing?"

First Lial, then Gabriel and now the Devil. They had all asked me to reconsider the concrete choice I was one gesture away from making.

I almost laughed at how ridiculous the whole thing was— the past ten years and the last couple of days, even the last few minutes. I wondered how many people had been in a position similar to mine throughout history. I doubted it was a high number. I kept my eyes on the Devil, who remained silent.

"I know that this is how my story ends," I answered.

He was satisfied and offered his hand to me once again. "After sunset you will walk into a world of fire and your sister will wake up to blue skies and sunshine. Does that please you? Is that what you want?"

"Yes."

"Let's shake on it," he winked.

I stopped thinking. I lifted my hand and placed it in his. The

Devil had a warm, secure grip. It was the way I remembered from years ago. He kept his hold on me for longer than seemed necessary. When I tried to excuse myself from the handshake, he tightened his hand around mine. I got the idea that the Devil was trying to make a point. I belonged to him now.

"There's my good girl," he whispered in a perverse, callous way that made my blood run cold. "We shall see each other soon, Sage. I am looking forward to it. In fact, I am counting the minutes. There aren't many," he mocked.

The Devil watched as I turned and distanced myself from him. He was certain that he would see me again soon. No matter what happened throughout the course of the day, come sunset I would have nowhere to hide.

25

Petrichor

I took my time walking through Bridgeview City, past red brick buildings and over unevenly paved roads towards the McGreevy's home. It was the early hours of Thursday morning and the night would live on for a while longer. At least I would be able to keep my promise to Ned. I would be with him when Lena was buried at dawn.

This was my final night on Earth and I was overcome with an inconsolable sadness. I looked up to find the moon staring down at me. It was full and bright against the blanketed sky. I wandered from star to star because I knew that these stars would be my last. They were brilliant.

I let myself get lost in the stillness of night. Apart from a wistful breeze, there was silence. If I had more nights ahead of me, I would look for this sense of peace over and over again. Instead I could only indulge in it this one time.

The streetlights flickered as they guided me back to O'Brien Circle, which was the only place that had ever really felt like home. The modest looking house was standing in the same place I left it. For some reason I was surprised to still see it there.

I was even more surprised when I walked through the front

door, and Jack wasn't there to greet me with sloppy dog kisses and a wagging tail. It was very early morning, every light inside the house was switched off, but Jack should have realized that I was downstairs. He should've had a sixth sense regarding my arrival. He should've smelled me coming from half a block away. I shut the door behind me. Where was that damn dog?

That's when I heard a ferocious barking erupt from somewhere upstairs. I immediately knew that something was wrong. I sped down the hall, past the kitchen and living room. I rushed up the stairs. I was moving so quickly I tripped over my own feet and stumbled.

I threw open the door to Ned and Lena's bedroom, but Jack wasn't there. He must have been shut in the guest room. I was about to check when I noticed something odd. It was well past midnight, but the bed was made and there was no one was in it. For a moment I thought Ned had gone out and left Jack in the guest room. Maybe he was worried that the dog would have an accident on the sheets. But that didn't make any sense. Where would Ned disappear to in the middle of the night? If he had gone for a walk, he would have taken Jack with him. My head was swimming with the possibilities of what could have happened to my godfather.

Jack continued his hysterical barking from the other room. I turned to leave a second time and once again I became distracted. The closet door had been left ajar, and I could make out a peculiar shadow from within. I ignored the dog's warnings and crossed the room towards the closet. As I reached for the handle, an eerie draft swept in through an open window. I froze where I stood.

I waited for my eyes to adjust to the dark. The moon acted as the only source of light in the house. It streamed in through the windows and poured onto the wooden floorboards and carpets. It was hauntingly beautiful, and yet I felt uneasy. I had never been afraid in the McGreevys' home before. I tried to brush off my discomfort but it persisted.

I gathered my courage and opened the closet door. What I saw made my jaw unhinge and I muffled a scream into my hand. I had found Ned. He was tied to a chair, severely beaten and barely conscious. Ned's eyes were half closed and his face was bloated and bruised. I could tell he hadn't shaved or showered in days, and his hands were turning purple from the knotted rope that held him to the chair. He was so disoriented; I don't believe Ned noticed me in front of him. I was afraid to touch him. I worried I might cause him further harm.

I crept closer. "Ned, can you hear me? Hey, old man."

He groaned and tried to open his eyes, but they were too swollen. I could hardly make out their blue.

"What happened to you? Who did this?"

He whispered a word so softly I couldn't understand him. I leaned in. He smelled rank, but that didn't bother me. I inched even nearer and was horrified to discover that Ned had soiled himself. The most righteous man I knew was sitting in his own waste. The asshole that did this to him was going to pay. In the few hours I had left on Earth, I would hunt down the man who had treated my godfather with such crudeness. Ned whispered to me again but I still couldn't make out what he was trying to convey.

"What?" I asked. "Ned, you have to speak up."

With a nod of his head, he gestured for me to move in even closer. I followed his silent instruction. I brought my face level with his and waited anxiously for Ned to speak. His voice was barely audible, but I was able to decipher two words. "Run, kid."

I ignored his order. I frantically tried to free him from his predicament. I clawed at the rope like a maniac, desperately trying to untangle the knots that held Ned captive. He raised his voice. "Run, kid."

"I can't leave you like this!"

Just as I started to loosen one of the knots, I felt a pair of arms wrap around my waist and pull me away from Ned. I was forcefully thrown backwards and my head slammed into the far wall. I was dazed for a moment. A low humming filled my ears and threw me off balance. I leaned against the wall and somehow managed to remain on my feet. A rough hand took hold of my waist. I looked up and was met with a pair of deep blue eyes, dark ruffled hair and soft freckles.

"Shane?"

"Not at the moment."

The young man's mouth curled into a fiendish smile. I was looking at Shane Forester's face, but he felt like a stranger. The boy who had tracked me down several days earlier wasn't the person with me now. His course body language, the sinister gleam in his eyes— everything about him contradicted the young man I'd met.

My head was throbbing. "Shane, what are you—"

"Shane Forester is not here at the moment, but I would be happy to take a message for you. However, I can't promise he'll be in touch."

"Who are you? Tell me your name," I was suddenly clear-headed. Shane was possessed. He hadn't tied up Ned and locked him in the closet. He hadn't slammed me into the wall. He wasn't running his hands all over me. It was the demon inside of him.

"Oh, Sage. I'm hurt you don't remember me. We had such a special night together once upon time." His mouth pouted beautifully. "I won't ever forget it, every last detail. I especially enjoyed the way you screamed my name."

The demon slipped Shane's hands under the front of my shirt and caressed my bare skin. I could feel my face growing hot with embarrassment. I was blushing and it made me sick. I couldn't control my physical reaction, but I was not taking pleasure from one second of this interaction.

The demon took a step towards me, like a predator closing in on its prey. There was only an inch separating us before he pressed all of Shane's weight against my body. I tried to shove him off but wasn't able to. He had me pinned firmly against the wall. If it had only been a human soul in Shane's body, I could have defended myself but I couldn't contend with the strength of a demon. I felt the hair on his arms brush against my skin. I felt his chest heave as he inhaled deep breaths. Mostly, I could feel the bulge in his pants pushing into my hipbone.

I took in a sharp breath and held it. Shane's hand moved from beneath my shirt to the top of my jeans. I struggled violently. The demon only leaned harder against me. I was unable to free myself from under him. When his fingers played with my zipper, I screamed.

"Stop!" my voice was high pitched.

"Don't you want to? I know Shane does. I'm doing this for him. I am just acting out what runs through his head when he looks at you."

The demon stopped playing with my zipper and grabbed my face with Shane's hand. His thumb pressed into my cheek and I winced. He brought his face uncomfortably close to mine, examining my eyes and nose and mouth with great interest. I didn't have the freedom to turn away so I shut my eyes.

"I don't know what he finds so attractive," the demon grunted. "You're so ordinary. You're not even that pretty."

I knew better than to let his words hurt me. Demons fabricated lies and played on insecurities to weaken their victims' spirits.

"You had a sister once, didn't you? She was pretty. Of course your parents preferred her. It's no wonder they decided to throw you away after she died. You could never match her beauty or her innocence. You could never live up to your sister's memory. Sage, you can't even compete with her ghost. I'm surprised you haven't committed suicide. You would have done the world a kindness."

"You can have me, just let Ned and Jack go," I said. "I won't fight. You can do whatever you want to me, but let them go."

The demon smiled and shook his head as if he pitied me. "Oh no. We're not bargaining. We're not searching for even ground. I can do whatever I want with you or the old man or the dog— You don't have a say in the matter, and for the record, I prefer when girls fight back."

I wondered if he was imagining me in a more vulnerable position. My stomach turned and I felt my eyes water. I felt his warm lips graze against my ear.

"Don't," I breathed against him. "I have one day— just one more day on Earth."

"What does that mean?"

"I made a deal with the Devil. He only gave me one more day to live. Just wait for me in Hell. I will be at your mercy. I know you would never show me compassion, but I will beg for it if you wanted me to. I will cry and scream just to entertain you. You can be the first in long line to deliver me endless humility and suffering. You can have me, just let me have today."

He was suspicious, and while he considered my offer the housegrew quiet again. Jack had stopped barking and Ned was probably unconscious. The demon and I shared a heavy silence, and in that time I almost forgot that the beautiful boy in front of me wasn't Shane Forester. I wanted him to be.

"I must decline your offer, Sage. I am impatient, you see. I want your blood and tears now. I am going to take your virginity too."

I lost my breath. How could this demon know such a personal secret? I was mortified and my alarmed nerves were screaming for help.

The demon laughed at my humiliation. "I can smell it on you. Virgins smell different from one to the other. Would you like to know what you smell like, Sage? Petrichor, the smell of rain on dry Earth. You might not be much to look at, but you smell lovely. I wonder what your little sister smelled like."

The demon buried Shane's face into my neck and took a long whiff. His ruffled brown hair tickled my cheek. His hands began to wander again. I tried to escape, but there was no running from him. I was a mouse and he was a lion. Soon I would be the lion's snack.

"Stop! Don't!" I shouted as his hands trailedback to my jeans' small metal zipper. "STOP! Get off of me!"

"You said you only had one day left on Earth, Sage. Don't you want every human experience? This one can be quite nice. Then again, it is your first time. I imagine there will be some discomfort on your end." He burst into a hard, callous laugh. "Oh, who am I kidding? I have no plans to make this a pleasant experience for you," he stated and unzipped me.

I lost my mind after that and fell into hysterics. I kicked and dug the heels of my hands into his face. I tried to rip out his hair and screamed louder than I thought I could.In my mind I said a silent prayer that the demon wouldn't go through with this.

The more I fought him the more I realized it was hopeless. I was too weak. Even though the demon said he enjoyed when girls put up a fight his actions contradicted that statement. He quickly grew tired to my objections and threw me into the wall. When my head hit the unyielding surface this time I was certain I had a concussion. For a second, the world went black and all the noise in it was drowned out. It wasn't long before my senses returned, but they were somewhat impaired.

"That got you to shut up," the demon laughed again before shoving a hand down the front of my pants.

I couldn't stop myself from crying at the point. It was the only thing I could do.

"I have been inside Shane's head, you know. I'm there right now. He liked you immediately, but I think we could change his mind. I bet he'd think less of you if he knew you were the reason Logan is dead. Shane came home one day and found his brother's broken body and no one to blame. Logan's blood is on your hands, Sage. Shane deserves to know the truth."

"How do you know about that?" I choked out through my tears.

"The thought must have crossed your mind. You know exactly who I am. I was there that night and you sent me away. I've never really gotten over it. And now I am possessing Logan's big brother, the other Forester boy. I think of it as poetic justice."

Murmur. The demon I exorcized from Logan two years earlier was now possessing Shane. This was his revenge, and it could not have come at a worse time. I tried to imagine myself somewhere else. I wanted to be far away from what was happening inside the McGreevy house. I found myself even wishing that I would pass out. I cried incessantly as Shane's hands explored the more intimate parts of my defenseless, trembling body.

"This is nothing compared to what waits for you in Hell. You are going to have to be stronger than this or you'll go mad in no time. If you're not careful, you are going to end up a demon yourself. That's what happens, you know. Sooner or later you are going to lose your humanity. You'll forget that you ever felt anything apart from pain, sorrow and rage. You won't be able to remember your name, so the Devil will give you a new one. The light in your eyes will die until they become seeping black holes. Oh, Sage. I can't wait to watch you turn. I'm getting excited just thinking about it."

I closed my eyes again. I felt the demon's hot breath against my neck. I heard a breeze rush past the house and rustle the trees' leaves and the sound of Jack's nails click across the floor in the guest room. Every time I started to drift off and get lost in some quiet part of my mind, Murmur brought me back to him. The demon would slap me or yank my hair. He wanted me to suffer through every bit of degradation. I felt myself giving up. I was at the mercy of this merciless dark creature.

In that cold and shameful moment, without hope or comfort, a rough voice found its way to me. "Blondie."

My eyes shot open and I turned my face towards the doorway. Lial stood there with his arms folded across his chest and his speckled gray eyes fixed on me.

"I wasn't gone two hours and you're all ready in trouble," he said.

"Lial. Did you get your wings back? I wish I could see them," I was so happy to see the angel I had forgotten the dreadful position I was in. Murmur stopped groping me for the moment, but kept me pinned against the wall.

"I haven't been given them back yet…" Lial trailed off.

I could see that he was disgusted by what had happened to me in his absence. I imagined he blamed himself for not being there to protect me from the demon's unwanted affections.

"Sage, is this the boy who was waiting for you on the porch the other night?" he advanced into the room.

"Not exactly."

"He looks like the same boy. Did he hurt the Ned or the dog?"

"I think Jack is okay, but Ned's tied up in the closet," I answered meekly.

Murmur had been an audience to our conversation up until then. He stepped forward with one hand still clutching my shirt. He squinted at the angel and studied his divine face.

"Belial, is that you?"

"Sorry, I don't recognize you," he shrugged.

"Ha! Of course! I'm wearing a meat suit. Belial, it's your old friend, Murmur. I cannot believe we're running into each other like this."

"Murmur," Lial repeated and his mouth formed a broad smile. "Murmur, it has been ages!"

The demon shoved me back and I watched them embrace. Murmur took a step back and ran a hand through Shane's tussled brown hair. He was thrilled by the chance encounter.

"I had no idea you'd gone topside," Murmur noted.

"Yeah. I mean it's only been a few days."

"What brings you here?"

"I'm sorry to say it's on business and not pleasure."

"The girl said you got your wings back, is that right? So you're on the side of the angels now— again." he corrected himself.

"Yeah, He gave me back my wings. I don't deserve them, but I would be lying if I said I wasn't looking forward to flying again."

"Hey, good for you, Belial."

"I appreciate that, Murmur."

I cleared my throat. I didn't want to give Murmur a reason to throw me into the wall, but I needed my guardian's attention. "What about Shane?"

"Oh," Lial said and remembered the scene he'd just walked in on. He looked back to the demon. "Murmur, I need you to give up that body."

"Really? Listen, I am glad that you've been accepted back into His kingdom, but those were all the kind words I have in me."

"Murmur, return that body to the boy it was created for."

"I can't do that. Your girlfriend cut my last vacation short. She and I have history."

"That's too bad because that business I mentioned early, she's it."

"I don't believe this! I know you play for the other team, but would you really deny a scorned demon his revenge? Belial, you and I shared a few laughs over the centuries and millenniums. You have to let me have her."

"No." His jaw tightened.

Murmur released a slow and haughty laugh. "You are the most feared archangel in Heaven and Hell second to Michael. Are you actually taking orders from a human girl?"

"Thou she be but little, she is fierce," Lial said. I recognized the quote as one of William Shakespeare's.

"Is that from the Old Testament?" The reference flew over the Murmur's head. "If you fight me, you risk causing harm to this young man's body. Why not let me walk around in his skin for a while? I promise to keep him in good condition until I find suitable replacement."

"No!" I shouted. "That is not your body. You don't belong here. You don't belong anywhere other than the circles of Hell."

Shane's eyes changed. Murmur drowned out all of the color until there was only black left. He spoke through clenched teeth. "I could say the same thing about you, Sage."

"I know, and come sunset you won't be able to find me anywhere else."

Lial's arctic stare flickered over to me and rested on my face. "Sunset? You mean tonight, like sixteen hours from now?"

"That was a condition of the deal I made. The Devil wanted me to leave with him after I shook his hand, but I asked for more time. He gave me until sunset, and that took a lot of convincing."

"That was generous of him. Lucifer won't usually change his mind after he has made a decision, even when he'd like to."

"I know one angel more stubborn than he is," I teased and a wry smile crept onto Lial's face. He knew I was referring to him.

Murmur cut in, annoyed that he was no longer the center of attention. "Would you two stop flirting?"

Lial took several large strides towards the demon. "Murmur, you've had your fun but it's time for you to leave now."

"Fun? I was just getting started! What if I refuse?"

"That won't change anything. Sure, it will take longer to exorcize you than it would for you to leave on your own, but I'm not picky."

The demon made a strange guttural sound, somewhere between a growl and car engine being revved. "Give him a pair of wings and he forgets who his friends are," he mocked. "Hey, you're not better than me, angel."

"I believe that's true," Lial answered. "Come on, Murmur." Give her the rest of today. Wait for her in Hell. I can't protect her there."

He kept his eyes on Lial for another minute. I believe he was weighing his options. Would fighting to stay in Shane's body be worth the pain and suffering Lial would cause him? Murmur tapped his fingers against the wall, deep in thought.

"Fine. You can have her for now."

Lial nodded, relieved that the demon had taken the easy road.

Murmur walked back over to me and wrapped his hands around my waist. He squeezed until he could see the discomfort in my scrunched up face. The demon applied so much pressure it hurt to breathe. His dark eyes were spiteful.

Murmur hissed in my ear. "Find a way to look forward to feeling like this, breathless and scared, because after sunset, this is all you are ever going to know. I am going to make sure of it." He kissed me on the cheek. "See you in Hell, Sage Barnaby."

After that Shane's eyes closed and his body collapsed. I managed to catch him before his head hit the floor. A line of black smoke escaped through his mouth, slid across the floor and out through the bedroom door. Murmur was gone. I brought my attention back to the boy lying at my feet. He started to stir and stretch, finally back in control of his body. He would be awake soon.

I knelt down beside him and watched as Shane's eyes gradually opened, revealing their normal color. And before he said a word, I could see that every trace of the demon had left him. Shane had returned to being a fragile, beautiful human.

"Shane," I whispered over him. "Um, are you all right?"

"Yeah," he sounded woozy.

"Do you know what happened to you?"

He nodded and his mouth turned down. He looked like such a little boy when he frowned. For a second I thought he might weep. Instead, he pushed himself up and took my hand in his. "Sage, I am so sorry. I wanted to stop him but I couldn't. I tried. I swear I tried," he told me. "Listen, there's a man in the closet. He might need to go to a hospital. Your dog was here too—"

"Don't worry. Everyone is okay. Do you have a place to stay in Bridgeview? Somewhere you can rest?"

"There's a motel just outside the city."

I shook my head. "You can stay in my apartment. Hell, you can have my apartment. I don't need it anymore."

"Are you going somewhere?" He crinkled his nose. "Where? For how long?"

I hung my head and lied. "I don't know… Out of town, for a while."

"Sage, you can't go without telling me what happened to Logan. I need to know— I heard what Murmur said—"

"Okay," I agreed. "Wait outside for me."

Shane did. After I heard the screen on the front door slam shut, I faced to Lial. We stared at one another for an all too brief moment. I wanted to run to the angel and wrap my arms around him, bury my face in his leather jacket and inhale. I wanted cry and laugh and thank him over and over again for coming back, but

I did none of those things. I was so overwhelmed that it took me some time to remember how to speak.

His name was the only thing that came to mind. "Lial."

"Blondie." His pale eyes were sad. He must have been disappointed in me. He probably wanted to curse me and tell me how stupid I'd been. I couldn't blame him after everything I had put him through. I deserved whatever horrible things he had to say.Instead he just repeated my nickname in that same sad way, "Blondie."

It was far worse than any lecture or scolding could have been.

"Would you mind letting Jack out?" I asked. "I'm gunna make sure Ned is all right. We still have to bury Lena."

26
Lial—

Ned was fine, thank goodness. It turned out that every text message he sent me, just checking in, was done at Murmur's hands. Ned had been tied up and shut in the closet for two days. Apart from being dehydrated and bruised, there were no serious injuries. The same went for Jack. They would make full recoveries soon enough. I left them in Lial's care, promising to return before sunrise so that we could all go to the cemetery together.

I met Shane outside. He was sitting on the front porch staring at a street lamp as it flickered on and off. I tapped him on the shoulder as I walked by. He followed me over to Sweetie, which I was surprised to find parked in the driveway. Lial must have driven the car back to Bridgeview from Sleepy Hollow. As I approached the Cadillac, I noticed that something disturbing had happened to her interior. The beige leather seats were soaked in pools of crimson blood. I realized that it must've to belonged to Lial. After we were separated in the cemetery, he suffered from spontaneous cuts and open wounds, which caused him to bleed all over everything he came in contact with. When Lial returned to Talbot Place, we were less than one hundred yards apart, so the bleeding stopped but the stains remained.

"Why don't we walk to my apartment?" I suggested to Shane.

He agreed with a quiet nod. I moved past Sweetie and into the street, leading the way. Shane stayed close behind me but not one word was exchanged between us. Eventually, we turned onto Gretchen Road and scaled the stairway up to my apartment. It was just as I left it the morning following my sleepover with Lial. Clothes were scattered on the floor, my bed was unmade and the refrigerator was empty. I also forgot to switch off the bathroom light, but that wasn't important. Things like electric bills and unfolded laundry didn't matter anymore (not that they ever really did.)

I sat down on the couch and proceeded to tell Shane everything while he paced in the kitchenette area, listening to my story of Logan Forester. I included almost every detail. I decided to leave out how I felt about his brother— how deeply I had come to care for Logan in the short time we were in each other's lives. Afterwards, I waited for Shane to say something. I gave him as much time as I could, but the sky outside my window began to change from the deep black of night to the first gray signs of morning. I tried not to show my impatience, but I knew that Ned was waiting for me.

"Shane, there's somewhere I have to be. You can stay here, as long you want. No one is going to bother you. I'm sorry there's not much food in the refrigerator, but I keep money in one of the empty cereal boxes in the cabinet. There's more hidden under the bathroom sink. You can have it."

"Thanks," Shane forced the word out of him before shuffling his feet across the apartment and collapsing onto the couch. He looked exhausted, which wasn't uncommon for someone who had just suffered a recent demonic possession.

"I hope that a part of what I said helped you somehow," I offered. "I know it wasn't what you expected—"

"Logan told me he was going on a date. He said that if things went well he might want to take her home," Shane remembered with a dazed, expressionless stare. "I was so excited for him, but he was with you the whole time."

I didn't know how to comfort him. There were no words that could make Logan's death beautiful or at the very least okay. Nothing could change the sadness of it and the guilt I felt.

Shane reminded me so much of his little brother then, leaning back on the couch with ruffled hair and freckles. His eyes were closing and soon he would be asleep.

"Sage," he said. "I think that under different circumstances you and I could have been friends."

"Me too," I heard myself say.It was a nice thought, friends, but not in this life. "Goodbye, Shane," I said with a touch of regret, but he was already asleep.

When I returned to O'Brien Circle, I made Lial drive Sweetie to the 1976 parking lot and leave her there. If I only had one day left with Ned, I didn't want to spend it explaining what happened to his beloved automobile. Ned didn't even seem to notice that his precious car was missing. We took a taxi to the cemetery. We had to pay extra so that Jack could ride along with us in the back seat. We packed into the yellow cab, squished against one another with no personal space to spare, but I relished the closeness. I wish that car ride had lasted longer.

Bridgeview Cemetery was just north of the city, stretching over several rolling hills that overlooked the rigid skyline and the Hudson River. The cemetery contradicted the seedy streets of Bridgeview with its serenity and cleanliness. Every time I visited, I wished that I'd gone more often. It was a perfect escape from the constant sirens and overflowing trash bins that littered the inner city area. The cemetery didn't have the history that Sleepy Hollow did, but it was no less quaint or lacking in beauty. The gray headstones complimented the changing sky as its morning palate exploded with pastels.

We trudged up the hillside and stopped at an open grave. I glimpsed over the edge and saw a dark brown wooden box inside. It seemed wrong that Lena was inside a coffin. She was supposed to be standing beside Ned, Jack and me. It was unnatural for her to be anywhere else. Ned took my hand in his and squeezed tightly. It hurt, but I didn't object. He could have thrown me into the ground with Lena and I wouldn't have objected. I would have been okay with anything if it made my godfather feel better.

I hung my head. My hair fell around my face, shielding me from the rising sun and hiding the tears that swelled in the corners of my eyes. Ned was sniffling on my left while Jack sat quietly to my right. I rested my free hand in the space between the dog's ears. Lial had chosen to stay a respectful distance from us. He watched as we said our goodbyes from several yards back in the shade of a weeping willow.

"So few people ever know the kind of love Lena and I had," Ned started. He kept his eyes on his wife's grave. "If I had forever with her, it wouldn't have been enough. "

"When someone dies, even the happy memories are sad. I hate that," I declared just above a whisper. "Every good moment you had with them is ruined because they're not here anymore."

"No," he squeezed my hand tighter still. "That's not true, kid. Death doesn't spoil life. Death helps make life important."

"You really think so?"

"You bet."

I wondered if my time on Earth had been important. I suppose it was worth something if I could trade my soul for Nola's life.

Ned knelt down beside me. He grabbed a fistful of dirt in his hand and tossed it into the open grave. It rained down onto Lena's coffin. I also grabbed a handful of dirt and let it fall into the Earth.

Ned stood up, took my dirty hand in his and pulled me away from her resting place. Jack followed at our heels. We started back down the hill and I looked over my shoulder to make sure that Lial was still there. He gave me a gentle wave and strolled leisurely after us.

Ned's blue eyes shimmered like the surface of a lake beneath the sun. He looked down at me and I received the full effect of his height. Ned still hadn't shaved and was beginning to resemble a brooding giant. I sent up a small prayer, asking that he would be okay without me. He had already lost so much; it didn't seem fair that he should suffer any more.

"I'm hungry," I whined.

Ned laughed suddenly, tears fell from his blue eyes. "I could really go for some pistachio ice cream. How about you?"

"Yeah." Pistachio ice cream was exactly what I was in the mood for.

The rest of that day was perfect, and if you don't mind, I am going to keep most of the details to myself. I won't tell you how beautiful that final sunrise was. I won't tell you how much I cried in the taxi back to O'Brien Circle or how quickly I settled down when Lial wrapped his arm around my shoulders. I won't tell you how nice it felt to take a hot shower one more time. I won't tell you which television series I watched that afternoon. I was upset that I'd never see the show's finale. I won't tell you how it sounded when Ned laughed at me after I spilled my ice cream, or how he looked at me when I told him I was just running downtown for a cup of coffee. I won't tell you how good that last cup of coffee tasted. I won't tell you how it felt the last time I rubbed Jack's stomach and buried my face in his white fur. I will let you in on the last few minutes I spent on Earth. I was in the company of an angel.

The day had flown by, as the good ones always do, and the sun was setting. The birds had quieted down and were nestled against one another in the treetops. An outline of the moon was sketched in the darkening sky, but the summer air was still warm on my face. Lial and I stood side by side in a city park overlooking the river. As the night settled in around us, it felt like we were the only two creatures on Earth. Even the crickets stopped playing their music while we said our goodbyes.

Lial stared at me with his outstanding blue eyes. "Run away with me."

God, I wanted to.

"If I run away, Nola stays where she is."

"I still don't know why that bothers you so much. People die."

I took a breath. I wanted to choose my words carefully, but as I watched the sun start to sink beneath the horizon line, I knew my time was fading.

"I know that people die; that's not what bothers me. I can't stand that some people never really live. I have been miserable, broken and in places so dark I doubted that the sun ever existed. I thought it was just something I made up, but even then I always knew that being alive is an extraordinary thing— Human life makes the angels jealous. What else can do that? I know this is the right thing to do, Lial. Nola is going to be amazing."

I could see that Lial still didn't understand me, or agree with me, but he left all further opinions unsaid. There was nothing he could do to change my fate now. I guess he didn't want our last moments together to be spent arguing.

"Are you scared?" his voice was low as he pushed a stray curl away from my face.

"Yes, but not of Hell. I'm scared of dying," I answered. "I'm not sure why. I know what I am going to find on the other side. I've known it for most of life, so why am I still so afraid to die?"

Lial reached out and took my hand. Its heat resonated in my palm. "Because death lasts longer. I said it before, life is the dream and death wakes you up to what's real. There is no death in death, just evolution and awakening."

I squeezed his hand and choked back the emotion rising inside me. The sky was firing off its grand finale of colors. The brightest pinks and deepest purples were displayed flamboyantly overhead.

"What's going to happen to me? Will the black gates appear before me or am I going to disappear and wake up in fire? Is the Devil going to give me a personal tour of the circles of Hell? What about the demons I exorcized? There were so many… Do you think they'll be waiting for me?" I'm not sure how, but I managed to keep from shaking as buckets of fear rushed through me.

"I don't know what's going to happen, Sage. That's not my area."

"Of course not," I smiled. I was so pleased for him. "Lial, you're getting your wings back."

He didn't return the happy expression. He was worried about me and scared for me, like a true guardian. I wish that Lial hadn't looked so sad. He had the most absurdly gorgeous smile, but there was nothing that could keep him from pouting now. He knew the horrors waiting for me in Hell. He had suffered them all.

"Will you look after Ned and Jack?"

He nodded and some blonde hair fell down onto his forehead.

"Will you keep an eye on Nola?"

"Your sister will have her own guardian angel. She won't need me."

"Please, Lial. I know I don't deserve to ask you for anything else—"

"No, you don't—!"

"Just check in on her from time to time. Please."

"She better not be as much trouble as you were," he narrowed his clear eyes. "No, that's not possible. Trouble should be measured on a scale from one to Sage Barnaby."

"Lial, please—"

"Fiiiine!" he whined and continued to act like a perfect grouch. "Yes. Okay. I will look after your sister. You have my word."

I breathed easier.

"Are you sure I can't convince you to run away with me?" he persisted.

Okay. Yes. Anywhere. Everywhere. As long as it's with you.

But I couldn't say that. I made a deal. I shook on it. I gave Lial and apologetic smile and he understood my meaning.

"I don't— I don't want you to go," he said in a rough voice.

"I am going to miss you, penguin."

"You might not. If you're down there long enough, you won't even remember me. That's what happens to human souls in Hell. They forget, and then they change. They become something else, something dark— minions, demons, shadows, tortured spirits… Your humanity is going to leave you and forgetting the life you had on Earth is the first step."

"Murmur already educated me on that matter."

Really, Lial? I thought to myself. His timing was awful. I had a minute or two left on Earth and he chose that moment to tell me the horrible truth about Hell. Maybe he hoped to scare me into running away from my deal with the Devil. It half worked. I wouldn't run, but I was scared. I felt my blood stream cold, which meant that I was still human. Being afraid is very human.

"I won't forget."

"Try not to." I could tell he didn't believe me.

The evening sky was still a riot of color. It had transformed beyond pink and purple to crimson red and blazing orange. The sun was no more than a sliver of burning yellow just above the horizon line. It was a spectacular sunset and even though it meant that this was the end, I found a way to enjoy it. I took a couple of deep breaths, appreciating those last moments of fresh air. There was only smoke and sulfur where I was headed.

"I wish time would just quit for a while," Lial announced.

"I wish there was more."

"If I could find a way, I would stop the sunset for you, Sage."

I would miss the way Lial said my name. I'd be torn away from his side at any moment. In a minute, maybe less... My life had flown by in a blink.

"Lial, I don't know how to say goodbye to you."

"Good. Don't."

He was still holding my hand when he pulled me into him. For a moment we were so close, I thought that we'd become one person. The angel was an extension of me. His hand was my hand. I saw the world through his unearthly eyes and it was all so beautiful, shimmering and alive. I would miss everything so much. I tightened my hold on him. Lial must have washed his clothes at Ned's house because the smell of blood and cigarettes was faint; they were overlaid with the scent of lavender laundry detergent. I breathed him in. I would never know Heaven, but I'd always imagine it smelled like laundry detergent and cigarettes.

He returned the embrace. I could feel the tip of his nose and his full mouth resting in my curls. We stayed like that for a while and I really believed that time stopped for us. I thought that He was sympathetic and briefly changed the rules of the universe, granting Lial's wish and giving us a few more seconds together. I couldn't prove it, but I believed it.

I felt Lial's soft lips press against my forehead with a kiss and it soothed me. The warmth present in his body and voice contradicted the ice in his eyes. I loved that about him. Lial had fascinated me from the moment he came into my world. I could never forget him, my angel.

"I never thanked you," I voiced a nervous whisper into his green leather jacket. I would be taken away soon, too soon.

I heard Lial stifle his laughter. These were our final words to each other, and there was nothing funny about that.

"Well, you really should. I saved your ass, Blondie. Just make it quick." A crooked, smug smile graced his mouth. I wish I had leaned in.

I kept my eyes fixed on his, which were lovelier and sadder than anything in this world. I felt the same way I did the first time I saw him, impassioned and breathless.

"Lial—"

It was a surreal, thrilling moment. I wouldn't change a single thing I've done. I would relive each mistake. I would retrace every heart-wrenching and brutal step because it brought us together.

This had been my beautiful and terrible life. I was not proud of many things, but I had found someone kind to hold me as it came to an end, and what else could I ask for? I mean, we all run out of time, but not everyone has someone with them when it's over. I was scared, but at least I wasn't alone.

I was not ready to leave this world. I tried my best to capture how it felt to have his hand in my hand. I guess part of me thought that would be enough to save me… but then the darkness came, and I was gone.

27
Nothing in Creation

She never did thank me. I just stood there and watched her go. What kind of a guardian angel watches their human being dragged to Hell and just stands there? Well, I never was any good at my job.

It was stupid to ask her to run away with me. When I dreamed up that idea, I should have known that it would stay a dream. I could still see her magnetic brown eyes in front of me. I could feel her dark curls, like threads of silk between my fingers. I would never forget her fair skin, soft curves or bow-shaped mouth. I wished I had spent more time memorizing her features when she was with me.

I resented the sentiment she had for her sister— that she doubted her own worth over such a little girl. I don't believe anyone could compare to the incessant bravery and heart that Sage Barnaby possessed. I cursed myself for asking her to leave with me. I shouldn't have given her a choice. I should have made her run— carried her away as she kicked and screamed. How could I have allowed her to go through with this? Sage may have released me from being bound to her, but I was still her guardian.

I have been around since before time was born and I have existed all that time without her. I can't figure out how I did that.

In five days she ruined me, the second most feared archangel in Heaven and Hell. I still can't believe she tricked me into taking back my place in His kingdom. Somehow she got me to put aside my pride and accept my wings, but I had saved her too, more than once, and she never even said thank you.

What did I get? I got a lousy pack of cigarettes, and cake and steak, which hardly seemed fair. I thought I deserved more than that, at the very least a thank you. Hell, I wanted another pack of cigarettes. I wanted to see her get angry when someone made a comment about her nickname. I wanted to watch her drink shirley temples and coffee and cry over the dog. I wanted to fight with her. I wanted to listen to her sing and push rogue curls away from her face. I wanted more.

Huh.

How very human of me? Funny. Me. Human. I may have studied humans for thousands of years, but I was too far removed to understand what it meant to be one. He saw to that when He made the angels. I think He feared that if we were more sensitive to our emotions, to others' emotions, we would interfere more often with life on Earth, and that would affect free will. For whatever reason, He believed that free will was kind of a big deal, the opportunity to choose, to question, to try, to fail. It was something I would never fully grasp being an angel.

I looked up to find a universe of stars littering the night. I watched as they winked at me, charming and playful as ever. A burst of energy rushed over me, and without warning a strange throbbing flooded through my body. The sensation reached down to my toes and stretched along my spine. A heaviness weighed on me, and it wasn't long before I understood what was happening. My wings were being returned, and they spanned from my shoulders to my knees. I could feel the lush white and gray speckled feathers sweep down my back, and I realized how much I missed them. This should have made me whole again, but I couldn't be, not without her. Sage Barnaby was somehow better than flying.

"Hello, Belial," a voice cut through the darkness. "You look like your old self. Can I share a secret with you? Will you promise not to tell? Come on now, cross your heart and hope to die."

I turned to find Lucifer treading towards me. He was still disguised as the bartender Sage met in Sleepy Hollow. I nodded, agreeing to keep his secret.

"I miss my wings every day," he said in a hoarse whisper.

I was not touched by his shallow confession, his weak attempt to gain sympathy from me. "What do you want?"

"I brought you a gift," he said. "And they say I'm not a nice guy."

Lucifer tossed a small object to me. I recognized the red leather cover immediately. Liber Alter. I furrowed my brow. "Why?"

"I am so pleased to have Sage for a trophy that I don't see the book as much of a prize," a cruel smile appeared on his lips. "What an incredible turn of events— the little girl who sold her soul twice, and for the same ridiculous reason!"

Lucifer started to roar with furious laughter. I felt the need to take a step back and distance myself as I watched him unravel.

I spoke over his obnoxious cackling. "It must be nice for you to win one, Lucifer. I know you're much more experienced at losing, over and over and over and over and—"

"Oh, you cannot break my spirit tonight. I have Belial's girl. That's what they call her, isn't it? Well, she's not yours anymore. Sage belongs to me now."

"I'm still her guardian."

"I don't see how that matters anymore. You would not believe how many demons have lined up for some one on one time with your precious human. I was amazed."

I knew he was telling the truth. I had listened to some of those deranged creatures rattle on and on about how they would punish Sage for sending them back to Hell. Although she'd only exorcized thirty-six demons, each of those demons was the head of a legion, and every one of those thousands of lesser demons would torment her on their master's behalf. I wanted to channel all of that pain into myself and spare her.

"Belial, you should see the look on your face right now! I have never seen an angel look so heartsick. I have to say, it's not becoming on you, old friend. If I didn't know better, I'd think you were about to shed a tear for the girl."

Was I? No… No? No. No, absolutely not. Heartsick, maybe. Crying, never.

"Actually, I have seen that look on you before. Belial, this is exactly how you looked when you agreed to follow me out of Heaven. You were heartsick, but not over a human, no. You and Michael had a falling out. Oh, big brothers can be so judgmental. I don't get along with mine either."

Count to ten, I told myself. One. Two— Oh, screw it. I wanted to be humble, I wanted to turn the other cheek, but instead I raced toward him. I smacked my fist in Lucifer's jaw and he fell forward, his hands flew up to cradle his face.

"OUCH!" he moaned. "Was it something I said? Millions of years have passed since you fell from Heaven. I cannot believe that Michael is still a sore subject for you."

I hit him again, and this time he collapsed onto his hands and knees. I watched him wince and twist his face in pain as I glared down at him with cold eyes. Lucifer pushed himself off the cool ground and staggered clumsily to his feet.

"I am stronger than you," I said. "You're a seraphim, remember?"

"No match for an archangel," he admitted in a somber voice. "Oh, yes I was— am— a seraphim. I was among the order of angels closet to Him. I used to be His favorite. Did you know that? Trust me, you cannot imagine the pressure."

"Am I supposed to feel sorry for you?"

I watched his expression soften and the corners of the bartender's mouth turned down. "You never really believed in my cause, did you? Belial, you were the last to fall. I know you wish you never followed me out of Heaven. I think you were just angry with your brother; you rebelled to hurt Michael. Now that I think about it, you've never even asked me why I opposed Him— why I was so desperate to separate myself from Him. No, you were angry with Michael, and you made a rash, naïve decision to run away to the dark side— like a child. I wonder, do you even remember why you and Michael were fighting?"

Of course I remembered. I could recall every word that was exchanged between Michael and I during that final, regrettable argument, but it was none of Lucifer's business. I had been so proud, so entitled, and he'd been right.

"Goodbye, Lucifer," I said.

I watched him hang his head and laugh under his breath, as if he pitied me. Lucifer still saw me as a misguided, ignorant young angel, but the truth was that he had no idea where I stood in the war of morality. He just liked to think he did.

"Goodbye, Belial." The bartender's blue eyes pierced through the veil of night and held my stare. "I am happy for you, by the way. I am happy that you have been given another chance. We both know how unforgiving He can be, and you never even had to say you were sorry."

With that Lucifer vanished, evaporated into the sharp night air.

I was alone again, but this time I welcomed it. If I couldn't be in her company, then I would rather be alone. I brought my attention back to the tiny, sacred object in my protection. I moved Liber Alter back and forth between my hands. I let my boney fingers trace over the gold inscription imprinted in the red leather. I was surprised that Lucifer offered it to me without the slightest degree of hesitation.

I don't know why, but I opened the book and read the Latin words written on the inside cover. I let my eyes rest on a blank page within. Soon enough the truth revealed itself to me, and I sighed with disbelief and exhilaration.

The inside cover offered a warning; I read it out loud. "For the truth is a dangerous thing." I should not have doubted that message.

The Other Book disclosed a world-shifting truth, something I would have never dreamed of otherwise. Five words, that was all. Five simple words that changed everything. I would see those brown eyes and wild dark curls again. There was nothing in creation that could stop me... *You can still save her.*

The Sage Barnaby Chronicles
will continue…

Acknowledgments

I want to keep this short and sweet. I used to believe that the only way to realize my dreams was on my own. Here are some of the people who proved me wrong.

Thanks to Katrina Bateman, Kelly Brown and Ann Forster for reading my first draft all the way through, despite its many blunders. I am truly grateful for your constructive criticism, edits and doodles.

Thanks to Alexander Herzig for dismissing your homework to read this book cover to cover, for your unique insight and excellent suggestions.

Thanks to Camie Salaz and Gabriela Seguinot for your continued support, excitement, and inspiring me with your own works of art.

Thanks to Anthony Laurino for your advice, interest, experience and much needed guidance along the way.

Thanks to Christina Dello Buono for your over the moon enthusiasm, and drive to make sure that people outside of my family know this book exists.

Thanks to Tara Chillemi for your brilliance and attention to detail. I feel very lucky to have had you edit this novel.

Thanks to Apprentice House Press for making my dream of being a published author come true. I want to thank you for your professionalism and care with my first novel. It has meant the world to me.

Apprentice House is the country's only campus-based, student-staffed book publishing company. Directed by professors and industry professionals, it is a nonprofit activity of the Communication Department at Loyola University Maryland.

Using state-of-the-art technology and an experiential learning model of education, Apprentice House publishes books in untraditional ways. This dual responsibility as publishers and educators creates an unprecedented collaborative environment among faculty and students, while teaching tomorrow's editors, designers, and marketers.

Outside of class, progress on book projects is carried forth by the AH Book Publishing Club, a co-curricular campus organization supported by Loyola University Maryland's Office of Student Activities.

Eclectic and provocative, Apprentice House titles intend to entertain as well as spark dialogue on a variety of topics. Financial contributions to sustain the press's work are welcomed. Contributions are tax deductible to the fullest extent allowed by the IRS.

To learn more about Apprentice House books or to obtain submission guidelines, please visit www.apprenticehouse.com.

Apprentice House
Communication Department
Loyola University Maryland
4501 N. Charles Street
Baltimore, MD 21210
Ph: 410-617-5265 • Fax: 410-617-2198
info@apprenticehouse.com•www.apprenticehouse.com

www.ingramcontent.com/pod-product-compliance
Lightning Source LLC
Chambersburg PA
CBHW030632020726
47493CB00006B/1676